LONELY FRIEND

Little Georgie was all by himself in the world, and he didn't have a soul to play with. That all changed when he met Bobby, because Bobby didn't mind that his new pal had been dead for decades.

GHOSTLY FRIEND

Happy at last, Georgie would do anything not to lose Bobby—and anyone who tried to take his new buddy away would have hell to pay.

DANGEROUS FRIEND

Then Bobby was killed by some local teenagers, and Georgie got mad. But he found a new game to play—a game filled with blood and terror—a game he wouldn't lose because he couldn't die twice.

DEADLY FRIEND
Keith Ferrario

KEITH FERRARIO

Book Margins, Inc.

A BMI Edition

Published by special arrangement with Dorchester
Publishing Co., Inc.

For Tammy Husby

I would like to express my deepest thanks to the following people for their help and patience: Annette Burmeister, Jane Hoeft, Bruce and Barbara Mulvaney, Darlene Stahl. If it wasn't for their encouragement and support, I may not have finished this, my first novel. I would also like to thank Janet Holmes for her advice, and Patty Larsen and Todd Wagner for finally convincing me to write.

Chapter One

May winds overpowered the dark clouds, pushing them slowly across the sky, turning the blue to a broken gray. The sunshine dimmed behind the large mass; only small patches of yellow light poked through. The cloud shadow crawled across the previous summer's tall growth of grass and weeds, which had become brown lifeless straw heaped upon the dried foliage of past years. Gusting winds pushed the dead growth back and forth like ocean waves slapping against the shore. The blackening sky threatened rain.

Peter Cowal and his younger brother Bobby ignored the threat. Instead, they focused their attention on a red-and-blue box kite flying high above their heads. Peter had spent many hours after school and on weekends constructing the special kite for his brother. It didn't have the standard design for a box kite; rather, it had an altered frame and flaps cut into the cotton cloth to give it better lift and easier control. The color scheme was Bobby's contribution. Red and blue were his favorites, but he couldn't decide on which color he liked best. So Peter had used them both, and by doing so, he made Bobby happy.

Of all the kites Peter had designed and built, that one gave him the most pride, because it enabled him to test some of the tougher aeronautical theories he had read about.

He spent a lot of his time reading, science books mostly. He would check out several books at a time from the library at Fulton High School, where he was in his senior year. Unfortunately, at Fulton High, that made him a target for ridicule by some of the other students.

Being smart wasn't as popular as being on the football team or the baseball team. That didn't bother him much; with the exception of track, school sports didn't interest Peter. His glasses did correct his slight nearsightedness, and with a little work his thin frame could be developed into a fine athletic tool. Still, he couldn't see himself wearing a silly uniform while catching or throwing or hitting one type of ball or another. Track wasn't like that. All he really needed was a pair of sweats and a good pair of running shoes.

Peter had once had it in his head to try out for the track team, and he had even gone to the field to practice. From the incredulous stares of the other teens, he knew right away he had made a mistake. The track team had become more a social clique of the popular than a team for athletic endeavors. After two relays in which he had been tripped three times by other runners, Peter left the field. He didn't need more hassles in his life. Besides, he really did enjoy spending time with Bobby.

"That one's up high," Bobby said as he watched the kite. Excitement bubbled from his voice.

"We have a good strong wind," Peter said.

The wind pushed hard against the kite as if trying to break the line, so Peter gripped the heavy string with both hands. He had made sure to use heavy-duty twine so that the kite would not break free, as so many had in the past. More than once, he had seen weeks of work simply blow away with a snap of a line.

Bobby laughed as the kite climbed higher and higher until it became a dark speck against the background of moving clouds. The colored swatches seemed to blend together in the distance. Bobby squeezed the ball of twine hard between his hands. It was his job to prevent the twine from tangling as it unwound, and he always listened carefully as Peter told him when to let out more line.

Seeing his little brother laughing brought a smile to Peter's usually somber face. He tried to spend as much time with Bobby as he could, but with school and homework those moments became fewer and fewer. Bobby was special. A large boy, he outweighed his older brother by a good 25 pounds, and he had the enlarged head and close-set eyes of all Down's syndrome children.

Peter never felt sorry for his brother. Bobby was born shortly after his fifth birthday, and Peter grew up thinking of him as normal. Not until other children started calling Bobby names did he even wonder about his brother. When Peter was old enough to understand, his mother sat down with him and tried to explain Bobby's differences. To Peter, however, all that mattered was that he loved his little brother, and no amount of name-calling would make him denigrate Bobby with pity.

"Want to try?" Peter asked, pulling the twine toward Bobby.

"Can I?" Bobby's eyes lit up. Then he dropped the ball of twine, which rolled about five feet and came to rest in the tall brown grass.

"It's your kite, isn't it?" Peter said. "Take hold of the line above my hands."

The kite pulled against Bobby's palms as his fingers closed around the line. He tried to position his hands like his brother.

"Now hold on tight," Peter said. "You got it?"

"Yeah, I got it."

"OK. It's yours." Peter let go of his end.

The kite tugged, then started to spiral. Bobby pulled back on the twine to gain control. "Look! Look! I'm flying it."

"Yep, you are. Let out a little more line."

"Look at it go! Look at it go!" Bobby loosened his grip and the kite climbed still higher. Then he tightened his fingers and held the twine tight with both hands the same way Peter had. "You found a real good spot to fly kites, Peter."

"It's about the only place left without power lines now that they started building houses over on Hennily Road."

"This will be my favorite place," Bobby said. "Can I let out more line?"

"Sure, you've done a great job so far."

"Oh, it's—" Bobby suddenly turned and stared at a large oak tree 30 yards right of the two boys. While the boy wasn't paying attention, the line slipped through his hands, and the ball of twine rapidly unrolled. Because there was too much slack, the red-and-blue box kite came crashing down.

"Did you hear that?" Bobby said, ignoring the kite.

"Hear what?"

"Someone's laughing."

"I don't hear—"

"Look . . . see . . . there he is." Bobby let the twine fall to the ground and ran toward the oak. "Come out! Come out!"

"Bobby," Peter said, following his little brother to the old, twisted tree. Some of its bare limbs looked like old wrinkled hands with long thin fingers grabbing at the clouds. A thick piece of frayed rope hanging from a lower branch banged against its trunk, making a slapping sound in the wind.

"He was here. He was right here," Bobby said, running to the other side of the tree trying to flush out the intruder.

"Are you sure, Bobby? I didn't see anyone."

"He was right here. He was laughing at us."

"Well, whoever he was, he almost made you ruin your kite."

The pained expression of Bobby's face made Peter regret his words. But after carefully inspecting the kite, they found it wasn't damaged too badly. Only one of the support bars had broken on impact, and it would be easy enough to replace.

The boys spent the next few minutes rolling up the twine. The whole time, Bobby kept glaring back at the dark oak tree, hoping to catch the intruder.

As the two brothers walked off the lot, Bobby lifted his arm and stretched it rigid, pointing back to the oak. His eyes opened wide. "See! See! There he is. You see him, right?"

Peter turned. Still nothing, just an empty lot. And although Peter hated to lie to his brother, he said, "Sure, Bobby. I see him. It's just someone trying to play a joke on us. That's all."

"It's not very funny."

"Just forget it. Here"—Peter handed Bobby the ball

of twine—"you keep this safe."

The brothers walked across the road and took the shortcut through the woods. During the ten-minute hike along the dirt trail, the two boys joked and laughed. Bobby even remembered the new knock-knock joke he had heard at his school earlier that day.

At one point, the trail widened and one side sloped down to the rocky floor at the bottom of a naturally formed cliff. Bobby stopped and stared at the sheer rock face. "Why does everybody call this place Crazy Man's Bluff? Is it really because some crazy man killed a whole bunch of people?"

"I don't know about a whole bunch of people," Peter said, his voice dropping. His eyes moved to the right, then to the left; then he said, "But I did hear how a patient escaped from an asylum one night and ended up killing three boys."

Bobby's eyes scanned the area. "Think he could still be around?"

"No," Peter said matter-of-factly, "that was way back in the thirties. The sheriff and his men had to hunt the guy down and—"

"Wow! Then they caught the crazy man?"

"Didn't have a chance. With the dogs right behind him he jumped off the cliff. Broke his neck clean."

Bobby gave his brother a doubting look. "You're just making that up."

Peter pointed to the top of the cliff. "See that fencing? The town put that there so others don't jump off."

"Oh, that doesn't prove anything."

. "I know." Peter snickered. "Some parents probably made the whole story up to keep theirs kids from playing on the cliff and the story just got around town. It's called an urban myth."

"Her-bin what?"

"Urban myth. They're stories that get started and are passed around until people start thinking they're real." Peter realized Bobby had stopped listening; his eyes were fixed on something back down the trail. "You OK, Bobby?"

"Look," Bobby whispered, "by that tree. He must be following us from the field."

Peter strained his eyes. "Which tree?"

"The one with the broken arm."

Peter saw the tree. The bottom limb had been snapped a foot or so from the trunk and hung down lifelessly. But he didn't see a boy standing by it. "Let's just keep walking. Maybe he'll get sick of his game and go."

The rest of the way home, as Bobby kept glancing back over his shoulder, Peter kept a close eye on Bobby. His actions seemed irrational, almost frantic. It frightened Peter to think that his little brother might be having hallucinations. The fear spread through Peter's body, starting in his stomach, cutting through his chest, finally lodging in his throat. The sickening feeling almost made him shake. For Bobby's sake, he kept the feeling under control and gave no clue that anything was wrong.

The skies grew darker with every passing moment. Sunlight no longer escaped through the heavy clouds, which had formed a rolling black mass. The pounding winds hit the boys as they left the protection of the woods. Except for a few pieces of litter pushed along by the gusts, the streets were deserted. Even the birds had disappeared to seek shelter from the coming storm.

It took only a few more minutes for Peter and

Bobby to make their way home once they hit
Fifth Street. The houses along the street appeared
dead because the clouded sky had stripped away
all the colors, leaving dull, cold shells. Even their
own house looked lifeless. The only motion was a
curtain flapping out an open side window on the
second floor.

"Good thing it hasn't started raining yet," Peter
said. "You left your window open again."

"I always forget," Bobby said.

He ran up the porch steps and through the front
door, leaving it wide open. Peter followed at a much
slower pace.

"Fifi! Fifi! Where are you baby?" Their neighbor
Mrs. Romun bellowed from her porch. Her dreary
orange bathrobe tried to hide her rather large shape—
tried, but failed.

Peter was only inches from the door when Mrs.
Romun said, "Peter . . . Peter dear. Have you seen
Fifi? I'm so worried."

Evil images of Fifi popped into Peter's head. The
nasty poodle had a high, whiny yelp and a quick snap,
which Peter would always remember because of the
small scar on his ankle. "No, Mrs. Romun. I haven't
seen Fifi."

"Oh, my. She's just a little thing, so defenseless,"
she said, then called for the dog again.

Peter smiled politely and entered his house. The
wind gave some resistance as Peter closed the door,
then died down for a moment causing him to slam the
door with a bang.

"What's all the commotion about?" Sharon Cowal
said from the kitchen.

"It's just us, Mom," Peter said.

She walked to the front door while wiping her

hands on a flowered hand towel. Her dark blonde hair was held back from drooping to her shoulders by two strategically placed hairpins. When the soft curls were down they perfectly framed her delicate features. "I know who it is. It was the number of you I wondered about. Sounded like an invasion. One of you charging up the stairs, the other banging doors. I wouldn't be surprised if the house came down right on top of us." She smiled at Peter. Her smile disappeared when she read the worry in his eyes. "What's wrong? Lose another kite?"

"No, it's on the porch."

"Honey, what's wrong?"

"Nothing, I suppose." Peter started up the stairs, then stopped after taking only four steps. "Mom?"

"Yes, dear?"

"Nothing." He continued up the steps. "I think I'll try to get some studying done before supper. Call me when it's ready."

As Sharon watched her oldest son disappear around the bend of the stairs, she couldn't help thinking of her late husband Max. She missed him a lot. At times like that moment she missed him the most. The boys needed a father to talk to.

Still thinking about Peter, she started back toward the kitchen when someone began to knock at the front door. The rapping was soft at first, but grew in intensity as she approached.

"I'm coming," she said. "I'm coming."

After she pulled the door open and started to greet the early evening visitor, Sharon snorted in disgust. There was no one to hear her words. Besides Bobby's kite moving slightly with the breeze, the porch was empty.

Sharon closed the door and called upstairs, "Bobby,

you better come down and bring your kite in before it blows off the porch."

"OK, Mom," Bobby said from the second floor.

Before she could return to the kitchen, she heard another knock. That time it was sharp and distinct. Again she opened the door, and again she found no one. But the kite was propped straight up against the house, apparently moved by the mischievous caller. She stepped out onto the porch and decided that some children must be playing games.

As Sharon stood on the porch, gripping the hand towel tightly at her side, Bobby came to the door and asked, "What are you doing, Mom?"

"Oh, nothing. Coming for your kite?"

"Yep," Bobby said. "This one's the best. Peter got it up a mile."

"He did?"

"Yeah, it was great."

"Well, you better bring it in before it rains."

Ten minutes passed before the rain actually started. The small droplets hit the windows with a soft patter. Sharon went around the house making sure all the windows were tightly closed. While she was securing the windows, she saw Bobby standing alone with his kite in his hands. He was standing near Mrs. Romun's yard and for a moment it looked as if he talking to someone. She turned the handle and cranked open the window. "Bobby, come in now. You're going to get soaked."

Bobby jumped at the sound of his mother's voice. "Yes, Mom," he said, his voice so faint she barely heard him.

Meeting Bobby at the door, Sharon wiped the small beads of rain water from his shoulder and asked, "What were you doing in the rain?"

"It's hardly raining," he said.

"I thought you were talking to someone."

"No. Just thinking."

"Thinking about what?"

"Nothing much."

"Guy stuff?" she asked.

Bobby nodded his head. "Yeah, guy stuff."

"Well, go get cleaned up. Supper's almost ready."

Outside the rain came down harder. Mrs Romun's poodle Fifi sniffed along the side of the Cowals' house, ignoring the pellets of water falling around her. She stopped. Her head shot up. She started to growl, exposing her sharp yellowed teeth. She backed away and then lunged forward, snapping and snarling.

The vicious animal was swept up into the air. Fifi yelped and fell back to the wet grass. Her body twitched once, then became still. Her pink tongue dangled from the side of her mouth. Her eyes rolled back in her head, showing only two white orbs. The cold rain washed at the red stain on the fur around her throat.

Two days later, Peter scrawled an extra tidbit of information from his physics textbook into the margin of the class notes, figuring that every little bit helped. The desk lamp filled his work area with a white-yellow glow, leaving the rest of his bedroom in shadows. His hand guided the black pen across the lined pages of the spiral notebook. It was all a part of his ritual of studying after supper.

When a knock sounded on the closed door, Peter recognized Bobby's firm rap and said, "Come in."

"Peter?" Bobby said, poking only his head into the semidarkened room. "Can I bug you a minute?"

"Sure," Peter said, closing his book, the black pen

acting as a bookmark, "and you're not bugging me."

"Well, Mom says not to disturb you when you study."

"It's OK. Really." Peter motioned for his brother to enter. "What's up?"

"Can I borrow your softball? The big mushy one. That one's my favorite."

"Let's see," Peter said, pretending to search his room. "I'm not sure I remember where I put it."

"Your closet. It's in your closet."

"You think so? I'd better look." Peter flipped on the ceiling light and walked to the closet. "Only a box in here."

"Yeah, that's right," Bobby said. "It's in the box."

"You're right." Peter reached inside and pulled out a tennis ball. "Here, you go."

Bobby laughed. "Oh, that ain't it. You know that."

"I guess this must be it." He pulled out a large white ball.

"Yeah, that's it. The big mushy one."

"That's strange. There seems to be something wrong with it," Peter said, returning to his desk. From a plastic holder of pens and pencils, he removed a black magic marker. He popped the cap off and wrote something on the ball. "But I can make it all right."

"What are you doing?"

"This." Peter showed the writing to his brother.

Bobby's eyes lit up when he read his own name on the spongy softball. "You mean it?"

"If it's your favorite, you should have it." He tossed the ball to Bobby.

"Wow, wait until Georgie sees this. You're the best brother in the whole wide world."

"You saw Georgie again?" Peter asked cautiously.

"He was waiting for me when I got off the bus." Bobby stared down at his name on the softball. "He wanted to play. I told him we had to watch out for Mrs. Romun."

"That's a good thing to tell him, I guess."

"Bobby, what have I told you about bothering your brother?" Sharon said, appearing in the doorway, her expression stern, but not angry.

"He's not," Peter assured his mother.

"Look what Peter gave me!" Bobby said, holding out the white ball, proudly displaying his name.

"That was very nice of him," she said, smiling at Peter. "But, young man, your brother wants to study. Take your ball back to your room. I'll bring you up a couple of cookies."

"The ones with the white stuff in the middle?" Bobby asked.

"OK. The ones with the white stuff. Let's go." She took Bobby by the shoulder and directed him toward the door.

"'Bye, Peter," Bobby said. "Thanks for the ball. It's real neat."

"No problem, buddy."

"How's the studying going?" Sharon asked Peter as Bobby marched out of the room.

"Fine."

"You sure? You look a little, well, upset."

"No, just a little tired. Got Ohm's law on the brain. That's all."

"You want me to bring you up a couple cookies, too?"

"No, thanks. Not hungry."

"All right then." She left her oldest son to wrestle with his schoolbooks.

It wasn't much of a match. After a few minutes

Peter leaned back in his chair. He had trouble returning to his physics book. The events of the last couple
days tugged at him, breaking his concentration.
Thoughts of how, while playing in the backyard
after school, Bobby had found Fifi dead around
the side of the house. Bobby seemed fine now;
nevertheless Peter worried how the whole incident
had affected his brother. Not the poodle's death, but
the events afterward, when the police were called.

During the storm that had hit two days earlier,
the heavy rains and strong winds had littered the
neighborhood with many large broken branches, and
in the opinion of the investigating officer, Fifi had
been fatally struck by one of those falling limbs.
The police thought it best to drop the case, but Mrs.
Romun refused their explanation. She implied that
Bobby had something to do with the dog's death.
"That sort of creature," she had told the police, allud-
ing to Bobby in her cruel, heartless way. Those words
had cut into Peter then and continued to do so every
time he heard them repeated in his mind. The worst
memory, however, was the look on Bobby's face. He
had just stared at the lifeless animal. He'd seemed
paralyzed by the sight of death, and he'd even looked
a little guilty.

And to top off the whole weird mess, Bobby had
created an imaginary friend named Georgie. Peter
couldn't remember Bobby ever mentioning Georgie
before. Not to say he hadn't, but Peter had been so
caught up in his schoolwork lately that he could've
missed Bobby talking about his new friend. He just
wasn't sure.

Peter's bedroom door had been left open and the
sounds of Bobby's laughter came from down the hall.
Peter pulled himself out of the chair. Walking down

the hall he expected to see his mother in Bobby's room with the cookies she had promised. When he peeked through the crack between the door and its frame, he saw Bobby laughing and talking to empty air.

"It's starting to get too dark outside for me to show you. Anyways, it's almost my bedtime," Bobby said and paused. Then he said to the nothingness, "Sure, we can play catch tomorrow."

Chapter Two

"Are you sure you have the right day?" Amanda Colins asked her associate David Jensen. A slight twinge crawled up her lower back. The wooden chair without the least bit of padding she was sitting on had to be a throwback to the Puritan age. She had to readjust her five-foot three-inch frame for the third time and, to make things worse, she needed a cigarette.

"It's right here," David said, showing her his appointment book. "Thursday, one o'clock, Fulton City Council."

The outer office, where Amanda and David had been told by a receptionist to wait, was a simple white room with two doors in opposite walls, a ceiling light with a white glass fixture, and a steel-gray desk. The only attempt at decoration was a watercolor print of a busy open-air cafe.

When Amanda looked at David she had to make sure she wasn't staring. It had been only two days since he had shaved off his beard, leaving a very

24

trim, very dark mustache. "It's for the summer," he
had told her. She liked the change. He looked good
and years younger. He was 44, but without the face
fur she thought he looked a lot closer to 32, her
own age.

Amanda admired David for his discipline. Every
morning he jogged seven miles, and the effort showed
in his thin, lean body. She had tried working out at
a swim-and-fitness club, but made the blunder of
wearing the form-fitting leotard she thought looked
so cute in the store. She found it had an adverse
effect on the males at the gym. After receiving three
dinner offers and one proposal of marriage on her first
night working out, she decided to wear the grubbiest
clothes she could find and to pin her long brunette
hair up in a sloppy heap. But even though she thought
she looked horrific, the guys hadn't. From then on,
she watched aerobic video tapes at home when she
had time.

"What's taking so long?" Amanda said at last.
"We've been sitting here for forty-five minutes."

"You're the one always telling me to be patient,"
David said.

"Patience is one thing, but this is ridiculous."
Amanda shook her head. Her hazel eyes found their
way back to the hanging print. She had noticed how
one of the men sitting at a table looked a lot like
Mark Twain. She kept examining the watercolor faces
to see if she could recognize any other characters of
the past.

From the inner office came strange mumbling. That
noise had been an on-again, off-again companion to
the twosome since they sat down. At times the sound
grew in volume and pitch.

"They came to you. I'll give them just another two

minutes." As she finished speaking the last word, the inner door opened.

"Please, come in," said a young man no older than 22. "They're ready for you now."

Amanda walked in first, then waited for David to enter before venturing too far into the room. The decor was much less bland than the outer office. The walls were nicely papered. On the farthest wall hung an oil painting of a very distinguished looking man wearing turn-of-the-century clothes. In the center of the room was a large polished mahogany table with matching padded chairs. There were five people already sitting around the polished table. Two men seated along the side had stood up as Amanda stepped over the threshold. Another man, who sat under the oil painting, and two women remained still.

"Good to see you again, Dr. Jensen," the taller of the two men standing said. "I'm sorry. I'm afraid I haven't met your secretary."

"I'm not—" Amanda began to say.

"Can we dispense with the pleasantries?" the seated man said. He was a large man with more than a double chin. His suit was well tailored, and it concealed, Amanda was sure, a very out-of-shape body. "Can we get on with it?"

Before Amanda and David sat, David said, "Gentlemen and ladies, this is Dr. Amanda Colins."

"Oh, I'm quit sorry," the tall man said. "Please forgive me. I—"

"Yes, yes, Murry, now sit down," the fat man said. "Please wait outside, Jeffrey. We won't need notes for this meeting."

"Yes, sir." The young man disappeared to the outer office, closing the door behind him.

"I'm Marcus Trulain," the fat man continued.

"Chair of the Fulton City Council. My embarrassed colleague is Murry Kampfer. To his right, Frank Currie."

"Good afternoon," Frank said. "Please, have a seat."

"And the ladies to my left," Trulain continued, after giving Frank a cold stare, "are Sarah Heepner and Opal Manky."

Opal nodded with a pleasant smile of subtle red lipstick. Through her thick glasses, Sarah just shifted her eyes back and forth between Amanda and David. She had a tight hair bun on the top of her head.

"Now that we have that out of the way," Marcus Trulain said. "I must start this meeting by saying"—his eyes moved around the table—"that this council is not unanimous in its decision to have a parapsychologist come in to solve our problems."

"I should say not," Sarah said.

"It was a majority decision," Frank said forcefully.

"By only one vote," she bit back.

"That doesn't matter. It was a majority."

"Order. Can we have order?" Trulain shouted over the two.

Amanda noticed David's glance at her. She smiled back, but not her friendly smile. *What has David gotten me into this time?* she thought.

David cleared his throat, obviously uncomfortable. "If you need more time?"

"No," Trulain said. "It has been decided. You are to proceed with the investigation."

"Fine," Amanda said. "If you can give me a copy of the file."

"Oh," Murry Kampfer said, "I thought Dr. Jensen would be handling the investigation."

"I see." Amanda stood up. First the waiting, then

the bickering, and finally the insult. She had had enough.

David also rose from his chair, but to stop Amanda. "I'll handle this," he whispered to her. "Please."

As Amanda reluctantly sat back in her chair, David said, "I'm afraid this misunderstanding is my fault. Mr. Kampfer, when you approached my department at Ohio State and asked me to investigate the site for paranormal activity, I never said I would be taking on the case myself."

"Well, that is true," Murry said.

"You are very fortunate to have Dr. Colins. She has headed many investigations in the past, as I have; however, she possesses certain insights that I do not."

"Then you will be assisting her."

Amanda smiled at David. She liked the way that sounded.

"Well, only with some of the very preliminary stages. Unlike Dr. Colins, who is on sabbatical, I still have classes to hold, followed by the inevitable grading of final exams and senior projects. The life at a university—I'm sure you all understand."

"That sounds reasonable," Opal said. "What else will you need from us, Dr. Colins?"

"I want to go over the files you have, and Dr. Jensen and I will visit the field after leaving here. If the case bears investigating," Amanda told the council, "I will simply need some office space."

"Office 117 is available," Frank Currie said. "We've been using it for storage."

"Fine," Trulain said. "Get it cleared out by—"

"Monday," Frank said. "You can have it by Monday."

"That's suitable," Amanda said. "It will give me

time to put my affairs in order before I start."

"I want you, Dr. Colins and Dr. Jensen, to know my feeling on this matter as council chair. I think this situation is a waste of time. But"—with a simple hand gesture, Trulain stopped Frank before he could interrupt—"I feel it is important we finish with this nonsense once and for all. Fulton, Ohio, is a growing community. Last year we were a town of fifteen thousand, and this year we will probably be adding another five hundred to that. We need to develop all our resources. We can't allow a piece of land to go undeveloped because of a lot of superstition."

"And if it's not superstition?" Amanda asked.

"Then take care of it or tell us how to. That's what you're here for."

"Very well," Amanda said, rising from her chair. "I will call you tomorrow with what I find."

On the edge of Fulton stood a piece of land that had changed little as the city grew around it. Save for a few chunks of charred wood hidden under tall grass, the only remnant of the building that once stood on the spot was its stone foundation, which had broken into many smaller pieces. Years of rain and wind had decayed the blackened ruin down to its brittle base; heavy grass patches forced their way through the cracks, and over the span of time, dirt had pushed up, distorting the crumbling rock.

For years, the old house remained desolate, its windows all broken and boarded up, its wood rotting. On quiet nights, passersby claimed to hear strange noises coming from the dead structure. Full of fear and superstition, people left the house to its secrets. Even after the structure mysteriously burned to the ground, townsfolk still stayed away. Rumors flourished that the land itself was haunted. A large, bent oak tree, untouched by the flames, rose high above the ruins. Even though the oak seemed perfect for climbing by playful children, the children stayed away. Only on a dare would the bravest child enter the lot with the challengers watching from the safety of the road. Most who tried failed and ran back screaming. The few who did cross swore they would never do so again.

When the boundaries for the town of Fulton had grown in 1945, the records on the property's true ownership were at best unclear and, with no one to claim it, the city took legal possession. Several groups of city workers tried over the years to get an exact survey of the lot, because the different mayors and council members were determined that the land would be cleaned up and sold. The workers all reported strange happenings and eerie feelings connected to the area. Even potential buyers didn't stay on the property for long. Some claimed to have been touched from behind, only to find no one standing there. Others claimed to have heard laughter. One woman insisted she heard a child calling out to her. Afraid the child was in need of help, she scoured the property—and found no one. The council members dismissed the stories as fantasies, as delusions, as silly superstition, and they refused to take the land off the market. But even buyers from outside Fulton, people who had no possible way of hearing any rumors or stories, didn't stay on the property long. At first, the whole matter was just scoffed at, treated like a big joke. But as the years passed, the city council refused to give up trying to sell the land—even if it meant calling in a para-psychologist to prove the rumors had no basis in reality.

*   *   *

David Jensen snapped a quick photograph of the field from the road. He advanced the film and snapped another shot. "Looks pretty normal to me."

"You should know better than to make such a hasty judgment like that," Amanda said, her eyes focusing on the grassy area. "Get a shot of the old foundation. And I'll need a close-up too."

"Sure thing." The sun was slightly behind him, which always made for better pictures. "I only said it looks normal. Let's move in farther and see what your insight has to say."

"Do you have to call it that?"

"Sorry."

The two walked together, wading through the thick grass. Amanda already felt a strange trembling coming from the old stone. The soft vibration against her skin would start one moment and end the next, as if someone were playing with a light switch.

"This place hasn't been totally deserted," David said, referring to another path trampled through the high growth of grass and weeds. He took a picture. "Probably just a deer or something else mundane."

"Follow it," Amanda said. "See if you can find anything."

"Like what?"

"I don't know. Deer droppings or something more mundane."

"Cute."

"The file said the house burned down over sixty years ago. I'm going to see if I can pick up any impressions from the fragments. I'm guessing the site of the old house will be the focal point of any activity."

"Not much left," David said. He took the close-up 'shot Amanda wanted.

"Enough for me."

"Smile," David said and snapped off a photo of Amanda. "Another candid moment."

"Don't waste film."

"I wouldn't call a photo of that gorgeous face of yours a waste." David smiled and started to trace the path.

When his back was turned Amanda felt herself smiling. She knew joking was his way of hiding his feelings. She knew the strength of his caring for her. Her insight told her, but she never let on she knew. Besides, she enjoyed their witty banter.

Amanda picked up a hunk of stone, which crumbled in her hand. As the small pieces fell between her fingers, the vibration covered her hand. At times she felt anger, at others, loneliness.

"Are you getting anything?" David said, coming up behind her.

"Yes, but . . ."

"But what? You feel a presence?"

"Not a presence, really, more like an afterglow. As if there was something here, but gone—only not gone. Almost like the feeling you get coming home to an empty house after a long trip. It still seems empty, but it's not. I can't explain it any better."

"I take it, then, that the investigation is a go."

"Yep, seems like a hot one," she said, brushing away the residue of stone from her hand. "What's that in your hand?"

"The path forked off. I found it at one end." David had brought back a broken wooden dowel. "It's pretty clean. It couldn't have been here very long. I thought you might want to give it the once-over anyway."

Amanda took the broken rod from David. She held it tight for a moment.

"Anything?" David asked.

"Yeah, it's a stick."

"Brilliant. Anything else."

"It's broken."

"Well, I guess we're done here for the present. Now what?"

Amanda glanced at her watch. "It's almost three-thirty. I have a dinner date with an old college friend at five."

"Really?"

Amanda felt a surge of energy come from David. "Yes, she and I were really a wild pair as freshman," she said and felt the energy fade. "Funny how we are both so respectable now. She teaches at the local high school—shaping young minds, as she puts it. I told her I must have dialed the wrong number."

"I bet she appreciated that."

"Molly has a good sense of humor. You could join us if you want."

"I wouldn't want to stifle all your girl talk. Ah, sorry, woman talk. Or is that person talk? It's so important to be politically correct these days."

"I'm being serious," Amanda said. "You can join us. I know she'd love to meet you."

"If you're sure I won't be disturbing the reunion."

"I'm sure. And think of it this way. It's a night away from your cooking."

"Can't argue with that. I accept your kind offer."

As the two started back to the car, David said, "Wait a minute. It's four hours back to Columbus, and I drove. How were you planning to get back if I hadn't accepted?"

"That was never a problem. I knew you wouldn't say no to a free meal."

"Come on," David said. "I'll buy you a cup of coffee while we wait."

"Great!"

David reached into his pocket, then looked at Amanda. "You got any money?"

"Great."

Chapter Three

The three o'clock bell rang. In the same instant, class-room doors opened and a wave of teenagers poured into the empty hall. Fulton High had finished yet another school day. The sunshine coming through the windows on that magnificent Friday afternoon reminded everyone summer was close at hand. Voices filled the hall with all the hopes and dreams a three-month vacation promised to the teenage mind. The voices mixed with the metallic clang of slamming lockers and soon the slamming surpassed the human tones in intensity. The lockers that lined both sides of the hall were painted with a light gray enamel; each had a combination lock built into its door with a slot in the center of the dial for the master key, which Principal Moorse used during his infamous locker raids.

Peter Cowal broke into an exhausted grin as he left his physics class, his books tightly tucked under his arm. The week had finally dragged to its conclusion and with the weekend came the chance to spend some extra time with his little brother. Bobby had been on his own more than usual of late, which meant more time with his imaginary friend Georgie. Peter blamed himself for making his brother so lonely he had to create a friend. He should have eased back a little from his studies, Peter had told himself, and given Bobby more attention, eliminating the need for Georgie. He hoped to make it up to his brother that weekend.

Peter had made a point to finish all his homework in study hall. He wanted nothing to interfere with his plans. He didn't have to worry about Bobby having any homework—he never did. Bobby's school had a very structured system of teaching, one that watched the progress of each student closely. All work was done at the school and carefully supervised to make sure it was completed correctly.

As Peter continued down the hall, he glanced down at his watch. Bobby's bus would have dropped him off by then. His pace quickened.

"Hey, look where you're going," an angry boy snapped at Peter.

"Sorry," he said. The main hall was crowded. It was strange, Peter had always thought, that the only time after the last bell that the halls were crowded was on Friday afternoons. Other days the halls were dead silent in five minutes. On Fridays, however, many students stood around the lockers gabbing.

Peter made his way through the teens as best he could. But halfway down the hall someone shoved the books from under his arm and sent them flying across the floor. He retrieved his books while ignoring the flood of laughter and cruel remarks. A few notebook pages were covered with dusty gray sneaker prints and would need to be recopied, but there was no real damage to his books, nor his pride. He picked the last

of his books off the floor and simply brushed away
a small patch of dust from the bottom of his pant's
leg. The laughing stopped and the normal hall traffic
resumed. A few heads still turned Peter's way, but for
the most part, the excitement was over.

As Peter hurried on, he turned the corner, then
froze. The sudden change in his forward momentum
caused his physics book to slip out of his arms and
crash to the floor a second time. When Peter bent
down to pick up the fallen text, his eyes strained to
the side and caught a covert peek of the two girls
chatting by the lockers.

The two stood in front of Judy Kilter's locker.
Mona Thompson gabbed on as Judy began dialing
the combination. Mona dug through her black leather
purse and pulled out a small bottle of red fingernail polish. Judy stopped turning the numbered dial
and edged over alongside her friend to examine the
color. Mona opened the small bottle, applied the thick
glossy liquid to her fingernail, then held the painted
nail out so they got a better look.

Peter glanced over at Judy, but quickly turned away
when Mona looked his way. Her voice caught his ear;
still he could not make out what she had said. He
heard a loud giggle coming from the girls and figured
he was the cause of their amusement.

He stood close to the wall wasting time by
straightening out his books, first by title, then by
author—anything to keep Judy within sight. He took
another quick peek. Her long, auburn hair was pulled
back away from her very pretty face and tied off in
a French braid, which hung down past her shoulders.
Her clothes weren't tight, but the short-sleeved white
blouse and the blue-denim skirt did nothing to hide
her soft curves.

Mona was pretty too, Peter thought, but nothing like Judy. Mona had strawberry-blonde hair, except for the dark roots that needed covering about every three months.

No one knew how Peter felt about Judy—not even Bobby. Whenever he saw her walking down the hall or in the occasional class they had together, they never exchanged more than a few words to each other. They had known each other since childhood. Years ago, when their fathers worked together at the Fulton Construction Company, the two families spent weekends together up at Myer's Lake. Max Cowal and Roger Kilter often talked about going into business for themselves as partners. Both Judy and Peter's lives had changed a lot since then.

His attention on Judy made the other girl fade away deep into the background and finally evaporate to nothingness. He heard no more sounds, saw no more sights. His mind wandered back to his childhood—to their childhood—to the simple event of two small children meeting for the first time while playing outside on a warm sunny day.

Young Peter had marched up to the tiny girl playing quietly with her Barbie doll, the white laced edges of her bright yellow dress tucked partially under her legs. A small blanket protected the pretty dress from the emerald grass that would have permanently stained the delicate fabric. The cloudless sky was royal blue and a slight breeze cooled the day. He stood there a moment scrutinizing the little girl. She was too content brushing Barbie's long blonde hair to notice.

"What's your name?" Peter asked.

She didn't look up, but answered, "Judy." She picked up one of Barbie's richly sequined evening gowns and placed it over the doll's body, deciding if she wanted to put that particular dress on her doll.

"My name's Peter Maxwell Cowal," he said, trying his best to sound the way he thought adults talked. "This is my house. I live here."

Judy kept playing with her doll and didn't respond. After a few moments of silence, Peter still didn't know what to make of the girl. His five-year-old mind came up with only one thing to say. "Dolls are stupid!"

"No, they're not," Judy said softly.

Peter sat on the ground next to the girl and watched her actions closely, examining every movement. "Wanna play a game?" he asked, after getting bored with his inspection. Judy looked up at him for the first time. "What?"

"I don't know."

"How about jacks?" she said.

"Jacks are for girls."

"No, my best friend plays jacks with me all the time. He likes to play." She glanced over her shoulder, then back at Peter. "He's not very good."

"He must be real dumb."

"Shhh, Georgie will hear you."

Peter looked around. "I don't see anyone."

"He's hiding. Maybe if he sees you playing jacks, he'll come out," she whispered.

Peter shook his head. "I don't want to play jacks," Peter said. "Let's play something else."

"What?"

"Do you like cars? I have real good ones."

She shook her head and went back to brushing Barbie's hair.

"I know," Peter said. "Let's play tag." He tapped her on the shoulder, then ran off laughing. "You're it!"

Judy started after him. "That's not fair. I wasn't ready."

"Can't catch me! Can't catch me." Peter shouted, laughing so hard he barely got his words out.

Peter's memories moved quickly through those times the two spent together as very young children. As they grew older, things changed. After the death of his father, Judy and her parents stopped coming over. Not right away, of course, but over time, their visits had grown more and more infrequent and finally stopped altogether. Peter and Judy ended up going to different grade schools. He had missed her at first; then, as the years passed, she drifted out of his thoughts. However, he had seen her on rare occasions.

"Hurry up, Peter," he remembered his mother calling upstairs one evening. "Bobby's sitter will be here soon."

Peter came stomping down the stairs dressed in his blue Cub Scout uniform. "Mrs. Olsen is an old crab. I don't like her, and neither does Bobby."

"Peter!" she said, her mouth open and eyes staring at her son. "Don't talk that way about your elders. And she's not an old crab. She just doesn't take any grief from the two of you. Besides, Mrs. Olsen can't come tonight. Her arthritis is bothering her again."

"She's always been stiff as a board. What's the difference now?"

"Young man, I want to hear none of that. She's a sweet woman."

"Old lemon puss, you mean," he said under his breath as the doorbell rang. But his mother had gone to answer the door and missed his remark.

"Hello, Mrs. Cowal," Peter heard a girl's voice say as he adjusted the gold pins on his shirt. He spit on his finger and rubbed the fluid on his good-conduct pin, then wiped the pin clean with his shirtsleeve.

"You remember Judy Kilter," Sharon said as Peter went downstairs. "You two used to play together."

"I remember," he said, diverting his eyes from Judy's face and burying his hands deep in his pockets.

"Hi, Peter," Judy said.

"Hi," he said, his face to the floor.

"We shouldn't be too long," Sharon said. "Just a few hours. I left the number of the school if there's any trouble."

"Yes, Mrs. Cowal."

Peter stood there twisting his right foot into the carpeting. His shoulders curled toward the floor.

"Let's go, Peter. You don't want to be late for your awards assembly, do you? And don't slouch."

Peter felt his face turning red. Then his mother put her hand on his back to hurry him along past Judy to the front door.

"Have a nice time," Judy said. " 'Bye, Peter."

As he left, Peter had looked at her, then turned away before he met her gaze. And standing in the hall of Fulton High, he realized he was still too shy to look Judy in the face.

Suddenly, a sharp metallic bang brought Peter's mind back to the present. Judy stood in front of her locker fighting with the handle. When it refused to open, she banged her fist against the door in frustration.

His heart started to pound as he realized Mona was nowhere about. He took a deep breath and strolled over by the locker, praying the wetness under his arms wasn't drenching his shirt.

"Having troub-bles, Judy?" Peter said, as composed as possible, thanking God that his voice hadn't picked that particular moment to crack.

"Oh, hi, Peter," Judy said, kicking the locker. "Stupid lock. It never opens right."

"Let me try," he said and reached out his slightly shaking hand.

"No. That's OK. Mr. Hedburg can use his key."

"You'll have a problem finding him. He's probably sweeping out the boys' locker room. Let me try. What's the combination?"

"I don't want to put you to any trouble."

"It's no trouble, really." For the first time in his life, Peter looked straight into her deep brown eyes without feeling the least bit embarrassed. His actions alone almost astounded him, but he knew they were worth all the effort when Judy smiled.

"Well, OK. Four, twenty-four, thirty-four." She grinned. "It's pretty easy to remember."

Judy watched as Peter carefully turned the locker's dial. She appreciated his help and had always thought he was sweet, but she was also a little worried. He was the kicking board for half the school, though she had never understood why. Whatever the reason, she didn't want to be the cause for any more of his torment. And although she wanted to ask about his family, she figured it would be better if none of her friends saw them together.

Peter turned to the last number and lifted up on the chrome handle—nothing. He pulled harder, and the locker snapped open. "There, I think the tumblers are good; it must be the door catch."

"Thanks, Peter . . . I . . . thanks." Judy flushed, suddenly embarrassed.

"Anytime!" Peter said, feeling good. "You know, I was just wondering if, you know, if you weren't busy. . . ."

"Peter, I really have to go. Martin is waiting and—"

Two large arms, seemingly out of nowhere, moved so quickly both Peter and Judy were caught off guard. They overpowered Peter; his body flew forward and landed partially inside Judy's locker. He felt a pair of hands pushing and shoving at his shoulder and waist, forcing him farther into the cramped space until he was surrounded by the narrow walls. His face was flush against the cold sheet metal, his arms pinned against his body. There was a loud slam, then darkness until Peter made out thin strips of light shining through the locker vents. Laughter erupted outside the locker until Judy's voice started to overpower it.

"Let him out of there, Ox!" Judy said, anger strong in her voice.

"He asked for it, trying to hit on another guy's girl. What would Martin think?"

"He wasn't, Ox," Judy yelled. "He was just helping me."

"Well, he shouldn't have been standing in front of an open locker. The dumb ass was asking to get pushed in."

Peter couldn't help thinking Ox was right on both counts, and he had only himself to blame for his current imprisonment.

"Come on," Ox said. "Martin's waiting to head down to O'Brian's."

"I've got to let Peter out of there," Judy insisted. "And I have to wait for Mona."

"Forget about them," Ox said. "We're late."

Judy tried to convince Ox to free Peter, but he pushed her along. She shouted for him to let her go, but gradually her protests faded away to silence.

Trapped inside the locker, Peter decided to wait a few minute before pounding, refusing to give his captor the pleasure of hearing him. And in the future, he'd think twice before talking to Judy at school.

Bobby stood alone in his backyard. Even though Peter had cut the grass the day before, the scent of the freshly mowed lawn still permeated the air. Small bits of grass slightly stained the white rubber trim of Bobby's black high-top sneakers. He wore his baseball glove snugly on one hand and gripped the large softball in the other.

"It's really easy, watch," Bobby said. He threw the ball straight up into the air and caught the ball firmly in his glove. "See, now you try." Bobby's gaze met with vacant air. "Try, just try. It's really easy."

Bobby tossed the ball. It sailed through the air and landed in Mrs. Romun's yard, and Bobby scooted after it.

"You get out of here!" Mrs. Romun yelled from behind her patio screen door. "You get off my property or I'll call the law again. And this time they'll lock you away. Like your kind should be."

The shrewish scream made Bobby jump. Shaken, he could barely made out the large shape hiding in the darkness behind the metal mesh. "I just wanted my ball back. I'm sorry. Me and my friend were playing and—"

"Your friend. What friend? I've been watching you, you little liar. You lied about Fifi and I know you're lying now."

"I'm not lying!" Bobby said. "This is my friend Georgie."

Mrs. Romun slid the screen door open with a screeching sound of metal against metal. She poked her head out of the blackness and glared across the yard, and her angry eyes scared the boy, who backed away to the safety of his own yard. "There's no one here, you dummy."

"Don't call me that!"

"You should be locked up—locked up forever!"

Tears started to run down Bobby's cheeks. "Don't say that! Don't say that!"

"That's what I'll do. I'll call the police. You're on my property. I'll call the police. They'll lock you in jail."

"Stop it! Stop it! I didn't do anything." Bobby ran off toward the back door of his house, the tears streaming from his eyes.

Mrs. Romun slipped back into the darkness of her house, smiling as she watched Bobby cry through her open patio door. Her fat arm shot out of the doorway. "You stay out of my yard!" she yelled, shaking her pudgy finger. "You retard!"

The word barely finished forming on the large woman's lips when the screen door slid across its metal guide and slammed against her arm, pinning the fat limb between the door and its frame.

Mrs. Romun screamed and tried without success to pull open the screen, which had jumped its guide and was wedged tight in the frame. Struggling in vain, the woman moaned in pain and her arm turned white as it dangled in the air.

Pedaling his old green bike down Wellesley Avenue, Peter was happy to be getting home. The afternoon sun felt good against his face, and a slight breeze at his back made the ride a little easier. His shoulders still felt a little sore, but he was content with the feeling of being freed from the locker.

He hadn't had to wait long for his release. He had heard a sound echoing through his confined space and recognized it as Mr. Hedburg's broom banging against the bottom of the lockers as the janitor swept the halls. Peter pounded on the locker door, hoping Mr. Hedburg had his hearing aid turned up. He pounded once more, waited a moment, then pounded again. His fist struck against the sheet metal door as it opened, causing it to fly forward and knock the broom out of Mr. Hedburg's hands.

The glare from the hallway light had stung Peter's eyes, and he'd raised his right hand and shaded his face until his eyes grew accustomed to the brightness. Seconds later Peter saw the half-surprised, half-angered face of Mr. Hedburg staring at him. As Peter stepped out of the locker, Mr. Hedburg chewed him out for playing in the locker.

Anger made Peter pedal harder—anger at old man Hedburg, anger at Ox, and anger at himself. He picked up speed as he turned a corner and headed down Fifth Street, only four blocks from his house. Even his feelings for Judy angered him.

"How could I even let myself think I could just go up and ask her out?" he asked himself. "I make an ass out of myself every time I get within ten feet of her. Why do I do it?"

Then he laughed and lost some of his anger. It was all too clear he liked Judy more than he would admit.

The blasting sound of a car horn halfway down the block snapped Peter out of his thoughts. He looked over his shoulder and recognized the blue-gray Dodge Charger from the school parking lot. Instinctively, he stood up on the pedals of his bike and pumped as hard as his muscles allowed. He felt the tension building in his legs as they moved up and down as fast as he could force them. He leaned his body forward, using his weight to gain speed. Again he looked back at the car, which had easily caught up with him. The Dodge Charger, still honking, was just inches from Peter's back tire, and for a few seconds, it stayed right there behind him. Even under the sound of the roaring engine and the blaring horn, Peter could distinguish raucous laughter.

"Eat dirt, Cowal!" a boy screamed out the window. The car pulled alongside Peter. One of the passengers stuck out her middle finger and screamed its meaning; then a boy spit at Peter. Fortunately, the wind redirected the slime and it missed him. As the car drove past Peter, a trail of dark smoke came from the tail pipe, and the heavy stink of burning motor oil polluted the air.

At first, Peter thought the worst was over, that the teenagers were going to leave him alone. Deep down, however, Peter knew that was too easy. And he was soon proved right. The car turned at a sharp angle in front of him, its black tires squealing against the street causing white patches of smoke to rise from the pavement. The odor of burning rubber mixed with the stench of the oil. Without thinking, Peter swerved to miss hitting the car. His front wheel wedged into a small crevice, stopping the bike dead. Peter flew over the top of his handlebars, flipped over once, and landed on his back. The soft dirt at the road's edge broke his fall. Somewhere between the flip and the landing, his glasses flew off his face.

Peter rolled onto his side. His arm was numb except for the tip of his elbow, which throbbed with dull pain. He was a little dizzy and his vision was blurry, but he could make out the fuzzy image of his bike lying flat in the street, its front wheel spinning unhampered. Just ahead of the bike, he made out two white back-up lights coming toward him. The ringing in his ears stopped, and in rushed the sound of teenagers chanting, "Run it over! Run it over!" Then came a loud crunch, followed by more tire squealing and laughter. As the Charger drove off, the laughter seemed to lag behind.

"Are you hurt?" asked a slightly accented man's voice that Peter recognized. His squinting eye recognized the familiar silver-gray hair, though the man's face was a blur. It was Alex Stein, an elderly friend of his family. Alex lived alone in a large Victorian house, and Peter often helped him with his yard work when the job ended up being too great a challenge for his aged body. Peter had known Alex for as far back as he remembered, and at least once a month Peter's mother invited him over for dinner. Alex always accepted; he loved her cooking.

"Just took a fall, that's all," Peter said in response to Alex's question. He reached over and picked up his glasses from the grass. When he put them on, Peter was relieved that both lenses were unbroken.

"Nonsense," Alex said, leaning down on one knee. "I saw the whole thing. Those kids could have killed you."

"It's nothing."

"No. I should call the police."

"No, please don't. It will only make things worse."

Alex reluctantly nodded his head. "All right. Let's get you cleaned up. I have some bandages in the house. Come." Alex helped Peter to his feet. Then he held Peter by the arm to steady him as they walked up the cement path leading to the large white house.

O'Brian's Arcade had three major attractions for the teens of Fulton: video games, junk food, and freedom from parental influence. An hour after school let out that Friday afternoon, the place was packed. The video games were beeping and flashing. The kitchen was turning out so many greasy hamburgers and french fries that the plates of food lined the pickup counter from end to end. Judy Kilter's eyes moved around the arcade from the booth where she sat next to Martin Welth and his omnipresent white-and-blue Fulton High School letterman jacket. The young couple had been dating since the start of the school year. At first Judy had enjoyed the jealousy of the other girls. As time passed, however, she wasn't too sure if there was really anything to envy.

"You're not still mad?" Martin asked, looking at Judy with his hard steel-blue eyes. He smiled and gently touched her bare forearm.

"Why don't you do something about it?" Judy said.

"Hey, I'm not their mother. They do what they want."

"That's bullshit and you know it." She pulled her arm away, letting his hand fall to the tabletop. "Ox and those other goons do exactly what you tell them. If you tell them to lay off Peter Cowal, they will, and you damn well know it."

"I'm sure it was nothing. Ox was just having a little fun. That's all." He ran his palm above his ear, smoothing back any strand of his sand-colored hair that might be out of place.

"Pushing someone into a locker," she said, "and slamming the door is not fun. It's cruel."

"He's just a little wound up. Hey, it's the week-end. Lighten up."

"Damn it, Martin! I'm serious."

"I know you are, baby," Martin said, reaching over to gently stroke her hair. "Peter Cowal's a loser.

Forget it. He's not worth the sweat."

She pushed his hand away. "He might not come from a rich family and have everything bought for him, but that doesn't mean he's less of a person than you."

"OK, OK. I'll see what I can do. Now can we discuss something more important like our plans for after the party tonight?" He caressed her leg. "Maybe a drive to the lake?"

When Judy didn't respond to his question or his touch, Martin moved his hand and changed the subject. "Bought a new tux for the big country club dance. Couldn't fit in my old one. Since I started lifting weights with Ox, I must have put three inches around my chest." He gave his arm a quick flex. "It should be one hell of a dance. Only the finest at Ridgeport Country Club."

"That dance is all Jessica seems to talk about these days," Judy said. "She keeps bugging me about what dress I'm going to wear. Do I have the right matching shoes?"

"Mothers are like that."

"She's my father's wife." Judy hated any reference to Jessica as her mother.

"OK, then, stepmothers are like that."

"Just drop it. She's the last person I want to talk about."

A waitress interrupted the couple. "Who ordered the cheeseburger with everything? Come on, I have other orders. Who gets the burger?"

Martin pointed to a spot on the table in front of him. "Right here."

"You OK, honey?" the waitress asked Judy, who wouldn't take her eyes off the woman.

Judy said nothing. She watched as a small stream

of blood trickled down the woman's hand to the end of her pinky and dripped onto the table. Judy jumped up and said, "Your hand. You're bleeding!"

The waitress dropped the tray with a loud crash. The two glasses full of Coke shattered on the floor, followed by the small basket of french fries, which soaked up the sweet fluid. The waitress looked at one hand, then the other, but found no blood. With an angry stare aimed directly at Judy, she shouted, "You trying to get me fired?"

"You . . . I thought I saw . . . I'm so sorry."

"You think it's funny?" the waitress said when Martin covered his mouth, trying to stifle a laugh. Martin shook his head, but a chuckle escaped from his lips.

"I'm sorry," Judy said again. "I really am. I don't know why I did that."

Something in Judy's solemn face calmed the waitress a little. "Oh, forget it. Just a couple of glasses, but I still have to charge you for the food and drinks, else it comes out of my tips."

"Hey, wait a minute," Martin said, "if you weren't so—"

"Shut up, Martin!" Judy said. "I'll pay for it."

As the waitress bent down to clear away some of the mess, Martin whispered his objection to her paying, but Judy said, "It was my fault. I'll pay."

"Damn!" the waitress kneeling on the floor shouted suddenly. She leaped to her feet, gripping her right hand tightly by the wrist as a small stream of blood trickled down her pinky and dripped onto the table.

Judy and Martin just stared at her, unable to say anything.

*　　*　　*

"Thanks, Mr. Stein," Peter said as they stepped outside into the cool air. "I'm sorry for the trouble."

"No trouble at all, my boy. You are lucky your arm's not broken."

"I just hit my funny bone. That's all. My elbow's not even scuffed that bad." Peter lifted his arm and eyed the piece of gauze Alex had fastened on with white medical tape.

"Well, you keep that bandage on it anyway," Alex said as they strolled down to the street. "Keep it clean, and tell your mother hello for me."

"I will."

"By the way, how is your brother doing?"

"Really well. The new school is helping a lot."

"Just make sure you encourage him. You're his big brother. He looks up to you."

"I try," Peter said. "I let him help me with one of my box kites. You should have seen his face as it went up. We found a good spot on an old field at the edge of town. There used to be a house or something there a long time ago."

"You must stay away from that field," Alex said, his friendly face twisting with fear. His tone made the boy take a step back.

"Why? There weren't any power lines, and there's only one big oak tree."

"Still, it's no place for boys to play." Alex's face eased. His voice became apologetic. "Please, forgive the ramblings of an old man, Peter. I worry about you and Bobby."

Peter just smiled and picked up his bike. The front tire was flat on its twisted rim, the frame bent into a crescent shape.

"This bike will never ride a straight line again," Peter said, his voice cracking slightly as he stared at the only real means of independence he had, which had become a twisted piece of metal.

"It's not really that bad," Alex said, trying to reassure Peter.

"I'll never be able to get it fixed," Peter said, gently tapping the bent frame with the tip of his sneaker. "It's going to be hard enough carrying the thing home."

"You can store the bike here, if you wish."

"Thanks, I don't feel too much like lugging it around right now. I can come back for it tomorrow."

"That would be fine," Alex said as he stroked his chin. "I'll see you tomorrow then. If you want, you can help me wax the Buick and earn yourself a little money. How about that?"

Peter smiled. He had never seen Alex drive the old car and knew he was trying to help.

"Sure," Peter said. "I can use the cash if I'm ever going to get my bike fixed."

"Fine, fine. You come back tomorrow. Say about ten o'clock."

Peter took five steps, then stopped, remembering his promise to spend the day with Bobby. Peter dashed up the walk. Alex had just opened his front door, but before he could enter, the boy called out, "Mr. Stein? Can we make it a little earlier, if it's no trouble?"

The old man smiled at Peter. "How about nine o'clock?"

Peter nodded and smiled back. He felt as if his luck was changing for the better.

At O'Brian's Arcade, two teenage boys and a girl couldn't contain their laughter as they thundered through the glass door. The two boys wore white-and-blue letter jackets that exactly matched those worn by Martin and Ox.

"Funniest thing I've ever seen," Suzy Kendell said. Her short brown hair was still slightly mussed from sticking her head out of the Charger's window.

"Yeah, did you see him wipe out?" Mark Turner said. His lanky arm reached over and slapped his friend Karl Warner on the back. Mark had a few small freckles that his girlfriend Suzy found adorable.

"My favorite was the sound when you laid rubber over that green piece of shit he rides," Karl laughed. He was average looking, average height, average weight. Nothing really stood out on Karl. So he compensated with a smart mouth. "Must have taken a half inch off your tires."

"Nah, maybe a quarter inch," Mark said, putting his arm around Suzy. "Still plenty left for driving up to Myer's Lake. It's the shocks I'm worried about. Suzy and I can really get that car of mine a bouncin'."

"Don't tell 'em that!" Suzy said, playfully pushing Mark away.

Snickering at Suzy's dismay, and Mark's expression of innocence, the group walked over to Judy and Martin's booth. Ox had joined the couple on the other side, along with his double-patty hamburger, large fries, and strawberry milkshake.

"What's with the chuckles?" Ox asked, holding the half-eaten burger in his large hand.

"We had a run-in with Peter Cowal," Mark said.

"More like a run over," Karl said, and the other two laughed. Everyone except Judy laughed even harder when Ox told how he had forced Peter into Judy's locker.

"You didn't hurt him, did you?" Judy asked, a look of concern and pity on her face.

"Nah," Mark said, "but that bike of his has seen its final days."

With a cry of dismay, Judy stormed toward the door.

"What's eat'n her?" Suzy asked.

"Martin eats her," Karl said, being his typical smart-ass self.

Martin smiled and gently smacked Karl on the side of his head. "She thinks we pick on Cowal too much."

"Well, he asks for it," Ox said, then shoved the last bite of his burger in his mouth.

When Martin saw Judy was serious, he rose from his seat and headed to cut her off. Grabbing her by the arm, he said, "What is it?"

"Damn it, Martin!" She pulled her arm from his grip. "You didn't hear a word I said."

"I heard. What do you want me to do?"

Judy took a sharp deep breath. "I want you to tell them to stop being so cruel to Peter. I mean it."

"OK, OK, I'll tell them. I will. I promise. Come back to the booth."

"No, I think I'll go home."

"Don't be mad," Martin said, standing close to her. "I'll take care of it."

Judy's expression softened. "I should really go. I have to get ready for the party."

"OK. I'll pick you up at seven." Martin touched the side of her face, then leaned over and kissed her.

"I'll see you at seven," Judy said, then walked out the door without looking back.

Martin watched her get in her car and drive away. He didn't notice anyone standing behind him until Ox took a large bite of his second hamburger and said, "What's her problem?"

Martin faced his oversize cohort. "Don't talk to me with your face full of food. It's gross."

"Hey, I'm hungry."

"You're always hungry."

Ox smiled as if he was pleased with Martin's observation. "What does she want?"

"Nothing. Nothing at all."

Peter turned the doorknob and entered his house. It wasn't the fanciest in town, but his mother had made it a good home. He always felt safe surrounded by its walls.

"I'm home," he bellowed.

"Where have you been?" Sharon called out from the kitchen. "I was starting to worry."

Peter thought about sneaking upstairs before she had a chance to see him, but before he made up his mind, his mother was rushing over to him at the base of the stairs.

"What happened?" Sharon said. Her eyes focused on the large rip in his pants, soaked with dried blood. "Are you all right?"

"I'm fine, Mom. Just fell off my bike."

"Go upstairs. I'll get the bandages."

"No, Mr. Stein saw me fall. He already helped me out." Peter displayed the bandage on his elbow. "I'm fine, really."

"If you say so," Sharon said, her voice full of concern. "Now go upstairs and wash up. Dinner's almost ready."

"All right," Peter said.

"And change your pants. Toss that pair in the tub. I'll wash them up and see if I can sew up the tear. They should be good enough to wear around the house when you do yard work."

"OK, Mom," he said.

Peter strolled down the upstairs hall toward his

room. The door was shut exactly as he had left it.
Even as far as halfway down the hall he spotted the
small piece of string he had placed on top of the
door. If anyone had opened his door the string would
be gone. He liked having this system; it gave him
some warning that his room had been entered and,
he hoped, time to come up with a story if his mother
found the *Playboys* he had hidden in his closet.

As Peter walked past the open door of Bobby's
room, his younger brother said, "Peter, Peter, come
see what I did in school today."

Peter backtracked to his brother's room, where
Bobby was sitting on the floor looking at a piece of
construction paper with stick figures drawn in several
different-colored crayons.

"Whatcha' got there, Bob?" he said in the most
adult voice his teenage vocal cords could produce.

Bobby smiled. He thought it was funny when Peter
called him Bob. "It's a picture I drew at my school.
Look. That's you, that's Mommy, and that's me."

"Why did you make me so tall?"

"You're my big brother, so I made you big."

"What's that?" Peter asked, pointing to a gray shape
that stuck out of the crayon ground. His words were
gently spoken so as not to hurt his brother's feelings
since it might be something Bobby thought obvious.

"That's where Daddy is," Bobby said, and Peter
realized the shape was Bobby's idea of a gravestone.

"Who's that?" Peter said, pointing to a small stick
figure standing next to what appeared to be a tree.

"That's my friend Georgie."

Peter swallowed. "Georgie, huh? Ya know, I got
big plans for us this weekend. Just the two of us. I
have to do something tomorrow morning, but when
I get back, we'll do stuff the rest of the day and all

day Sunday. How about that?"

"But Sunday is your birthday," Bobby said. "Don't you remember?"

"I remember," Peter said slowly. It might be his birthday, but it was also the anniversary of the day his father had died in a car accident. Max had left work early to pick up ice cream for the party celebrating Peter's sixth birthday. Another driver had run a stop sign, and Peter had lived with the memory of his father's death on every birthday after.

"We're going to have cake and everything," Bobby added. "Don't ask me about your present. I can't tell you. Mom told me to keep it a secret. It's a real good one."

"Not even a little hint?" Peter asked, trying to shake his gloomy thoughts.

"Nope."

"You're a tough one, Bobby. I guess I'll have to wait until Sunday. But first we'll do something tomorrow. Maybe go fishing for bullheads down by the dam."

"OK, I can play with Georgie until you come home."

"About Georgie—he won't be with us tomorrow when we hang out together. OK?"

"He's my friend."

"I know, Bobby, but how about tomorrow being just for the two of us?"

"I'll tell him," Bobby said, glancing down at his picture lying on the floor in front of him. "He won't be happy."

"If he's your friend, he'll understand."

Bobby looked up at his brother. "OK, Peter. You really like my picture?"

"It's a fine picture, Bobby." Peter felt a lump in his

chest. The mock adult voice came out again when he said, "Are you ready for supper?"

"Almost," Bobby said with a giggle.

"Well, get movin'. You know how Mom gets. I'll see you downstairs," Peter said, continuing down the hall and opening the door to his room.

It had been a hot day and the air was stale. A pungent smell told Peter something in his room cried out to be washed. It was a good thing, he thought, that his mother hadn't entered his room that day.

Because of the sunlight shining through his window, Peter had no need to switch on the ceiling light. He walked over to his dresser, opened the bottom drawer, and pulled out a fresh pair of jeans. The bottom hem of the right pants leg was frayed a little, but they were good enough.

Peter smelled the food as he went downstairs and approached the dinner table—roasted chicken with sage and onion stuffing—his favorite. Bobby poured milk into the three tall glasses he had brought from the kitchen, then he placed them beside the brown stoneware plates sitting on the tabletop and sat down in his usual chair. Sharon had just placed a basket of warm sourdough buns on the table and then she took her chair.

As Peter slipped into his place, he said, "Tomorrow I'm goin' back over to Mr. Stein's house." He tore off a small piece of dark meat from the steaming chicken leg lying on his plate and hungrily tossed it in his mouth. "He's got my bike."

"Don't talk with your mouth full, dear. And you know better than to eat with your hands."

"Yes, ma'am," Peter said, swallowing his food.

"I hope you're not bothering Mr. Stein."

"No, he said it was OK. I'm going to help him wax

his car." When Bobby giggled at his words, Peter looked up from his plate and caught his mother giving the boy a peculiar look. Puzzled by the exchange, Peter said, "I like Mr. Stein."

"I'm not surprised. Mr. Stein and your father were friends too."

"Really?"

"In fact, when your father was just about your age, he would go over to the Stein house and help cut the grass, rake the leaves, whatever Mr. Stein needed help with. My, that was a long time ago. Well over twenty years now, I would say. Mr. Stein has never been a strong man. He was in the hospital for some time when he was young. I never knew why. He almost died, I understand. I'm surprised he didn't pass on years ago."

"Like Daddy," Bobby blurted out.

"No, dear. Your father died in an accident." Sharon glanced over to Peter. She prayed his next birthday would be a happy one for him. "I just meant that as a person gets older his body starts to tire and one day it's time for him to sleep."

"Mr. Stein's not that old. Is he?" Peter asked, picking at his chicken with the prongs of his fork.

"You know, come to think of it, he seemed old when your father and I were young. I guess all adults looked older to us then."

They continued to talk about Mr. Stein throughout their dinner. And each time Peter mentioned the man's car, Bobby would giggle and his mother gave him a look of warning. Peter didn't know what their behavior meant, but he guessed it had something to do with his birthday. It wasn't long before he found out he was right.

Chapter Four

Peter liked Saturdays: no school, no hassles. The hardest part of the day was getting out of bed. The sunlight penetrated the curtains that Saturday morning, filling the room with a soft glow that helped Peter out of his night's sleep. After he lazily rolled on his side, Peter reached across the small table at the side of his bed and pulled the digital clock close to his face—8:35.

Suddenly wide awake, Peter jumped from his bed, grabbed a clean set of clothes, and ran to the bathroom. A five-minute shower, a three-minute breakfast, and he was out the door, still chewing on a piece of toast smothered with grape jelly. The pleasant odor of cooking bacon filled his nostrils and made his mouth water as he shut the front door. He wished he had remembered to tell his mother what time he had to be at Alex's. In his mind, he still saw her surprised face when he dashed into the kitchen proclaiming he was late. It was her idea to at least make toast. He would have settled for a glass of orange juice.

He hurried down Fifth Street and covered the four

blocks in just a few minutes. On his way he passed two small boys playing pirates, but for the most
part the street was quiet. Drawing closer to the Stein
house, Peter saw the dark-green hose rolled tightly on
its stand next to the porch; it was already attached to
the outside faucet.

Alex emerged from the front door of his Victorian
house, carrying a large yellow bucket. "Hello, my
boy. You're a little early."

"I was afraid I'd be late," Peter answered. He
felt grape jelly sticking between his fingers as he
approached the bottom step of the porch.

"Come," Alex said to Peter, who followed close
behind the elderly man. Against the side of the house
leaned a large sheet of black plastic. Even though it
was covered, Peter knew his bike lay twisted beneath
it, covered as if it were dead.

"Would you be so kind as to lift open the door?"
Alex said after unlocking the garage door with a
brass-colored key from the set he pulled from his
pocket. Peter gave one tug and the door rolled up
along its metal tracks. Inside sat a bone-white Buick
covered by a huge canvas drop cloth. Alex lifted the
front end of the heavy cloth and started to peel it
back. The large round headlights were the first thing
exposed to the morning air, and the sunlight beamed
off them as if they were made of fine crystal.

Peter quickly grabbed his side of the canvas and
helped Alex remove the rest of the drop cloth. He
used extra care as he pulled, making sure the heavy
material did not catch on any part of the car's metal
work. He stood there a moment gazing at the auto.
He had never seen the Buick totally uncovered and
up close.

"What year is she?" Peter asked.

" 'Fifty-nine. I've had her since the day she was new." Alex smiled and patted the car on the fender as if patting a small child. The car didn't have a speck of rust anywhere. The tires were black as coal with a deep zigzagged tread; they were mounted around half-sphere hubcaps. The original chrome bumper and trim gleamed when the sunlight struck them through the open garage door.

" 'Fifty-nine. Wow, fifteen years before I was even born."

Alex nodded. "Yes, that was a long time ago."

"It's still in perfect condition," Peter said, his fingers gently gliding across the smooth paint job.

"A simple feat really. You want something to last, just take care of it." With that Alex handed the keys to Peter, whose eyes opened wide. "Here, you start her up. We can't wash and wax her in the garage, now can we?"

"No, but I—"

"You know how to drive. You have your license."

"Yes, but—"

"No buts. You can drive it ten feet along the driveway. What can go wrong?"

"OK!" Peter's face beamed as he dashed over to the driver's side and jumped in. He was surprised to see how much room there was inside. With his left foot on the clutch, he pumped the gas pedal twice with his right and turned the key. The engine roared to life, then died. As Alex waved his encouragement, Peter turned the key again, and again the engine roared. When Peter gave the car a little gas, it purred. He smiled at Alex, who signaled him to drive forward. Peter took a breath and put the car in gear. The shift stick slipped smoothly into place and the car pulled forward. Peter drove at the speed of about three miles per hour, but still the Buick seemed to fly. When Alex gave the signal to stop, Peter stepped on the brake pedal and realized why power brakes were invented.

"It was like a dream," Peter said, getting out of the car. "Why don't you drive her anymore?"

"I'm too old to drive on the public streets, and I haven't for about ten years. I just start her up once a week, drive her to the end of the driveway, then back her into the garage. I can't hit anything going in straight lines."

"You don't even drive her to get gas or oil or anything?"

"My friend owns the gas station down on Third Street. He comes over about every three months to change the oil and give her the once-over. He brings gas if she needs it. Of course, you don't burn a lot of fuel on a driveway. She just needs a little attention now and then, and that's about all I can give her. No, my driving days are behind me."

"It's a fine car," Peter said, looking at the white Buick bathed in sunshine.

Alex's eyes also fell to the car. "She is. Let's wash her down and give her an extra good waxing. She has to look her best tomorrow."

"Tomorrow? Why tomorrow?"

The old man didn't take his eyes off the car. "She'll have a new owner tomorrow," he said. "And I want him to see how really special she can be."

"New owner! Why?"

"You said it yourself: she's a fine car. She should be driven." Alex took a deep breath, then let it out. "Let's get started."

The telephone rang with a short series of high-pitched beeps, then beeped once more. Judy lifted the cordless phone off the long walnut table in the front hall, pulled out the antenna, pushed the small button, and said, "Hello."

"Judy? It's Mona."

"Oh, hi, Mona," Judy replied, pinning the phone between her shoulder and ear, freeing up her hands to finish buttoning the blouse she had just pulled from the dryer. Her stepmother Jessica walked into the hall from the living room and gave her a questioning look. Judy covered the mouthpiece with her left hand. "It's for me."

"You still there? Judy?"

"Yeah, sorry about that. Jessica just crept by."

Hearing her name mentioned, the slender woman peered at her stepdaughter. Her tight-lipped scowl exaggerated the crow's-feet around her narrow eyes. Jessica had already touched up her salon-permed hair, but her bitter expression robbed that youthful look she had paid plenty for.

Over the telephone, Mona said, "Do you think we can stop by Rod's house on the way to the mall? I left my sweater in his car last night after the party. By the way, if anyone asks we were with you and Martin at your house. OK?"

"Can you hold on a moment?" Judy said. Not waiting for a response, she again covered the mouthpiece and glared at Jessica. "Could I have a little privacy, please?"

Jessica didn't say a word. Instead, she gave Judy a cold stare before walking away.

"I'm back," Judy said into the mouthpiece.

"Any problems?" Mona asked.

Judy peeked over her shoulder, making sure she really was alone. "No, not really. Jessica's just being a snoop."

"I still can't figure why you don't get a phone in your room," Mona said. "It's not like your father can't afford it."

"That's not the point. I like knowing I can go in my room and not be bothered by a ringing phone."

"Bothered by a phone? You're joking, right?"

"What was that about Martin and me?" Judy asked to change the conversation.

"Well, I just need you to cover for me. I got home a little late and I needed a good alibi. So I used you. That OK?"

"What time did you get home?"

"Around one-thirty."

"What were you two doing? Never mind. I don't think I want to know," Judy said. "What if your parents call here?"

"They won't. I told them that your parents went to bed early and the four of us ended up watching a few rental videos. They were convinced."

"Why tell me then?"

"Hey, they're not stupid. They may bring it up when you're over here. It would be a little hard to explain if you don't know what in the hell they're talking about."

"Guess you're right," Judy said.

"What did you and Martin do after the party?"

"Not much."

"Come on. The hottest couple in the school? I'm your best friend, aren't I?"

"You are. And I'm telling you we didn't do much. It's not as hot as you think."

"What do you mean by that?"

"Nothing," Judy said, regretting her words. Mona was her best friend, but she was also the biggest gossip in school. "Listen, if we want to get to the mall by ten I'd better leave now."

"Sure thing," Mona said. "See you in a bit. 'Bye."

" 'Bye." Judy held the phone a few moments before replacing it back on the table.

"Where do you think you're going?" Jessica said from behind, causing Judy to flinch.

"Do you have to sneak around like that?" Judy said, lifting her purse from the large table.

"I asked you a question, young lady."

"You're my stepmother, not my keeper." By the look on Jessica's face, Judy knew that her answer wasn't sufficient. "I'm going to the mall with Mona."

"I hope you'll use the time to buy a dress for the club dance."

"The dance is still weeks away. There's no rush."

Jessica walked over to the hall closet and pulled out her purse. Opening the shiny bag, she asked, "Do you have enough money?"

"Yes," Judy said. "I don't know what the big deal is. It's just a dance. I might not even go."

Jessica snapped her purse shut. "I expect you to be there. Your father expects you to be there. You will be there."

"I'm late," Judy said. "I've got to go. Can we talk about this later?" She didn't give Jessica time to answer before she rushed out the door, slamming it behind her. As she walked down to her red Ford Probe, she pulled the keys from her purse. She had just inserted the key into the lock when she heard a car horn honk. As a large white Lincoln Town Car pulled into the driveway, Judy smiled and hurried to the other side of her car.

"I didn't know you were up and around so early," Judy said.

"What? You think your old man's a bum," Roger

Kilter said, stepping out of the car.

"No way." She reached over to give her father a hug. In his early fifties, he had a muscular body and rough hands, the result of his years of working construction—long, hard years that had finally paid off when he had opened his own company.

"Jessica didn't say anything about you being gone, Dad. She leaves a lot of those little details out of our conversations."

"You two weren't fighting again."

"Not really. It's just—"

"I wish you two could get along a little better. She's part of our family. I will always love your mother, but I can love Jessica too."

"I'm sorry."

Roger kissed his daughter on her forehead. "Besides, it's my fault Jessica didn't tell you I was out. I asked her not to. I forgot something at the office and went to pick it up."

The image of a gleaming silver bracelet nestled in black velvet flashed in Judy's mind. "It's for me. Isn't it?"

"Just like your mother. I couldn't keep secrets from her either," he said, smiling. Detecting the impatience in his daughter's eyes, he removed a small box from his jacket pocket. "OK, yes, it's for you. I saw this downtown and thought you might like it." He lifted the top open, revealing a bright sterling-silver bracelet surrounded by black-velvet lining.

"Oh!" Judy gently took the bracelet and put it around her wrist. "I love it. Graduation's not for a month."

"It's not for graduation. It's for my daughter."

"Thank you, Dad." She gave him another hug. "Wait until I show Mona."

"So that's where you're off to."

"The mall really. And, yes, I have enough money."

As the two walked around Judy's car to the driver's side, Roger said, "You'd better get going. Drive safe."

"Oh, Dad."

As Judy backed out onto the street, she let out a short toot from her horn. She stuck her arm out the window and waved good-bye to her father, without giving any thought to the fact that her new bracelet was identical to the one she had envisioned.

A few miles away, Sharon Cowal opened the front door after hearing loud pounding. She hoped it wasn't yet another boy trying to sell her a subscription to the newspaper she already had. Sharon's eyes opened wide at Mrs. Romun standing on the stoop with her arm wrapped in an ace bandage and supported by a sling.

"Your boy is the cause of this!" Mrs. Romun blurted out, skipping the common courtesies.

"Peter?" Sharon said in utter disbelief.

"No, that other one!"

"His name is Bobby," Sharon said, her voice taking on a resentful tone, "and I'm sure you're mistaken. He has never harmed anyone."

Mrs. Romun's forehead wrinkled, and her eyes became two thin slits. "Are you calling me a liar?"

"No," Sharon said, straining to keep a calm voice.

"There are institutions for creatures like him. You should consider sending him to one and make life easier for everyone."

Sharon felt her face flush. Her breathing became very irregular as if a heavy weight had been placed on her chest. Without warning her words slipped out.

"You broken-down old woman! I've had to put up with your shit for years! Bitching and moaning about every little thing. If there's anyone who needs to be institutionalized, it's you. And damn it, don't you dare talk about Bobby like that again! Ever!"

Mrs. Romun's face changed from anger to shock. She had never heard Sharon use such language. She was caught off guard for only a moment before the hate lines reappeared on her face. "There are ways for innocent people like me to protect themselves. I bought a gun. If that boy comes on my property again, the law says I can use it. And I will!"

"Well, now you're on my property!" Sharon said, firmly gripping the door. "And I suggest you get off it now!"

With that she slammed the door on Mrs. Romun. Even though she knew that wasn't the civil thing to do, it gave her a very satisfied feeling. She walked to the base of the stairs leading up to the second floor, but before starting up them, she took a few deep breaths to calm herself. As she climbed the steps, she told herself over and over again not to get worked up again.

The short distance from the top of the stairs to Bobby's room that she had walked countless times seemed somehow longer. Then she realized that she unthinkingly was taking a few steps, then hesitating, then taking a few more steps. This pattern continued until she reached her youngest son's bedroom door, which she was surprised to find closed.

"Bobby?" she said, her voice calm and gentle.

The door opened and Bobby peeked out at his mother through the small gap he had made. "Yes, Mom?"

"Can I talk to you?"

"Sure."

She caught the look of tension on Bobby's face as he opened the door wide enough for her to enter. "Let's sit down."

"Am I in trouble?" Bobby asked as they sat on the edge of his bed.

"I'm not sure," Sharon said calmly. Her words came slowly. "Mrs. Romun came to the door and said you were in her yard. Is that true?"

Bobby diverted his eyes from the wall to the floor, then nodded. "I threw my ball too hard. I had to go get it."

"What else happened?" she asked, putting her hand gently on Bobby's shoulder.

"She came out and started to yell at me," Bobby said, the tone of his voice dropping almost to a whisper. "I got scared and ran away."

"Did anything else happen? Did you do anything because you were scared?"

Bobby nodded again, and she asked, "What?"

"I cried."

The anger at Mrs. Romun began to erupt again, but Sharon kept it in check. She placed her arm around her son and said, "That's OK, Bobby. It's OK to cry if you're scared or hurt. You understand?

"From now on," she said after Bobby nodded, "I want you to stay away from Mrs. Romun. Don't go in her yard, for any reason. Is that clear?"

"Yes, Mom."

"If you have any trouble—"

"Like my ball?" Bobby said, finally looking up at his mother.

"Like your ball. If you have any trouble at all, you tell me or your brother. We'll take care of it," she said, then added, "How about a hug?"

"Sure."

Moments later Sharon left Bobby's bedroom, content with the feeling that the matter had been settled, at least as far as Bobby was concerned.

In his room, Bobby watched the door close and waited until his mother walked down the hall. Then he said, "I told you I wouldn't tell. I promised."

After a five-minute drive to Mona Thompson's house, Judy sat in her red sports car parked next to the curb. When she honked for the third time, Mona finally came running out the front door, her purse and spring jacket hanging loosely in her right hand. Climbing in the car, Mona apologized for keeping her friend waiting.

Driving down Fifth Street, the girls chatted about the previous evening's highlights. Judy kept changing the subject every time Martin's name came up, but Mona never noticed. She was more interested in the volume of the radio.

"I love this song!" Mona said.

"You love anything loud."

"No, I love songs with meaning," Mona said, tilting her head so her hair blew out the open window.

"What's the name of the song?" Judy asked.

"Huh?"

"The name of the song—what is it?" Judy pressed down on the brake as she drew closer to the red stoplight.

"I don't know, but I love it anyway."

Judy laughed. She watched in her rear-view mirror as a car pulled up behind her. She thought she recognized the car, but didn't get a good enough look at the driver to be sure, so she tried looking in her side mirror. She didn't know the man—wrong car.

Then she glanced up from her mirror and happened to look across the street, where a boy rubbed a towel across the body of an old car. As the boy moved around the car and wiped off the last of the wet spots, Judy recognized Peter Cowal and instantly felt a pang of guilt.

"You in there?" Mona said, intruding on Judy's thoughts. "It's green."

Judy said nothing, but wished she had been alone so she could apologize to Peter. Since she wasn't she eased her foot on the gas pedal, and the two girls were back on their way to the mall. She'd just have to make up for her friends' cruelty another time.

Amanda Colins strolled down the quiet streets of Fulton, glad she wasn't wasting such a beautiful afternoon in her car. Her errand took her only a few blocks from her motel room—the perfect excuse for a walk. She had always found her previous visits to Fulton to be a pleasure, though there had been few. Everything seemed to move at a much slower, more peaceful rate—a quality her home city of Columbus needed more of. And the people of Fulton seemed friendly; many even said hello as she passed. When she needed directions to Philips's Drug Store, she asked an elderly couple, who were more than glad to help her.

Over dinner, two nights earlier, her friend Molly Nordine had asked Amanda if she would lecture her psychology class the following Monday morning. Amanda felt a little nervous about lecturing; after all, how could she keep a class full of teens interested in what sometimes put the most studious grad students to sleep? With the fresh air and a firm idea in mind, however, that nervousness vanished.

Amanda made her way to the end of the block. She turned the corner, and right where the couple had said it would be stood Philips's Drug Store. The large front window had the familiar Rx stenciled on front in deep red paint. Glancing through the window, Amanda saw rows of greeting cards, paperback books, candy, and cosmetics.

She headed to the back of the store, where a gray-haired man wearing round wire-frame glasses and a white coat rang up a purchase. Amanda approached the counter, pulling the white slip of paper from her purse and nodding at the other customer—a thin, middle-aged woman.

"Hello," Amanda said to the pharmacist, whose nametag announced he was Ed Philips. She handed him the slip. "Would you be able to fill this? I should have had it filled back home."

"I'm sure I can. It will be just a moment." The gray-haired man examined the paper; then he moved over to his left and started typing on a computer keyboard. "My, that was easy enough. Here you are."

"Excuse me?"

"In the computer network. I'm connected to a pharmaceutical network. A lot of the big chain stores have them. They let us little guys connect up. Makes things a whole lot easier. All I need is a picture ID."

"Certainly." Amanda pulled out her wallet and displayed her university ID card.

"Oh, Dr. Colins. MD?"

"No, PhD."

"I see. It'll only be a minute." He stepped out of her view between two large shelves filled with glass bottles.

"Pardon me." The words came from behind Amanda, but she made no move until she felt a light tap on her shoulder. "Pardon me. Are you Dr. Amanda Colins?"

"Yes, I am."

"I thought I heard you say so. I'm Gale Harper."

"Have we met? If we have, I'm sorry I don't remember you."

"No, we haven't met. Frank Currie said you would be coming around to speak with my grandmother about the field. She lives with me. I take care of her."

"Harper? I don't remember seeing a Harper on my list."

"No, you wouldn't," Gale said. "Her name is Margaret Able."

"No need to apologize, it was my mistake."

"And here's your order," Ed Philips said, reappearing at the counter. "That will be $10.32 with tax."

Amanda handed him the exact amount, then turned back to Gale. "I guess we'll be seeing each other again."

"Please," Gale said. "My grandmother is very old. And I'm afraid she's not well."

"Has she seen a doctor?"

"Not that kind of well. I mean that her mind's not very strong."

"I can cross her off my list. I'm sure Frank would understand."

"No," the woman said. "Frank Currie has done so much for my family. I just thought maybe a short visit. One that wouldn't tax her too much. And maybe if you had time today, you could come with me now."

"Yes, as a matter of fact I do have time. It would be as good a place to start as any. I'll need to walk back to the motel to get some things. Could I met you? I'm sure I have your address."

"No need. I'm parked right out front. I can drive you to your room and then to my home. It wouldn't be any trouble."

"That would be fine."

After a brief stop at the motel, the two women drove to the home of Margaret Able. On the way Amanda read over the report of Margaret Able's experience with the field. Unlike other reports about the field that Amanda had read, it hadn't been made by Margaret Able, but about her. Twenty years earlier, the police had received a missing persons report on the elderly woman, who was sixty at the time. Given her age, the police decided on an immediate search.

They found Margaret Able within several hours. She had managed to make her way to the field in question. When the police found her, she was babbling about being called to the spot. Because of the woman's history of mental illness, no further action was taken concerning her or the field.

"Your grandmother," Amanda said, after finishing the report, "has she always been afflicted?"

"Before my mother died, she told me what a lively and caring person Grandmother Margaret was." Gale turned the steering wheel, taking a sharp right. "I guess she felt she had to tell me that. I can't remember ever seeing my grandmother any other way."

"Did your mother ever explain what happened to her?"

"It's a pretty awful story. During the Depression, my grandfather lost his job, and my grandmother found work at the Amherst Mental Institution as a nurse. She didn't like the job, but she desperately wanted to support her family. While she worked there, one of the patients killed another. My mother never told me exactly what happened, but I gather it was quite gruesome. Anyway, my grandmother found the body, and it was a great strain to her—especially because the boy who committed the murder was one of her favorite patients. She tried to help the boy, but he escaped and killed some local teenagers. When the police were about to catch him, he threw himself off a cliff near the field you want to know about. Everybody calls that Crazy Man's Bluff now."

"That is an awful story."

"Yes, and like I said, the whole situation put a lot of pressure on Grandmother. She had a nervous breakdown and never really recovered." The car slowed and lurched to a stop. "Here we are."

The small house had a fresh coat of paint and a newly trimmed lawn. Gale guided Amanda to a back bedroom, where the smell of violets almost overwhelmed them even though no flowers were in evidence. Wincing slightly at the odor, Amanda spotted a can of air freshener sitting on a dresser.

"Grandma," Gale whispered, not wishing to startle the old woman, who was resting in bed. "We have a guest."

The old woman turned her head toward the bedroom door as the two women entered. She had thin white hair and sunken eyes. The blanket covered most of her body, but both her arms stuck out and lay straight at her sides.

As Amanda ventured farther in the room a dull throb started in her mind. She had always liked the smell of violets, but the odor in the room was beginning to disagree with her.

"Grandma?" Gale said. She pulled up a chair from the vanity and signaled for Amanda to sit. "We have a guest. She's the friend of Frank Currie I told you about. She would like to talk with you. Would you like that?"

"Hello, Mrs. Able," Amanda said, sliding herself and the chair closer to the bed. "My name's Amanda. How are you feeling?"

"I feel fine," Margaret said, her voice shaking with age. "Has it stopped raining?"

"It hasn't been raining, Grandma," Gale said, adjusting her grandmother's pillow. Then she walked over to the window and propped it open. "Please excuse the violet aroma, Dr. Colins. It's Grandmother's favorite. Sometimes I use a little too much."

Although she was thankful for the fresh air, Amanda still felt the throbbing. Uncertain as to the source of her continued discomfort, she forced her attention on the elderly woman.

"Too drafty?" Gale asked.

"No, it's perfect."

"Grandma," Gale said, returning to the bedside, "Amanda wants to talk to you about the field. You remember the field? We talked about it just the other day."

"Yes, I remember."

The throb in Amanda's head became more distinct, but she tried to ignore it. "Do you recall going to the field, Mrs. Able?"

"Yes, I do."

"Why did you go to the field?"

"One of my patients had committed suicide nearby, at the cliffs, I felt sorry for him. When I went out there, I passed through the field and saw that strange little boy."

Amanda winced when the throb became a sharp cutting pain, as if someone were turning a long screw from her forehead all the way down to the nape of her neck. Amanda couldn't hold back a moan.

"Are you all right?" Gale said. "Can I get you something?"

"Maybe some water," Amanda said, the pain beginning to recede.

After Gale left, Amanda felt a hand grab her arm, and suddenly the pain shot back through her head. Luckily Amanda was better able to steady herself against it that time.

"He killed that Stein man," Margaret Able wheezed out. "That little boy killed him. Jimmy was a good boy. It wasn't him. The other—he killed them all. Right there in his room, he killed him. He called to me and laughed. He laughed."

The old woman's grip loosened. Her hand slipped off Amanda's arm and fell back onto the bed. Her wrinkled eyelids fluttered, then closed. As the woman surrendered to sleep, the pain in Amanda's head dissipated.

"Here you go," Gale said, reentering the room and handing Amanda a glass of cool water. "I brought some aspirin if you would like some."

"No, thank you. The water is fine."

"I see Grandmother is asleep."

"Yes, she dropped off just now."

"I hope you got the information you needed. I hope coming wasn't a waste of your time."

"No. I can't say it was," Amanda said, glancing at the sleeping woman.

Sharon Cowal sat alone in her living room reading an old issue of *Redbook*. Peter had returned earlier from helping Mr. Stein and kept his promise to spend the day with Bobby—it was a toss-up between fishing or the movies. The movies won out, and Sharon was enjoying the solitude.

Sharon really didn't mind the noise her sons made. It gave her a warm feeling and made their house a home. However, it was important to have some quiet whenever possible.

But her serene afternoon was suddenly ended when Peter and Bobby raced through the front door. Sharon closed the cover of her magazine and returned it to the rack next to her chair. She had been so caught up in the article that she hadn't noticed that the sun had already set and the sky was growing darker by the minute. The night would soon sweep over the town and, Sharon thought, creep into their home. She wasn't sure where the feeling had suddenly come from—it just overpowered her.

"You two could wake the dead," she said, trying to dispel the morose feeling.

"Sorry, Mom," Peter said.

"Yeah, sorry," Bobby added.

"Did you two eat?"

"Yes, ma'am," Peter said. "We grabbed a couple of burgers."

"Oh, Peter. You know I don't like you two eating junk food."

"It's not that bad. I made Bobby get milk."

"Can I go to my room?" Bobby asked, looking over to the stairs. When Sharon nodded, Bobby walked quickly to the staircase, then ran up the steps, skipping every other one.

"Peter," Sharon said after Bobby left, "something happened today I think you should know about."

Peter stood there puzzled and said nothing. He waited for his mother to gather her thoughts. Something he heard in her voice told him that whatever was on her mind must be serious.

"Mrs. Romun came over today." Thinking about

her neighbor's mean words instantly brought back Sharon's anger, but she didn't want Peter to see it. She forced the anger away, then said, "She says she's been having trouble with Bobby."

"What kind of trouble?"

"I don't know. She was saying some pretty awful things. I told Bobby if anything happens to come and get one of us."

"What things did she say?"

"That's not important. I just want you to promise me that you'll look out for your brother. I'm afraid Mrs. Romun is looking for any reason to accuse your brother."

"Accuse him? Accuse him of what?"

"Anything, I would say."

"Did you talk with Bobby? What did he do?"

"Yes, I did. And I'm convinced he didn't do anything. He told me he entered her yard to retrieve a ball. Beyond that, nothing. Just watch out for him."

"I will." Peter's face grew very still. "Mom, about Bobby."

Sharon looked carefully at her oldest son, and for the first time, she detected his father in him. His adolescent face had started to take on many of Max's features, yet it was more than that. His voice was taking on that same protective tone that Max had always used.

"Bobby has a friend." Sharon tilted her head in bewilderment, and Peter added, "An imaginary friend."

"That's normal, honey. At one time or another all children make up friends. It's all part of growing up. Do you remember when we brought Bobby home from the hospital for the first time?

"I guess you wouldn't since you had just turned

five," Sharon said when Peter shook his head. "Well, we had to give your brother some special attention, and you thought we loved him more than you. So to deal with your feelings, you made an old toy lion your constant companion. You used to talk to it and carry it every place you went. I remember once you were very angry with your father, and in a fit of rage you threw your lion across the room. When you picked it off the floor, you saw the top half of one of its big plastic eyes had broken off. You started to cry. You kept telling your lion how sorry you were you hurt him and that he was your best friend.

"You see," his mother said, as she smiled at Peter's embarrassment, "it's OK to have an imaginary friend sometimes."

"I guess," Peter said, shrugging his shoulders.

"It's your big day tomorrow," she said, trying to ease the concern in Peter's face. "Your eighteenth birthday comes only once. I hope it will be a happy one."

"I'm a little tired. If it's OK I think I'll follow Bobby's lead and go to my room." Peter walked to the stairs, though not with Bobby's speed. He turned when his mother called him.

"It's OK. Bobby's fine," Sharon said.

Peter didn't say a word. Only time would tell whether his concern for Bobby was warranted or not.

Chapter Five

The orange glow reflected in Peter's eyes as he watched the candle flames flicker and grow. He inhaled, filling his lungs to capacity, feeling the strain deep inside his chest. He held his breath for only a moment, then was forced to release it. With one tremendous huff, Peter blew out all the candles on his birthday cake. Bobby and Sharon applauded with approval.

The smell of burnt wax filled the room as thin streamers of smoke rose from the darkened wicks of some of the candles; others were still topped with small red embers.

"Did you make a wish?" Bobby asked as Sharon gently pulled the candles from the cake, being careful to allow very little of the vanilla frosting to stick to the wax.

"Sure I did," Peter said and smiled, "but I can't tell you."

"I know." Bobby chuckled.

Sharon cut the cake and placed the yellow slices

on small plates she had stacked next to her. She passed one plate to Peter and one to Bobby; she kept one, then she set another in front of the only empty chair.

"Four pieces? Why four pieces?" Peter asked.

"I'm expecting someone," Sharon said, glancing at her watch.

"Who?"

"You'll see."

"What's going on, Bobby?" Peter whispered when his brother giggled.

"I'm not telling." Bobby covered his mouth as if to trap his laughter when Peter gave him a stare of mock anger.

The doorbell rang and Bobby laughed harder. Knowing the answer must be waiting at the door, Peter said, "I'll get it."

But Sharon pushed him back down by the shoulders. "You stay right here, young man. Don't let him peek, Bobby." Without another word, she disappeared into the hall leading to the front door.

"OK, Mom," Bobby said.

"Come on," Peter said. "Give me a little hint."

"No. You'll see . . . you'll see."

Peter heard only bits and pieces of the whispers coming from the hall. He strained to hear more without success because the wall blocked most of the sounds from the front of the house. But he caught the slam of the door closing and more fragmented whispers. Then Sharon returned with her guest. "Look who's here."

"Happy birthday, Peter, my boy," Alex said, walking into the dining room, his hand extended to Peter.

"Thank you," Peter said. He stood up from his chair and shook the elderly man's hand.

Behind Alex came another man—a rather large man, wearing clean blue overalls and holding a gray baseball cap.

"Would you like to join us? We have plenty," Sharon said to the stranger.

"No, thank you," he replied. "I have to get back to the garage. The work's piling up."

Alex turned his head to the stranger, then back to Peter. "Come, I want you to meet my friend Raymond Hursch. And this fine young man is Peter Cowal. Peter and I are good friends, as his father and I once were."

"Nice to meet you, Peter, and happy birthday," Raymond said as he and Peter shook hands.

"Thank you. This is my brother Bobby." Peter had to coax his brother to meet the large man; Bobby's shyness surprised him.

"Raymond was kind enough to drive me here," Alex said.

Peter thought that was strange. On clear sunny days like that day, Alex liked to walk. The thought that something might be wrong with Alex caused a lump to form in Peter's throat.

"You wonder what I'm doing here, right?" Alex said, his hands folded in front of him and a big smile on his lips. "I came to bring you your birthday present."

Peter gawked at the elderly man. Then he thought how stupid he must look, standing with his mouth hanging wide open, not knowing what to say.

"Come," Alex said, walking over to the front window. "Come see what your mother has done."

"Go ahead, dear," Sharon said, signaling Peter to follow.

"Are you ready?" Alex asked and Peter nodded.

Then Alex pulled back the curtain, revealing the white Buick parked in front of the house. The two coats of wax Peter had applied the day before made the car shine in the afternoon sun.

Peter wasn't sure what his old friend meant until Alex held out the car keys and placed them in his hand. The smile on Alex's face convinced Peter that it was no joke. The car was now his.

"Happy birthday, Peter," his mother said from across the room.

Peter was speechless. Then he rushed over and hugged her. "Thank you! Thank you!"

"Take me for a ride, Peter," Bobby said.

"There will be plenty of time for that later," Sharon said. "We still have company."

"Mom's right," Peter said, seeing Bobby's disappointment. "I'll take you with me the first time I drive it. OK?"

Bobby forced a smile, but he didn't fool Peter. So Peter rubbed the top of Bobby's head and said, "I'll let you honk the horn."

Bobby smiled again, this time sincerely, and Peter returned the smile. Turning to Alex, he said, "I thought you loved that car."

"I do. And I cannot think of anyone I would rather see have it than you. It's a shame to have such a fine car just sitting in a garage. It should be on the road where it can be seen."

Peter looked outside at the white Buick and silently agreed. "You said she'd have a new owner."

"What? Did I lie? Your mother told me that she was having trouble finding you a gift. That's when I got the idea."

"It's a combination birthday and graduation present," Sharon said.

"I helped," Bobby said. "I saved up my allowance for a whole month."

"I'll take real good care of it," Peter said.

Mr. Stein placed his right hand on Peter's shoulders. "I know you will, my boy. I know you will."

"And if you have any problems," Raymond said, "you bring the car around to my shop and I'll help you out. It's a fine vehicle. You're a lucky young man. Now, I should really get going. I got my truck parked on the wrong side of the street over at Alex's."

"Are you sure you can't stay for cake, maybe a little coffee?" Sharon said.

"I'd love to, but I can't. Thank you. A few of my customers are expecting their cars back first thing tomorrow morning."

Sharon gave him an understanding smile. "My husband used to put in a lot of overtime himself. Thank you for bringing Alex. I'm sure I can convince Peter to drive him home later." She accompanied the large man to the door and thanked him again for his time while Peter and Bobby stared out the window at the car.

"Come back to the table, you two," Sharon said as she walked to the table herself. Then she pulled out the end chair. "Alex, your usual place at our table."

"Thank you," Alex said, "for inviting me. It was very kind of you."

"I should be thanking you," Sharon said, shaking her head. "You gave me the opportunity to make this a very special day for Peter."

For over an hour, the small group sat around the table talking and laughing. Alex told some tales of Max at Peter's age. Some of Max's great adventures, Sharon called them.

"This is fun," Bobby said, eating his third piece of

cake. "I wish Georgie was here."

Alex's hand jerked, bumping his coffee cup and spilling its contents on the tablecloth. "Oh! I'm very sorry," he said, grabbing the napkin from his lap and desperately trying to soak up the black liquid. Peter stood up and tried to help with his napkin.

"Accidents happen," Sharon said calmly. "It's an old tablecloth, no harm done." She went to the kitchen and emerged a moment later with three small towels, which she used to blot up the spill. After sponging up the remaining coffee, she removed the tablecloth and took it into the kitchen. As she returned, Alex apologized once more for being so clumsy, but she reassured him everything was fine.

"Why don't we go to the living room?" Sharon said.

All four got up from their chairs and went into the other room. There, Bobby and Peter sat on the couch. Alex sat in the stuffed chair at a right angle to the couch, and Sharon pulled in a chair from the dining room.

"Who was that you mentioned, Bobby?" Alex asked.

"Georgie? He's my friend."

"How did you meet Georgie?" Alex asked.

"Georgie is Bobby's special friend," Sharon said, catching sight of Peter's worried glance. "When Peter's busy with his studies, Georgie comes over to play with Bobby."

"Oh, I see," Alex said, the tenseness in his voice disappearing. "He is a neighborhood boy?"

"No. Not exactly," Sharon said, trying not to say anything that might upset Bobby. "Well, let's just say Bobby has a very good imagination."

"Georgie followed us home," Bobby said. "Didn't he, Peter?"

"Are you feeling all right, Mr. Stein?" Peter asked, ignoring his brother. "You look a little tired."

"No. I'm fine. It's just all the excitement of the day."

But Alex's whole manner had changed and his face seemed pale, and Peter couldn't help wondering if the old man was as worried about Bobby as he was. Whatever the case, the joy the youth had felt only moments earlier was gone.

Several blocks away from the Cowals' house, the heavy sound of rock music blasted from the windows of Martin Welth's Trans-Am. At the side of the street, a black-and-white speed-limit sign read 30 miles per hour, but the needle of the speedometer embedded in the dash of the car pushed past twice that speed. The view through Martin's amber sunglasses was clear and sharp. He barely noticed because his surroundings weren't half as important as his destination. After all, he had an image he had to uphold.

Martin pulled up to the curb and stopped the car with a squeal. He drove the silver car another five feet to get out from under the branches of the large oak tree that reached out from the Kilters' front yard. Removing his sunglasses, he carefully placed them lens up on the dash. He pushed a button, sending the windows up with an electric hum. Finally, he pulled the chrome-plated handle to open the door. Before getting out, he took one more look in his rearview mirror. "Not a hair out of place," he said, treating himself to one of his toothy smiles. He stepped out onto the street and shut the car door, giving the outer handle a quick yank to ensure himself the door had locked. Walking around the front of his car, he stopped to wipe a small speck of dirt from the left fender.

Martin strolled up the narrow walkway that ran parallel with the Kilters' driveway, his letter jacket hanging open. When the lilac bush at the front of the house started to shake, Martin crouched down to get a better view. He saw nothing, so he picked two smooth stones and threw one into the bushes, which made a loud smack when it struck the cement foundation behind the leafy lilacs. Judy's large tabby cat Caesar dashed out from his hiding place.

"Stupid cat," Martin said, throwing his last stone and hitting the frightened orange cat on the left hind paw. Screeching in pain, Caeser escaped, making a sharp turn around the corner of the house. Martin smirked and wished he had picked up three or four of the round stones instead of just two.

Martin was about to knock on the door when it opened. Judy's startled expression didn't bother him. He knew she hadn't expected to see him standing on her doorstep.

"Surprise," he said, taking a step inside and kissing her on the mouth.

"I thought I was going to meet you at the park," Judy said.

"I didn't want to have to wait for you. And I don't want Ox and the others to get the wrong idea. You're my girl, so you should show up with me."

"Tough what they think. I—"

"Oh, hello, Martin," Jessica said, coming up from behind Judy and talking over her shoulder.

"Hello, Mrs. Kilter."

"How are your parents? I understand your father was nominated to head the board of directors for the country club."

"Yeah, Dad's pretty busy with work and everything. Mom, too. Otherwise they're OK. I guess. Don't see them a lot."

"Are you looking forward to the dance?" Jessica asked.

"Pretty much. I know my mother sure is."

"Twenty-five years—an important milestone for the members of the club."

"I guess," Martin said. "We should be heading out. The concert probably started by now."

"Judy," Jessica said, "I hope you're not keeping Martin waiting. You should be more considerate."

Judy didn't dignify Jessica's snide remark with a response. She simply pulled the strap of her purse up around her shoulder and pushed Martin out the door, following close behind.

The trip to the park was a 20-minute ride. Judy was looking forward to hearing the bands. She remembered the fun she had had the previous year with Mona, before she'd started dating Martin.

"I have something for you," Martin said. "Behind you."

Judy's eyes fell to the back seat, where a long white box sat alone. "What is it?"

"Don't ask. Open."

Judy leaned back and lifted the box off the seat, pulling it onto her lap. It was very light and an edge of thin wrapping tissue poked out from under the cover. Beneath the tissue lay a long-stemmed red rose with white baby's breath nestled up by the red petals. Mildly impressed by the gift, she leaned over and kissed Martin on the cheek. "That's sweet. Thank you."

"It's nothing. I just wanted to show you I care." He watched Judy inhaling the flower's fragrance. When he reached out and took her hand, she responded in kind.

They held hands and sat quietly until they got to the park. There, the concert was already going strong. It didn't take the two much time after leaving Martin's car to find their friends because the boys stuck out in their blue-and-white letter jackets.

"Have a Coke," Ox said to Martin, handing him an open can.

Martin took a sip, and the liquid burned slightly as it went down his throat. "I love that real thing."

"You want one?" Ox asked, holding out a can for Judy.

"No, thanks. Where's Suzy?"

"Had to work. She tried to change her hours," Mark Turner said with a shrug. "No luck."

"That's too bad," Judy said.

"Huh, he's 'whipped," Karl Warner said.

Judy glanced at Martin, thinking about the rose. He gently put his arm around her and took another swallow from his pop can, but Mona tugged on Judy's arm.

"Come with me," Mona said.

"Where?"

"Where do you think? I gotta go, bad."

"You should have gone earlier. I hope you know the lines will be impossible."

"Hey, Mona," Karl said, pouring out some of his laced pop, which made a loud splash as it hit the ground. "How about a drink?"

"Asshole!" Mona said while the guys laughed at the strain on the girl's face.

"Stop it, Karl," Judy said. "I'll go with you, Mona."

The girls disappeared through the crowds, leaving

the boys to themselves and their booze. After five minutes, there was a break in the music. On stage, the next band hurried to set up their instruments on the outdoor stage. After a quick sound check came over the enormous speakers, the new band started their set.

"Look over there. Hillsbury." Karl pointed to a young couple standing off from the crowd listening to the music. The boy from the rival high school wore a black-and-yellow baseball cap. A large H surrounded by a diamond emblazoned the cap's front above the bill. The girl had long blonde hair tied back in a simple ponytail.

"Looks like we'll be playing them for regionals," Ox said, taking a drink from his can.

"We'll kick their ass," Mark said. "Their pitching stinks. They can't hit. No problem."

"That's why they have a sixteen and three record, right?"

"Haven't you heard of luck, Ox?" Karl said.

Bored by his friend's chatter, Martin checked out the crowd. The girls were still nowhere in sight. With nothing else to do, he let his mind take a devious turn. "You guys want to have some fun?"

The group collectively agreed, and Martin signaled for them to follow him. He knew by their faces they understood what he had in mind. Ox crushed his soda can and tossed it through the air as the group sneaked up on the two Hillsbury students. Standing behind their unknown rival and his date, Martin pulled the baseball cap off the body's head, uncovering his red hair.

"What the hell?" The boy turned around to find Martin dangling the cap on the end of his index finger; extending the cap, Martin dared the boy to take it back.

"You're a little off your turf," Martin said.

"Let's go, Tommy," the girl said, moving closer and entwining her arm with his.

Tommy swept the girl behind him. "We're here to see the concert. We don't want any trouble."

"I don't think so." Martin dropped the black-and-yellow cap to the ground, slowly twisting it into the dirt with his foot.

"You asshole." Tommy made the mistake of rushing Martin. He took a step before a fist came seemingly out of nowhere and smashed him square in the face. A steady flow of blood dripped from his nose as the fist pulled back. Stunned, Tommy fell to his knees and his girlfriend screamed. He buckled over and fell flat as the pain of a foot kicking him against the rib cage coursed through his body. Then he rolled on the grass, gasping for breath.

"Stop! Stop! God! Please stop!" the girl screamed, trying to pull away from Mark Turner, who had pinned her arms behind her back. Tears poured down her face as she watched Martin, Ox, and Karl kicking her downed boyfriend.

Mark laughed as the boy writhed on the ground, trying in vain to protect his body. Then, out of the corner of his eye, Mark spotted two security guards running toward them. "Let's get the hell out of here!"

He released the girl and pushed her to the ground. She immediately rushed over to Tommy and tried to push Ox away. With one sweep of his large hand, Ox knocked her down to Tommy's side, then ran off with the rest of his friends.

"Get in the car! Get in the car!" Martin yelled.

"What about the girls?" Karl said.

"Forget them! Come on!"

The four rapidly piled in. Martin already had his

keys out. Almost in one motion, he shoved the ignition key into its slot and turned, starting the car with a loud roar as his foot pressed heavily on the gas pedal.

"What's this?" Karl said from the back seat, pulling the crushed flower box from under his butt.

"Nothing," Martin said.

"My car, what about my car?" Mark yelled to Martin as they pulled out from the parking lot.

"It'll be OK. We'll get it later."

Ox hadn't finished closing the car door when Martin sped off. The tires squealed as the car turned the corner, and Ox had to tighten his grip on the door. They were soon a good distance from the park, laughing and cheering over their victory. But Mark still worried about his car.

The joy Sharon felt hadn't stopped since the moment Peter had peered out the window at the white Buick that she had given him for his birthday. The smile on Peter's face and the wonder in his eyes made the day one she would always keep with her. She thought how proud Peter must be driving Alex home. He hadn't had to ask Bobby twice if he wanted to tag along.

The house was quiet once again as Sharon walked to the laundry room off the kitchen, which had just enough room for the washer and dryer. The striped wall paper tried to fake a roomy look, but failed.

While the dryer still tumbled, Sharon pulled open the metal door, and the heat rose up against her face and arms. A wash cycle and a dry cycle—Peter and Bobby had been gone about 45 minutes, Sharon thought, pulling the clothes from the dryer. She hung one of Peter's shirts on a hanger, since it might still need some ironing, then she separated a couple of pairs of Bobby's underwear from the tablecloth and placed them in a plastic basket. She held the tablecloth up to the light and turned it carefully, looking around the edges; finding no coffee stain, she placed the cloth in the basket. After folding the wash, she headed upstairs.

In Peter's room, Sharon found an open math book on the floor. It was propped up next to a notebook covered with scribbles and pencil scrawl. Her first impulse was to pick up the book, but she immediately caught herself. Peter was old enough to keep his room the way he wanted. As she hung Peter's shirt in his closet, she reflected on how quickly her son had grown.

A loud thud interrupted her thoughts. Then a second thud, and still another.

"Peter? Bobby? You two home?" she called out, sliding the hangers back across the aluminum bar. She stopped shifting the clothes and repeated her call when no one answered.

She listened carefully. No sounds now, but there had been something. She left Peter's room and walked down the hall, whispering, "Peter? Bobby?"

A thud from Bobby's room stopped her cold. Slowly, Sharon reached for the brass doorknob, but at the last moment she pulled back. Instead she raised her hand and lightly rapped on the door with her finger tips. "Bobby? When did you get home?"

When no one answered, she turned the knob and opened the door a crack. A cold blast of air blew across her bare arm, and the door pushed back against her and slammed shut. Caught off balance, she stumbled back.

Surprised and a little angry, Sharon regained her footing and knocked louder. "Bobby? Peter? What's going on in there? Open this door, or I'm coming in."

Silence filled the hall, and Sharon frowned, quite displeased at her sons' apparent joke. Again taking the brass knob in her right hand, she steadied her left hand against the door itself. When the door opened wide, she had a clear view of the entire room—an empty room. But Bobby had left his window open again, and Sharon felt foolish for assuming that her sons were up to no good when she discovered the cause of the strange noise. With a sense of relief she walked over to close it. After the window came down to rest in its frame, Sharon turned the latch, securing it in place.

She looked out the window and wondered where her boys were. Outside the sky was a cloudless royal blue. The trees were dead still on that perfect spring day. Her smile returned until her peripheral vision caught something strange in the room. It took a moment for her brain to process and react to the fact that someone was standing by the bed. She gasped and shouted, "Who's there?"

But there was no one. Her breath rasping in short sobs, she tried to calm herself. For a moment, she could have sworn she had seen a small boy standing by the foot of the bed holding something white in his hands.

After a few moments, her composure had all but returned only to be shattered by the slamming of the bedroom door. The sound penetrated Sharon's body, and with it came a surge of fear. The natural instinct of escape forced Sharon to bolt for the door. She grabbed the knob, turning and pulling, but the door would not open. She twisted the knob back and forth, desperately yanking with all the strength she was able to muster. Still, the door remained closed. That feeling of dread she'd had the night before returned with greater force. She had to fight the impulse to slam her fists against the door.

From behind her came the thud again. As if being called to, she released her hold on the doorknob and slowly turned to see Bobby's softball rolling across the floor and stopping at her feet. The sound of faint laughter echoed through the room. Sharon thought she was losing her mind until Bobby yelled, "Mom, we're home."

A sense of relief flowed over her. She wanted to yell back for help and barely stopped short of doing so, but she wouldn't frighten Bobby for anything. Instead, she grasped the doorknob again and said, "I'm in your room. I can't open your door."

The words were still ringing in her ears when the door clicked open. Only the edge of the door left its frame, but that was enough for her. Sharon yanked the door and made her escape. She couldn't help feeling a little foolish because in her haste she bumped into Bobby, who gave her a puzzled look.

"What's the matter?" Bobby asked, noticing her anxious state.

"Nothing," Sharon said softly, her heart still pounding. "I was putting away some of your clothes."

Sharon's explanation was far from convincing, especially since she had left the clothes basket in Peter's room. But what could she tell her son? That she had been trapped in his room? That she had become frightened when the door wouldn't open? That she had become frightened over nothing—nothing but the image of a little boy?

Chapter Six

"Hi, baby," Martin said to Judy the following Monday morning, as he stopped on his way to his first-period class.

"You hear something?" Judy said, turning to Mona.

"Not a thing," Mona said. "Why? Did you?"

"No, I guess not. Someone must have farted. It sounded like something coming from an asshole," Judy said, and the two girls laughed to themselves.

"Don't be angry. I tried to explain what happened. We couldn't help it," Martin said, but Judy ignored him and tried walking around him. He cut her off, then said, "You act like it's all my fault."

Judy said nothing and refused to let herself get angry all over again, though Martin had it coming. She and Mona, had wandered around the park for a half hour looking for Martin and his cronies before giving up and going home. Judy had fumed the entire ride back because Martin was always pulling that kind of crap. That same evening, he had called her with an unlikely story, but Judy was too disgusted to listen.

As she walked to her first class, she dismissed Martin from her mind. She only wished it were so easy to dismiss him from her life.

A few students walked into the psychology class before the bell rang; most would come in at the bell. They settled into their seats behind long formica tables. There were eight tables in the classroom— four on each side of the room—leaving a wide aisle down the middle.

At the front of the classroom, Molly Nordine chatted with her friend Amanda Colins. "Thanks for coming," Molly said.

"It should be fun," Amanda replied, surprised by how much simply wearing a pair of glasses and pulling her hair back had changed Molly's appearance. Though it seemed to be more than that, her bubbly friend of two nights earlier had been replaced by an authoritative high-school teacher.

"I have to admit," Molly said, "I felt a little guilty after you left Friday night. I didn't mean to twist your arm."

"What twisting? I'm in town anyway. And it gives me a chance to pay you back for that wonderful dinner. David loved it, too. He thought I was crazy to turn down your offer."

"It still stands. I wish you would reconsider. There's no reason for you to stay at the motel. I have plenty of room."

"Trust me, it's better this way. I'll be tramping in and out at all hours. What is it people say: both fish and houseguests stink after three days. And I'm sure I'll be in Fulton more than three days. Don't worry, I'll be fine."

"If you're sure?"

"I am."

"Here we go," Molly said when the bell rang. She pushed her glasses closer to her face. "Time to put on my teacher's face."

Amanda watched the expressions of the students as they came in. A mixture of sleepy eyes and broken smiles was what she expected in the first class after the weekend. Amanda remembered how hard that class had been for her back in high school, especially on a beautiful spring day like that day.

"Hurry, please. We have a guest today," Molly told her students as they entered. "You won't be needing your books."

Those words perked up the class and produced the sounds of both glee and relief. The teens settled in their seats, and all faced forward.

"Good morning, class. We are very fortunate to have with us Dr. Colins." Molly smiled at Amanda as she made the introduction. "She's a friend of mine who has been kind enough to come and speak to you today. She's from the Ohio State University Psychology Department."

"What? Is she going to analyze our minds?" Mark Turner blurted out and the class laughed.

"If you had a mind," Martin said and the class laughed louder.

"That will be enough, Mark and Martin," Molly said, immediately taking back control of her classroom. "As I was saying, Dr. Colins is from the university. Her field is the subject of parapsychology."

"You are now entering the twilight zone," someone shouted, which made Molly give the teen a stern look.

For her part, Amanda smiled at the comment. "I see some of you already have an idea about parapsychology. But let me make it clear that parapsychology is not about all the spooky stuff you see on TV or at the movies. It is a study of the human mind and its locked potential. Joseph Rhine, an American psychologist, pioneered the study of extrasensory perception and psychic phenomena. He brought these events under objective, scientific scrutiny and coined the term parapsychology. In more cases than not, parapsychology will disprove an event rather than prove it.

"Yes?" Amanda said when Mona raised her hand.

"Isn't it just about reading minds and stuff like that?"

"You mean telepathy. Partially. Parapsychology includes the study of clairvoyance, precognition, telepathy, astral projection—a whole host of topics. Sometimes the list seems endless. However, telepathy is one of the most popular. Let me show you something."

Amanda walked over to the side of Molly's desk and lifted a leather briefcase off the floor. After setting the case on the desk top and snapping it open, she removed eight large cards with black symbols on their faces.

"We use these cards to gauge a person's ESP rating. A typical ESP study might require subjects to try to perceive the symbol on each card presented in a random order. When subjects can consistently name the cards at rates exceeding chance guessing, there is said to be evidence of ESP."

Mona raised her hand again. "Isn't it true that the odds will allow a person to pick the right card some of the time?"

"Correct. We use the odds to determine the rating. For example, here I have eight cards, all having different symbols. When I hold out one card, a subject has a one-in-eight chance of guessing it correctly.

That's just for one card. There's over a one-in-forty-thousand chance of guessing all eight cards correctly. In testing we use a deck of seventy-five cards, which unquestionably makes it somewhat harder."

"You still get some right by guessing," Karl Warner said from the back of the room. "Doesn't that mess up the results?"

Amanda forgave the interruption and answered the boy's question. "No. The average person, with a normal ESP rating, would guess about five percent correctly. That's about four cards out of the seventy-five. It's when a subject's average is higher that the study becomes more interesting." Amanda looked around the room. "Would some of you like to try?"

A few of the students snickered, but no one volunteered.

"Come on. It doesn't hurt, really." She paused, then said to the boy who had interrupted her, "How about you? Give it a try?"

At first Karl shook his head. After a little coaxing from the other students, he agreed to try. He got up from his seat and walked to the head of the room, the thumb of his right hand hanging from the lip of his faded blue jean pocket. He stopped a comfortable distance from the woman. He glanced back to his classmates and gave them a nervous smirk, then asked, "What do I do?"

"First and most important, relax," Amanda said. "Could we have a couple of chairs, please?"

As the chairs were brought forward, Amanda focused her attention on the boy. "What's your name?"

"Karl, Karl Warner."

"Mine's Amanda," she said with a warm smile, then looked back at the class. "It will help if we all feel comfortable with each other. So I want you all to call me Amanda. All right?"

After murmurs of agreement filled the room, Amanda positioned the chairs so they faced each other. "This is how we will proceed. You sit facing the class, and I'll sit with my back to them. That way when I hold up a card they can see the symbol before you make your guess. All right?"

"Sure, whatever."

"Don't get too excited," she said and heard some snickers. She held up the first card so that the class had a clear view of the square symbol card. "Now the rest of you remain quiet. Karl, concentrate and tell me what you see."

All eyes were on Karl, while he sat quietly for a moment. "I don't know. This is stupid."

"Relax and give it your best try."

"A circle," he said immediately, causing some of Karl's classmates to laugh at the guess.

"Actually, that was quite good. The two are very similar." Amanda showed Karl the card. Then she held up another one to the class. That one had three wavy lines. "Put everything out of your mind and try again."

"A star?" Karl smirked at his classmates, but only Martin and Mark laughed.

"You're doing fine," Amanda said, turning the second card to him. "Now, how about this one."

"A triangle?" he said, and the class came to life with amazement.

"See, you can do it," Amanda said, showing Karl the face of the card. "It is a triangle."

Karl's remaining guesses were wrong. And Amanda went on to test other class members, none of whom fared much better. A few minutes before the bell,

Amanda dismissed her latest subject and said, "I see we have time for one more person. Who will it be?"

Many hands went up. But Amanda made eye con-'tact with Judy. The girl wasn't raising her hand, yet something inside Amanda clicked.

"How about you?"

"I'm not really interested," Judy said, surprised the woman selected her.

"Go ahead, Judy," Mona said. "It's fun."

"All right." Judy walked to the front of the room and sat in the chair as the others had before her. Taking her established place, Amanda carefully watched the girl, trying to evaluate her without making her nervous. Amanda felt something strong about the girl.

"Judy, is it? You know how this works. Clear your mind. What's the symbol on the card?" Amanda asked, then held up the card with the star.

"A star?" Judy glanced at Mona, who enthusiastically waved to her friend.

"Yes. Very good. And this one?"

"A square."

"Yes. Right again. Now?" Amanda asked, the students suddenly buzzing with interest.

"Wavy lines?"

"Yes. Terrific."

"She can see them through the back," Mark blurted out, but Martin didn't laugh.

"Ignore them. Keep up your concentration." Amanda held up the circle card. "How about now?"

"Circle?"

"Now?"

"Crescent."

By this time the classroom was dead silent as if all the students were holding their breath. Amanda picked up the triangle card. She could see fear in Judy's face.

"Tri—" Judy started to say. "Square. A square."

"Ha, she blew it," Karl said.

"That's OK. How about now?" The card had two crossed lines. Amanda knew Judy had the image in her mind. But she could sense the girl was going to guess wrong. A talent like hers would set her off from others.

"A heart," Judy said, confirming Amanda's suspicions.

"No," Amanda said, "but I think—"

The bell rang, ending the class. As the students herded toward the door, Molly said, "Before you leave, I'd like to mention Doctor Colins's fine book, *ESP in Today's Society.* I will have a copy reserved at the front desk in the library for you to check out, if anyone is interested. And read chapter sixteen for tomorrow."

The assignment produced a few moans, but not from Judy. Shaken by the experience, she ignored her friends' questions. After they went on to their next classes, Judy went back to her table to collect her textbooks.

"Wait a moment, will you, Judy?" Amanda said, seeing the girl leaving the room.

Judy nodded and stood by the door. Amanda briefly spoke with Molly, then returned to Judy. "Where's your next class?"

"Just down a floor."

"Let me walk with you," she said and the two left the room. "You missed the last card on purpose. You knew it was a cross. And the card before—you started to say triangle. You changed your answer. Why?"

"I'm not sure. I just felt weird."

"You shouldn't. You have a great gift."

"No, not me."

"Yes, you. I would like you to come to the university. I can test you more thoroughly there. We can do it during summer break. You won't need to miss any school."

"No. I don't think so."

"Judy, you have nothing to be ashamed of."

Judy pulled her books close to her body, trying to shield herself. "It's not that. I just can't. That's all."

Reading the tension in Judy's eyes, Amanda reached into her purse and pulled out a small white card. "Take this. If you change your mind give me a call. I'll be in Fulton for a few days. That card has the phone number for my office here in town, and my hotel room's phone number's there too."

Judy reluctantly took the card. "I really have to get going or I'll be late for my next class."

Amanda smiled at the girl. "Please, give it some thought?"

Clutching her books tighter, Judy walked down the stairs to her class. Behind her, Amanda stood considering the confused girl and the gift she so wanted to deny.

"I'm home," Peter called out as he went through the front door to his house. Going into the living room, he dropped his schoolbooks on the couch. "Mom?" When no reply came, Peter dashed up the stairs. Through the bathroom doorway he saw his father's red metal toolbox open on the floor and the handles of the bathroom faucet lying next to it on a piece of old newspaper. His mother was wearing an old flannel shirt and jeans flecked with spots of brown paint.

A sudden curse from his mother made Peter laugh.

"I could've done that for you."

Sharon gasped and dropped the wrench in the sink at the sound of Peter's voice. The color in her face disappeared. "Peter, you nearly scared me to death! Must you sneak around?"

"Sorry," Peter said, eyeing his mother with concern, "didn't mean to scare you."

"No, it's not you," Sharon said, regaining her composure." I'm just a little jumpy lately. That's all."

"How's the sink?" Peter asked. He hoped changing the subject would smooth his mother's nerves. "Will it live?"

"Well, I think this washer's had it," she said, holding a small black ring that had been flattened out of shape. She was glad her son was too levelheaded to let her skittishness upset him. But since that day in Bobby's room, she couldn't shake the feeling of being watched. "Can you get me another from the toolbox?"

"Ah, Mom," Peter said, restraining a laugh.

"What?"

When Peter pointed to her face, Sharon looked in the bathroom mirror and saw a dark smudge across her nose down to her cheek. She wiped away the grime with the sleeve of her flannel shirt. Then she and Peter burst out with peals of laughter. All her tension released, Sharon relaxed.

"We're out," Peter said as he fingered through the metal box.

"Hmmm?"

"We're out of washers."

"You sure?"

"I know what a washer looks like, Mom."

"Of course you do, dear. I just thought I saw some last time I looked. I must have been wrong."

"Guess so," Peter said. "Sorry."

"Would you do me a favor and run down to the hardware store to pick up a couple? I look too much of a mess."

"Sure thing."

"Here, take this." She handed Peter the spent washer. "It should help you get the right size."

"Can I take Bobby?"

"If he wants to go," she said, picking up a rag and wiping off her hands. "I think he's in the backyard."

When Peter went out the back door, he had the eerie feeling someone was watching. Looking around, he saw Mrs. Romun glaring through the small space between the curtains of her kitchen window. Peter stared back at her and she pulled the curtains closed. Peter hoped she hadn't been calling Bobby names again. And from the way his brother was playing, Peter didn't think she had.

"Hey, Bobby, you want to go with me to the hardware store?" he asked his brother, who hadn't noticed him until he spoke. "Mom needs some washers for the upstairs sink."

"Sure! Can Georgie come with us?"

"Sure," Peter said.

"Did you hear that, Georgie? We're all going to ride in Peter's new car." Bobby paused a moment and gazed into empty air. "Georgie says it will be fun. He likes your new car. He remembers seeing it before."

"How could he?" Peter caught himself and smiled. "Let's go. Mom's waiting."

Peter and Bobby drove uptown to Anderson's Hardware Store, and all the way, Bobby talked to his friend. It seemed to Peter as if he was eavesdropping on a one-sided phone conversation. But it seemed real enough to Bobby; the pitch of voice even changed as though he really did hear someone talking back.

The afternoon traffic was very light, which put Peter at ease. He didn't have much experience behind the wheel to start with and this car, without power steering or brakes, took a lot more skill to drive than his mother's station wagon. Anderson's Hardware Store wouldn't normally have been Peter's first choice, but it was close, and the shorter the trip the better.

Peter drove up the hilly part of Wellesley Avenue. The more daring skateboarders rode down the hill for its steep incline and semisecluded location. Both sides of the street were lined with sporadic tree growth and no homes. Other small businesses were set on the other side of the hardware store, which sat atop the hill at a point where traffic was never heavy.

After signaling his left turn, Peter pulled into the small parking lot next to the store. He got out of his Buick, proudly started off to the entrance, then stopped. "Let's get going," Peter called out and waited for his brother, who was still sitting in the car.

The passenger door opened and Bobby stepped out. He held the door for a moment before closing it. "Can me and Georgie stay out here?"

"Well, I don't know," Peter said.

"We'll be good."

"OK, if you promise to stay by the car and out of trouble."

"We promise."

"All right then. I'll be right back." Peter disappeared into the store.

Bobby stood by the car, talking to Georgie. He picked up a handful of small gray stones and made a game out of imagining what they were by their shape. He laughed, then threw two of the stones down the hill and watched them bounce out of sight. From behind Bobby came the loud sound of a muffler badly in need of repair. He ignored the rumble, but he couldn't ignore Mark Turner saying, "Hey, isn't that Cowal's retard of a brother?"

Bobby glanced up toward the noise as a mustard-colored Ford Maverick with large rust holes pulled up and stopped alongside the curb. Inside the car, three boys watched Bobby as he dropped his remaining stones to the ground and whispered something to the air.

"Look at the dummy talkin' to himself," Mark said, pointing and chuckling. Karl Warner, the driver, strained to look out the passenger's side, and Ox poked his head out the back window.

"Don't listen to them, Georgie," Bobby said, and his odd remark caused all three boys to roar.

"Georgie?" Karl said.

"Listen to the freak!" Mark said. "I think he's talking to a troll."

"Shut up!" Bobby yelled. "He's not a troll."

"What then? A leprechaun?"

"No," Bobby said, "he's my friend."

Karl pushed open the car door and leapt out; the other two boys followed close behind as he strutted toward Bobby. "I don't see anyone, you shit."

"I don't care. I see him," Bobby said.

Karl waved his hands through the air where Georgie was supposed to be. "Look, you little moron, there's no one here."

"Yes. He's here."

"I said there's no one here."

"Yes, he's here," Bobby repeated.

"Anyone home?" Karl's face tightened and he slapped Bobby on the side of his head.

"Stop it," Bobby cried out.

"Where's your friend Georgie now? Oh, there he is, down there." With that, Karl shoved Bobby down to the pavement. Then the three boys started back to the car, laughing all the way. Once there, Karl leaned against the car door, crossing his arms against his chest. "Tell your friend to take better care of you next time."

His taunting stopped when something hard smashed him in the middle of his chest. The other two boys watched him drop to the ground, gasping for breath. As Karl went down, he tried uselessly to stop his fall by grabbing at the side of the car. There was a loud ripping sound as his jacket sleeve caught on the sharp edge of rusted metal.

"Shit!" Karl wheezed out. He got to his feet and started to move away from the car, but he couldn't take a single step because his sleeve had become wedged and twisted in the exposed metal of the door. He tugged at the sleeve and the fabric tore a little more, but would not come free. He tried to open the door to get a better angle without any luck. The door latch was jammed by the jacket's material.

"Help me get loose," Karl said, still having a little trouble breathing.

Mark and Ox ran around to Karl's side. Mark pulled on the sleeve while Ox worked on the door.

"It's stuck pretty good," Mark said. "Maybe we should cut you lose."

"No way," Karl said. "Just get the door open. I can pull my jacket free."

As Mark and Ox pulled hard enough to shake the car back and forth, the car started to roll forward, slowly at first, but the pace changed quickly.

"Get inside and set the parking brake," Karl said.

Then Ox ran to the passenger's side and tried the handle only to find that door wouldn't open either.

"What are you waiting for?" Karl asked.

"It's locked," Ox said. "I didn't lock it." As he tried the back door and got the same result, the car picked up more speed.

"Hurry up, will you!" Karl yelled, his voice starting to shake.

"Take your jacket off!" Mark said when the car edged closer to the crest of the hill.

"What?" Karl shouted, panic making his voice shrill.

"Take your jacket off. Now!"

Karl grabbed for the zipper and, in his haste, jammed the metal teeth in the jacket's lining. While his feet moved faster to keep up with the car's speed, Ox kept pulling on the handle, but the downward hill got closer and closer each second. Karl tore at the zipper, his quick pace becoming an outright run.

The car rolled faster and faster, and Karl barely kept on his feet. The door handle pulled from Ox's grip as the car began down the hill. Then Karl lost his footing. Sliding across the ground he struggled to force the jacket off and over his head. The jacket worked its way up his body, but stopped when the zipper caught under his chin. The steel teeth cut deep into his skin, followed by a warm gooey sensation running down his neck as blood came from the chewed flesh. Behind him, Mark and Ox watched helplessly.

Karl's eyes opened wide with a jolt as they focused on a cluster of large oak trees at a bend in the road. Frantically pulling at the jacket, too scared to feel any pain, he attempted to break the meshed teeth of the zipper apart. As the car continued to gain speed while heading directly toward the huge oaks,

Karl squirmed violently, trying to free himself. The jacket at last came loose from his chin; the metal teeth raking up and across his face. The jacket shrouded his head, blinding his view, but he couldn't stop. At any moment, the car would crash. With one final desperate shake, Karl freed himself from the jacket. His body rolled off the road into a muddy ditch as the car spun to its side and collided with an oak, pinning the jacket between the crushed passenger's door and the solid tree. The danger over, Mark and Ox raced down the hill, Mark heading for Karl and Ox for the twisted car.

At the top of the hill, Bobby watched the boys for a few minutes before returning to Peter's car. He opened the door and jumped in, then slid across to the middle of the seat. "Hurry up," Bobby said and the car door closed.

Peter came out of the store carrying a small brown bag. Because the bend of the hill hid the wreck from his view, he had no idea of the strange scene that had just taken place. "Any problems?"

"No. Nothing Georgie couldn't handle."

Peter smiled, but he wondered why Bobby looked so serious.

In office 117 of the Fulton municipal building, Amanda Colins sat at a large paneled desk; her cigarette burning in the ashtray had a long gray ash. She sat, her hands knitted together in a tight ball before her face, her elbows planted firmly on top of the desk. The phone rang, but she didn't react. It rang again, snapping Amanda out of her thoughts. Picking up the receiver, she said, "Yes."

"How are the accommodations?"

"Hello, David," she said, resting her free hand in

her lap. "Not bad, actually. There's even a plant."

"I had a moment. Thought I'd call and find out how your lecture went."

"Today I met the most amazing girl at the local high school," she said, not really hearing David's words. "Her name's Judy Kilter."

"What was so amazing, except her listening to your lecture?"

"Ha. Ha. Funny guy. No, I gave the standard ESP test to about eleven kids. Most did quite average, but this girl, Judy—she was remarkable. I only brought a few cards with me, but still. Five out of seven. She got five out of seven, and I know she had the sixth one. She deliberately tripped up. And something tells me she had the seventh too."

"Luck, maybe?" David said.

Amanda reached over to crush out the burning ember of her forgotten cigarette, which was starting to eat away the filter. "It wasn't luck. It couldn't have been. She was terrified about the whole thing. Still, under her fear, I sensed her mind reaching out."

"So, you think she's legit," David said.

"I do," Amanda said. "I've been on both sides of the testing process enough to know that level of ability."

"You don't have to convince me. Remember, I've tested you myself on several occasions when you were a grad student. You were the best part of my paper."

"Yes, subject K. I remember. How flattering."

"Hey, anonymity is important."

"I know, but subject K. Why not Dick or Jane?"

"Well, what do you plan to do about the girl?" David asked, getting back to the subject at hand.

"Don't know yet," she said, tapping her fingers

against the desk. "I gave her my card. I hope she'll call."

"By the way," David said, "a couple of files got sent here to your office. Someone must have got his instructions wrong. I'll express them to you."

"Great. I met with Frank Currie. The city council wants me to meet with the head of the construction company doing the development on the land."

"A good first step. Let me know how things turn out."

"Will do."

There was a pause on the phone. "Maybe if you get bored," David started, "I could drive to Fulton. I'll buy you dinner."

"David," Amanda said, taken back a bit. "Are you asking me for a date?"

"Hey, a man's got to eat."

Chapter Seven

"Gonna eat your pickle?" Mona asked as they sat together in the school cafeteria.

"No," Judy said, pushing her plate across the table, "go ahead."

"Bad sandwich?" Mona said, seeing Judy picking at the top slice of whole-wheat bread. "Take it back. Sometimes I think the school cooks serve the sandwich meat left over from last year."

"It's fine. I'm not very hungry, that's all."

"I know Martin can be a creep now and then," Mona said, "but I think you did the right thing."

"I guess," Judy said.

"Hey, a lot of girls in this school would love to go with Martin. They're like vultures waiting to strike."

"I guess."

"Besides, he does care about you. It's hard for him to show it, that's all." When Judy nodded, Mona asked, "You going to meet him after school?"

"No, he and his buddies already have plans."

"Translation," Mona said, "they got their hands on

117

beer or something harder, and they're going to get themselves blitzed."

"Mona," a girl called out.

"Speaking of vultures," Mona whispered.

As Diana Codling walked through the cafeteria to Judy and Mona's table, not one male head went unturned. She had jet-black hair draped down the middle of her back and sparkling green eyes. Her clothes were always tight, and it was a popular boys' room rumor that she never wore underwear.

"I just wanted to tell you I can't make track practice this afternoon," Diana said.

"Why tell me?" Mona asked.

"Well, you are head of our relay squad."

"That never mattered before."

"Sorry if I'm going to mess up the timing. It can't be helped. You can get the alternate to take my place." Diana smirked at Judy and added, "Though, I know it won't be the same."

"Sure," Judy said, smirking back at Diana, "I can cover for her. It won't be tough. She does run the weakest leg."

"Sorry," Diana said, "if I wrecked any plans—if you had any."

"No, not a one."

"Well, that figures."

"If you're finished," Mona said, "you can leave now. We're trying to eat."

"Tell Martin I said hi." Diana batted her green eyes at Judy, then waved her fingers and swayed off.

"Drop dead," Judy said under her breath.

Mona giggled. "Forget her. We can practice one person short. Who knows? It might push us harder to get a faster time."

"No, I'll take her place. It's no big deal."

*   *   *

Sometimes Tuesdays could be a little dull, and for Peter Cowal that day had begun slowly and died by lunchtime. The clocks seemed to fight against reaching three o'clock, and when the day's last bell finally chimed out its permission to leave, Peter found himself hurrying to do just that. It was one of the very few times when the sound delighted his ear.

It wasn't until Peter arrived home that things started looking up—for him anyway. The letter from Ohio State University he'd been waiting for had arrived in the mail. He dashed around the house calling out to Bobby, and to his mother. Peter had expected to receive some scholarship money from the college, but he had to read and reread the last paragraph, then read it still a third time. It said the university was pleased to inform him that he would be receiving a full scholarship for his first year, which was renewable for the next three years with a 3.90 or higher G.P.A. Full scholarship—room, board, tuition, books—all of it paid for. In that one moment all his hard work, all his extra studying—all of it paid off.

The letter did not make everybody happy. Bobby had gotten home from his school about 40 minutes before Peter and found the mail waiting to be opened. He had heard his mother and brother discussing the college plans and had misgivings about it all. Bobby stared at the letter with the return address of the university stenciled in bold black letters. For a moment he thought of hiding it, but knew that wouldn't be the right thing to do. He went to his room and waited for Peter to come home.

"What's wrong, Bobby?" Peter asked later, when he found Bobby. The sadness in his brother's eyes was painfully obvious.

Bobby pointed to the letter in Peter's hand. "You're going away."

"Bobby, the university is only a few hours away. We'll still see each other a lot. Maybe I'll live here my first year. I don't know."

"No, you won't. I heard you and Mom talking. You want to be on your own. You want to move away to the big school."

"I haven't decided yet. And if I do, that doesn't mean I wouldn't come and visit. I can come home on weekends and holidays."

"You won't. You won't!" Bobby shouted. Suddenly, he started out of the room. "You want to leave us! You don't care about me anymore!"

"Bobby, come on, don't be like this," Peter called from the doorway. He started to follow his brother until he felt a hand on his shoulder.

"He's scared of losing you," Sharon said. "This is hard for Bobby. You've always been here for him. He'll adjust. You'll see."

Outside, Bobby ran away from his house. As he got farther and farther away, his breathing got heavier and heavier. His direction was guided by his instincts, and he found himself at the foot of the same woodland trail he and his brother had used as a shortcut when returning home from flying kites the previous week. He looked back once before starting down the path. Too upset about his brother's leaving, Bobby didn't hear the voices coming from Crazy Man's Bluff.

Alex stood at the edge of a road looking out across the brown and green field. Its tall, snaky grass, waving back and forth in the breeze, seemed to welcome him home. Almost 60 years had passed since he had last walked on that soil. Deep in a far-off corner of his mind he wished, almost prayed, he could have forgotten, that time and an aging mind would have washed away all the memories.

The lines cut into the tall grass were as he expected and feared. Peter had been there. It was the field he had spoken about so innocently. Alex still regretted shouting at the boy; he had no way of knowing what horrible things had happened there.

Alex's eyes followed the trails. Most people stayed clear of the rubble that was once the foundation of his childhood home. All, but one. A trail ran along the outer rim of stone. The only other trail away from the main cluster led to the old oak tree. As the breeze picked up, Alex heard the slapping. Hanging from a branch, a tattered piece of rope moving with the wind banged against the bark.

Alex recalled the long climb to reach that limb and how he had carefully tied off the rope, making sure the knotting would never slip. Obviously he had done quite a job.

He also recalled the beating he received from his father for using the best piece of rope he had. It was one beating he hadn't minded getting for something that at the time was so important. Besides, after his father had cooled down he had allowed the swing to remain.

"What am I doing in this foul place," Alex said out loud. "The whole thing is craziness. It's over. I ended it, years ago."

Alex blinked. And in the split second between the closing of his eyes and their subsequent reopening, a small boy appeared standing next to the tall oak. A flood of emotion poured over Alex as he focused on the small child. His pace slowed as the tall grass

twisted around and against his ankles. His legs tired
quickly as he pushed through the brush, yet some
surge of energy, some unknown force, carried him
onward to his little brother—his little brother Georgie.

Bobby stopped running when he heard the loud
voices coming from up ahead at the base of the cliffs.
The cliff wall rose 30 feet. A gradual slope began at
the base, which became a vertical wall ten feet from
the cliff floor. At the top was a safety barrier made
of a chain-link fence with wood strips between the
metal loops.

Bobby took only a few more steps when he spotted
the group of boys, some standing, some sitting, but
all drinking from bright gold cans. He wondered what
kind of pop they were drinking; he'd never seen pop
cans like that before. He stood quietly watching the
group and counted four of them. All wearing jackets
with a large blue F on the front.

"Hey, Martin, look," Karl Warner said and pointed
at Bobby. "We've got company."

The youths scurried to hide their cans behind large
rocks, under their jackets, behind their backs, anywhere out of sight of the intruder. Meanwhile, Ox
carefully tried to extinguish his tightly rolled joint
without destroying it. When he burned his fingers in
the process, he cursed.

"Relax," Martin said, "it's only Cowal's retard
brother."

On hearing the intruder's identity, the other boys
relaxed and uncovered their beers. Karl chuckled at
Ox, who was sucking on the edge of his finger. The
sneer on Ox's face made Karl get up and walk over
by Martin and Mark.

"I'll take care of this," Martin said, his voice cold

and emotionless. "Bobby. Hey, Bobby, come here. I have something for you."

Bobby reluctantly walked off the trail. The loose rocky floor under the cliff caused him to slide on his first step, but he quickly regained his footing. He approached the group of boys, who quickly encircled him.

Bobby remembered Karl, Mark, and Ox from the day before—from outside the hardware store—and took a step back. He saw a large white bandage taped to the left half of Karl's face. Dark-brown spots soaked through the gauze in a curved line from top to bottom.

Karl pulled away from Martin and glared over at Bobby. He managed a single step when Martin grabbed him by the arm, pulling him back. When Martin whispered in his ear, Karl nodded.

Martin broke from the circle and stood in front of Bobby. "You weren't spying on us, were you?" Martin asked, a wide smirk on his face.

"No, no, I wasn't spying." Bobby's eyes were drawn to the golden can in Martin's hand. "What kind of pop is that?"

"The best kind. Want some?" Martin said, holding out the can.

Bobby heard faint snickers. He looked around at the boys circling him and saw Ox mumbling to Mark, who let out a shallow chuckle. Bobby glanced back at the gleaming can.

"OK," Bobby said, taking the can from Martin's hand and placing it to his lip. The fizzing liquid went down his throat with a slight burn, and with a gagging reflex, Bobby forced it right back up out of his mouth and onto Martin's letterman jacket.

A tremendous roar of laughter came from the

group, except from Martin, who stood there with beer dripping off his precious jacket.

"You asshole," Martin said. He hadn't yelled, but his tone still frightened Bobby. "Wipe it off."

Bobby, with beer dripping from his chin and a foul taste in his mouth, felt sick. "I'm sorry. I didn't mean—"

"I said wipe it off!"

"I don't have anything to wipe it off with."

"Use your shirt. I don't give a damn! Get this shit off my jacket!"

Bobby's eyes started to tear and his bottom lip quivered. "I want my brother."

"Your fag brother couldn't help you if he was here," Ox said.

"I want my brother. Peter! Peter!" Bobby cried out.

"Clean this off, you freak." Martin grabbed Bobby's arm and rubbed his shirtsleeve against the large beer stain, but Bobby pulled away.

"Clean it up! Now!" Martin shoved Bobby to the rocky cliff floor. When Bobby tried to crawl away, Karl jerked him up by the shirt and pushed him back to Martin, who shoved him to Ox. Soon it was as if they were playing catch with Bobby as the ball. From Martin to Ox to Karl to Mark back to Martin. Round and round the boy spun.

Bobby whimpered as the ground whirled faster and faster. As the faces passed him in a dizzy blur, his head began to feel heavy and his stomach heaved violently.

The boys finally stopped and Bobby fell to the ground. Instinctively, he picked up a handfull of dirt and threw it at his attackers, pelting both Martin and Ox with small pebbles. In the confusion Bobby got up and ran, but the ground still seemed to sway. He couldn't tell which way led back to the trail, and his escape was cut off by the rocky cliff and the angry group on his heels.

"So you like throwing things. Well, so do I." Martin grabbed a fist-sized rock and hurled it at Bobby. The sharp stone grazed Bobby behind the temple. At the speed Bobby's heart was beating, blood quickly ran down the side of Bobby's head and dripped off his ear. The other boys followed Martin's lead and began pelting Bobby.

"Stop! Stop! You're hurting me!" Bobby pleaded. He backed up closer to the face of the cliff, working slowly up its incline. The blood continued down his face and dripped off the tip of his chin. When another rock hit him on the bridge of his nose, there was a loud crack and pain shot through his head. His tears mixed with the blood on his face and dripped onto his shirt. Turning away from the flying stones, Bobby pressed his bloody nose against the cliff. Then a heavy stone clipped the top of his shoulder, making his arm go numb for a second.

"Please! Please! Don't hurt me no more!" Bobby cried out, the blood and tears trickling into his mouth with each word. But Martin and the others ignored his plea.

Higher and higher Bobby climbed. The small pieces of gravel made it hard to maneuver. He had to use the larger rocks as handholds to pull himself up and away from the stones that struck him on his back and legs. He had cleared 13 feet of rock when a stone smashed the back of his right hand, snapping his index finger at its lowest knuckle. Bobby screamed out. His arm dropped to his side as his hand swelled. His entire body weight was supported by his left arm alone.

His feet kicked out hoping to catch hold of one of the many groves in the rock. The tip of his sneakers pushed against a ledge in the cliff's face as he tried to regain his balance. The large shelf of rock moved slightly under the pressure. Dirt spilled from the fracture between the rock and the cliff.

Then Bobby's right foot slipped off, and the jerky motion made his handhold rock shift position. Dirt poured out onto his face, stinging his tear-soaked eyes. His eyelids closed tight; his head kicked back. What little footing Bobby had gave way. The rock, no longer able to support the full weight of his large body, broke off. Both the rock and Bobby went tumbling down the incline. The motion started other rocks falling, rolling down behind the boy.

The boys below watched Bobby's plunge. Ox and Mark just stood staring, Karl let out a laugh, and Martin opened another beer.

Finally, Mark said, "We have to help him!"

"We do?" Martin said.

"Yeah, lighten up, Mark. He screwed himself," Karl added.

Bobby rolled to the bottom of the cliff, pain shooting out from all parts of his body. A large dark shadow followed close behind him and seemed to blot out the sunlight. Bobby felt the air being forced out of his lungs as the falling rocks blanketed him. His legs and arms went numb. The last thing he heard was a loud snap.

When the avalanche ended, Mark and the others walked slowly over to Bobby's motionless body. Only Bobby's jeans, his sneakers, and one hand stuck out from under the large pile of rubble.

"He's dead," Mark said.

"No-dah! We can see that from here," Karl said, his hand shaking.

"This isn't funny!" Mark yelled. "We're all in real deep shit! Do you assholes understand?"

"Don't shit your pants, Turner," Martin said. "If we all keep quiet, nobody's gonna know we were ever here."

"I don't know, Martin," Ox said. "Maybe we should go for help."

"No, he's dead," Mark said. "God, I'm gonna be sick."

"We killed him," Karl said.

"What do we do now, Martin?" Ox asked. He put his trembling hand to his mouth. "We have to tell somebody."

"No," Martin said, sipping his beer. "No, we don't. Somebody will find the body and figure the retard tried to climb the cliff. They'll think he fell."

"Then let's go! Let's go now!" Mark said, his voice trembling.

"Will you calm down!" Martin said. "Get your empties. We can't leave any signs of being here."

The boys grabbed the empty beer cans and made the area appear unvisited. The whole operation took 30 seconds.

"Now," Martin said, "let's get the hell out of here. And nobody say anything to anyone—not even your babes. Got it?"

All nodded their heads. Then the boys hurried off and cut through the woods back to town. Only Mark looked back.

With each step, Alex uprooted long shreds of grass, cutting another path from the road. Some of the green blades caught around his ankles and jabbed the old man through his socks, but he didn't slow down to relieve the irritation. As he walked across the field, his mind slipped back to the days he and his brother had passed the hours together. Georgie's favorite thing was that tire swing—Alex would push him for hours. It had been worth a few welts to make his tiny brother so happy.

The images of the past raced through Alex's mind as he walked, almost trancelike, across the hard ground. He tried to hold the thoughts back, but found he didn't have the will. They forced themselves to the surface with painful clarity.

The day was almost 60 years ago, and the images were sharp and clear in Alex's mind. He remembered pushing his little brother on that tire swing. He still heard the way Georgie laughed while he pushed.

"Higher . . . higher," Georgie called out.

"You'll hit the moon if I push any harder," Alex said.

"No. The moon doesn't wake up until night."

"Where is it now?" Alex asked, teasing his little brother.

"Don't be dumb," Georgie said seriously. "He's home sleeping before he gets up and goes to work like Daddy."

"Just wondering."

Georgie laughed. "Higher . . . higher."

"Where in the hell are you?" their father's angry voice shouted from the house.

"Daddy's home," Georgie whispered to his older brother as Alex stopped pushing and brought the tire swing to a stop.

Alex silently motioned for Georgie to get off the swing, then said, "It will be OK, if you stay next to me. Are you listening?"

"Yes. Alex, I'm scared."

"I know. It will be all right."

Isaac Stein appeared at the back door and stared down at his two sons. Above his dark stubble beard, his eyes were two black slits. He had a scowl full of yellow teeth. "I knew you two lazy kids would be out here goofing off with work to do. Where's my supper?" He started down the stairs. His right foot slipped off the step's edge, and he slid down the next two steps. He caught himself on the railing, which saved him from landing face first on the hard ground. He was drunk.

Georgie pulled closer to his brother, hiding behind Alex's longer body. Only his head poked out as he watched his father stagger back to his feet.

"I want my supper now," Isaac growled.

"I'm sorry," Alex said, easing Georgie back, hiding him from the view of their drunken and angry father.

The realization that he had stopped walking snapped Alex away from his thoughts of the past and back to the present. He found himself looking down at the small boy he once called his brother.

"Why have you come back?" Alex said.

Georgie didn't speak. Instead, he reached up and wiped the tear from the old man's cheek, then faded away.

Peter went huffing and puffing along the trail to Crazy Man's Bluff. He had searched for Bobby in his usual hiding places, first the backyard, then his favorite fishing spot down by the dam. The field was Peter's last chance. He was running out of places to look for his brother.

From a small rise, his view stretched far down the path. Bobby was nowhere in sight. "Where can he be?" he said to himself, trotting along the trail a little farther when he heard far-off voices. The words were only mumbles and garbled phrases. Still, he hoped one of the voices belonged to his brother. He dragged himself along the trail and followed the voices, which seemed to evaporate to nothing.

The cliffs were deserted, though Peter thought he detected some brush moving in the woods. He stepped off the trail and looked at the base of the cliff, where he saw the pile of rocks and the body underneath. The sight of the black high-top sneakers sticking out from the rubble made his whole body tremble.

"Bobby?" Peter said softly and without taking a breath. The word couldn't be coming from his mouth. To his ear the sound seemed like some cruel echo. "Bobby!"

Chapter Eight

Two days of anger and guilt had passed since Peter had found his little brother crushed to death. His hands had many small cuts and bruises from pulling the heavy debris off Bobby's body. The dress jacket he wore to his brother's funeral hid the scratches that ran up past his wrists and along his forearms.

Sprays of flowers garnished all sides of the shiny brown casket, and a large bouquet of freshly cut lilies rested on top. On that sunny day, Peter, his mother, relatives, and friends stood in a semicircle around the coffin with Pastor Goodwell at the head.

Great care had been given in the preparation of the site. The grave had been neatly dug by hand, not heavy machinery. Thick planks, hidden under a large piece of clean Astroturf, covered the hole. The heavy lumber easily supported the weight of the casket. Ten feet from the grave a large green tarp securely covered the mound of dirt that would be used to cover the casket. Only the smallest of dirt clumps leading to the pile could be seen in the grass if anyone troubled himself to look close enough.

Peter couldn't bear the sight of Bobby's casket any longer. His stinging eyes moved from face to face of those people who stood with him and his mother. Bobby's teacher wept into a tissue. Alex stood with his hands folded together, a black yarmulke on his head. Aunts and uncles and several cousins—some he hadn't seen in years—were all there for one reason. To say good-bye to Bobby on that warm day.

My fault, Peter thought, blaming himself as he had since finding Bobby. *All my fault.*

"Our Lord, accept this child into your. . . ." Pastor Goodwell was saying.

Why didn't I go after him sooner? Why? Peter watched his mother wiping the tears from her eyes with the soft blue handkerchief Bobby had given her the previous Christmas. Peter remembered her telling Bobby that she would always keep it with her. *I'm sorry, Mom. I'm so sorry. I didn't take care of Bobby. It's all my fault. Bobby's dead because of me!*

" . . . the shepherd watches over his flock. . . ."

Peter started to feel as if his head were going to spin off. He forced himself to remain standing. Then he felt someone take his hand. It had been years since he had felt the tenderness of his mother's hand in his. She gave him a soft squeeze, and Peter squeezed back. The simple act gave Peter the strength he needed; he would not let her down here.

" . . . and the innocence of this child in the eyes of . . ."

Beer on his clothes? The police said they found beer on his clothes? How? Where would Bobby get beer? The questions filled Peter's waking hours. Both Sharon and Peter couldn't believe the police report. Sharon told the investigators they were wrong. Later, the officer informed her there was no alcohol in Bobby's bloodstream, but there were slight traces in his saliva. Peter had heard the man's words, but he couldn't accept them.

"Let us pray."

And the service was over.

The pastor's wife helped Sharon arrange the small get-together after the funeral. Mrs. Goodwell offered the church for the gathering, but Sharon preferred her home.

At the house, Peter talked with his cousins, but he spent more time with Bobby's teacher, who had only praise for his little brother. Still, he was brief because he had an important task.

Peter made his way across the living room. There he found his mother pouring coffee for his great-aunt Carol, a sweet old woman who lived across town. Peter knew by the look on his mother's face that Aunt Carol was in an advice-giving mood. Sharon nodded her head at Carol's comments and smiled a lot.

"Excuse me, Mom," Peter said, stopping his Aunt Carol in midword.

"Yes, dear?"

"There's something I have to do."

"Can it wait?"

"No, it can't. Would it be all right if I leave for a little while? I'll come back when I'm done."

"Honey, we have guests," Sharon said, noticing Aunt Carol glaring at Peter. "It wouldn't be polite to leave."

"I know, but I feel trapped here—smothered sort of. Know what I mean?"

Aunt Carol took a long sip of her coffee while watching mother and son talk.

"I think so. All right, dear. If it's that important."

"It is." Peter kissed his mother on the cheek and headed upstairs.

"Now, Carol, where were we?" Sharon said.

Peter went down the stairs two minutes later carrying a shoe box under his arm. The path to the front door was crowded with people, so Peter left through the back door. Mrs. Romun sat snugly in her patio chair reading a copy of *Cosmopolitan*. Although she glared over at Peter, he ignored her, but thought she made a good argument for euthanasia.

As he walked to the front of the house, he realized there was a very good possibility his car would be blocked in the driveway by one of their guests' cars. Fortunately, he found he had a clear path to the street. Peter slowly backed out of the driveway, expecting to hear the sound of his car scraping the blue Toyota next to him. After backing into the street without a scratch, he drove off.

"Mark? Mark, I'm talking to you," Suzy Kendall said, gently pushing her boyfriend on the shoulder. The young couple sat comfortably alone in the corner booth at O'Brian's. They faced the wall, their backs to the rest of the world.

"What?"

"Where are you today? You seem miles away."

"Sorry. I'm just worried about trig class. There's going to be a quiz. You know how I get when it comes to tests."

"Sure," she said and snuggled closer to him. "You're going to take me to the stock-car races tomorrow night, right?"

"Races? Yeah, I'm taking you. You're my girl."

"For now, anyway," she said and smiled at his hurt

look. "Only kidding. You just try to get rid of me. But what's the matter? I know you. No test has ever made you this much of an airhead."

"You're right. If I tell you, you have to promise me you won't tell anyone or even hint that I told you anything."

"All right."

"I mean it. No one. Not Mona. Not Judy. Promise me! No one!"

"OK. OK, I promise."

"Promise what?" Martin suddenly said from behind, causing Mark to jump in his seat.

"Hi, you guys," Suzy said to both Martin and Judy, who joined their friends in the booth.

"What are you two doing way back here?" Judy said.

"Nothing yet," Suzy said. "Just kidding. We wanted to be alone."

"We can leave," Judy offered.

"No," Suzy said. "It's OK. Maybe you two can liven things up a little."

"Promise what?" Martin repeated.

"Well, I. . . ." Mark started to say.

Suzy detected the tension in Mark's eyes. She had seen that troubled look only once before. Mark tried to hide his fear and did well. Only Suzy picked up on it. Coming to his rescue, she said, "He wanted me to promise him that I wouldn't ever leave him. Isn't that sweet?"

"Yeah, sweet," Martin scoffed.

"Martin," Judy said, "it was sweet. It wouldn't hurt you to act the same sometimes."

"Yeah, right. Act like a pansy."

"Martin!" Judy said.

"Hey, I'm joking. Don't have a cow."

Judy turned to Mark and Suzy. "You guys ordered yet?"

"No, not yet," Mark said.

"Mark," Suzy said, "we ordered five minutes ago. Remember?"

"We did? Oh, yeah. Sorry. My mind's all over the place. You guys want something?"

"No, I'm dieting," Martin said sarcastically, staring at Mark, who turned his eyes down to the tabletop.

"Well, I have to go to the girls' room," Judy said.

"Again?" Martin said. "You're always going."

Judy ignored his remark. She had heard his complaints often enough to know there was no point in a reply.

"Wait," Suzy said, "I'll go with you. Our food won't be here for a couple of minutes. I can use a touch-up." She reached over and wiped the small lipstick print off the side of Mark's mouth. Mark got to his feet and let Suzy slide across the seat and slip out of the booth. "We'll be right back."

As soon as the girls were out of ear range, Martin said, "I told you to keep your fuckin' mouth shut!"

"I didn't say anything," Mark said, picking up his glass of ice water. A small amount splashed over the rim and ran down the side.

"You would have."

"I wouldn't. Do I look stupid?"

"Don't ask!"

"Mark seems jumpy," Judy said as she finished brushing her hair and shoved the green plastic brush back in her purse.

"He's been like that the last couple of days. Can I borrow your lipstick?"

"Pink or red?"

"Red, of course."

"Of course." Judy pulled the stick of lipstick from the side pocket of her purse and handed it to Suzy. "Martin's been his usual sweet self."

"You two OK?" Suzy asked, the words sounding distorted as she applied the red tint to her puckered lips.

"I guess. It's just sometimes he can be a real asshole and other times he can be the sweetest. And lately it's been more sour than sweet."

"Well, I bet things get better when school's out."

"Maybe."

"You two got any plans for tomorrow night?"

"Nothing set in stone. Why?"

"Want to come with me and Mark to the stock-car races?" Suzy asked, handing the lipstick back. "My uncle has a car entered. My father's been working with him for months to get it ready. The way they talk the other entries might as well stay home. What is it about men and cars?"

"Got me. I can't figure out the guys our own age. They say one thing, then do another."

"I know what you mean." Suzy wiped a small flake of red lipstick from her right front incisor with her pinky finger. She smiled in the mirror to check the work on her lips. "And some are so hung up on themselves. So self-absorbed. You want to come then?"

"I don't know. I'll talk to Martin about it."

"Oh, God!" Suzy said.

"What?"

"A zit!"

"Oh, no, you should run home. You don't want to frighten any little children."

"Funny."

Judy suddenly collapsed against the sink and held

on, trying to prevent herself from falling to the floor. Suzy rushed over and grabbed her friend by the arm.

"You OK?" Suzy said, holding Judy upright.

Judy's face eased. "Just a headache."

"I have some aspirin in my purse. Want some?"

Judy regained her balance and stood up. "No. Thanks. I'm better now. It hit me so quick."

"You sure you're OK?"

"Yes, I'm fine. Don't tell anybody about this."

"Sure, I guess, but a headache's no big deal."

"I know. It's just that I don't want anybody worrying." She gave herself one more glance in the mirror. "We should be heading back to the table."

"Sure you're ready?"

Judy nodded. "Let's go."

Suzy gave her friend a reassuring smile. "The guys probably think we fell in."

"It's been two days," Martin said, "and nobody has even batted an eye our way. The other guys are fine with this. Why can't you? You have to get your shit together. We're in the clear."

"Only a matter of time," Mark said. "The cops have ways to figure things out."

"No way. If the cops suspected anything, they would've come down on us by now."

"Maybe they're watching and waiting for us to make a mistake. Waiting to get evidence."

"Calm down. Lower your voice. There isn't any fuckin' evidence. None."

"I hope you're right."

"I am. Now shut up. Here come the girls."

"You miss me?" Suzy asked Mark as the two girls sat back down in the booth.

"We thought you fell in," Martin said.

Suzy smiled at Judy. "Told ya."

"Told her what?" Mark asked.

"Nothing. Girl talk, you know. What were you two philosophers talking about?"

"Just about—" Mark started to say.

"The regional championship," Martin said, interrupting his friend.

"Baseball?" Suzy said. "Is that all you two can find to talk about?"

"Hey," Martin told her, staring at Mark, "we're gonna kill Hillsbury!"

"Yeah, right," Mark said; taking another small sip of water. "Kill Hillsbury."

After three hours of driving around town and along the back roads Peter finally found himself at the gates of the cemetery. The sun had started its decline in the western sky, and its color took on a reddish-orange glow.

He sat in his car with his forehead resting against the top of the steering wheel. He took a deep breath and opened the door. With the tip of his index finger, he pushed the bridge of his glasses up the bridge of his nose. Peter stepped out of his car, carrying the shoe box that had been sitting on the front seat. At Bobby's grave, two men were starting to fill the hole. The older man had a hard, tan face, black hair with several strands of gray, and large callused hands. The other man, much younger than the first, was tall and thin, but had large muscular forearms.

"Excuse me," Peter said.

"What the hell you doin' here, son?" the older man said, wiping the dirt from his hand onto his sleeve before reaching into his front shirt pocket for his cigarettes. He tapped one out and stuck it in his mouth.

"You-ou sh-shouldn't be h-here," the young digger stuttered. "It-t's ta-too late. You'll hav-ve ta leave."

"How'd you get in?" the old man asked through the cigarette hanging out of his mouth.

"The gate was unlocked. I just walked in."

"No. Gate should be locked. Arnie, you lock the gate?"

Arnie looked down at the ground. "N-no, H-harland. N-not yet. I-I meant t-to, but I-I . . . we b-been so busy. I d-didn't get t-to it."

"Sorry," Peter said, "I didn't mean to cause any trouble."

"Ahhh, it's no trouble, I guess. Arnie's right. We've been busy today," Harland said. "I ain't angry with ya, Arnie. I hate when we're busy with this kind of work. Don't mind mowin' and trimmin'. Even don't mind wiping the bird dung from the stones. But fillin' the holes. That's hard. Don't get me wrong, son. It ain't the doin'. It's the loss. Each hole we fill means a whole bunch of hurt for somebody."

"He's my brother," Peter blurted out.

"I'm sorry, son. I won't trouble ya with any more questions. I can see the hurt on your face."

"Thanks. I'd like to leave something with him." Peter held the box under his arm close to his side. "Can I? Please?"

"Sure you can. Ain't no rules against it, I guess. What about you, Arnie? You know anything about any rules?"

Arnie shook his head. "N-n-no. N-not me-ee."

"Go ahead, son. Come on, Arnie. Let's get some coffee and leave the boy to his task."

Arnie plunged the tip of his shovel into the mound of dirt and waited for Harland. As Harland passed

Peter, he patted the boy on the back and said, "Take all the time you need."

"Bobby," Peter said when he was alone. "Bobby, I miss you. I'm so sorry. I don't believe them. I don't!"

Peter lifted the top off the box and let it drop to the ground. "I thought you might want this. You said it was your favorite." Peter reached into the box and pulled out the large softball with Bobby's name written in large letters. Without a second thought, Peter let the box fall to the ground. "I know it's not much." Peter got down on his knees and gently tossed the ball onto the thin layer of dirt that Arnie had already shoveled in the grave. He got back to his feet, took the shovel by its long dirty handle, and covered the softball with dirt from the pile.

"I let you down," Peter said. "I would do anything to. . . ."

Peter had cried so much over the last two days that he thought himself empty of tears. But to his surprise, more tears covered his face. He wiped his face, smudging a dirt streak across and down his cheek. All the while, he felt as if someone was watching him. He turned, expecting to see Harland and Arnie. Instead, a small boy stood next to a tombstone topped with a stone angel. The boy remained perfectly still, not moving a muscle. He simply stood there watching Peter.

"'Scuse me, son," Harland said, coming up behind Peter. "You finished?"

"Yeah, I guess so." Peter picked up the shoe box and its lid. "Someone else is here. Some little kid."

"K-k-kid?" Arnie said. "No k-kid here, 'cept you."

"He's right there." Peter looked back at the tombstone with the angel. The little boy was gone.

"Like I s-said, no k-kid here."

"He must have run off," Peter said.

"Sure," Harland said, "some of the kids in the neighborhood get a big kick running through the graveyard. I think it's all sort of sick, but it takes all kinds. Arnie, make sure we give the grounds a good search after we lock the gate."

"A-all right."

"I should be heading home," Peter said. "Thanks for your trouble."

"No trouble, son. You gonna be OK?"

"You two have work to do," Peter said. "I'll go now."

Both Harland and Arnie looked at Peter, but the two men said nothing. On his way back to his car, Peter stopped for one more look at Bobby's grave site. Harland had filled his shovel blade and dropped the soil into the open grave, and Arnie copied him.

The setting sun cast dark tombstone shadows across the green grounds. The shadow wings of the stone angel stretched out touching other stones around it. Peter paused for a moment, bothered by his memory of the little boy. Then it hit Peter. He replayed the image clearly in his mind. The shadow. It hadn't been there. The little boy had had no shadow.

Chapter Nine

When his alarm clock buzzed for the third time, Peter reached over and pushed the plastic switch off instead of hitting the snooze button again. He watched the blue electronic digits change: 8:15 . . . 8:16. Finally he pushed the covers off his body. They fell to the floor in a soft heap next to his bed. He lay on his back for a moment, covering his eyes with his forearm. No real thoughts went through his head, and he wondered if he should go back to sleep.

"No, I'll get up," he said without enthusiasm. "Why not? School's waiting. And I don't want to blow it now."

He let out a huff. It had never been difficult to face Monday mornings. Although he had heard other students and even a few teachers remark how hard it was to show up at school Monday mornings, it had never been that way for him—until that day.

He lifted himself up, planted his feet on the cool wooden floor, and sat on the edge of his bed. He put his right hand on his forehead, then brought it down and gently rubbed his eyes. With one smooth motion, he drew his hand straight back through his hair, stopping at the nape of his neck, which he stretched. After taking his glasses from the dresser, he headed for the bathroom.

He passed Bobby's room, and the door was still closed. He stopped and reached out for the knob, then pulled back at the last second. His mother had been in the room to straighten it up some, but he couldn't find it within himself to enter. It didn't seem right; it didn't feel right. He had never entered his brother's room without Bobby's permission. And he wasn't going to start.

"Peter, are you up?" Sharon called from downstairs.

"Yeah, Mom. I am."

"What would you like for breakfast?"

"Anything's fine," he answered and continued on to the bathroom.

Once there, he turned on the water for a shower. The falling water drenched his arm as he pulled back, then it beaded and dripped off the ends of his fingers. With his wet hand, he reached to the shelf for a towel, which he hung next to the shower curtain.

Taking a step back to disrobe, he caught his reflection in the cabinet mirror. He stared at his face. It was cold and hard except for the hurt deep in his eyes. As if his reflection angered him, Peter slammed his fist against the sink. Nothing would ever be the same again.

Judy and Suzy stood next to the railing overlooking the huge foyer of Fulton Senior High. They passed the time chatting about the events of the previous weekend. From down below came the slams of lockers and voices raised in excitement because of the end of the school day. Martin, Ox, and Karl came scrambling up the stairs, but the girls didn't see the three until they were only feet away; then Judy greeted the trio with a forced smile.

Martin put his arm around her waist. "Saw you standing up here and figured you must be waiting for me. Well, here I am." He pulled her close and kissed her.

When Karl put his fingers to his mouth and started making smooching sounds, Ox shoved him and said, "Can the lip noise."

"I hate to disappoint you," Judy said, "but we have track practice, and we're waiting for Mona to show up before we head down to the field."

"We're always waiting for Mona," Suzy said. "For everything!"

"Sorry I'm late," Mona said, coming up to the group. "I didn't expect such a reception. I'm flattered."

"Don't be," Martin said, releasing his hold on Judy's waist.

"You're your usual sweet self," Mona said.

As Martin and Mona went through their usual cuts and comebacks, Judy noticed Peter coming up the stairs, keeping to the far side of the staircase. She thought he would fall over the handrail if he leaned any farther. He had his head down as if watching each step.

"We should go say something to Peter," Judy told the others. "His little brother was killed. I'm surprised he's back in school already."

They followed her eyes to Peter, who at the moment was almost at the double doors to the second-floor main hall. Suddenly the boys became silent and Karl's face went white.

"What's wrong?" Judy said. "It won't weaken your tough-guy reputations to say something."

Ox made a noise. It might have been a word, but came out as only a grunt.

"Say something?" Martin said. "What the hell for?"

"Yeah, I don't understand you sometimes," Mona said. "Who cares? He's a creep."

Martin's reaction didn't surprise Judy. It was Mona's words and bitter tone that stumped her because she had always thought of her friend as having a big heart. Judy watched as Peter walked out of sight through the double doors. She wanted to run after him, but she didn't.

Mona pulled at her sleeve. "We better get down to the field or we'll be doing extra laps."

"You could use them," Karl said, but his joke fell flat.

As the girls walked down the hall, Judy couldn't shake the feeling that the guys had done something wrong—and she wasn't sure at all that she wanted to know what it was.

Outside the sky was overcast, threatening rain. Judy wished it would because she didn't feel like running. Seeing Peter had given her a bad feeling, and she couldn't shake the suspicions about Martin and his friends. The three girls were halfway through the parking lot, when she opened her mouth to speak, but Mona started to say something before she got a single word out.

"Is it safe to assume," Mona said, "that you two have heard about the party at Diana Codling's house this Friday night?"

"I'm sure the whole school knows," Suzy said, "the way she strutted around telling everyone. I hate the way she's always throwing her boobs around. It would serve her right if no one showed up."

"You're not gonna go?" Judy said.

"Are you serious?" Suzy replied. "I wouldn't miss it. You and Martin going?"

"That's the plan."

"It should be great," Mona said. "I guess her parents are out of town all weekend."

"I can't believe they trust her," Judy said. "She's always in some kind of trouble."

"Some parents are like that," Mona said.

"Not mine!" Suzy said.

"My dad's OK," Judy told her friends, "but Jessica is always on my case about something. Who am I out with? Where am I going? What my father sees in her, I'll never know."

"I hope my mom never remarries," Suzy said. "I couldn't stand the idea of a stepfather—some man I don't know living in the same house. That would give me the creeps."

"Oh, shoot," Judy said. "I forgot my shorts back in my locker."

"Your locker?" Mona asked.

"I took them home and washed them. I know that might seem a little strange to you."

"Hey, I wash my shorts too," Mona said.

"Oh," Suzy said, "is it leap year already?"

"I'll meet you guys down on the field," Judy said, leaving her friends and heading back up to the school.

It took only minutes for Judy to hurry to her locker and retrieve her running shorts. On her way back through the parking lot, she saw Peter walking between the cars. He stopped by the big car she had seen him wiping dry the week before. Although she wanted to say something to him about his brother's death, Judy just stood and watched as he drove away. Without knowing why, Judy felt tears come to her eyes. She shook her head and sniffled, then wiped her eyes, hoping her friends wouldn't notice the unexpected emotions they would undoubtedly belittle. Her feelings once more in check, she headed off for the track.

Karl scratched his chin as he and his buddies left the school. "I can't stand this itching." He was careful not to tear open the scab along his chin and the side of face. He didn't need the bandage any longer since the wound was now more like a red line dotted with crusted spots every half inch or so.

"I'm glad Mark wasn't around to hear all that about Cowal's brother," Ox said. "Probably would've shit his pants on the spot."

"He'll be OK," Karl said. "I can't say having Judy talking about Cowal's brother made me feel too easy myself. I keep looking over my shoulder expecting to see some cop about to grab me."

Martin laughed. "You sound as bad as Turner. Maybe you should run home and hide under your bed."

"Cut it out, Martin," Ox said. "I've been feeling a little tense myself. This isn't the easiest thing to live with."

"You too? God, give me a break. You guys sound like a couple of girls. Maybe you should be on the track running around with them. I'll tell you what I've been tellin' Turner. It's over . . . done . . . finished. There's no way anyone's gonna connect us with the retard's death. So forget about it."

Neither Ox nor Karl said anything more as the three got to their cars. Then Karl asked, "You guys want to head for O'Brian's?"

"Holy shit," Ox said, standing behind Karl's car. His eyes were locked on the car before him.

"What?" Karl said.

"I think you might want to see this yourself," Martin told him. He too stared at the car.

"Not another dent?"

"No. It's not a dent."

Karl shut his door and started around the car, the expressions on Ox and Martin's faces making him hurry.

"What in the hell!" he said.

On the back side panel of Karl's car, several words were scratched into the paint: *Hurt you! Hurt you bad!*

Chapter Ten

Amanda Colins unlocked her office door. She entered and placed a cup of steaming black coffee on her desk. She noticed that the ashtray had been emptied, along with the garbage can. The plant had been moved to get more sunlight. She had no doubt it had also been watered. Amanda dropped her briefcase to the side of the desk. She hated lugging that thing around.

She stepped around the desk and pulled out the chair. Before sitting, she flipped the page of the desk calendar. Under the bold letters for the date, she saw her pen scribbles: *9:00 A.M.—Frank Currie and pres of const comp.*

"Wrong day to be late," she said to herself, glancing at her watch. With only a few minutes to spare, she grabbed the handle of her briefcase, yanked it to the desktop, and snapped it open. She had pulled out the first file when a knock sounded on the door.

"Come in," she called, taking out a second.

"Good morning," Frank Currie said with a broad

smile. He wore a brown suit and matching shoes, but no tie. Behind him stood another man who towered over him. That man's suit and tie were of an expensive cut, yet Amanda thought the husky man looked as if he would prefer more casual attire. "May I introduce Mr. Roger Kilter?"

The man stepped forward with an extended hand. "Nice to meet you, Dr. Colins. And it's Roger."

"Amanda," she said, shaking his hand. He had a gentle grip, yet the muscles of his hand and fingers felt powerful.

"All right, Amanda."

"Please," she said, taking her seat, "pull up a chair. I'm glad it's only the three of us. That's all the chairs I have."

"If you need more," Frank said, "I can certainly have more sent up."

"No. Actually this is the first time I've had this many people in this office at any one time." She waited for both men to be seated, then said, "Let's begin."

Amanda went over all the information she had gathered up to that date. She explained to the two men that there were still a few leads she had to track down. Of the several townspeople she had interviewed, however, many told very similar stories. Of course, some common reports could be grouped together by people with common acquaintances, which she explained as normal when experiences of that nature were discussed between friends and families. Still, some reports fit into the cluster of similar experiences, and the people had no apparent connection with any other.

Frank Currie seemed pleased with her progress. Amanda figured that he must have started the whole campaign to develop the land, and it was his reputation on the line if whatever was causing the disturbance turned out to be nothing more than a mother raccoon guarding her nest or the like.

"Please excuse me," Amanda said, when the phone rang and interrupted her report. "Hello? Yes. Yes, he is. It's for you, Frank."

"Yes," Frank said into the mouthpiece a second later, clearly irritated. "Can you handle it? I'm in a meeting. . . . Very well, give me a minute. Goodbye." He placed the phone back on its cradle. "I'm terribly sorry. Something has come up that needs my personal attention."

"No harm done," Amanda said. "We're almost through. I'm sure Roger and I can finish up."

"Very well." Frank rose from his chair. "I will check back to see how things are faring for you, Amanda. You have my private number if you need anything."

"That reminds me," Amanda said, "if you need to contact me after hours, I'm in room 11 at the Blackstone Inn Motel. Feel free to call. If I'm not there, leave a message at the front desk."

"How is the staff at Blackstone treating you?"

"Fine. In fact, great."

"Good. Now if you two will excuse me." Frank extended his hand to Roger, then did the same to Amanda and left.

"He seems to be a very busy man," Amanda said.

"No seems about it. He is. He has a lot of authority in this town. He could be chair of the city council if he had the desire to. Hell, he could be mayor. He was the one who persuaded the council and the mayor's office to give my company the contract."

"You two are friends?"

"Yes, you could call us friends. But don't get the wrong idea. He didn't award me the contract because of that."

"I'm sure. I didn't mean to imply any impropriety."

"Forget it." Roger laughed. "To be totally honest with you, my wife is always telling me I should use my connections more. But I believe a man should get ahead because of what kind of a man he is and what he does, not because of who he knows."

"Though there's nothing wrong with having friends who can help you out either."

"Granted. In fact, by all rights, you can say that helping out a friend does have something to do with my being here. Not Frank Currie helping me, quite the opposite. One of the reasons Frank wanted my company is that I have had my own experience with that particular piece of land."

"Really?"

"It was about fourteen, fifteen years ago. Before I started my own construction company. I suppose Frank figured I would take this whole investigation seriously."

"Do you take it seriously?"

"Yes. I can honestly say I do."

"Well, then, Frank Currie chose wisely. Tell me about your experience. I didn't see your name in any of the files."

"It wouldn't be there. Emmit Jackson, my boss at the time, threatened to fire the whole crew if we opened our mouths. It wasn't worth losing our jobs over, so we kept it to ourselves. I can't say I remember the first time I ever mentioned what happened, except it was after I started my own company."

"What did happen?"

"At first nothing real special. Things disappeared, nothing big. One guy lost his lighter, another a watch. The guys started talking and comparing notes on the lost items. Nothing like that happened to me, so at first I thought they were trying to get a rise out of me. You know, playing a joke.

"Then," Roger said, "surveying equipment started being destroyed right on site in broad daylight with men ten feet away. One moment the equipment was in perfect condition: Then a guy walked away for a minute, and when he went back, his scope was smashed to pieces."

"Mind if I take notes?" Amanda put her pen to paper.

"Feel free."

Amanda scribbled the date at the top of the pad and the initials R.K. "Continue, please."

"The final straw was broken when one of the trucks started up by itself and took off down the road. After that, no one, including myself, wanted anything else to do with that land."

"Interesting." Amanda scribbled a few more words, then asked, "One final thing: would you happen to remember about what time of day it was?"

"Yes. Yes, I do. It happened after lunch. I remember, because my wife and daughter stopped by the site. I forgot my lunch box and they brought it to me. Not a place for a little girl, but Judy wanted to see where her daddy worked."

"Judy? Judy Kilter?" Amanda asked. She felt like bolting up from her chair. "I should've put that together. Kilter is not a common name."

"I'm sorry, I don't understand."

"There's no reason you should. I met your daughter

last week in her psychology class. You have a very special girl in Judy."

"No need telling me."

"I've asked Judy to take some tests."

"Tests?"

"I teach courses in parapsychology at Ohio State. You know, ESP, telepathy, the lot."

"I've heard of it, from TV mostly. And I've read a couple things. Nothing much, though."

"As I was saying, Judy is very special. She has certain abilities."

"Abilities? What kind of abilities?"

"Precognition for one. Under the right conditions, she can tell what will happen before it does."

"Oh, that. She gets it from her mother. Used to drive me up the wall. On anniversaries or birthdays, Carol always knew what I got her before I gave it to her. She used to laugh about it."

"Really? This might seem unusual, but would it be possible for me to speak with her sometime? That is, if she could spare a few moments."

Immediately after she spoke, Amanda knew she'd said something wrong. "Roger?"

"I'm sorry. You caught me a little off guard. Judy's mother died seven years ago."

"Oh, I'm terribly sorry. You mentioned your wife earlier."

"Second wife," Roger said.

"Please forgive me. I assumed—"

"Give it no mind. You had no way of knowing. And it's my fault really. When I talk about Carol, I forget to mention she's my first wife. It's a habit I can't seem to break."

"Thank you. That's very understanding. You said

Judy gets her gift from her mother. Has she displayed
it for a long time?"

"No, not really. You know, I don't think she even
realizes she's doing it."

"Maybe." Amanda tapped her pen against her
notepad. "After her class we talked for a few minutes.
I got the impression she knew something. But then
again, I'm not sure. That's why I'd like to test her.
She may be capable of many different things."

"That's up to her."

"She seemed very reluctant. I gave her my card,
hoping she would change her mind. Maybe if you
speak with her."

"She's like her mother in that respect too."

"Oh, how's that?"

"Once she's made up her mind, it's made up. No
talking from me or anyone else can change it. Any
changing to be done will have to come from her."

"I see." Amanda smiled again, trying to hide the
guilty feeling that was developing. She couldn't
believe she had asked the man to speak to his
daughter on her behalf. "Well, I've taken enough
on your time. Tell Judy I said hello."

"Sure will."

"Thanks for your time, Roger." She stood up and
extended her hand.

He followed her lead. "You're certainly welcome.
If I can be of any more help, you need only ask."

"I will. Do you have a starting deadline for the
construction?" Amanda asked.

"Not really. As soon as I hear from Frank to go
ahead I will. I have a few men ready to survey and
subplot the land."

"I hope not to cause your men any more delay."

"No need to worry. We have a large addition project at our local country club, adding on four more meeting rooms and enlarging the sauna. That will keep my crew plenty busy for the next couple of weeks. When it's time, I'll pull two men away for a couple of hours to do the plotting. Simple and quick."

"Fine," Amanda said, "I'm sure we'll be seeing each other again."

Chapter Eleven

Martin had finished his last class for the day. He had eagerly awaited the weekend and found the drive home relaxing. Driving fast always made him feel good, and the fact that it was Friday afternoon didn't hurt either. As he pulled into the driveway, he hit the white button on the remote to open the garage door. Finding the garage empty surprised him. He had expected his father to still be at work, but to find his mother gone at that time of day was an unexpected delight.

Once in the garage, he pressed the remote button again, closing the large door with a dull thud. He hurried from the garage to the kitchen, making a beeline to the refrigerator, where a plate with two fried chicken legs tightly covered with plastic wrap waited. He pulled back the wrap, pinched off a hunk of meat, and popped it in his mouth. With the cold chicken and a bottle of catsup he headed toward his bedroom.

He had only stepped one foot out of the kitchen

when the phone rang. For a moment, he considered letting it ring, then changed his mind. Still holding the plate of chicken, he picked up the receiver.

"Yeah?" Martin said, his tone laced with hostility.

"Hi, Martin. This is Diana. I wanted to make sure you're coming to my party tonight."

"Sure am," Martin said, Diana's large breasts flashing through his mind.

"Great. Should be a blast."

"I'm counting on it."

"Make sure you come see me. I don't want you ignoring me all night."

"How could I do that? We'll show up around eight, I guess."

"You and Judy?" Diana asked sarcastically. "That will be just great. See you then."

Before Martin had a chance to respond, he heard a click. Martin shook his head and smirked, then headed upstairs to his room.

After eating the chicken and discarding the bones and plate on the floor next to his bed, Martin reached over and lifted the headphones from the top of his stereo. He switched the power on. The equipment lit up as the electricity surged through its circuitry. The volume meters immediately began to pulse back and forth from the compact disk he had left in the player that morning.

Martin put the headphones on and turned the volume up another notch. As he lay back on his bed, his father passed his door.

"Dad," Martin said.

Darwin Welth, a tastefully dressed man in his late forties, stepped into the room. "Yes, Martin?"

Martin pulled the headphones down around his

neck. "Dad, I pitch Tuesday night. You can make it, right?"

"I wouldn't miss it. To see my son win the regional championship. Let someone try to stop me."

"It won't be only me winning. The whole team—"

"I don't want to hear that. In life, if you don't do it yourself, it won't get done. What have I tried to drill into you?"

"Self-reliance," Martin said, remembering all the past lectures and feeling another coming on.

"That's right. You can only rely on yourself. Don't trust anyone else to do it for you—you do it."

"Yes, Dad."

"Don't even rely on friends. You must control your own life. Don't let anything or anyone stop you from obtaining your goals. I might sound harsh now. When you're older you will understand."

"I understand now."

"We'll see," Darwin said. He reached into his jacket pocket and pulled out his billfold. "You need anything? Shoes or whatever?"

"No, Dad. I don't need your money."

"Take it." He placed $50 on top of the dresser. "Only the best for my boy."

"Sure, Dad. Thanks."

Darwin nodded and left the room. After removing the headphones, Martin walked over to the dresser, grabbed the bills, and shoved them in his pocket. If that was all his father could give him, he might as well take it.

With her parents out of town for the weekend, Diana Codling took full advantage of their absence by throwing a party. Diana had some college friends who helped her get a few kegs. Somebody even brought some pot, which was being smoked out in the backyard.

Around midnight, Karl took a sip of beer, but the alcohol did little to relax him. In fact, he was a wreck because he had been watching Mark go from nervous to drunk to bombed out of his skull. And all evening long, Suzy had been questioning Mark about his erratic behavior. For the most part, Mark didn't give her any answers. But as the night had progressed and each drink had gone down, Mark began blabbering about rocks and cliffs. A couple of times, Karl feared Mark would spill the whole story to Suzy and to anyone else who would listen. Sticking around was the only assurance he had that Mark would not do that.

Fortunately, Mark had drunk himself into a stupor, and he was in no condition to say anything. With Mark no longer a threat, Karl decided it was a good time to leave. He made his way through the crowd and into the kitchen, where he found Ox bent over the counter munching down a ham sandwich.

"Want some?" Ox asked, his face slathered with mustard. "It's pretty good."

"No, thanks. You seen Martin?"

Ox nodded his head and swallowed. "He was out back."

"You sure?" Karl opened the kitchen door. Along with the night air came a familiar odor. Outside, a group of teenagers huddled together smoking pot. Karl saw no faces, only a small red ember floating through the air. "Martin, you back here?"

"No," a boy said, "he said something about being horny."

"He's probably upstairs with Judy," another boy said. The others made catcalls at the remark.

"Help us finish this joint," the first boy said.

"No," Karl said, wishing he could, but fully aware that his father would kick his ass if he caught Karl using drugs. "I'm heading out."

"Well, tell Ox to get his big butt back out here or we'll finish it without him."

"You heard?" he asked Ox, who gave him another mustard-covered grin.

Karl should have known Ox would be wherever the pot would be. He raised the sleeve of his shirt to his nose and sniffed the fabric, making sure that he didn't pick up any of the strong odor. Then he found Mona and quickly confirmed that Martin and Judy had retreated upstairs to one of the bedrooms.

Upstairs, in Diana's parents' room, Martin and Judy were making out. Martin bit her neck gently because he had learned over the months of dating her the quickest way of getting what he wanted. He continued kissing her, moving up her neck and across her cheek until their mouths met. She responded exactly as he knew she would. As their tongues interlocked, their heavy breathing escaped from the sides of their mouths. All the while, their bodies tossed and turned, and they drew closer together as if they were starting to melt into one.

Martin felt the lightness of Judy's body as she rolled atop him. As their deep kisses became more intense, Martin pulled the bottom of Judy's blouse free. She was too caught up in the moment to notice. He carefully slid his hand up the opening and placed it on the lace that covered her breasts.

"Stop it, Martin," Judy said, sitting up and tucking in her blouse.

"What? I thought you wanted—"

"You thought wrong."

"Come on, baby. What's wrong? It's not like it's our first time. Why are you making it so tough?"

"I don't feel like doing that. OK?"

"OK. OK. Come back. I'll be good."

"All right," Judy said and slid back across the bed.

"So how about a little kiss?" he said in a soft gentle tone. "It will make it all better."

Even in the dark Martin could make out Judy's smile. Their lips met again, then their tongues. Since Martin was from the school that believed that when a girl said no she meant maybe, he repositioned his hands on her breasts, not bothering with her blouse.

Judy pushed Martin away and jumped off the bed. As she stormed out of the room, she said, "I said no and I meant it. I'm going home, and I don't need you to take me, creep."

As Judy stomped down the stairs, she rushed past Karl, who leaned to one side so he wouldn't get trampled. He watched her hit the floor and disappear, then he continued up the stairs. By the time he reached the last step, Martin was sauntering out of the bedroom.

"She seems in a hurry," Karl said.

"She's mad because I messed up her hair," Martin said, knowing Karl wouldn't believe him.

"So, how good was she?" Karl asked, a knowing smile on his face.

"As good as always. So what do you want?"

"I'm heading out."

"Why so early?"

Karl shrugged. "Gotta be at the school tomorrow morning. Mr. Bobwin's gonna open the auto shop for me so I can finish up fixing the dents in my car, but I have to be there early."

"Don't you get enough of that place during the week? And seeing Bobwin's ugly face that early on a Saturday would make me nuts."

"He said Saturday or in two weeks for class. What other choice do I have? I'm not too happy about it either. But after that weird accident and those scratches, I'll have my car back as good as new."

"You never had it as good as new." Martin smirked. "Come on, you could stay a little longer."

"Why? The party's a drag. Besides, I really want my car back. I had to grab a ride over with Mark and Suzy. Normally, I wouldn't mind, but the way Mark's been, he almost drove us off the road twice."

"Aren't they leaving too?"

"Nope, they're staying. I'm gonna walk home." Karl glanced over his shoulder to make sure he would not be overheard. "You've got to do something about Mark. He's gonna crack."

"Me? Why me? I've already talked to him."

"If someone doesn't do something, I tell ya he's gonna get us all screwed."

"He'll be fine," Martin said, reassuring his friend.

"I hope you're right. I don't want to spend the rest of my life behind bars."

"Don't worry. Besides, it wouldn't be the rest of your life. Only twenty or thirty years." Martin laughed.

"I thought I was the one with the jokes," Karl said, not finding any amusement in Martin's words.

"Who's joking?"

"Terrific," Karl said and turned to the stairs.

Martin laughed again. He had started to follow Karl down when Diana Codling emerged from the bathroom. She wore faded jeans and a tight-fitting blue tank top; her nipples were erect under the clinging material.

"Martin. Hi. Where's Judy?"

"Ahmmm, she left." He had to force himself to meet her gaze and keep it. "Had to get home. You know how it is."

"Sure, I guess I do." She gave him a leering smile and sauntered closer to Martin, almost pressing her body against his. When Martin didn't retreat, she touched his shoulder and glanced toward the bathroom. "That's too bad. Now you're all alone. Plenty of hot water for a nice long shower. It's good for taking away all kinds of stress."

She squeezed his shoulder and ran her fingertips up and down his arm. "Oh, my. I can feel all that tension. Something wet and warm will take all that bad tension away."

"I don't know." Martin smiled and pushed her long black hair off her shoulders. "What about Judy?"

"You said she left."

"She did." Martin kissed Diana below her right ear.

"Come on," Diana said, taking Martin by the hand and leading him back to the bathroom.

"Somehow," he said, closing the bathroom door, "I think this will still cause some muscle tension."

"Maybe at first, but I guarantee you'll be relaxed afterward."

Behind them, Mona stood on the landing halfway up the stairs. Her eyes were at floor level, and she witnessed the whole scene between Martin and Diana. She walked up to the closed door. The sound of rushing water came through the door, then Diana's giggles. There were some whispers, but they were too soft to be clear over the running water. Angry at Martin's betrayal of her friend, Mona was tempted to break in on the couple. But she decided against doing

so and went back downstairs. She'd find another way
to see that Martin got what he deserved.

A block away from Diana's house, Peter drove
down the road, going nowhere. He had felt trapped at
home and needed to get out for a while. He couldn't
concentrate on his homework anymore that night, and
since Bobby's death he couldn't go near his kites.

From out of the clear, dark night came cool air,
which rushed through Peter's open window and
soothed his face. Wilmore Street was lined on both
sides with cars parked bumper to bumper, and the
sound of loud music and laughter destroyed the peace-
fulness the youth sought.

Peter slowed his car down to a crawl. He recognized some of the cars from school and one in
particular. Parked in a driveway was the blue-gray
Dodge Charger that had run him off the road in front
of Mr. Stein's house. The loss of his bike meant very
little to Peter at the moment, but the bitter memory
of the incident still made him angry. As he drove
on, Peter's ire mixed with his grief, and together
they gnawed at his gut. There had to be some way
he could make those kids pay for what they'd done
to him. There just had to be.

Karl wormed through the crowd over to Suzy and
Mark. On the way, he said his good-byes. Although
some of his friends tried to persuade him to stay, he
told them he had other plans. One tried to shove a
half-empty beer glass into his hand, but Karl refused
it.

He found Suzy and Mark on the couch, exactly
where they had been 40 minutes earlier. Mark held
an empty glass tightly with both hands, and Suzy

watched him with a concerned look on her face.

When Karl told her that he'd decided to walk home, Suzy didn't say much and didn't bother to make the gesture of offering Karl a ride, which was fine with him. Mark sat slouched back, his eyes glazed over. Karl wasn't sure if Mark had even heard a word he said.

Outside, Karl walked down the incline of the Codlings' driveway and over to Mark's Charger. He took his jacket off the seat and threw it over his shoulder. At that moment, he realized how much he depended on having his own car. He actually missed the gas-guzzling beast. His only consolation was knowing he would have the paint job finished the following morning and by suppertime would be driving it home.

It was a moonless night, and the darkness gave Karl the eerie feeling he was being watched. He looked around, then laughed at his paranoia. Yet deep down he still felt something.

Two blocks away from the Codling house, Karl paused. The street light overhead gave him a stubby shadow. Behind him, the whole Codling house was lit up, filled with his friends drinking and having a great time. He hated that he had to leave so early, but when Mr. Bobwin said 7:30 he didn't mean 7:35. And he wouldn't get a second chance to paint his car's side panel if he messed up because he was too tired.

"Who's that?" Karl called out when a sudden noise made him jerk his head to the right. As he spoke, the light above him flickered, then exploded, dropping small sharp shards of glass on him. Without thinking he pulled his jacket over his head as a shield from the fragments.

"Shit!" Karl said as the bits of glass hit against the cloth dangling above his head.

Steps came up from behind Karl, and he held his jacket open like the flaps of a pup tent as he spun around to see who was approaching. In the suddenly darkened street, all Karl could make out was a large formless shape of blackness.

"Who's there?" Karl said, his voice a little breathy. The black thing moved closer into view, but he couldn't make out the passerby. To get a better look, he lowered the jacket off his head. The bits and pieces of glass chimed as they hit the sidewalk. "Who is it? Are you following me?"

Karl waited for some reply, but got only dead silence. Unnerved, Karl summoned up his courage and took a step forward toward the intruder. Before the sole of his shoe touched the sidewalk, some force slammed him down to the ground.

More surprised than hurt, Karl tried to speak, only to cough out his words. From behind him, the intruder dragged him to his feet. Strong fingers dug into the flesh where his arm met his shoulder, the pressure so great he felt his muscle tissue tearing.

"Why are you doing this?" He wanted to ask, but was silenced when his head snapped back. There was another flash of light and the crackle of breaking bones. Then a stream of blood rushed from his crushed nose.

The pounding continued until Karl's whole being became one numb mass of flesh. Blood trickled from both sides of his mouth, from his nose, and from a large gash below his right eye.

Then, as suddenly as the beating started, it stopped. Karl's limp body fell to the strip of grass next to the sidewalk, and he rolled into a shaking heap. As the intruder stood over Karl's beaten and bruised body, Karl tried to crawl away by digging his fingers into the soft earth and dragging himself across the ground, but his leg was grabbed and given one hard sharp turn. Karl tried to scream as his leg snapped at the knee, but the blood running out of his mouth turned his cry into a gurgle.

Whimpering, Karl tried once more to pull himself away from his attacker. He could barely see as he dragged himself to the road's edge. The streetlights seemed to be moving closer. He shook his head, trying to clear his sight, but wished he hadn't when the action sent back waves of pain. Through the stabbing sensation, he saw lights getting closer, but he couldn't understand why until he heard the loud diesel engine of a truck. Rolling on his side, he lifted his arm to try to flag down the truck.

"Help me!"

As the truck drew closer, the tight grip closed around Karl's wrist and pulled him off the ground again. The burning pain caused Karl to black out for a moment. But he woke instantly when he was hurled to the ground. The oncoming truck headlights shone in his face, bringing him more and more into awareness. He felt two hands holding him high in the air—one hand still on his left shoulder, another on his right hip. The light came closer, burning his already swollen eyes.

"No," Karl said, his voice barely a whisper. "No. Please. No, don't. Please."

Karl Warner's body flew through the air and hit the grill of the truck with a loud thud. The massive vehicle lurched as the brakes caught. The loud, high-pitched squeal made the truck sound as if it were in pain.

The driver pushed open the heavy door. He jumped from his torn leather seat to the street below. An empty bottle on his lap fell to the blacktop and shattered. He ran to the front of his truck. The headlight's beam came through a filter of thick blood, which ran down the grill and under the front of the cab. The trembling man got to his knees and peered under the truck. What he saw couldn't really be called a body.

Chapter Twelve

"I don't wanna play jacks no more," the little boy said, dropping the small red ball, which bounced twice before rolling away. With one sweep of his hand he pushed aside the 12 metal jacks, ending the game.

"Jacks is your favorite," the little girl said. "Let's play again."

"No, I don't want to. Let's play something else."

"What?"

"I don't know."

"Look, here's something." The little girl held out a GI Joe doll. "When did you get him? I have a Barbie doll."

"I don't ever play with him."

"But, he's real fun. See how he can stand up all by himself." She balanced the doll on its feet. "Barbie can't do that. Her feet are too funny."

"He's a bad guy. I only play with good guys." The little boy raised his hand and brought it down on the plastic figure, knocking it over.

"Don't do that!" she shouted. "You'll hurt him."

"He's a bad guy. Bad guys hurt people, so I hurt him."

"He's not a bad guy," she said, picking up the plastic soldier doll and hugging it. "Play with something else then."

"I will. I have a much better toy." The boy turned his back to his friend, hiding his new plaything with his body.

She could see his elbow and shoulder moving back and forth and strained to look around him, but the little boy kept moving to block her attempts. "What do you have? Let me see."

"Nope," the boy said, his back still turned to the little girl. "This is mine. You can't see."

"Please . . . please."

"OK," he said, pushing a silver truck around into view. "Varoom. Varoom. This is a real good truck. It's real fast and strong too."

"Is that all? I don't want to play with a truck. I know, I'll go get my Barbie doll and we can have a wedding. That's fun."

"No, that's real dumb. Bad guys don't get married to Barbie."

"He's not a bad guy," she said, clutching the doll tight against her body.

"He is! He is!" The boy snatched the doll by the leg and yanked hard. The plastic leg snapped off in his hand and the force propelled the doll out of the little girl's tiny hands. The doll landed face down between the two children.

"Look what you did!" the little girl yelled. "You hurt him! You hurt him bad!"

"He's a bad guy. Only a bad guy." The boy reached for his truck and started pushing the toy 18 wheeler *toward the one-legged doll. He rolled his truck over the doll, then stopped the truck with the soldier doll under its small black tires. "He's a bad guy!"*

The two children stared down at the broken man. Neither said a word. The little girl reached out for the broken plastic soldier and began to pull the toy man from under the plastic tires. The doll felt warm and sticky wet. Something about it frightened her, so she let go of it. She brought her hand up because it still felt wet. She screamed as blood dripped between her small white fingers.

Judy bolted up from her bed and frantically wiped her hand against the sheets. Her breathing was hard and fast as she tried to remove the blood. Then she stopped, her vision clearing as the dream left her. She saw no blood. There was no blood on her hand, no blood on the sheets. Her eyes saw only the familiar trappings of her room.

Settling back on her bed, Judy shivered. Why had the dream seemed so real? she wondered. No answer came to her as she tried to fall back to sleep. But since the dream mixed with memories of the party she had run home from earlier that night, Judy tossed and turned until the following morning.

"You did a fine job, as usual, Peter," Alex said, handing the boy an open bottle of pop. They were in his living room. "But it's not my idea of a good way to spend a beautiful Saturday afternoon—mowing the lawn. It could have waited until tomorrow morning or even next week." Alex sat in an old rocking chair, then turned the chair to face Peter, who sat forward on the edge of the couch.

"It did me good," Peter said and took a sip of his drink. "I needed to get out of the house for a bit. Sorry

I came so late. The sun's almost gone now."

"That's all right, Peter. You finished in plenty of time." Alex glanced down at the newspaper on the table in front of Peter. "Did you know the boy who was killed last night?"

"Yeah, I knew him—one of the jocks at school. I couldn't stand him. He and his friends all think they're so great. They're idiots if you ask me . . . all idiots." He put the pop bottle to his lips, then pulled it away. "There're more important things than sports and fast cars and things like that. They don't really mean anything. What good are they when it all comes down to it?"

The old man detected pain in the young boy's eyes. He had first seen that look the day of Bobby's funeral. "Peter, it's not your fault. You mustn't punish yourself for what happened to your brother."

"It is my fault. Bobby's dead because I was being selfish. I only thought of myself."

"I don't want to hear such rubbish, Peter. Your brother's death was an accident."

"Mom tries to convince me of that too, but I don't believe it. Bobby would've never climbed the cliffs at Crazy Man's Bluff. He wouldn't. And the beer, how did he get beer on himself?" Peter's voice started to grow in volume, reflecting the anger building inside him. "There was someone else there. I know it. Someone else! Someone killed my brother."

"Peter, Peter, calm down. You mustn't—"

"I been thinking about this whole thing. Someone must have killed my brother. I should have stopped them. Bobby, please forgive me."

"If there was a way," Alex said, putting his arm around Peter, "I'm sure he would. I know deep in my heart Bobby would never blame you."

"He was my little brother," Peter said, wiping his eyes. "I was supposed to protect him. It's my fault he's dead."

"Peter," Alex said, barely loud enough for Peter to hear. "Sometimes, no matter how hard we try, there are times we can do nothing. We try and try to protect the ones we love and sometimes it's not enough."

Peter looked down to the floor, holding back more tears. "I should have been with him."

"Believe me when I tell you that I know what you're going through. But it's not your fault."

A half hour later, still confused and upset, Peter left for home, and Alex made his way from the front door back to the coffee table, where he picked up the pop bottle. On the way to the kitchen, Alex's mind kept focusing on Peter's words. Alex understood the boy's anger, his wanting to lash out at the world for his loss. There was something more in Peter's words: *I was supposed to protect him.*

The words struck a cord in Alex that sent ripples through the old man's being. Those words clicked something down in the trenches of Alex Stein's mind. Something he had tried to bury away forever. The images flashed for only a moment, but he felt as if he were reliving his past in that brief second.

One day while he was in high school, Alex had arrived home late from school because his math teacher had kept him after class for talking out of turn. The boy rushed in the house hoping his father wouldn't be home from work yet, but he was not that fortunate.

"Damn kid!" Isaac Stein yelled, backhanding Alex across the mouth, knocking the boy to the hardwood floor.

Alex scrambled away from his drunken father, sliding across the floor on his butt until his back ran up against the living room wall. Blood dripped from his broken lip and spotted his white school shirt.

"When I come home, I expect food on the table. You're just like your mother. Lazy good for nothing." He took the last swallow from a bottle of whiskey, then dropped the bottle to the floor. It made a loud clank, but didn't break. "She thought I was crazy, and I'll tell ya maybe I am. Putting up with you brats. I'm glad she's dead."

Alex's little brother Georgie walked into the room holding his pet rabbit in his arms. "Are you sick, Alex?"

"No, Georgie. Go upstairs."

"Is Daddy sick again?"

"Yes, Georgie. He is. Now go upstairs."

"Maybe Bunny will make him feel better."

"Georgie!" His sharp tone made his little brother jump. Forcing himself to be calm, Alex said, "Georgie, go upstairs."

"Where the hell were you?" Isaac yelled.

Alex tried to move closer to Georgie, but a new pain in his elbow stopped him. He touched the sore spot and found that the bend of his arm had become swollen due to his fall.

"I was playing with Bunny," Georgie said. He proudly held the rabbit to his father. "See?"

"Dirty animal," Isaac said.

"No," Georgie said, "he's very clean."

"Please, Georgie," Alex said. "Go upstairs."

"Get that animal out of my house. I don't want rabbit shit everywhere."

"Bunny wants to sleep with me."

"I said I wanted the animal out of my house." Isaac staggered up to Georgie and pulled the rabbit from the small boy's hands. The animal squirmed violently in the drunk man's grip. The rabbit's powerful back paws scratched Isaac's bare arm, but Isaac felt no pain. He threw the small bunny toward the window. Although the window was closed, the rabbit went through the already cracked glass with a loud crash. "When I say out, I mean out."

Georgie stood frozen with tears running down his face.

"Damn it!" Isaac yelled at Georgie, raising his hand to strike the boy. "See what you did? That's gonna cost me a day's pay to have that fixed!"

Alex jumped up, forgetting his pain, and dashed over to his little brother. As his father's hand was about to hit Georgie, Alex shielded his brother's body with his own. The blow hit Alex in the middle of his back, forcing him to his knees.

"Go upstairs, Georgie. Please go upstairs." Alex pushed his brother. Georgie finally obeyed him and ran up the stairs, tears streaming from his eyes.

"You come back here!" Isaac started after Georgie. Alex grabbed the man by the leg before the drunk could reach the stairs. "You little bastard. I'll teach you to stop me."

Isaac kicked Alex in the chest with the side of his foot, but Alex wouldn't let go. Then Isaac began slapping Alex hard against his head and Alex still held tight. The beating went on for several moments before the alcohol finally caught up with Isaac and he passed out.

After he rolled his father away from the door, Alex went outside to move the dead rabbit's body, which rested amid pieces of broken glass. A large fragment stuck out of the poor creature's body just below its right front leg. There was very little blood. The animal had died very quickly. Alex took the body around

back and gently placed it in a small wooden box. As
he lifted the box, a wave of pain shot through his
chest. Ignoring his injury, he put the corpse on the
top of the shelves standing alongside the house, which
were high enough that Georgie wouldn't find it. He
would bury the animal later, after his little brother had
gone to bed.

Suddenly dizzy from his father's blows, Alex
leaned against the house for support. It was not
enough to keep him upright when he passed out,
landing hard as the pain fully caught up with
him.

The sun had already gone down by the time Alex
woke, and it took a moment for him to orient himself.
As he stood up, both his lip and back throbbed in the
same painful rhythm. As quietly as he could, Alex
crept back into the house. Every light on the first
floor was turned on. He figured that his father must
have been hunting for another bottle to replace the
one he had finished earlier.

Passing the living room, Alex saw his father sitting
in his chair with a bottle of his favorite whiskey
glued resting on his lap. The man's gaze was aimed
straight at him.

"I was outside," Alex said, slowly walking into the
room, expecting a loud scolding and possibly another
beating. He moved to the side, but Isaac's empty stare
didn't follow. "Father?"

Alex touched his father's shirtsleeve. The man did
nothing but blink. The house was absolutely dead
quiet. Something was very very wrong.

"Where's Georgie?" Alex said, but didn't wait for
his father to speak. He yelled out his brother's name
as he ran up the stairs and to his brother's room. With
the hall light filling the room, he saw his brother on

his bed covered by a blanket. Only the top of the little boy's head poked out.

"Georgie?" Alex said. "Georgie, you OK?"

He walked over and turned on the small bedside lamp, then gently touched his brother on the shoulder. No response, no movement of any kind.

"Georgie?" his voice cracked. He carefully pulled down the covers. Georgie lay there motionless, his little brown eyes open and his neck twisted back the wrong way.

Even as the memories flooded through his mind all those years later, Alex couldn't bear the image of his brother's broken body. And like Peter, he broke down and wept over the loss he still felt so dearly.

Chapter Thirteen

As the new week began, the halls of Fulton High were alive with chatter about Karl Warner's death. The story had appeared in the Sunday newspaper and on all the local TV channels, but there were still some who couldn't believe that Karl's death was due to a drunk driver. He would have gone out with a little more style. Some of the stories passing from mouth to mouth were way off from the reported events. A few had Karl crushed in his car after a high-speed chase. Others had him running his car off the route 29 bridge.

At the moment, however, not all the students were concerned with the storytelling. The chatter along the second floor hallway was abruptly broken by the metal-on-metal slam of a locker door. The clamor made heads turn.

"Leave me alone, Martin!" Judy shouted. They were through! Mona had called Judy the day before and told her about Martin and Diana's jaunt to the shower.

"It's all a lie," Martin said. "Nothing happened. Nothing."

"Oh, really?" she said, walking away from her locker.

"What do I have to do?" he said, following her down the hall. "I tried calling you all day yesterday."

"I wasn't home."

"All day? I don't believe you."

"How does it feel? Then again, I don't give a damn how you feel. Just leave me alone!"

"Talk to me."

"Talk to you," she said. "I'll talk to you. You are so full of shit. You think I'll believe whatever you say, don't you? Well, fuck you!"

"Can you keep it down? We're not exactly alone here," Martin whispered, the blood rushing to his face. He grabbed Judy by the arm, but she pulled her arm out of his hand. "Whatever you heard. It's a lie."

"I see. It's all a lie. You and Diana were only doing each other's back in the shower. Hope you didn't run out of hot water."

"Oh, that." Martin smiled as if he had unraveled a bad punch line. "Somebody started this joke and I guess it got out of hand. I'm not even sure who started it."

"Now who's lying? It's true, Martin. It's all true. I know you. You don't care about anyone except yourself. I was too stupid to see it earlier."

"Judy, will you wait a minute?" he called out, trailing after the furious girl. As he reached out to touch her, she pulled back. "It was just one of those things. It doesn't mean anything. You're my girl."

"Martin," Judy said, "you know, I'm glad this happened. You're a real asshole. Drop dead!"

Judy hurried down the hall, feeling surprisingly good. She peeked over her shoulder once and was relieved to see Martin had decided not to follow her anymore.

As she turned the hall corner, she saw Peter Cowal coming from the library, his arms full of books. A deep sadness poured over her as she approached him.

"Hello, Peter," she said, making a point to smile.

"Hi," Peter said. Even though his arms were full, he pushed his glasses up with his index finger.

"You must have a lot of studying to catch up on."

"A little," Peter said, feeling awkward. "A history report, that's all, really."

"Listen," she said, her eyes brimming with tears. "I'm very sorry about Bobby."

Peter didn't know how to respond to her emotion. She had baby-sat Bobby a few times, but that was a long time ago.

"I mean it, Peter," she said, reaching over and gently touching his arm. "Is there anything I can do?"

When Peter shook his head, Judy said, "I hate how the others treat you. It's so cruel."

"Forget it," he said, not wanting any sympathy. "I'll probably never see most of them again after graduation. I can hold out two more weeks."

"Can I tell you something?" she said. "You have very pretty eyes."

Peter stood there dumbfounded. Where did that remark come from? he wondered.

"You look surprised. Oh, I embarrassed you, didn't I?"

"No, not really . . . well, maybe a little."

"I'm sorry, but I meant it. Why do you wear glasses?"

"I can't see without them."

"No, silly. Why don't you wear contacts?"

"I have a pair, but they hurt my eyes a little. Anyway, I never had a reason to wear them, I guess."

"Well," she said, glancing at the hall clock. "I should get to class."

Peter nodded, but he didn't want her to go. He had to do something, anything. Then it came out. He didn't think of the consequences or the risk he was taking. The words came from his mouth too fast to stop. "Maybe we could go to a movie . . . or something . . . sometime." He half wished he could have swallowed his words, but it was too late.

"Maybe," she said.

He watched as she turned and walked away. Before she was too far down the hall, she turned back to Peter and gave him a smile.

The ache in Amanda Colins's stomach made her wish she hadn't skipped breakfast. She promised herself that after meeting with Jonathan Cain she would grab some food—a couple of tacos maybe. She had been waiting for over 17 minutes. It was her own fault, she admitted to herself, dropping by without an appointment and close to the lunch hour. She was lucky the director of the Amherst Institution had granted her an audience at all.

The Amherst Institution—Amanda had noticed the absence of the word Mental from the brass plate affixed to the stone wall at the entrance when she drove up. Her first impression of the building wasn't what she had expected. Instead of dark stone and mortar, she had found glass and steel. It looked more like a high-tech research lab than the last hope of the mentally ill. And the office she sat waiting in reminded her more of an office for the president of a *Fortune* 500 company than for an administrator of a mental institution.

As she sat in a very comfortable chair, doubts began creeping into Amanda's mind. Maybe she was grasping at straws, and slim straws at best. She had run out of other leads, and her experience at Margaret Able's home had been floating in the back of her mind. A definite case of psychic feedback. Some trauma had forced open Margaret's psychic channels, and it had caused either a mental breakdown or some other equally intense reaction. The old woman's thoughts about the field triggered some release of mental energy, and Amanda's questioning brought it to the surface with painful results. Had she suspected such a thing sooner, Amanda thought, she would have been better prepared to deal with it by putting up the necessary blocks and barriers.

Anyway, they were her best leads—a death that happened 60 years earlier and the name Jimmy.

Behind Amanda's chair, the office door opened. The man entering was in his late forties. He had a receding line of brown hair and an average build, and he wore an off-the-rack suit.

"Hello, Dr. Colins," he said, extending his hand. "I regret having to keep you waiting. We had a slight problem downstairs."

Amanda remained seated as they shook hands. "Thank you for seeing me on such short notice. I'm sorry to be stealing your lunch hour."

"It's quite all right." The man walked around behind his desk and sat. "To be frank, normally I would have turned you down flat, but. . . ."

"But?"

"Actually, I'm quite an admirer of your work. I've seen you speak several times. I've read all your papers.

I even own a copy of your book."

"I don't know what to say. I never thought of my work as being interesting enough to attract such praise."

"Don't be so modest. I'm sure there are many others, like myself, who are fascinated with the paranormal and find your work very interesting. But you're not here to hear me babble on. What can I do for you?"

"I'm currently involved with an investigation. A woman I interviewed, Margaret Able, worked for the institution very briefly. She told me of a killing of one of the patients and—"

Jonathan's face went white. "I can assure you, Dr. Colins, none of our patients have been killed. Some older patients have died, yes, though I can assure you from natural causes only. This Margaret Able is either mistaken or out-and-out lying. In fact, I don't recall ever hearing that name before."

"I should've been more clear. Margaret Able worked as a nurse for the Amherst Institution back in the thirties."

"The thirties," Jonathan said with a chuckle of relief. "I guess that clears my staff."

"I would, if it's possible, like to go through any old documents, patient records, anything you have for the decade. Maybe as late as the earlier forties."

"Yes, we have records that date back that far."

"May I see them?"

Jonathan lifted the handset of his phone and pushed a button on its base. "Janet, will you call Wallace Rannet and have him unlock storage room A, please? Thank you."

He rose from his chair and indicated for Amanda to do the same. Then, after an elevator ride to the basement, Jonathan led her down a small corridor. By the last door at the end of the hall stood a small man in blue overalls who opened the door. He slipped his hand into the darkness and groped his way along the inside wall, then the room filled with a yellow glow.

"You only have to pull the door shut," the man said as he passed Jonathan and Amanda.

"Thank you, Wallace," Jonathan said. Extending his open hand toward the doorway, he directed Amanda to enter the room. "You wanted to look at the old records."

Amanda's mouth almost dropped, but she held it tight. As if being confronted by a wild animal, she would not show any fear. All the shelves were overflowing with boxes, and along each wall more boxes were stacked five high.

"You must understand that these files have been inactive for over fifty years. Anything more current is stored elsewhere, and I can't give you access to them without a court order."

"That won't be necessary. Anything later than nineteen-forty or so is too late."

"Ten years, that's still a lot of paper. The records are supposed to be sorted by year," Jonathan said, "but don't count on it."

Amanda's eyes moved back and forth along the boxes and boxes of yellow documents. "I won't."

"Those boxes were moved from the old building to the second-floor records and finally found a place down here. Dig in—so to speak."

"Thank you—I think."

Jonathan chuckled. "Listen, I'll leave word at the front desk that you can have access to the records for as long as you need. I knew the moment you asked the work you had in store for yourself. One day won't cut it."

"That's very understanding. This could take a week to go through."

"At least," Jonathan said. "I should apologize for my little melodrama of suspense, but when I try to explain the vast task involved in going through the old files, my estimates aren't taken seriously. So now I show whoever's interested the mess and let him see for himself the burden of the job."

"You have that many people wanting to see these files?"

"No, maybe one every few years. Usually to trace a family line. My first year as administrator, we had a man claiming he was a third cousin to Howard Hughes. He was trying to trace back to his great-grandmother."

"Really? Was he related to Howard Hughes?"

Jonathan tilted his head thoughtfully. "I don't know. He saw the boxes and, well, I guess we'll never know for sure."

Outside Fulton High, the afternoon sky was clear except for a few thin clouds, which appeared more like wisps of smoke coming up from the horizon. There was no breeze, yet the air was quite cool, making it a perfect day to be on the field for an after-school practice. The girls' track team was on the side track going over their events. Diana Codling had just handed off the relay baton to Mona, who started her leg. Judy continued her stretching. With the baseball team on the far side of the field chasing the ground balls Coach Murphy batted out, the track team was forced to use one track for all running events.

On the field, Coach Murphy blew the whistle that

had hung around his neck for the past 14 years, and the ball team took a break from their practice. The players ran across the field and swarmed around the water boy. Grabbing for a plastic squirt bottle from the ice-filled metal tub, Martin glanced over at Judy, then slowly broke away from the thirsty mob.

Martin kept glancing over his shoulder, making sure that his teammates were too busy cooling off to notice him leaving. His talk with Judy might get messy and he didn't need the extra attention. He hesitated for a moment and thought about putting it off, but when would he get a better chance? Judy couldn't hang up on him, no one could tell him she wasn't there, and she couldn't even run away. She'd have to listen. That's all he would need. She would melt as he spoke; he knew it. That was all it would take.

"Judy?" he said, smiling. "Can we talk now?"

"No," she said and walked away toward a sideline bench.

"Hi, Martin," Diana said, throwing back her long black hair.

Martin ignored her and rushed after Judy. He caught up with her and grabbed her by the arm. "Judy, please. I won't leave until we talk."

"What?" she said, without meeting his gaze.

"Come on. Don't be that way. I miss you." His eyes darted around the field. Some girls in a tight group stared back his way, a few of them giggling. Without another word, Martin led Judy around the side of the bleachers, out of view of the girls, but not his teammates. "Judy, I'm sorry. I made a mistake. I admit that."

"I made a mistake too," she said, her eyes still cast downward. "Going out with you at all was a big mistake."

"Will you at least look at me?" He tried to keep up his best hurt expression and to force back any smirk that hid just below the surface.

Judy complied, but with such an angry glare that Martin wished he hadn't asked. "You are the biggest asshole in this whole goddamned school! You think because your goons follow you around, kissing your butt, I will too! Well, I never want you around me again."

Martin stood there helpless as Judy stomped off. He had just taken a tongue-lashing from a girl, and the guys had picked up on the action. Their grins told Martin what they were all thinking—Judy had made a chump of him. He clenched the fingers of his left hand into a tight fist, the tips digging into his palms. In his mind he heard snickers become laughter—laughter aimed at him. *Nobody dumps on me like that,* he thought as he charged after the girl.

"Judy!" Martin yelled. Catching up to her, he grabbed her arm and spun her around. "Is that any way to treat your boyfriend?"

"You're not my boyfriend. It's over."

"It's over when I say it's over. You got that?" Martin squeezed Judy's arm.

"You're hurting me."

"I'll do more than that"

"Lea-ve her alone," a trembling boy's voice suddenly said. "Leave her alone."

"Get lost," Martin said when he saw that it was Peter who had spoken. "This is between me and my girlfriend."

"I'm not your girlfriend!" Judy struggled to break Martin's hold, but failed. "Can't you get that through your thick skull?"

"I think she made that clear enough," Peter

said, forcing his voice not to quaver. "Now leave her alone."

As spectators started to move closer to the trio, Martin released his hold on Judy's arm. He didn't want to look like the type of guy who would hit a girl, although he wanted to.

"What in the hell do you think you're doing?" Martin said, moving toward Peter, sizing him up, but Peter held his ground. "You must have a death wish, you freak."

Without so much as a blink of his eye, Martin slugged the other boy in the stomach. Peter gave one loud gasp as his breath rushed from his lungs, and as he fell to the ground, his glasses flew off his face.

The other players swarmed around the two, pushing Judy off to the side. "Fight! Fight!" someone shouted, which caused more kids to run over and crowd around the action.

"Martin!" Judy yelled. "You're sick. He didn't do anything."

"I think he did. I think he needs a hand up." He grabbed Peter by the shirt. The sound of the fabric ripping seemed to please the crowd. Martin grinned as he saw his friends nodding their heads in approval.

"Kick his ass," one of the boys yelled out.

"Martin," Judy said, "don't do this!"

"He has it coming." Martin cocked his fist.

To Peter, the whole fight was all just a blur. Even if he wanted to strike back, Martin's first blow had ended any chance of that. He could barely catch his breath, let alone find the strength to throw a punch. He could only wait for Martin's fist to find its mark on his face or whatever other body part Martin would decide on. His only hope for survival was a miracle.

The miracle came in the hulking form of Coach

Murphy. "What's going on here?" The group of teens parted in the wake of the husky man. Murphy had his well-known 25-laps look in his eyes as he canvassed the mob.

"Just helping my friend here up. He fell," Martin said.

"Right. Hit the showers. All of you. Hit the showers," Murphy said, the irritation in his voice coming across loud. As the crowd broke up, Murphy walked over to Peter. "You OK, son?"

When Peter nodded, Murphy said, "OK. You best get yourself home."

After he thought everyone had left, Peter sat on the ground, coming to terms with his pain. Then he felt a light touch on his shoulder.

"I'm sorry," Judy said. She handed Peter his glasses, which were broken at the bridge. "Someone must've stepped on them. Are you sure you're OK?"

When Peter tried to speak, his chest burned. So he nodded his head and grimaced.

"Thank you for trying to help. That was the sweetest thing anyone has ever done for me."

Peter managed to raise his hand and gasp out, "No problem."

"Really. That was very brave and very stupid."

"Gee, thanks."

"Oh, I'm sorry," Judy said, putting her hand to her mouth. Hoping to cover her remark, Judy changed the subject. "How did you even see what he was doing to me?"

"I was going to my car, and I saw you two over here. Martin didn't seem to be acting very friendly, so I thought I'd ask if you needed any help."

"You are so sweet. Is the movie offer still good?"

Sure that the fight had rattled his hearing as well

as the rest of his senses, Peter didn't respond. He'd made enough of a fool of himself for one day.

"You know," Judy said, "earlier, by the library, you said something about a movie."

"Sure," Peter said, convinced finally that he had heard her correctly.

"Let me give you my number. I don't suppose you have a pen."

"I don't need one," Peter said quickly. "I'll remember it."

"Are you sure?" she asked. When Peter assured her again, she recited her phone number. "Got it?"

A short while later, Peter stared at his fuzzy reflection in his bathroom mirror. He knew what had to be done. He didn't want to go through life half blind. He rolled the smooth plastic handles between his fingers, took a deep breath, and pushed the home-repaired glasses on his face until they came to rest on his nose. His vision cleared immediately, and the large wad of tan masking tape wrapped around the broken bridge was the only thing he saw.

"Oh, God!" Peter said to the face staring back from the mirror. He tried shifting the rims, but it was a useless gesture. He could already hear the future jeers: geek, nerd, spaz, dweeb. "Don't I have enough troubles?"

He yanked off the glasses, and the haze came back. "Maybe if I'm careful—yeah, maybe if I'm careful I'll only break one leg."

Peter replaced the glasses on his face, but he was unable to look in the mirror a second time. He ran to his bedroom, pulled a tiny white plastic case from the top draw of his dresser, then hurried back to the bathroom and closed the door. His thumb popped up the round cap with an L embossed in the plastic. Inside, surrounded by a clear liquid, Peter found the soft plastic lens he had worn only once since he had bought them six months earlier.

Peter gently put the lens on the end of his finger. With his other hand, he held open the lid of his left eye. As the lens approached his eye, he felt his eye muscle trying to close. It was then or never, Peter thought, popping the first lens on his retina.

There was an immediate burning sensation. Tears dripped down the corner of his eye, and Peter shut his eyes tight. After a moment, the burning diminished somewhat and Peter opened his eyes. He took the second lens from the plastic case and repeated the whole process with his right eye. After another go-around with the burning, Peter looked in the mirror. His eyes were red, but he could see. In fact, things seemed a little clearer.

Chapter Fourteen

The next morning, Peter found Judy sitting alone in the school cafeteria. Several books were spread out across the tabletop, one of which was propped open in front on her. Peter watched through the window of the door as she read from the book, then jotted down a few words in her notebook.

Some students used the cafeteria as a study hall before and after the lunch hour. But Peter had always found the talking to be too much of a distraction and preferred the solitude of the school's library.

Peter entered the cafeteria, took one step, and froze. Although he had searched half the school for Judy, he had to drag himself to talk to her. He took a breath and continued on.

"Hi, Judy," he said, hoping he didn't look like an idiot. "So what do you think?"

"I was right. You do have pretty eyes." She moved two of her books across the table, clearing a spot next to her. "Here, sit down."

"If I'm not bothering you."

"You're not. I could use the break." She closed her book. "Look, about yesterday—"

"Forget it. I know I'm trying to," Peter said, cutting her off. Desperate to change the subject, he tilted one book to get a better view of the cover: *ESP in Today's Society* by Dr. Amanda Colins. "Parapsychology? That's pretty heavy stuff."

"We had a guest speaker in psych class last week— a professor from Ohio State. She said some things I wanted to check out. And who knows? Ms. Nordine will probably have some of it on the final exam on Thursday."

"I had Ms. Nordine last semester. She probably will." Without thinking, Peter rubbed the corner of his eyes with his thumb and forefinger.

"Are your contacts bothering you?" Judy asked.

"They sting a little."

"You shouldn't wear them too long at first. Your eyes need time to adjust."

"My mother said the same thing last night. I didn't tell her about my glasses. I think those are details she's better off not knowing. I'll have to manage the best I can, stinging eyes and all."

"My friend Mona wore her contacts ten straight hours without a break her first day. She said she'd never wear her glasses again. But she's just stubborn."

"I wish I had the choice."

"Are you going to the baseball game after school?" Judy asked.

"I wasn't planning on it."

"You should. It'll be fun."

"I don't know. I've never been to a game."

"Seniors get the best seats," she said, smiling. "Third row up has the best view. We always grab it. There'll be plenty of room for one more."

She's asking me to go to the game, Peter thought in disbelief. *With her?*

"So what do you say? I'm sure my friends will like you once they get to know you better."

Friends? Of course, she's going with her friends. "Thanks, but"—*I hate your friends*—"there's something I have to do after school."

"I see," she said. "Well, if you change your mind, remember third row up."

The crowd of spectators hurried through the gates and quickly filled the seats surrounding the high school's ball field. Sounds of excitement and anticipation accompanied the fans, some of whom were certain that their team would surely win and move on to the state championship plateau. A steady buzz encouraged the ball players and taunted their rivals, only to be returned with similar chants from Hillsbury's fans. The argument would have to wait until the game's conclusion to see which chant was the right one.

The student sections on the Fulton side were the first to fill to capacity, though with the constant movement of the teens it seemed that no one really had a seat at all. Of course, anyone trying to take a saved spot would most assuredly find himself looking for another place to sit.

Fresh from an early session of track practice, Judy and Mona had taken the same seats they had had for most home games, from which they had a good view of home plate and the pitcher's mound. Sitting there had seemed important when Judy was dating Martin, because he waved to her between batters sometimes, and other girls would inevitably sigh in envy. But before that day's game, Judy had asked Mona if she would mind if they found other seats. When Mona asked why, Judy dropped the subject. It wasn't worth the discussion.

While Mona gawked over to the visitor's dugout, she commented on how cute some of the Hillsbury players were. But Judy didn't hear Mona's appraisal of the other team. Instead, without thinking, she rested her forehead on her fingertips and planted her elbows firmly on her thighs.

"You OK?" Mona asked, seeing her friend stooped over.

"I'm fine," Judy answered, lifting her head, "just a little tired. I'll be OK."

"You want a pop or anything?" Mona asked. "I can run out and get some."

"Maybe later."

"Looks like a case of heartbreak to me," Diana Codling said from where she sat behind Mona.

"I don't think so," Mona said, but she didn't bother to turn her head to reply.

"Poor baby," Diana said, "maybe she should run home to her daddy. He'll kiss her and make it all better."

"How I feel," Judy said, glaring at Diana, "has nothing whatsoever to do with Martin. I wouldn't give the creep the satisfaction. Nor you, for that matter."

"Who are you trying to fool?" Diana said. "The whole school knows about the breakup of the perfect couple. Practically half the school saw the show firsthand."

"You want him?" Judy asked, standing up from the bench. "He's yours. You don't know it, but you did me a favor. I should be thanking you. And I hope you two are happy. You two make the perfect couple. He has a swelled head and you're an airhead."

"You bitch," Diana said, almost pouncing toward Judy.

Mona stepped between the two girls. "That's enough, Diana. Shut your mouth."

"You can't talk to me like that, Judy."

"The hell I can't. Or would you like me to rip the black straw you call hair out by the roots?"

"Now there's a threat," Diana said sarcastically.

"Is there a problem here?" said Mrs. Brewer, the watchdog teacher for the section. By her tone, all three girls knew her question was rhetorical.

"No, ma'am," Judy said, getting in one final stare at Diana as she sat down.

For the next few minutes, while Mona was two sections over talking, Judy kept her eye on the crowd coming through gate A. There were several other entrances, but gate A was the closest to the student section of the bleachers, which started behind home plate and ran halfway up the first baseline.

"What's so interesting?" Mona said as she returned to her spot next to Judy.

"Just people watching, that's all."

"I guess there's a group going down to Myer's Lake after the game. Want to go?"

"Does that include Diana let-any-guy-in-my-pants Codling?"

Mona laughed. "Unfortunately, it does."

"Then count me out."

"Come on. You can ignore her." Instead of answering, Judy looked back up at the entrance. Mona's eyes followed along and she said, "Are you looking for someone?"

"Sort of. I don't think he's coming. He said he

wasn't, but I was hoping he would've changed his mind after all."

"Who?"

"Peter Cowal."

"You can't be serious," Mona said with a sneer.

"Why not?" Judy asked, watching more people pour in.

"Because," Mona snapped, "he's so . . . so. . . ."

"So what?" Judy turned back to her friend. She had never understood why people disliked Peter. "Have you ever said more than five words to him?"

"No, why would I?"

"Mona, you're my best friend, but sometimes I don't understand you. Peter is kind, gentle, caring. He's everything Martin and the other goons aren't. He's not a fake like that whole bunch."

"I'm part of that bunch. You think I'm fake?"

"No, Mona. That's not what I meant at all. I know it sounds stupid, but I feel something when I'm with him. When we were growing up, before my mom died, our families were close. Our dads worked together in construction and—"

"Your father worked construction?" Mona said, her eyes and mouth wide open. The revelation that her best friend came from a blue-collar family shocked her. She couldn't imagine Judy as middle-class with a father who made his money by digging around in the dirt.

"How do you think he got his company?" Judy said, sounding a little put off by Mona's question.

"I guess I always thought he bought it."

"No, he worked for it. He worked hard. Does that change me? Make me a different person somehow?"

"Of course not. So what happened? Between your family and Cowal's, I mean."

"Peter! His name's Peter."

"I know," Mona said, startled by her friend's reaction. "Are you going to tell me or what?"

"I don't know, really. Peter's father died in some kind of accident. I'm not sure how. After that our families grew apart." Judy looked back up in the stands. "He's not coming," she said sadly. The relieved expression Judy caught on Mona's face didn't make her any happier.

The Fulton team was finishing their warm-ups by throwing the baseball back and forth. They had already taken their batting practice, and the only thing left for them to do was to wait for the Hillsbury team to finish theirs.

"We're going to kill those guys," Ox said, before putting the tube of his water bottle to his mouth and squirting out a long, cool drink. He watched the Hillsbury players as they took their practice swings. Then a tall, red-haired boy stepped to the plate. Something about the batter made Ox do a double take. By the time the boy had completed his second swing, Ox remembered him.

"Hey you guys. Isn't that the asshole from the concert? You know, the guy we beat the crap out of."

"Yeah," Mark Turner said, stopping in midthrow, "that's him."

"Tommy," Martin said, "that's what the girl called him."

"Hey, Tommy!" Ox shouted. "Getting any good hits?"

"Hey, lay off him," Mark said. Nervously, he pulled off his glove and headed for the dugout.

"What's your problem?" Martin said.

"There's no reason to bug the guy."

"Get him," Ox said, taking another drink from his water bottle.

"Hey, easy on that stuff," Martin said, pitching him a ball. "You know you can't hold your water."

"Ha. Ha. Real funny, Welth, real funny," Ox replied. Martin's throw was wild and Ox missed it. The ball landed in the soft dirt behind Ox. "Pitch like that and we'll lose for sure."

"Don't worry about me," Martin said. "I'll be my usual greatness."

"Judy doesn't think you're so great anymore," Ox said, and a taunting roar broke out from the other players.

"Hey, don't think I'm not doing anything about that," Martin said, glancing over to Judy in the stands. He had spotted her the minute she and Mona took their seats in the bleachers. Inside, he was still angry, but he wouldn't let his friends know. To admit the anger, he would be admitting to the hurt. "She'll be back. You watch."

"Pretty sure of yourself," Ox said, signaling for another throw.

"Sure am," Martin replied as the ball left his fingers.

Top of the third inning. Two outs. Martin would have pitched a perfect game so far, except Mark had mistimed two grounders during the first inning. Martin had never pitched better, so he still got out of that inning without Hillsbury scoring. On the mound he pounded his fist hard against the webbing of his glove while waiting for Ox, who was playing catcher, to throw back the ball. Mark's stupid errors weren't the only thing grating on Martin.

"She'll come back," Martin whispered as he dug

his cleats into the firm dirt. He shot a quick glance to the stands and Judy. He punched his fist into his glove once more and sneaked another glance. "She'll come crawling back. But maybe I won't take her back. No one calls me an asshole."

"Play ball!" the umpire shouted, breaking Martin's thought. Martin caught Ox's throw and waited for the signal. Ox adjusted his catcher's mask, then signaled for a fast ball. Martin wound up and threw. The ball soared across home plate, and with a loud thud, it hit the dead center of Ox's glove.

"Strike!" the umpire called out.

"Easy out," Ox said, tossing the ball back to Martin.

"That bitch called me an asshole," Martin said under his breath. He raised his glove and caught the ball. "I should have hit her."

Ox gave the next signal, then Martin threw.

"Strike two!"

"One more," Ox called to Martin, tossing back the ball.

"She made me look like a fool."

Martin held the ball in his glove as he stared down the batter. His fingers wrapped tightly around the hard ball, turning white as he squeezed. His hand shook with the tension. He clenched his teeth hard, then threw the ball. The white sphere flew through the air and hit the batter on the hip. The batter dropped to the ground and a loud gasp came from the stands. The Hillsbury coach called for a time-out and rushed out to his player. He looked up at the mound and glared at Martin, but the boy merely shrugged his shoulders in response. "Yeah, right, I'm really sorry," Martin said, turning his back to the man.

When the player got to his feet and jogged down

to first base, rubbing the sore spot as he went, the Hillsbury fans applauded his effort.

"Batter up," the umpire bellowed out.

The next batter was the redhead named Tommy. As he approached the plate, Ox noticed the dark ring under his right eye and the short scab at the bridge of his nose.

"Nice eye," Ox said, his voice loud enough for Martin to hear him. "What's the odds you get another?"

"Don't know. This one took four to one," Tommy said, then tapped the side of his shoe with his bat. "Really easy when you got group odds, ain't it? But one to one. Different story, I'd say."

"Give it up," Ox said, throwing the ball back to Martin, then signaling for a curve ball.

After five pitches, the count on Tommy was three balls and two strikes. But Martin wasn't worried. As Tommy stared down to the pitcher's mound, he made eye contact with Martin, who returned the gesture with a smirk. Then Martin wound up and threw a fast ball.

Tommy swung hard, and there was a loud crack, after which the ball soared back over the right-field fence. Tommy laughed at Martin on the mound. Before he started his trot around the bases, he said, "What are the odds on that, I wonder."

Two-Zero, Hillsbury.

With Fulton behind, the game continued scoreless for the next three innings. The Hillsbury team was already on its second pitcher. But Martin was having his best game ever. He hadn't given up a second hit and had struck out over half the batters he faced.

In the sixth inning, Hillsbury was at bat with one out, no one on base. It was Tommy's second time stepping to the plate. Ox called for a time-out. On the pitcher's mound, he and Martin talked for a moment, then Ox returned to his position behind home plate.

After Ox positioned his glove low between his knees, Martin wound up and threw the ball. Tommy swung and hit the ball to right field. Ox jumped up, pulled his mask off, and watched the ball go.

"Shit!"

The ball dropped off the tip of Mark's glove and rolled deep inside the left-field foul line. The crowd moaned, and someone yelled for Coach Murphy to take Mark out of the game. Tommy was well on his way to second by the time Mark found the ball. His only play was to stop Tommy's advance to third base.

The next batter hit a fly ball to deep center, which was easily picked off by the fielder. After the catch, Tommy tagged up and started toward third. He came running across third base, and as his foot hit the bag, his eyes still were on the ball. He saw the relay from deep center to second. Tommy was between third and home as the second-baseman threw the ball toward home. He was only feet away from home plate when Ox caught the ball. As Ox held the ball down low, blocking the plate, Tommy started his slide.

At the last second before the tag, Tommy's leg shot up, driving his foot into Ox's glove, then on toward Ox's chest. When Tommy struck Ox, the ball dropped out of the catcher's glove and fell to the ground.

"Safe!" the umpire screamed as Tommy slid across home plate.

Full of rage, Ox lunged at Tommy and began punching. From the ground, Tommy returned the blows, and the players cleared the benches and the field. Cursing loudly, the coaches rushed out to stop their players.

After the fighting had been stopped and order restored, the umpire threw Ox out of the game. Coach Murphy had some nose-to-nose words with the umpire, but his bravado changed nothing. Ox was finished.

Ox's footsteps echoed as he walked down the deserted school corridor. His hand smacked loudly when he shoved the swinging door to the locker room open. He made his way to a sink and turned on a faucet. Cupping his hand under the cool water, he threw some against his face.

"I should've broken the asshole's arm when I had the chance," he muttered.

Ox kept his eyes shut tight as he groped his way along the sinks to find a towel. When the cold feeling of the porcelain sink ended, Ox knew the towels were inches away. Reaching out, he pulled one from the shelf. He shook it open and wiped his face dry, then threw the damp towel into a hamper, and started to his locker. But a scuffling of feet arrested his motion.

"Who's there?" Ox said, but he didn't see anybody. "Whoever it is, get the hell out. I'm not in the mood for any shit."

Still enraged from being tossed out of the game, Ox was ready to fight anybody. So when the unknown intruder giggled mockingly from behind a row of lockers, Ox rushed toward the noise. But he stopped short because no one was there. Shaking his head, the boy thought he was losing it—until a hand clamped on his wrist and forced his arm downward. Ox strained against the force that held his arm. His wrist began to throb, yet his fury drove him on. With a loud crack, Ox's wrist snapped back, and he screamed in agony as he fell to his knees.

Ox barely had time to deal with his pain when his unknown assailant attacked from behind again. The grip closed around his throat and lifted him off the floor, the hands becoming tighter as his feet dangled aloft. Ox tried to pry the fingers around his neck loose with his uninjured hand. Ox gasped for air as his vision started to blur and his head spun with dizziness. As Ox was about to lose consciousness, fresh air filled his lungs. He thought he imagined he was flying through the air, but the feeling of hitting a solid brick wall told him it was not his imagination. Whatever air he had managed to breathe in was driven out of his lungs as his back hit the hard surface. He landed on the floor in a heap, gasping and wheezing.

The trespasser approached and cast a long shadow over Ox. Desperate to escape, he dragged himself across the cold floor to the large wooden doors, pushing off with his feet and steering his body with his one good arm. He tried pushing the door open, but it snapped back against his hand. Although he pushed again, the door would not give way as if something on the other side were blocking its motion. He pounded his fist against the wood, but the door held fast.

As his attacker approached, Ox lifted himself off the floor. Although his head hadn't cleared, he managed to support his body against the obstructed door.

"What do you want?" Ox cried out as the cheers of the spectators in the stands mocked him. "I'll kill you."

The attacker moved quickly, grabbing the large boy and throwing him across the room as if he were a tiny child. A metallic thud rang out as Ox crashed into the weight bench that some players used to limber up without having to go to the workout room. A rod of weight disks resting across the bench's support bars prevented it from moving, so Ox absorbed the full impact. His large body dropped to the floor.

Using the frame of the bench as a brace, he tried to pull himself up. But he was able to rise only about two feet before collapsing again to the cold floor. The lights overhead spun in circles as his eyes began to focus.

The spinning slowed enough for Ox to watch the vaguely familiar outline of his attacker yank the weight bar from the bench, hold it high above him, then release it. The sound of Ox's skull being crushed was followed by the clank of the metal disks hitting the concrete floor.

Holding a full cup of soda, Judy was heading back to her seat when she saw a familiar figure watching the game from behind the wire fence that blocked the spectators from the playing field. As she approached him, she recognized the thin-framed boy.

"Peter?" she said.

"Hi," he said with a shy smile.

"I didn't think you were coming," Judy said.

"I had some things to do," Peter said. "Pretty good game—what I've seen of it, anyway."

"I guess." Judy looked back to her seat. Suzy had moved to her spot, and she and Mona were gabbing and laughing up a storm. Judy's attention returned to Peter. "I know the game's not over, but would you mind leaving with me?"

"No, I wouldn't mind if you want to." There was a small tremor in his voice.

"I'm not really in the mood for baseball anymore. I don't know what's come over me. We can go get a pizza or something. OK?"

"Sounds great."

"I'm glad you changed your mind about coming," Judy said.

"Me too."

Before leaving the stadium, Peter looked at the pitcher's mound—at Martin Welth—and he smiled. Leaving the game with Judy was the best revenge of all.

Chapter Fifteen

Judy sprang up from her sleep. Another bad dream. During the night she had torn the sheets and blankets from her bed, exposing the bare corners of her mattress. The top sheet was wrapped tightly around her right leg and the blanket ended up by the headboard. Her breathing was hard and fast, her sweat-drenched hair was matted to her forehead, and her soaked nightshirt clung to her back. The morning air hit the wetness and made her shiver.

Her head cleared quickly and she was able to catch her breath, bringing it almost back to normal. She pulled her nightshirt over her head, and the wet fabric made her shiver more as it slid up her bare back. She walked to her closet and pulled out a blue robe. The robe covered her only to the top of her thighs, but she felt warmer immediately. She headed for the bathroom and a hot shower.

After ten minutes under the spray of water, she felt better—not perfect, just better. Down in the kitchen her father was in the midst of his morning ritual of newspaper and coffee. Jessica was putting her breakfast dishes in the dishwasher. And Caesar was eating his favorite brand of cat food out of an old plastic dish.

"Morning," Judy said, her hair still wet and hanging down her neck. She had put the short robe back on after drying off, and when she sat on the kitchen chair, the robe rode up, exposing the edge of her panties.

Jessica scowled when she saw the pink silky fabric. "Can't you put some clothes on?" she snapped while pulling out the top rack of the dishwasher.

"You talk like I'm naked," Judy replied. "My mother gave me this robe."

Roger peeked over the top of his paper. "Honey, you were eleven then. I don't think it fits quite the same now."

"I think it fits just fine. Anyway, who's going to see me besides you two?"

Jessica pushed back the dish rack, reached for a fork lying on the counter, and placed it in the silverware basket. "You should be more considerate to those around you."

"What does what I wear have to do with being considerate?" Judy asked.

"Terrible thing," Roger said, trying to change the subject.

"It may be a little short," Judy said, her finger running across the hem, "but I wouldn't call it terrible."

"No, I'm sorry, honey." Roger lowered his newspaper to get a clear view of his daughter. "I meant terrible about Gary Oxten."

"Ox deserved to get kicked out of the game," Judy said matter-of-factly. "He started punching one of the Hillsbury players."

Roger set the paper aside. "The paper said something about that too, but I meant after the game."

"What? We . . . I didn't stay to the end."

"He was one of your friends, wasn't he?" Jessica asked.

"No, not really," Judy said, turning to Jessica, then back to her father. "What happened, Dad?"

"Some sort of accident. The other players found the poor boy dead in the locker room. It says here that he was apparently lifting weights unsupervised when his wrist snapped under the strain. The weights crashed down on him, across his eyes and forehead."

In her mind, Judy heard a loud clank. The sound made her jump in her chair. She felt her arms go numb. The numbness moved quickly down her body and continued along her legs.

"Judy? Are you feeling all right?" Jessica asked. The concern in her voice made Roger look at his daughter. "You look very pale."

"I'm fine," Judy said, pushing herself away from the table. "I should get ready for school." Her voice was soft and shallow. She stood up, took a step, then fainted.

"Judy!" Jessica called out.

Roger rushed over to his daughter, who lay deathly still on the floor. "Call 911!" he shouted.

As Jessica raced to the phone, Roger picked his daughter up and carried her out to the living room couch. He massaged her temples gently, but the young girl didn't respond. She lay as if in a trance, and nothing Roger did could revive her.

The school seemed frozen in time as Principal Moorse finished his announcement about Ox's death over the P.A. system. The noise that usually drowned out his daily recitations gave way to the heavy words. The students were still as they stared up at the speakers in each room.

Out in the hall after homeroom ended, the volume of the stunned students was only half the norm. Visibly shaken, Mona Thompson stood in front of the small mirror she had hanging on her opened locker door. After checking that her tears hadn't made her mascara run, she used a small touch-up pencil to recover a blemish that had poked through her morning makeup when Peter Cowal came up behind her. She saw his reflection in her mirror, but didn't recognize him at first without his glasses. In fact, she thought the face she saw was cute—until she realized who he was. Then she felt disgusted that he would come talk to her.

"Hi, Mona," he said, his tone calm and friendly. "I'm Peter Cowal."

"I know who you are," she said, turning to face him. Her eyes, moving up and down, examined him, and she mentally listed his faults.

"I was wondering if you've seen Judy. I—"

"No, I haven't." Her voice was sharp with contempt. "You should do both her and yourself a favor and leave her alone. That's the best thing for all concerned."

Although Mona's nasty words would have struck Peter down in the past, his newfound friendship with Judy had bolstered his confidence. No one was going to hurt him without a fight anymore. His voice fired by a surge of adrenaline, he said, "I think you should be concerned with your own problems! If Judy doesn't want me around that's fine, but that's for her to decide. Not you!"

Peter took a step forward, leaving him only inches away from Mona. "I can still see your zit."

"I'm fine," Judy insisted, but her words were ignored by the paramedic kneeling on one knee alongside the couch. His gloved hand quickly squeezed a black bulb, inflating the blood-pressure cuff around her arm; then he watched the needle move across the gauge. He had entered the house so quickly that Judy had never gotten a clear look at his face.

"Don't talk, please." The paramedic turned the silver valve on the bulb, releasing the air from the cuff with a hiss. With his stethoscope, he listened for her pulse.

As Roger and Jessica watched over the man's shoulder, Roger gave his daughter a reassuring smile, trying to hide his concern.

"Pressure's a little low. Nothing to be too worried about, though it might explain the fainting. Have you had other fainting spells?" The Velcro strips crackled as the paramedic removed the cuff from Judy's arm.

"No," Judy said, folding her arms in front of her body.

"It's all right dear," Roger said. "Tell us if you have."

"No, I haven't."

"Are you currently dieting?" the paramedic asked.

"No . . . well, I watch what I eat, but nothing serious."

"How about sleep. Are you getting enough sleep?"

"Sure, fine," she said, and a twisted fragment of the previous night's dream flashed in her mind—the image of playing a game with a little boy.

"Look up, please." The paramedic clicked on a

shiny penlight. He directed the beam into Judy's eyes, then pulled it away. He repeated the action three times on each eye. "Pupil response is normal. Please sit forward a bit. I'm going to check for any bumps or soft spots on your head. Tell me if any area feels tender. All right?"

Judy nodded; then the paramedic's fingers moved over the surface of her skull. There was only a firm pressure. No pain.

"That's fine." The paramedic got to his feet. "No need for worry. She's fine. However, I would suggest you inform your family physician of this call. I'll leave you a copy of my report. It has my number if your doctor needs to reach me."

"Thank you," Roger said, smiling at Judy again.

"She should stay quiet for a while, and if the fainting recurs anytime over the next five days, report it to your doctor. He may want to run some tests."

"Thanks again." Roger walked the paramedic to the door, Jessica following close behind.

Judy pulled up the blanket that covered her until it met her chin. She tried to remember the dream. It was like walking in and out of a movie, missing all the important parts. At times, the vivid images jumped out at her, and at other times, only blackness came. But the feelings associated with the dream, both physical and emotional, were almost overwhelming.

Clutching her arms tightly across her chest, Judy shivered. Maybe she wasn't all right. Maybe she did need help. Maybe she should make the phone call she had been dreading for weeks. But if that was what it took to get rid of the nightmares, that was what she'd have to do.

*   *   *

Alex set a cup of black coffee on the table. His hand shook, and a small amount dribbled over the side and down the ceramic face. The dark liquid came to rest in the saucer and surrounded the foot of the cup. He sat and took a sip of the brew, then leaned back and reflected for a moment. Only the ticking of a grandfather clock penetrated the still air.

A fear inside him began to grow. After the first death, he had told himself simply that it was tragic misfortune, nothing more. Then another boy died. Coincidence? Two in one week—just like when he was a boy?

He lifted the pair of scissors he had placed on the table before getting his coffee, then picked up the morning paper. With a strong grip on the scissors, he carefully cut the front page, making certain not to cut into the story about Gary Oxten's death.

Alex had lived through that hell 60 years earlier, and he knew all too well who the culprit was. What he didn't know was how he was going to stop Georgie— or who Georgie was using to get his revenge.

The door chimes rang out and woke Judy from a very light sleep. Above the couch, the wall clock read 3:35. Her father and Jessica had been gone for two hours. They wouldn't have gone at all except for Judy's reassurance that she felt fine. She would have said anything not to have had to spend the whole afternoon home with Jessica.

When the chimes rang again, Judy went to the door and was surprised to find Peter on the other side. For Peter, her appearance also was something of a surprise. Judy still had on her short robe along with an old pair of kneeless blue jeans. The way the cotton top rested across her body made Peter feel uncomfortable, since the curves of her body were fully outlined.

"Hello, Judy," he said, looking her straight in the eyes.

"Peter. Hi."

"I just came by to make sure you were OK."

"I'm fine. It's nothing really." She couldn't tell him that she had had a fainting spell—or that she had stayed home because of a bad dream. "I had a great time last night."

"Me too." He started to say more, but the phone rang, cutting him off.

"Come in. I should get that."

"No, I should be going."

"Please stay. It'll only be a minute."

Peter nodded and stepped into the house. He couldn't stop himself from scanning the interior, even though he felt as if he were snooping. From the outside, the house looked great, but the inside topped it.

"Hello? Oh, hi, Mona," Judy said, and Peter cringed. "No, nothing serious. A flu bug or something. . . . Yes, we did. We went for pizza. . . . He said what? What did you say?"

Peter could hear the electronic murmurs of Mona on the other end and wondered if he could sneak away.

"When? OK. I should go. I'll call you later. Right. 'Bye."

He watched her put the phone back on the table. As she walked back to him, he started his apology. Within the three-second delay at least ten opening lines came into and went out of his mind. Maybe pleading for mercy would be the best move.

"That was Mona, but I guess you heard that. She said you two . . . talked."

Peter nodded with a half smile, preparing himself for the worst. But it never came.

"If there's one thing I can't stand, it's when my friends tell me what I should do. Mona included. I like you, and I want to go out with you. You're sweet and kind. I like talking with you. Why can't she understand?"

Peter didn't have anything to add, but he did know her reaction was great for his ego.

"Did you really tell her she had a zit?"

"Actually, I told her I could still see her zit."

Judy laughed. "That wasn't very nice."

Peter shrugged his shoulders. "It slipped out."

"I hope you weren't hurt by anything she said. Mona's not a bad person. In fact, she's very nice. She just needs to be a little more understanding, that's all."

"I should get going," Peter said. He reached over and opened the door. "See you tomorrow at school."

"I'm glad you came over. I feel better already."

Peter smiled and started out the door, but Judy called him back. She took a step, then put her hand behind his neck and gently pulled him toward her. To Peter, the movements seemed to proceed in slow motion. As she drew him closer, Judy leaned forward and kissed his lips.

At that moment, a car pulled up into the driveway. Then Jessica came up to the front door with her husband trailing far behind.

"My, my," Jessica said, her eyes cutting through Peter on their way to Judy, "who do we have here?"

"A friend, Jessica."

"Does this friend have a name?"

"Yes, he has a name. This is Peter."

"Peter Cowal," Roger said. When Roger extended his hand, Peter returned the gesture and shook it. "It's been years."

"Yes, sir. It has."

"How have you been? And your mother?"

"We're fine, sir. We're both fine."

"What's this sir stuff? And your little brother—"

"Daddy," Judy said when Peter's eyes fell to the ground.

Roger realized his mistake. "Oh, I'm terribly sorry, Peter. How thoughtless of me. Bobby was a fine boy. A loss to your family. I'm very sorry."

"Well," Jessica said, "are we going to stand out here all day?"

"Jessica dear," Roger said, "this is Max Cowal's boy. Max and I went way, way back. We started digging holes for building foundations together."

"I wouldn't know about such things," she said.

"Jessica, for Christ's sake, don't be such a snob. I worked with Max before I met you. We would have been partners if things had turned out differently."

"I should be leaving," Peter said, his voice soft.

Judy picked up on the change in the boy. "Wait a minute, Peter. Can Peter and I have a moment together"—Judy stared at Jessica—"alone?"

"Come on, Jessica. Let's leave them alone."

"It was great seeing you again, Mr. Kilter."

"Send your mother my regards, and if she ever needs anything, tell her to call."

"I will," Peter said. "And it was nice to meet you, Mrs. Kilter."

"I suppose," she said, giving Peter the once-over.

Judy waited for the door to close behind her father and Jessica. "She can be such a bitch sometimes. I have never understood why my father married her."

Her words caused the image of his mother to pop in Peter's head. He had always thought how lonely she must get sometimes since her husband's death. "I think I understand."

"Peter, the drive-in opens for the summer this Friday. I thought maybe we could go. That's if you don't already have plans."

"Sure, what's playing?" he asked, although he was too excited to care.

"I think, *Friday the Thirteenth, part something* and *Toolbox Murders*."

"Oh, it must be culture night."

Judy laughed. "I better warn you. I jump real easy."

"That's OK. I'll catch you."

Chapter Sixteen

"I can't wait," Martin said, leaning back against the railing overlooking the atrium of Fulton Senior High. "One more week and we can kiss this school good-bye. Good riddance!"

"The same for this stinkin' town," Mark said.

"Marky . . . Marky," Martin said, "you don't sound too happy today."

"Stick it."

Martin laughed. "And I would've bet anything you'd be getting all excited about graduation and all."

"If it wasn't for my parents—"

"They do make it a big deal," Martin said. "Last night, out of the blue, my father gave me the you've-really-accomplished-something speech. The only thing we've accomplished was to rid the world of one sorry-ass retard. Boy, talk about getting stoned!"

"Will you shut the hell up! Someone might hear you."

"It was a joke."

"It's not funny." Mark glanced over his shoulder and spotted Gary Bruns walking toward them.

"Hey, you guys," Gary said. He was taller and thinner than most of the other boys at Fulton, yet very coordinated.

"Got any plans for tonight?" Martin asked.

"I have to work," Gary said.

"Hey, check it out," Martin said, putting his hand on Gary's back as if he had performed some great feat. "Gary here works at the drive-in. It opens tonight and he can get us in free all summer."

"Really?" Mark said, clearing his throat. "How'd you swing a job like that?"

"I got the job last year. Mr. Hansen hired me back for this summer. That's all."

"So," Martin said, "you up for some free movies tonight, Mark?"

Mark spotted Peter Cowal waiting in the foyer below. His mouth went dry and his heart bashed along the inside of his chest. Suddenly, a hand pushed Mark's arm. "What?"

"You deaf?" Martin said. "Free movies . . . the drive-in. Do you want to go?"

"I don't feel like it. You know—with Ox and all. How can we go to a drive-in like nothing's happened?"

"Hey," Martin said, "he'd go if you bit it. He was always up for a good time."

"I don't know. I'll call Suzy and ask her if—"

"Stop being such a wuss. You can do some things without her. You sound whipped. Be a man."

"Shut up," Mark said. "You should talk. At least I can keep a girlfriend."

"Like I said before, I'll take care of that when

the time's right. In the meantime Diana Codling will do fine."

"I think you're fooling yourself," Mark said.

"If you're so convinced Judy will come back," Gary asked, "why do Codling?"

"You've never seen her naked," Martin said.

"Well, no, but I have a good imagination."

"Believe me, it can't be that good," Martin said.

As Gary and Martin enjoyed the joke, Mark witnessed Judy joining Peter at the school's main entrance. Hoping to keep Martin from throwing a fit, Mark tried to distract him. "How about heading to O'Brian's? Get some food or something?"

Still laughing hard, Gary turned his back to the others. He looked over the railing and immediately stopped laughing. "Can you believe that?" Gary blurted, glaring down at Judy and Peter talking.

"It's nothing," Mark said. "Let's go."

"What's nothing?" Martin asked.

"Judy with that dip-shit Cowal," Gary said. "How can she stand being seen with him?"

Martin moved closer to the railing and stared down at the couple. "Don't worry about it. She's just trying to make me jealous. She'll come back to me. Just wait and see."

Meanwhile, in the high school's front corridor, Judy and Peter were unaware that Martin and his friends were observing them.

"Don't forget to pick me up tonight," Judy said jokingly.

"Would I do that? What's your address again?" Peter put his index finger to his temple as though he were trying to remember something. "Kidding. I'll pick you up at eight-thirty."

"Make it nine."

"Won't that be cutting it a little close?"

"We'll have plenty of time," Judy said. "The drive-in isn't very far from my house."

"You OK?"

"Fine. Why?"

"You seem a little distracted. It's . . . it's not me, is it?"

"No, silly. It's not you."

In her mind, Judy heard a loud clang echoing over and over again. It had awoken her the night before, and afterward she had taken an hour to fall back to sleep. She wanted to tell Peter about the noise, wanted to tell anyone. When she started to talk about it and heard the words coming out, she stopped, afraid she would sound crazy. People would think something was wrong with her. She once even tried to call Amanda Colins because her book contained a whole section on dreams. But after dialing the number of Amanda's office she only reached a secretary who offered to take a message. Judy had hung up and lost her nerve; so she didn't even try Amanda's hotel room. For all Judy knew, Amanda had left town already.

"Really, it's not you," Judy said again.

Peter smiled. "I'll walk you to your car."

"You go on. I want to get a book from my locker."

"I can wait."

"No. You go. I'll see you later." Judy kissed Peter and watched as he walked to his car. Something made her look up to the overhang, where the trio of boys stared back at her. Martin looked the angriest of the three. But Martin didn't matter to her anymore. Without even acknowledging the presence of the three boys, Judy made her way to her locker. And for the first time in a long while, she was at peace with herself.

A short while later, Judy lay on her bed and reread the three chapters on dreams in Amanda Colins's book. The first dealt with dreams and the subconscious, the second their symbols. The third was about how dreams were connected with precognition. Though the text was all very specific, nothing really matched Judy's dreams in either symbols or intensity. She regretted not having left a message for Amanda after all.

A light rapping interrupted her concentration. Then her father asked, "Can I come in?"

"Sure." Judy closed her book.

"Jessica sent me."

"Now what?"

"Don't sound so fretful. It's nothing bad. She wanted me to ask if you had bought a dress for the dance."

"I've been looking, but. . . ."

"I know the dance isn't for another two weeks and it might seem like we're rushing you—"

"Don't you mean Jessica is rushing me?"

"She wants you to look your best. That's all. I'm sure if you ask her she'll help you find a lovely dress."

"No, thanks. I can manage. I've seen a couple I like. I should have one picked out in plenty of time. Tell Jessica to relax."

"I'll tell her you'll have a dress in a couple of days. That will relax her more than anything else I can say. Are you staying in tonight?"

"No, Peter and I are going to the drive-in."

"How's he dealing with his brother's death?"

"All right, I guess. He doesn't really talk about

it, and I don't want to push it. Though, there is something—I don't know what. It could just be my imagination."

"Well, you two have a fun time." Roger turned to leave.

"Daddy," Judy said, before her father took a step, "do you know anything about dreams?"

"Only we all have them. What are you reading?" Roger took the book from the bed. He read the title and the author. "I see. Amanda Colins. I had a meeting with her. Very nice woman."

"When did you meet her?"

"Last week. She's working with Frank Currie to resolve a few problems with a piece of land. She asked about you. Said something about speaking at your school."

"She's still here?"

"For a while. She told Frank she was staying at the Blackstone."

"Thanks, Daddy." Judy jumped off her bed and rushed downstairs, where she grabbed the phone off the hall table.

Before she could dial, the doorbell chimed. Peter had arrived for their date. While debating over whether she should still try to contact Amanda, the bell chimed again. Judy returned the phone to the table. Her call would have to wait until later.

A long line of cars waited to pay their way into the Stardusk Drive-in theater. Peter's car was three down from the ticket booth at the gate entrance. The sun had just disappeared below the horizon, so Peter knew the movies would start as scheduled. The butterflies in his stomach had started an hour earlier.

One by one, the cars moved ahead. When his turn

came, Peter was greeted by a thin teenager with light brown hair and large freckles across his nose and cheeks. The freckled youth peered into Peter's car. Then, with a knowing leer, he asked, "Two? That's seven dollars."

Peter reached into his pocket and pulled out two ones and a five. He tried the best he could to smooth the bills before handing them to the youth in the ticket window.

"Pull ahead—and enjoy the movie."

Peter wanted to crouch down, but then he glanced over at Judy. He grinned and sat up a bit instead.

"What's so funny?" Judy asked, as they waited for the car in front of them to move up.

"Oh, nothing. It's just—"

"What?"

"I was so nervous about bringing you here."

"Why?"

"It'll sound stupid. You'll laugh."

"No I won't. Tell me, please."

"You're one of the most popular girls in the school and I'm, well, you know. Sometimes I think I must be dreaming. I'm afraid I'll wake up."

"That's sweet," Judy said, her brown eyes meeting his. "It's not a dream. I'll prove it. Does this feel like you were dreaming?" She leaned over and kissed him.

"That's no good," Peter said. "I dream that all the time."

"I could pinch you if you want," Judy said and they both burst out laughing.

After Peter found a parking spot on the far side of the lot, Judy slid across the seat closer to him, and he put his arm around her. He was surprised how natural the action felt. "I know you said the drive-in was near your house, but I didn't realize how close."

"It's closer than you think. Look. See those specks of light though the trees? The lights five from the end."

"Yeah, I see."

"That's my house. If those trees weren't there, you could see it all. When I was ten, I used to have sleep overs. A couple of my friends would bring binoculars, and we would take turns watching the R-rated movies from my bedroom window. There was no sound, but it was fun anyway."

Finally at ease with one another, Judy and Peter cuddled up and chatted all the way through the first movie—a bloody slasher with no plot but plenty of gratuitous sex. As the second movie began, Judy snuggled closer to Peter, but as much as he wanted to kiss her, his stomach growled and would not be ignored.

"You want something to eat?" Peter asked. "A hamburger or a hot dog?"

"Popcorn would be great."

"OK, popcorn it is. I'll get us a couple of Cokes too," he said, heading for the snack bar.

"Make mine a diet."

Anxious to get back to his date, Peter was relieved that the line at the concession stand moved quickly. He paid for the snacks and walked carefully out the door, the closed box of popcorn under one arm and one large drink in each hand. Suddenly he realized he'd forgotten to get straws. Without watching where he was going, he turned back to get some and bumped into Martin, who had intentionally blocked his way. Peter pulled up short, but the plastic lids kept the pop from sloshing out of the large paper cups.

"I think you've made a very big mistake," Martin

said. "You must realize that."

Gary Bruns grunted his agreement, but Mark said nothing. Mark and Martin were both in their varsity jackets, and Gary wore a white work apron, tee-shirt, and paper hat.

"Yeah," Gary said, "I'd kill ya if you stole my girl."

Martin smirked. "That's the idea."

"I didn't take Judy from you," Peter said. "I didn't have to. You lost her long before I—"

"She's mine," Martin said, grabbing Peter by the shirt. Then he pushed Peter back a few feet. "She's using you to make me jealous. Why else would she be with a freak like you?"

"She is because she wants to," Peter said, "you Neanderthal."

"What's that supposed to mean?" Gary said.

"That figures," Peter said.

"Come on, Martin," Mark said. He took a few steps forward. "Leave him alone. He's not here to fight."

"It won't be much of a fight," Martin said in a monotone.

Mark glanced at Peter, but diverted his eyes the instant Peter looked back. "What's the point? Let him go."

"When I'm done." Martin gave Mark a cold stare, and Mark stepped back. Then Martin jabbed Peter in the chest with his finger. "Prepare to die."

Peter took one of the drinks and hurled it at Martin. The top flew off, and the cold drink hit him square in the chest and dripped down to the front of his pants.

"What's going on here?" an adult voice said.

"Mr. Hansen," Gary said, his voice cracking. "Nothing's going on."

Martin backed away from Peter. In disbelief, he said, "He poured his pop on me."

The man ignored Martin, and his attention focused on Gary. "I'm not paying you to stand around socializing with your friends."

"I'm on my break, sir."

"Get back to work or you'll be on a permanent break. You understand?"

"Yes, sir," Gary said and quickly hustled back to the kitchen.

"And as for the rest of you, I don't want any trouble. I'll bounce you all out on your ear." Martin and Mark took off without a word. They knew the man meant what he said. Then Hansen looked at Peter. "Who are you? I've never seen you here before. You new in town?"

"No, sir. I'm Peter Cowal. I didn't—"

"Cowal . . . Cowal? Name sounds familiar. You Max Cowal's boy?"

"Yes, sir," Peter said hesitantly.

"I knew your father. He was a good man."

"Thank you, sir," Peter said, not knowing what else to say.

"But that don't change nothing. I don't like trouble in my drive-in. I catch you making trouble and you're out for the rest of the season. You understand?" Without waiting for Peter to respond, Hansen disappeared through a brown wooden door next to the entrance to the snack bar.

"Here you go," Peter said a moment later as he handed the popcorn and drink to Judy. "Did I miss anything?"

"No, not really," Judy said. "Jason just embedded a machete into some guy's head."

"Again? Didn't he do that in his last movie?"

"Probably." She took a handful of popcorn. "Were the lines long?"

"Not too bad. Why?"

"You were gone for a while. I was afraid you ran off."

"No chance of that," Peter said.

"Didn't you get yourself something to drink?" Judy said.

A few drops of Coke had landed on Peter's hand, and they were starting to become sticky. "I had a little accident. I spilled it on the way back."

"Oh, well, you can share mine," Judy said.

Sliding over to him, Judy realized that she hadn't once thought about her nightmares while she was with Peter. But no matter how safe she felt for the moment, she had to call Amanda Colins the next morning. If the dreams came again, she didn't know what she'd do. She had to stop them while she still could.

Chapter Seventeen

The ring of the phone jarred Amanda from her sleep. She pulled the pillow over her head, trying to drown out the noise. The third ring made her wish she had told the front desk not to allow any calls through. The last three days and well into each night, she had spent digging through the files at the Amherst Institution, and the work had exhausted her. When the fourth ring forced Amanda out of her grogginess, she reached for the phone, knocking over a glass in the process.

"Hello," she said in a raspy voice.

"Dr. Colins, this is Judy Kilter. You talked at my school a couple weeks ago. I need to talk to someone. You gave me your card."

"Who?" Amanda said, fighting back a yawn. She felt her eyes becoming heavy again.

"Oh, I'm sorry. Did I wake you? I didn't mean to. I'll call another time."

Amanda shook her head to snap herself awake. "Judy? Don't hang up. You still there?"

"Yes," the girl said. "I'm sorry to call you so early."

"It's OK. I told you day or night." Amanda removed the washcloth from the digital clock face—9:22 a.m. She didn't remember covering the clock face. She must have out of sheer habit, because she always had trouble sleeping unless the room was totally dark. The clock digits gave off enough of a glow to bother her, and the thick cloth assured darkness.

"Maybe I should call back later."

Amanda heard the tremor in Judy's voice. "No, really. We can meet somewhere. How about the cafe here by the motel? Let's meet there. Can you meet me in about thirty minutes?"

"Yes. Yes, I can. Dr. Colins . . . thank you."

"Whatever it is, it will be fine, I promise," Amanda said, but as she hung up the phone, she hoped she hadn't made a promise she couldn't keep.

Judy was still nervous about meeting with Amanda, but she was able to calm herself enough to drive. In the parking lot of Maxie's Diner, she pulled into the first space she found. There were already three other cars parked in front of the diner and two parked along the side.

The morning air was cool, but not too cold because the sun was climbing fast in the early morning sky. Its glow illuminated the thick clouds, surrounding the orb with an orange-tinted haze.

Inside the diner, a waitress, coffeepot in hand, walked away from a booth occupied by a heavyset, bearded man. The woman walked back to the counter, where a thin man wearing a blue baseball cap sat picking at a plate of eggs and sausage. The waitress offered the thin man another cup of coffee. He accepted and took a bite from his toast. In a corner booth, Amanda sat alone. When she waved to Judy, the girl joined her.

"Hi, Judy," Amanda said, smiling. The ashtray in front of her held two spent cigarettes and the air smelled of heavy smoke. When Judy apologized again for calling at such a bad time, Amanda assured the girl it was all right.

"I'm here," Judy said, " because of the dreams I've been having."

"Oh?" Amanda said, reaching for her purse and another cigarette. Then she stopped herself.

"Do you know about the trouble at Fulton High?" Judy asked.

"Yes, I think so. Some accident at a baseball game. One of the players was killed. Dreadful stuff."

The waitress interrupted her. "What can I get you?"

"Just coffee for me, thanks," Amanda said.

"How 'bout you, honey?"

"Nothing. I'm fine."

"Go ahead," Amanda said. "My treat."

"I'll have a Sprite."

"7up OK?"

"Sure, anything without caffeine."

Judy waited until the waitress was out of earshot. "It wasn't an accident and there was another death. Karl Warner—the police said he was hit by a drunk driver. I know it's not true. I've been having dreams about them. The deaths, I mean. I don't know how, but I know they're connected."

"That's not so uncommon," Amanda said. "You knew the boys. When you heard about their deaths, the shock could have stayed in your subconscious and been released in your dreams."

"No. That's not it." A tear welled in the corner of

Judy's eye. "The player who died—Ox, Gary Oxten. I didn't find out about him until the next morning after I had the dream."

"I see." Amanda's cigarette craving increased.

"There's more," Judy said. "In my dreams, the deaths weren't accidents. Ox and Karl were killed by someone or something. The images weren't clear; I couldn't remember them very long after I woke up."

"And that's why you called me? To help you with your dreams?"

"Yes, I know it sounds stupid." Tears trickled down Judy's face. Amanda reached in her purse, passed her cigarettes, and pulled out a tissue. She handed it to Judy.

"They're so real," Judy said after wiping her face. "He's going to kill someone else. I know it. Someone's going to die. He has to be stopped before that happens."

"How do you know it's a man who's responsible?"

"I don't know how," Judy said. "I just do. You don't believe me, do you?"

"Judy, dreams can be very subjective. They are a combination of the real and unreal, of events in daily lives, the good and the bad. Sometimes when those elements combine in our psyche, the results can be terrifying." Amanda touched Judy's hand, and instantly images and feelings almost overwhelmed her. She hadn't felt such sensitivity in any one person since her undergraduate days at the university as a test subject for David Jensen's research project. Her cigarette craving disappeared. "I believe you."

The waitress returned and set a steaming coffee cup in front of Amanda, then a glass of 7up in front of Judy. "If you need anything else, just give a holler."

"We will. Thank you." Amanda took a sip from her

cup, and her face crinkled. "My, they make strong coffee here."

Judy almost laughed. It was the first time since the dreams had started that she didn't feel totally helpless.

"Any messages for room eleven?" Amanda asked the desk clerk at her motel.

A short chunky man wearing red-and-black suspenders over a white, button-up shirt sat far behind the counter on a black vinyl bench. His back propped up against the wall, he was watching a portable black-and-white television. He had to stand on his tiptoes to peer into the mail slot for room eleven. "No, ma'am, no messages."

"Thank you," she said, then glanced at a newspaper lying on the counter. "Excuse me. This is yesterday's paper."

"It is?" The clerk checked the date. "You're right. Sorry. I must've put today's paper in the recycling box by mistake. Thanks for noticing."

"You wouldn't happen to have last Wednesday's paper in your recycling box, would you?"

"Had it until yesterday morning. Friday is pickup day for all the recycling material."

"Would you happen to know where I could buy an issue?"

"Maybe at the newspaper's printing office, but not until Monday morning."

"Any local bookstores?"

He shook his head. "I doubt it. You could try. The worse is that they say no. Or you could try the public library. You can't buy their copies, of course. But the reading doesn't cost anything."

"Could you give me directions?"

"No problem. I take my young ones there all the time." The man put a pad of the motel's logo paper on the counter in front of Amanda, then drew a pencil from his shirt pocket. "Here's whatcha do. . . ."

The air smelled fresh as Alex took his after-lunch walk. One of the things Alex enjoyed and was still able to do was take long walks. It didn't matter what time of year, he always enjoyed his walks.

Behind him he heard giggling that made him alter his pace. Quickly he turned around. "Georgie?" he called out. He took in a deep breath as he saw two little girls playing catch with a big green ball.

The sound of the children laughing threw Alex's thoughts back to a time many years ago. The courts had found Isaac Stein mentally insane and had him placed in the Amherst Mental Institution. No one was even sure if Alex's father knew or understood what he had done. He didn't utter a word after Alex found him in his chair.

The custody of Alex was given to his mother's sister May and her husband Ben. Even though May and Ben lived in Fulton, only a few miles from his home, Alex hadn't seen them since his mother's death. He liked living with his aunt and uncle. May was kind and a good cook. His uncle Ben was a strong man, but very gentle. Alex quickly overcame the fear that he would be beaten for his mistakes. When he did do something wrong, Ben would sit down with him and explain why what he had done was wrong. On those occasions when Alex had an accident, such as the times he dropped a glass or spilled his soup, Ben would simply say, "Those things happen."

One night, after Alex had gone to bed, there was a knock at the door. Unable to sleep, Alex sneaked to the top of the stairs to see who had come. He stayed in the shadows so May and Ben couldn't see him.

Outside, Sheriff Longstreet stood on the stoop, holding his uniform cap at his side. From his expression, Alex guessed he was not making a social call. May asked him to enter and offered the man a chair.

"How about some fine tea?" May asked in the living room, where the sheriff was greeting Ben.

"No, thank you. I can't. This is official business."

"Aaron Clark Longstreet," she scolded, "you know better than that. I always serve up some tea and maybe even a few cookies. Don't make me change my ways now."

"I'm sorry, May, but—"

"No buts. Whatever it is can wait a moment or two. My mother always said that tea makes bad news easier to bear and good news that much more enjoyable."

"All right, just a little," he said.

May disappeared to the kitchen and returned moments later carrying a silver tray with three steaming cups of tea.

"Thank you," the sheriff said, amid the clinking of cups and saucers.

"Now, what's the trouble?" Ben asked.

Standing in the shadows at the top of the stairs, Alex shuddered as he listened. He hadn't seen the sheriff since Georgie's death, and he feared the lawman had come to bring news about his father.

"Something's happened to the boy's father."

"Oh, Ben," May said. "He's escaped, hasn't he?"

Anxious and upset, Alex creeped down the steps to better hear the sheriff.

"No. Nothing like that."

"Spit it out, man," Ben said. "If it has to do with the boy—"

"Not the boy, really," the sheriff said. "The boy's father—well, he's dead. He's been killed."

"Oh, my," May said.

Cloaked in darkness, Alex was surprised by his own feelings. He didn't have any. He wasn't sad or happy. He didn't care.

"How did it happen?" Ben asked.

"One of the other inmates killed him. Some boy named Jimmy Selly beat him to death, nearly twisted his head off. Excuse me, May. I shouldn't be so heedless with my words. It's a funny thing. This inmate—he'd been institutionalized for most of his life. The doctors said he never showed what they call violent tendencies. Never hurt anyone or anything—until now that is."

"What do we do now, Sheriff?" Ben said.

"Well, since you're the closest adult kin to the man, I need to know if you want to claim the body. I only ask because I'm required to by the law. The asylum will dispose of it, if you want nothing to do with it."

"No," May said, "he was my sister's husband and the boy's father. We'll do the right thing and make the arrangements."

Alex listened until the sheriff finished his tea and left. Then he was about to go back to his room, but stopped at the sound of his uncle's voice.

"Should we wake the boy?" Ben asked.

"No," May said, "it can wait till morning."

"We don't have to tell him. We could wait until he's older."

"No," May said, "it would be best if he knows. Then he'll never have to worry about the evil man again."

Alex shuddered when he heard his aunt's words. Somehow they conjured up the image of Georgie lying so deathly still in his bed.

The next morning Aunt May and Uncle Ben had gone up to Alex's room. They told him about the sheriff's visit and, excluding certain details, the death of his father. Alex gave no sign of showing he already knew. They told him he didn't have to go to school that day if he didn't feel well. Both May and Ben were a little surprised by Alex's wanting to go.

The funeral was held two days later. It was a simple closed-coffin service. Only Alex, his aunt and uncle, and Rabbi Koleman were there. May and Ben debated on taking Alex to the funeral, but decided that, no matter what the circumstances, Isaac was still the boy's father. And they both hoped that by seeing the burial Alex would put any hatred of the man behind him once and for all.

As the three left the service, Alex could have sworn he heard the sound of giggling—Georgie's giggling. He had no idea at the time what Georgie was capable of. All he knew was his little brother was dead.

"Mister?" a little girl's voice snapped Alex back to the present. "Mister, can I have my ball back? Please?"

"Why of course, my dear," he said and picked up the ball at his feet; then he handed it to the little girl.

"Thank you," she said, taking the ball from Alex.

"My, aren't you quite the little lady?"

When the little girl giggled and ran back to play, Alex stared ahead indecisively. "I have to be sure."

Amanda entered the three-story stone building that housed the public library. The directions the motel clerk gave her were right on the money. She had never been in the building, but it reminded her a great deal of the library she had gone to back in her high-school days. The odor, the silence, the book checkout counter—all seemed to have jumped right from her memories. The building's layout was also the same. The books and other reading materials were on the first two floors. The third floor was used for storage, and it was off limits to the general public.

The newspaper morgue, located on the second floor, had two long tables running end to end down the middle of the room. The newspapers were stored on shelves that lined the back wall; magazines were to the right, microfilm readers off to the left. The newspapers were placed in 52 neat stacks; each stack represented one week's worth of papers. After a year the papers were converted and stored on rolls of microfilm.

Amanda found the stack she needed; she was surprised that the issues were consecutive. Finding newspapers so neatly stacked would have been a small miracle at the university. It took her hours to thumb through all the papers for the information she wanted. She not only looked for the stories about Ox and Karl, but for anything else out of the ordinary as well. It was a painstaking task, but she had done worse. She recorded any event in which someone had died somewhat peculiarly. Her list included two car accidents, one rock slide, three gunshot wounds, and, of all things, one slip in the bathtub.

After she had been working steadily for some time, the squeaking sound of metal against metal made Amanda glance up from her reading. An elderly librarian was pushing her book cart past the door, putting the returned books back in their proper places. Soon the librarian was in the newspaper morgue placing the magazines in the correct piles.

Amanda was busy jotting down the account of Gary Oxten's death when the librarian interrupted her.

"Horrible thing, isn't it?" the woman said.

"Excuse me?"

"The death—a horrible thing to happen. I couldn't help see you reading about it. Did you know him?"

"No, I didn't." Amanda returned to the paper.

"A thing like that can really tear at a town. Like before."

Amanda nodded, then looked at the woman. "Before?"

"They called them accidents then too, at first. Fulton was a lot smaller back then. People minded their own business."

"What about the deaths. Who died?"

"Oh, they were a tough group. I remember because Fulton had only one schoolhouse. They would strut around the school doing no good. Most of the other children were scared of them. I know I was, and I was pretty wild for my age. My mother used to call me a tomboy. Can you believe that? Just because I liked climbing trees and digging up worms to go fishing with my brothers. 'Why can't you be like your sister Emily?' my mother would say. Well, Emily was already married, and it was only me and my brothers."

"It must have been very nice, but do you remember any names?"

"Oh, my, yes," the librarian said, peering at Amanda. "I'll always remember their names. How could I forget the names of my brothers?"

"No, I mean the boys killed when you were a young girl." Amanda had to hold back her frustration.

"I'm sorry. That was a long time ago, but they

were troublemakers. Believe me. Always fighting and bullying. There was a big to-do about them putting another boy in the hospital and having to spend a night in jail. It caused quite an uproar. It was after that the deaths started. Like I said, accidents they called them, but they were some mighty funny deaths. I can't say I remember much more. My mind isn't as clear as it used to be."

"That happens to everybody," Amanda said, smiling understandingly.

"I'm sure there's something on the microfilm. We put the old stuff on film; otherwise, it turns yellow and brittle. And the room—it took a whole room itself to store the papers."

"What year?"

"Let's see; the town bought the film equipment in—"

"No, I'm sorry. I meant the year of the deaths."

"Nineteen hundred and . . . thirty-six. That's right, I remember. It was early autumn. My sister Emily had a little girl. Her first. Cutest little baby and grew up to be a lovely woman. And would you believe she has three little ones herself? Well, they aren't really little anymore. The oldest boy, he graduates from high school next week. Would you like to see a picture? I have one on my desk. I have pictures of all my family."

"Thank you, but maybe another time."

"All right then. I should get back to stacking these magazines. It was lovely chatting with you, dear. You know, people today are too busy to stop to talk with a neighbor. I'm glad you're not like that. I enjoyed our little conversation." And with that, the woman was back to her tasks.

Amanda rushed over to the microfilm files. She

worked her way through the racks of drawers until she found what she wanted. She spooled the film on the rollers and scanned through the black-and-white film, which took another couple of hours; however, her patience paid off. She found the stories she was looking for.

Being a careful researcher, Amanda wrote down all the facts, no matter how small or trivial they seemed. Though all the articles had something of interest, the final installment was the most telling. The killer was a mental patient, one James Selly, who had become violent. The staff at the Amherst Mental Institution could not explain his escape, nor how he had broken his bonds and escaped through locked security doors. The tragic tale ended when Selly was tracked down by the sheriff and his men with bloodhounds. In the chase that followed, the suspect fell to his death from the cliffs, which had immediately been dubbed Crazy Man's Bluff.

"Hello, Jimmy," Amanda said to herself. Jimmy Selly. Amanda had noted down every Jimmy, Jim, and James who had been a patient at the Amherst Institution in the Thirties. There had been almost two dozen. Most of the last names had blurred together, but she remembered the name Selly.

"Madam?" a man said. "We'll be closing in fifteen minutes."

"Almost five already?" Amanda stared at her watch in disbelief. She gathered up her notes and headed back to the main entrance. On the way she passed the old librarian.

"Excuse me, dear," the librarian said. "Oslow."

"I'm sorry."

"Oslow. He was the leader, and mean as night is black."

"Are you sure?"

"Absolutely. He comes in occasionally. Delbert Oslow was the only one left alive. He's still a mean, old cuss."

Amanda thanked the librarian. Armed with the information she had unearthed that day, she had some strange suspicions about the deaths that had occurred almost 60 years earlier. Somehow they might be connected with Judy and her dreams. Whatever the case, the pieces of the puzzle were falling into place slowly, and with any luck, Delbert Oslow might help her put everything together.

Chapter Eighteen

Peter peeked out the front window for the tenth time in as many minutes. That time, it was the sound of a car door slamming that had summoned him. But it was only the family across the street returning from church.

"Peter," Sharon said, coming up behind him, "you're ignoring Alex."

"Sorry, Mom."

"She'll be here," she said, gently touching her son's arm, which made Peter blush. "Don't be embarrassed. She's a lovely girl."

"Oh, Mom."

"Help me set the table."

Peter obeyed his mother's wishes, but the next 15 minutes dragged on like hours. He was so anxious he was almost sorry he'd invited Judy to dinner. When the doorbell finally rang, Peter had to fight the urge to bolt to answer it.

"Am I OK where I parked?" Judy said, standing on the porch.

Peter glanced down to the street. "You're fine."

"Here," she said, handing Peter the package she had hidden behind her back.

"What's this?"

"A present. What else? I saw it and I had to get it for you."

Peter opened the small package. Inside, he found a hardcover copy of *Understanding Physics* by Isaac Asimov. On the title page, Judy had written an inscription that made Peter blush again: *Thanks for understanding me. Love, Judy.*

"This is great. Thanks," Peter said. "Come with me. I want you to meet someone."

Peter lead Judy through the house to the couch where Alex and Sharon sat talking.

"Excuse me," Peter said, interrupting their conversation. "Judy Kilter, this is Alex Stein."

Alex rose to his feet. "So, this is the girl who has been keeping you so busy. It's very nice to meet you, Judy."

"Thank you. It's nice to meet you. That's a beautiful car you and Mrs. Cowal gave Peter."

"I thought Peter needed a way to get around on his own. He's all grown-up and a fine young man."

For the third time within a half hour, Peter blushed. But all in all, he hadn't felt happier since Bobby's death.

"Well," Sharon said as she stood, "dinner's almost ready. There're just a couple things left to do."

"Can I help you?" Judy asked.

Sharon grinned. "It would be nice to share the kitchen with another woman. You sure you don't mind?"

"Not at all. It would be fun."

"Your mother and I spent a few hours together

in the kitchen," Sharon told Judy as they left the living room, "except when it came to barbecues. Then the men always took over and left the dishes for us women afterward."

Peter saw Judy glancing back his way. He smiled at her, then realized that she wasn't looking at him, but at Alex. She disappeared through the kitchen door.

"I've never seen that look in your eyes," Alex said.

"What look?"

"Oh, Peter." He chuckled. "She seems very nice."

"She is."

As Sharon promised, the roast, mashed potatoes and gravy, warm rolls, and vegetables were on the table five minutes later. Then the four of them sat down to the fine meal.

"It's nice to have a full table once again," Sharon said, "if only for a little while. I hope I made enough food."

"Enough?" Peter said. "We'll be having leftovers for a week."

"Is something wrong?" Alex asked Judy, who was studying him closely.

"No," she said, embarrassed. "I didn't mean to stare, but you seem very familiar to me. I'm sure we've met before?"

"Who can say?" Alex said. "Fulton is not that big."

"I bet I know when you met," Sharon said. "Alex has been a friend of this family for quite a long time. It's possible that he visited on the same day you and your family were here."

"That's probably it," Peter said, hoping to change the subject. "Mom, can you pass the potatoes?"

"Peter?" Sharon gave him a stern look.

"What?"

"We're in the middle of a conversation." She said no more, not wanting to scold her son in front of his girlfriend.

"Sorry," Peter said.

"I don't remember such a meeting, but I'm an old man," Alex said. "I've forgotten much over the years."

To Peter's relief, neither Alex nor Judy gave any more thought to the matter, and the afternoon passed without incident. Later, before Judy left, she and Peter stood at the bottom of the porch steps. Peter kept checking for any curtain movement—not because his mother would spy on him, but because Judy was the first girl he'd ever had over for dinner. And, like at the drive-in, he felt a little uneasy.

"I'm stuffed," Judy said. "Your mother is a terrific cook. Thank her again for me."

"Do you really have to leave now?"

Judy reluctantly nodded. "I promised Mona I'd stop by. You want to come with me? I'll only stay a little while."

"I don't think I'd be welcome. Better go without me."

"Maybe I will stay a little longer."

"No," Peter said. "If I'm ever going to get along with Mona, it won't help if she thinks I'm stopping you from seeing her. You go."

"You sure you don't mind?"

"I'm sure."

"Is that your car parked in front of my house?" Mrs. Romun suddenly yelled from her door, pointing at Judy's Probe. "Move it or I'll have it towed."

"It's public parking, Mrs. Romun," Peter said, trying to be polite.

"You Cowals always think you're right about everything! So perfect, never wrong about anything!"

"There's no reason to yell," Judy said. "I'll just move my car."

"Damn right, you'll move it."

"She said she would," Peter said. "Now would you please leave us be?"

"A back talker," Mrs. Romun said, "like that dummy brother of yours. At least, that dummy is out of my hair."

"Listen you dried-up old witch," Peter said, starting across the lawn. "All you do is bitch about the damnedest things!"

"That's right," Mrs. Romun said. "Come on my property. I have something for you."

"Well, stick it up your ass, you crone! The world would be a whole lot better if you were dead, not Bobby! And if you ever say as much as my brother's name again, I'll make you wish you'd never lived."

Judy rushed over to Peter and grabbed him by the arm. "Walk me to my car. Please, Peter. She's not worth it."

Peter walked away with Judy, but nothing she said calmed him. He would have gladly beaten Mrs. Romun to knock some sense into her, and he wouldn't have felt the least bit guilty. It wasn't until after Judy left that Peter realized that Bobby's death had changed him. If he couldn't get his emotions under control, there was no telling what he might do.

Chapter Nineteen

The dilapidated building at 1600 Milton Street was in a run-down section of Fulton. In that neighborhood, most of the houses were in disrepair. The alleyways were cluttered with overflowing trash cans, whose contents spilled onto the cracked cement slabs between the buildings. The shabbiness of the area didn't comfort Amanda, but it was home to Delbert Oslow—the one man who might be able to answer her questions about James Selly.

Scattered along the apartment house's second-floor landing were scraps of paper, bottles, and other assorted bits of garbage. A broken pane of glass covered an empty fire extinguisher compartment, and a darkened exit sign hung from the ceiling by a single strand of electrical wire. Amanda knocked on a door in the middle of the hall, but no one answered.

"He's not home," an elderly woman said in a belligerant tone after Amanda knocked again. Amanda turned and found an eye staring at her through a slightly opened door. Below the eye, a chain draped the door from the inside.

"Don't come no closer," the woman said when Amanda took a step toward her door. "I don't want no trouble."

"I'm looking for Delbert Oslow," Amanda said in the most pleasant voice she could muster.

"Delbert? Ha! Yeah, you call 'im that. You'll see." The old woman laughed again. "He's not home."

"Would you happen to know when he'll be back?"

"He plays chess on Sundays down at the senior center. Every Sunday for the last eleven years, and probably every Sunday until the city closes it down."

"Could you give me the address?"

"Could, but it won't do you no good."

"Why's that?"

"It closes at three o'clock on Sundays, and it's just about three now."

"Would you know where Mr. Oslow will be after that?"

"How would I know a damn fool thing like that? Ain't none of my business."

Amanda had the urge to laugh, but knew that doing so would only make things worse. "Could I leave a note with you to give to him?"

"I ain't no mailman."

"Please. It's important I talk with him."

"You have a dollar?"

"Yes, I do."

"Well leave it with the note and I'll see he gets your message."

Amanda reached into her purse and pulled out a small notepad and a pen. She scribbled her name and number and a short message to call her. She looked at the eye still staring at her and included a line about paying Oslow ten dollars for his time. She folded the note in half, took a dollar from her wallet, and started to hand both to the eye.

"Leave it on the floor where you're standing. I'll get it after you're gone."

Amanda followed the woman's instructions, wondering if she would ever hear from Delbert Oslow. But at the moment, she couldn't wait. She had arranged to meet David Jensen for dinner, and if she had to go chasing all over Fulton for Delbert Oslow, she'd never be able to keep the date.

"I'll have the snow crab," Amanda told the waitress, handing back her menu. Instantly, she lit up a cigarette.

"And you, sir?" the waitress asked.

David Jensen ran his eyes down the list of food one more time. "I think I'll have the prime-rib dinner."

"How would you like that cooked?"

"Medium."

"Very good." After the waitress took his menu, David said, "So what's the big news you've got for me? A breakthough on our haunted field?"

"Of sorts. Remember me mentioning Judy Kilter?" Amanda said, pulling the ashtray from the center of of the table.

"The girl from the local high school. The one you feel is gifted."

"That's her, but I don't feel she's gifted—I know she is. Anyway, she called yesterday morning, and she told me she's been having strange dreams—dreams about the deaths of her classmates."

"Well, that's easy enough to explain," David said.

"But how does that tie to the case at hand?"

"Wait. There's more. Shortly after I arrived in town, I met with a woman named Margaret Able. She mentioned a man named Jimmy."

"Jimmy? Just Jimmy? Nothing more?"

"Not exactly," Amanda said. "She mentioned the name in relation with a nursing job she had."

"Jimmy was a coworker? A patient? What?"

"A patient at the Amherst Institution."

"Amherst? The mental hospital?"

"Yes, that Amherst. After going through miles of paperwork, I found a few patients named Jimmy."

"How many?"

"Twenty-three."

David chuckled. "You're going to track them all down?"

"Don't need to. The Jimmy in question was one James Selly."

"How can you be so—"

Amanda raised her hand, stopping David. "Please, all will become clear."

"I certainly hope so, because I can't see how Judy Kilter's dreams could possibly be connected to a field with a history of almost sixty years of paranormal activities."

"It's her dreams, and the deaths of those two boys. Judy says she saw the two boys being murdered in her dreams, and I think she's right."

"That insight again. Oops, I'm not supposed to call it that. Forgive the slip. Your feelings aside, must I remind you that accidents are the leading killer of children and teens?"

"According to the news articles, the police do think both deaths were accidents."

"See, let cooler heads prevail."

"And that was what the police thought about some other deaths that occurred in Fulton sixty years ago, until they couldn't be so easily written off. It seems the killer was an escaped mental patient."

"Let me guess—James Selly."

"On the money, but you still have to pay for dinner." Amanda tapped her cigarette against the lip of the ashtray. "He killed four boys, all friends, before he himself was killed. There was a fifth boy, Delbert Oslow. I tracked him down to a seedy apartment building across town. I left word for him to contact me. Though I'm not too sure how reliable the messenger will be."

"That's out of your hands."

"I know. It's just frustrating. Judy's dreams, whatever is causing the disturbances in the field, the deaths in the thirties, the deaths now—I'm sure they're all connected somehow, but I still don't have a solid link. I'm missing a few pieces. I hoped Mr. Oslow could shed some light. In the meantime, I need to investigate the circumstances around the deaths of the two Fulton boys. That might lead somewhere. It's a place to start."

"The only place."

"The first boy, Karl Warner, was hit by a drunk truck driver, but the paper didn't mention his name." Amanda didn't tell David that simply saying the boy's name bothered her, because Karl had been one of the Fulton students she tested that day. He would tell her she was losing her objectivity.

"That's odd," David said. "Newspapers love to drop names like that."

"Apparently not this one."

"So how do you plan to find this truck driver?"

"I thought a trip to the friendly Fulton Police Department might be in order."

"Well, good luck," David said as the waitress arrived with their entrees. "Now, can we forget about ghosts for a while? I'm starving."

Chapter Twenty

Alex climbed the steps of the local police department, which had changed quite a bit since his youth. Sheriff Longstreet had always worked out of a three-room jail with only two cells. Alex remembered how the sheriff had known everybody in town and, of course, everyone had known the sheriff.

Alex entered the station and made his inquiry of the desk sergeant, who told him he would have to talk with the detective in charge of the case. After signing in as a visitor and receiving a green-and-yellow rectangular badge, Alex approached what he hoped was the right desk.

"Excuse me," Alex said to a large, square-shouldered man. "Are you Det. Landers?"

"Yeah, I'm Landers. What can I do for you?"

"I would like some information, please."

"That depends on what you want to know."

"I would like to know about the two deaths."

"Two deaths? You're going to have to be more specific."

"The boys from the high school, Karl Warner and Gary Oxten."

"What about them?"

"Then you are the officer in change of the cases."

"I was. There's not much of a case for either. Both accidents."

"Are you sure? It's important that you're sure."

A look close to anger came over the detective's face. "It's my job to be sure. They were both accidents."

"I understand the Warner boy was struck down by a vehicle."

"Struck down? More like flattened. Semitrucks have a nasty way of crushing the human body when given the chance."

"The driver—did he say anything or see anything out of the ordinary?"

"Maybe pink elephants. He was pretty juiced up. Stunk of booze from head to toe."

"Please, I would like to speak with him myself. Could you give me his name and if possible his address?"

"It's not possible," the officer said. "Criminals have a right to privacy too. I can't divulge that information."

"Please, it's terribly important."

"I've already told you that I can't give out that information. If that's all, I have paperwork to do. You can turn in your visitor's badge with the desk sergeant on your way out. Now, can I help you, ma'am?"

Unaware that anyone was standing behind him, Alex turned to leave and bumped into Amanda, who had walked up while he was talking to the detective.

"Please forgive me," Alex said. "So careless of me."

"It's quite all right," Amanda said with a sincere smile. "No harm done."

"I'm a tired old man," Alex said. "I should be more careful. I don't make a habit of knocking ladies down, especially not one as lovely as yourself. Good day."

"Det. Landers, my name in Amanda Colins," she said, turning to the officer. "I'm doing some work for Frank Currie. I would like some information on a boy named Karl Warner, who was killed a little over a week ago. He was hit by a truck. I would like to see the file."

"You would, huh?" He put down his pen and pushed his notepad across the desk.

"Yes, I would. Also, there was another boy, Gary Oxten. They were friends. It wouldn't hurt to see his file either."

"What is the fascination with these cases? Both are simple accidents. I went fishing for the weekend and I had a fine, relaxing time. Now, when I get back to work, headaches. You're the second person to ask about these boys. And I'm going to tell you exactly the same thing I told that old guy who just left—nothing."

Amanda wondered what the elderly gentleman had wanted to know about the deaths, but her curiosity would have to wait until she dealt with the detective.

"As I tried to explain, I'm working with Frank Currie. I'm sure he would appreciate you helping me."

Landers leaned back in his chair. "You know, anyone can come in here and start throwing names around. Lady, I don't know you from Eve."

"I'm not sure she was a brunette."

"Huh?"

"Forget it." Amanda pulled a slip of paper from her

purse. "Here, call this number. I'm sure Mr. Currie will verify my identity."

Det. Landers took the paper. "Right, I know all the numbers at city hall. They're in sequence, starting with 3700 and ending at 3815. This number is out of range."

"It's his private number."

"I'll tell you what I'm gonna do," he said, smiling as he stared at the small slip of paper. "I'm gonna call this number, and if Frank Currie doesn't answer himself, I'll arrest you on a nuisance charge."

When Amanda smiled and pointed to the phone, he picked up the handset and pressed out the numbers.

"Good bluff, lady, but it's one bluff I'm callin'. Have a seat. I think you're going to be the first paperwork I fill out today."

Before he could come back with more witty banter, his call was answered. "Good morning, sir. . . . Det. Al Landers. . . . No, sir, no trouble . . . I . . . Yes, sir, I realize you're very busy. There's a woman down here at headquarter s claiming. . . . Yes, sir, that's her."

Amanda watched as the color drained from the man's face. She wanted to laugh, but didn't. She wouldn't lose what advantage she had just gained by satisfying a whim.

"Yes, sir, I will. Of course." Landers hung up the phone, then wiped away a small bead of sweat that had formed under his right ear. "I'll get the files."

Moments later, the detective returned with two thin folders. "Here you go. There's not much here. As I said, we're treating them as accidents, plain and simple."

"You said the gentleman who was here earlier also asked about the deaths. Do you know his name?"

"No. Is it important?"

"I don't know." Amanda started to page through the files, "I don't know."

"Mr. Smelnerk? Joe Smelnerk?" Amanda asked as she approached a gruff-looking man raking his front yard. He had on torn blue jeans, a tan tee-shirt from under which his potbelly peeked out, and dirty white sneakers. Workgloves covered hands that gripped a rake and pulled it across the grass.

"Who's askin'?" He stopped and held the rake like a weapon, pointing the round tip toward Amanda.

"My name's Amanda Colins." She held out her hand. "I'd like to talk to you if you have a moment?"

Smelnerk glanced down at Amanda's open hand, then to her face. "You a lawyer? I bet you're one of those sharks who advertises on the TV. You cut deep into a man's pocket so you can collect your thirty-three percent. I ain't talkin' to you."

"No, Mr. Smelnerk," Amanda said. "I'm not a lawyer. I'm a teacher."

"A teacher? What would you want to talk to me about? It ain't about reenrolling in high school, is it? Probably came up on somebody's computer that I never finished high school and you're here to try to convince me to finish my education. Well, I'm too old."

"I'm a professor at Ohio State. I'm Dr. Amanda Colins."

"Got any ID?"

"Of course." She reached into her purse and pulled out her university identification card.

Joe took the card and studied the picture. "Not a very good picture, is it? You're much prettier."

"Thank you."

"Now, what do you want?" Joe asked.

"I'd like to talk to you about your accident. A boy was killed."

"Goddamn it!" He threw down the rake. "I knew the moment I laid eyes on you that you had something to do with that mess. You're a lawyer for that boy's family."

"I've already told you I'm not. I have a doctorate in psychology and parapsychology."

"If that is a fact, what would I have to say to someone like you?"

"Tell me about the accident. I assure you whatever you say will be held in the strictest confidence."

"What good could it do you? Me tellin' the police my story certainly didn't do me any good. If it weren't for the trucker's union bailing me out of jail, I'd be stuck there now. But what good has it done me? My license has been suspended until the trial and my truck's been impounded. What good I ask you? What good?"

"Let's just say I'm doing my own investigation."

"Sounds like a waste of time. I can tell you only what I already told the police. Seems it would have been a whole lot easier to read their report."

"I have. I wanted to hear your account directly from you."

"Well, first off, I want to tell you it wasn't my fault. I wasn't drunk like they must have told you. Sure I took a couple of sips from my bottle. Hey, I'd been driving eighteen straight hours. Beside, I spilled most of what little I had left on myself." Joe threw his hands in the air. "You're not going to believe me either."

"Try me."

"OK, but don't say I didn't warn you. I was driving down route twenty-nine and made the turnoff down

Wilmore Street. That cuts a good half hour off the trip home. Well, I'm driving along and I see something real queer down the road. At first, I thought it was simply two guys settling a difference of opinion by knocking each other's blocks off. At least, I think it was two guys; it was too dark to tell. Anyway, the one guy who's winning—he has the other stretched out on the ground. Quick fight, I thought. Then the guy grabs the other off the ground and hoists him high overhead. When I realized what was going to come next, I almost got sick. I slammed down on my brake, but they wouldn't grab. Then the steering wheel seized up on me. I headed right toward them. There was nothing I could do. I tried downshifting, nothing. The shift seemed to freeze right in my hand. I couldn't even turn off the ignition. After I heard a loud thud, the brakes finally caught. I got out and . . . I'm sure you get the rest."

"What about the other guy? Where did he go?"

"Don't you think if I knew that I would have told the police?"

"I can make it possible for you to describe him to a police sketch artist. I have a little pull. If you have a face to go along with your story, it might help your case."

"An artist won't do no good. I didn't get a good look. Like I said, it was too dark, and by the time my headlights were shining on their faces, I was too busy trying to stop my truck to get a look. For all I know, it could have even been you out there that night."

Amanda concluded her interview quickly. She didn't want Smelnerk to realize that his story had set her mind reeling. For the first time, she had a piece of evidence that corroborated the theory she was developing. If Amanda was right, time might be running out for some other unsuspecting victims—just as it had 60 years earlier.

The next day, Amanda got off to a bad start. She had overslept and still felt tired. She had been up the previous night until 1:30 going over all her notes and files. When she finally arrived at the office at 9:30, she found a phone message waiting for her on her desk. Delbert Oslow had left word for her to meet him in a local park at 10:00, and he wouldn't wait long.

Not wasting any time, Amanda drove to the park, then made her way to the sidewalk surrounding the lush green tract. She scanned it quickly. Not knowing what Delbert Oslow would look like, she reasoned that if she appeared to be searching for someone he would approach her.

After a few moments, she realized her plan wasn't working, so she tried a different approach. She carefully observed the activities of the men in the park. Two men were playing chess at the far end of the park. Since Oslow's neighbor had mentioned that he played chess, Amanda started toward them. But she stopped short when a disheveled man approached her.

"You're late," he said. He was unshaven and reeked of body odor. His wrinkled shirt didn't match the pants he wore. "You got my ten dollars?"

"Yes." Amanda pulled a crisp clean bill out of her purse. "Here."

He snatched the bill and shoved it in his pocket, then extended his empty palm. "And a quarter for the phone call."

She handed him a quarter, then asked, "Would you mind if I record our conversation?"

"Makes no never mind to me. I can't figure what you want with me no how."

Amanda pulled a microcassette recorder from her purse. She pressed the play and record buttons, then stated the date and time. "I'm speaking with Delbert Oslow."

"I still don't know what this is all about."

"I understand that some friends of yours were killed when you were young."

"Why in the hell do you want to drag up that old dirt for? I don't want to waste my time." He began walking away.

Amanda followed him. "Please, Mr. Oslow. It's very important."

"What's so damn important about deaths that happened that long ago?"

"It just is. Please, tell me about it."

"Fine. Anything so I can get the hell out of here. That moron sheriff suspected that I was killing my buddies. Yeah, but he was proved wrong. Old Longstreet would've loved to have pinned the deaths on me. It must have broken his heart when he couldn't."

"Because the real killer was found?"

"Yeah, that's what they said at the time. But I don't know."

"You think the sheriff got the wrong man."

"I ain't saying that. I just think there was more to it. That's all."

"I don't understand."

"Well, back all those odd years ago, me and my friends tried to do our part to make the town safe for us God-fearing Christian folk. We had a little run-in with a Jew. Mind you, we only wanted to protect our town." Oslow cleared his throat and spit out a large chunk of greenish phlegm.

"We had a place down off Tavern Road," Oslow said, ignoring Amanda's disgusted expression. "We used it as a hangout. It was nothing really, just a small clearing in the trees. Me and my buddies would sit on the rotting logs for hours telling lies about girls we dated or trying to outdo each other with tales of how great our lives would be after getting out of this one-horse town. It didn't matter much what we said or did in the clearing. What mattered was being together at the clearing. None of us had much, and after school, there wasn't much to do.

"One day, my friend Russell showed up late. He told us his pa had been sacked. We might have been young, but we weren't stupid. We all knew the Jews controlled the banks and the businesses. They would keep their own kind working and fire the rest like Russell's pa.

"It was getting close to suppertime, and we were about to leave when this strange kid came walkin' down the road. Natt, he was one grade down from the rest of us, knew the guy from his class. He thought the guy was sort of weird, because he never talked to anyone. And it only fueled the fire when Natt told us all he was a Jew.

"We all looked at each other. I guess we figured we could get a little revenge for Natt's pa. We blocked the road and told him if he wanted to walk on our road he would have to pay us. He refused, which was exactly what we'd hoped he'd do. We aimed to collect our money and that's what we did. All I can say about the whole thing now is that he shouldn't have fought back. He only made things worse for himself. He ended up in the hospital, and me and my chums spent a night in the pokey. You would have thought old Longstreet would have thought we'd done a public service. After we got out of jail, strange things started happening. One by one, my chums died."

"But not you?"

"Obviously, else you're talking to a ghost. And I don't know why not me either. But I think that Jew had something to do with my friends dying. Just the way he looked at me after that. Even now, when I see him around town once in a blue moon, I get that same feeling."

"Around town? You mean Fulton?"

"Yeah, I mean Fulton. What other town do you think? You're not too sharp for a university egghead, are you?"

"Can you tell me his name?"

"I think your ten dollars are about up."

"Please, Mr. Oslow. His name?"

"Stein," Oslow said. "His name's Alexander Stein."

A short while later, Amanda knocked at Alex's door and waited. When he opened the door, Amanda was startled that she recognized him from their encounter at the police station. "Mr. Stein?"

"Yes?"

"I don't know if you remember me. We bumped into each other at the police station. I was coming in and you were going out."

"I remember. I hope you weren't injured."

"Not at all," she said. "My name's Amanda Colins. I'm in Fulton doing some investigation work for Frank Currie and the city council."

"What is it you want from me?" he asked.

"Please bear with me. Many years ago a group of boys were killed," Amanda said, and Alex's face immediately became grave. "The newspapers at that time reported the sheriff had caught the killer. But now the same thing is happening all over again. I was told that you might know something about—"

"Why ask me questions about what happened so long ago? Let the past be. I have nothing more to say. Good day." Alex started to close the door.

"Please, Mr. Stein, I'm trying to help a young girl. There have already been two more deaths. That's why you went to see Det. Landers. Please help me."

"I'm sorry," Alex said, slamming the door shut.

"Mr. Stein, it's important I talk with you. I'll leave you my card. I've written the local number where I can be reached. Call me if you change your mind. Please, Mr. Stein." She wedged the card between the door and its frame.

After returning to her car, Amanda saw Alex retrieve her card from the door. Driving away, Amanda felt hopeful that at last she had found the missing link that would end all the mystery about the deaths in Fulton. With any luck, Alex would contact her before someone else died.

Alex stood in the middle of the grassy field. It was the second time in as many weeks that he stood on the foul soil. How he hated the place, the tall oak tree, the remnants of the house, and the memories. Alex knew what had to be done. He had no choice. He had read about the deaths of the boys and had his own suspicions. Amanda Colins had strengthened those suspicions, and his conscience forced him to act. He loved his brother, but the killing had to stop.

"Where are you?" Alex called out in an angry tone. "I know you can hear me. I know it's you."

A coldness swept through the old man's body. Something had heard Alex's call. Then a childish giggle filled the air.

The large oak tree swayed and bent as if some

great gust of wind had blown. Alex's eyes scanned across the vacant property. Only the trees in the lot were moving.

Alex's face went stern, but he was not frightened. "Why are you doing these things? Why are you killing?"

A giggle again answered him.

"Answer me!" he yelled. "Answer me!"

"They hurt my friend Bobby," Georgie said. "They hurt him really bad. Now I have no one to play with."

"That can't be!" Alex said, trying to force the shock from his voice. He had to keep a cool head. "Bobby Cowal's death was a tragic accident. That's all."

"No, no, no! They hurt Bobby. Now I hurt them."

Alex was stunned. Without realizing it, Peter had been right: there were others at the cliff with Bobby. "Georgie, you must stop. Don't kill anyone else. It's wrong to kill. I'll go to the police. They will punish the boys for what they did to Bobby. I promise."

"They killed Bobby," Georgie said and anger made his voice sharp. "I kill them."

"Where are you? Let me see you."

"No," Georgie said, "I don't trust you no more. You'll try to make me go away again. Like before. But I came back. I won't let you stop me. I won't let you send me away. You can't send me away. I get so lonely."

"But you're not lonely, are you? Who are you using this time? You must stop." Alex listened, waiting for an answer. "Georgie? Georgie? You cannot do these things!"

Alex pleaded with Georgie again and again, but

no voice answered. A short while later, the coldness Alex had felt was gone—and, Alex knew, Georgie was too. Alone in the field, the old man trembled. He had failed to stop Georgie, and for all he knew, Georgie was off to kill again.

Chapter Twenty-one

Amanda had three open files spread out across her desk, from which she double-checked her facts in preparation for her two o'clock meeting with the city council. She had several hours to make any last-minute changes to her report, which included a brief summary of each interview. She was careful, however, to include only the information she could verify. Also, at that time, she thought it best to leave out any mention of Judy Kilter. There was an unknown connection between the girl and the field, but in her mind, Amanda saw a clear distinction between Judy's plea for help and the council's need to know. One was a question of privacy, the other of doing her job. One did not exclude the other. Besides, if the daughter of the man hired to develope the land came into the picture, it could cause some headaches for Frank Currie. With what Amanda had seen in the past, other council members might use the information to try to bring Frank down a few pegs.

Engrossed in her work, Amanda was easily startled

by the ringing of her phone. "Yes?"

"Miss Colins? This is Alex Stein."

"Hello, I'm glad you called," she said.

"Who are you trying to help?" Alex asked, his voice cold and suspicious.

"I'm sorry. I can't tell you that."

"Good day, then," Alex said.

"Wait," Amanda said, hoping to stall Alex. "May I come over? I'd rather not discuss this matter over the phone."

"I'll be expecting you."

The trip to the Stein house took 20 minutes. As Amanda was about to knock at the door, she heard the sound of a dead bolt being released. Alex opened the door, greeted Amanda, and led her into his living room, where he gestured for her to sit.

"Can I get you some tea? I remember my Aunt May always serving tea in this room. It's such a rare occasion that I get the opportunity to do the same."

"I'd love some coffee," Amanda said.

"Do you mind instant?"

"No, that sounds great."

"All right, then. Please excuse me." While Alex went to the kitchen, Amanda studied her surroundings, hoping that she might find a clue about what kind of person she was dealing with.

"Microwaves," he said when he returned. "They make instant coffee instantly."

"Do you mind?" she asked, displaying her micro-recorder. Since Alex shook his head, she switched on the recorder and carefully placed it on the table in front of her chair.

"Is that you?" Amanda asked, pointing to a yellowed picture sitting inside a glass cabinet.

"Yes, it is."

"Who's the little boy with you?"

"Tell me the girl's name," Alex said, ignoring her question.

"I wish you would reconsider. Do you really need to know?"

"The name—tell me the name."

"Judy Kilter," Amanda said.

Alex's face turned white. "Peter! I was right."

"Right about what?" Amanda asked.

"How are you to help this girl?"

"I'm not sure. I thought maybe you could help me help her. She's been having these dreams about the deaths of some of her classmates. She's very special. In the years I have spent in the field of parapsychology, I have never come across anyone with her potential."

"She is in grave danger," Alex said, his face hard and rigid. "Has she told anyone else about these dreams?"

"I don't really know."

"If he finds out she knows, he may fear she will try to stop him. He will strike back, killing her . . . or worse."

"Who? Who is he? Stop him from what?"

"Tell me what else you know," Alex said.

"I know about Delbert Oslow," Amanda said, "and about his friends. And how Sheriff Longstreet found the real killer—an escaped patient from the Amherst asylum."

"The patient's name was James Selly," Alex said.

"Yes, that's right. I believe there's a connection between those deaths and several deaths that have recently occurred. You do know something, don't you?"

Alex rose from his chair and walked over to the glass cabinet. He stared at the old yellowed picture. When he turned to face the woman, Amanda was surprised to see a tear run down his cheek. "Yes, I do. But you have one thing wrong. The sheriff never found the real killer. Jimmy Selly didn't kill those boys."

"I don't understand."

"I thought I could stop him, put him to rest. And all these years, I thought I had."

"Stop who?"

"My little brother Georgie, or what's left of him. He killed Delbert Oslow's friends because of what they did to me. He used Jimmy, took control of his body. Georgie would come to me. He could never stay for very long. After a few minutes, he would start to fade, then disappear altogether. He would come back after a couple of days. At first, it was very frightening, but over time I got used to seeing him. He's my brother, after all."

In amazed silence, Amanda listened to the old man's painful tale of his brother's death, Sheriff Longstreet's visit, and Alex's encounter with Delbert Oslow and his cronies.

"Somehow Georgie never left this world," Alex said. "He remained, but full of anger, full of hatred. I was in the hospital for weeks. My Aunt May and Uncle Ben never told me about the deaths of my attackers. It wasn't until I returned home that I heard. You have to understand that my brother wanted to protect me from those ruffians as I had tried to protect him from our father. I loved him very much, but I knew I had to stop him. No more people could die because of me.

"So I went back to our old house. Georgie never told me so, but I knew that's where he would be. I had to sneak out after my aunt and uncle had gone to bed. The night seemed especially black. I had hidden an old kerosene lamp out back behind the toolshed. That old lamp shined barely enough to see a few feet in any direction. I must have walked five miles that night."

Amanda held her coffee cup, but was too enthralled to drink as the man's story unfolded.

Decades earlier, on one pitch-black night, Alex stared at the place he had once called home. The cool autumn night wind blew across his face; the heat of his lamp warmed his hand. Knotted boards covered the windows as if trying to blind the house from the real world. The abandoned house stood alone, isolated.

Alex tore the loosely nailed boards away from the entrance. Then he reached out for the door, but pulled back at the last second. He hadn't realized that his hand was shaking. Taking a deep breath, he tried again. His fingertips touched the brass knob and the door inched open with a moan. His other hand tightened around the handle of his lamp. When he pushed the door, it swung easily, but then stopped with a screech as it knocked against a warped floorboard. Alex tried to force the door farther, but he found it stuck fast. But the door had opened enough for him to slip his body through, though not enough for him to see what awaited him on the other side.

Alex waited a moment, then followed his lamp into the darkness. He held his lamp high overhead, and its light seemed trapped by the dust Alex kicked up. As he started to call out his brother's name, the dirty air made his words choke back down his throat.

"Georgie? Are you here? I want to talk with you."

"Let's play a game." Georgie's voice came from all sides of the house.

"No. No games. I must know—are you killing those boys?"

There was no response, just dead air.

"It is you. Do you hear me? I want you to stop what you're doing. It's not right!" As he spoke, Alex could feel his heart beating in his chest. He wasn't sure if it was from fear or anger. "Answer me! Or I won't let you come see me anymore. I will never play with you. You will be alone forever."

"They were bad. They hurt you. So I hurt them back. I made them never hurt you again."

"How?"

"It's easy. Jimmy helps me. I don't have to go away when I'm with Jimmy."

"Jimmy? Who is Jimmy?"

"He's my friend. He can see me, too, like you can, but he's not as smart. He lives at the same place Daddy did. But he doesn't live there no more. He wanted to leave that place, so I helped him. I opened the doors so he could go out."

"Where is Jimmy now?"

"I don't know. I just find him when I want to—like when I punished Daddy for hurting me."

"Did you hurt Daddy, Georgie?"

"Yes. I went inside Jimmy. I don't get tired when I do that."

"I want you to stop hurting people!" Alex yelled, then caught himself. "It's not right. Please stop."

There was a long pause; then Georgie said, "All right. Now will you play a game with me, Alex? A good game."

Many years afterward, as Alex sat telling Amanda of that night, he could still recall Georgie's joyful laughter.

"I stayed with my brother," Alex said. "After he tired and faded to nothing, I called to him again all night, but he didn't answer me. When I was sure he wasn't going to return, I used my lamp to burn down the house. I thought by destroying the house I would finally put Georgie to rest. I was wrong."

"Don't be too upset with yourself. It's never that easy. Georgie is caught on our plane of existence."

Amanda could tell by Alex's expression that she was speaking too technically. "He can't pass over. He's stuck in limbo with no way to get to the other side and no one to guide him there. He's literally trapped in our world. And with few exceptions his interaction, contact with this world is slight at best."

Amanda felt the man's sadness, and she wanted to reach out to him, but she had to stay objective. If she was going to stop Georgie, she had to know everything Alex knew. "Why is Georgie killing these boys now? Did they do something to you?"

"No. Not me. Georgie had a friend named Bobby who was found dead not too far from here. Somehow Bobby could see Georgie and had befriended my brother. When Bobby died, Georgie was alone again. Georgie hates being alone. I believe the boys who were killed had something to do with Bobby's death."

"If you're right, you should contact the police."

"Remember our first meeting? I was there to simply get information on the boys who died. I was bluntly refused."

"If you explain—"

"And tell them what?"

"Yes, I see. It would be a tough story to sell. I find it hard to believe myself. But if you question the boy's death—you know, make an official inquiry—maybe that will start something to form a link between Bobby's death and the others."

"The police have the cause of Bobby's death listed

as an unfortunate rock slide."

"Yes, I came across the story during my investigation, but still. . . ."

"Bobby was retarded," Alex said, bluntly, "and he was very upset at the time. The police consider it nothing more than an accident."

"That explains a lot."

"I don't understand."

"It's quite simple actually. When we're children, we all believe in fantasy. Our minds are more open, more receptive. As we grow up, the adults in our lives tell us that Santa Claus and the Easter Bunny don't really exist, which makes us close down that part of our minds. Bobby still believed. He was innocent, childlike, so he could see Georgie. And on the other hand, for Georgie, Bobby was a contact with a world he could only see as if peering through a large picture window. Georgie would have clung to him for companionship. He would've used all his energy to keep the contact with Bobby viable. And from what you've told me, I suspect your brother couldn't keep it up too long without help."

"But I've seen him too," Alex said. "And I'm not what you yourself would call innocent."

"You're his brother. You love him very much. I think you would always see him. Strong emotions can break through the barriers of the mind."

After Alex stood silent for many moments, Amanda asked, "There's more, isn't there? Something you're not telling me. Do you know who Georgie is controlling now?"

"I have my suspicions, but I pray to the Almighty I'm wrong. You see to the girl's safety, and I will try to do what little I can to stop Georgie. It's my fault he is the way he is. I should have protected him better

than I did. I failed before. I pray this time I have more
success."

No matter how much Amanda argued, Alex refused
to give her any more information. At last, frustrated
and not a little vexed, Amanda left him. She had
almost forgotten about her meeting with the town
council, and so much time had passed that she'd
never be ready in time.

"You're miles away, Peter," Judy said. It was noon,
and the two of them had decided to eat their lunch
off school grounds. They sat across from each other,
a pizza—half cheese only, half pepperoni and black
olives—on the table between them. Judy had noticed
how Peter only picked at his food and directed her
comment at his sober mood.

"I guess I am."

"Want to talk about it?"

"Nothing to say."

Even though they had been dating for a short while,
Judy could read Peter. "It's about Bobby, isn't it?"

He reluctantly nodded. "Today is—was his birthday. His thirteenth. I bought him a new baseball glove
a month ago. It's still hidden under my bed. Wrapped
with a bow. I know I should get it out of there, but I
can't. When I lie in my bed at night, I think about it
being there. I just can't take it out. I must sound like
a real idiot."

"No," Judy said, reaching across the table and gently touching Peter's hand. "You sound like a caring
brother. We all have things that bother us."

"Right. Look at you."

"Yes, look at me. I have my own worries."

"Like what?"

"If I tell you, you promise not to laugh?"

"I promise."

"Or not think I'm crazy?"

"Crazy? Why would I—"

"Promise?"

"Yes, I promise."

"I've been having strange dreams. About Ox and Karl." Judy told Peter the details, as vividly as she could remember them, about the little boy making her play his games. She told him about her meeting Amanda Colins and the doctor's promise to help her. And most of all, she told Peter how afraid she was. "You must think I'm pretty messed up."

"You're half right. I think you're pretty, not messed up. Don't let a few dreams bother you. Dreams can't hurt you."

Judy silently agreed. But deep inside, a twinge of doubt remained. And try as she might, she couldn't totally ignore it.

Spiritual intrusion and possession was the official term for what was going on in Fulton, and Amanda couldn't wait to tell David about it. At the moment, she sat alone on a green park bench with only her thoughts and a cheeseburger. She decided the park was the perfect place to reflect and digest both the burger and the story Alex had told her. And since it was the same park where she had met Delbert Oslow, it seemed the right place.

Because of a general lack of interest, half the members of the town council had not bothered to show up for their meeting. Frank Currie had been embarrassed and apologetic, but Amanda couldn't have been happier. She was too full of Alex's story to put up with the council members anyway.

With her notes at her side, she played back her

taped conversions with Alex and Delbert Oslow. She carefully wrote down the key points from each interview without making them sound as if they had come from a late-night movie.

"This whole thing is fascinating," Amanda said as she rewound and played Alex's tale once again. The warning of danger to Judy, the killings, Georgie—all the bits and pieces roamed around in her mind.

Amanda took another bite from her burger, which she decided could use a little more mustard. After she rummaged around in the white paper bag for the small yellow packets she had dropped in, she was startled to find a small boy glaring at her.

"Hi," she said, swallowing her mouthful of food. "What's your name?"

Although the little boy stood silently in front of her, Amanda recognized his face after a moment.

"I saw you," the boy said. "I saw you talking to him."

"I didn't . . . I—"

"My brother. You're the one who talked to my brother. I saw you."

"Georgie, I'm a friend of your brother Alex."

"No, you're not. You want to stop me. Well, I won't let you."

"No, I want to help you." Amanda's heart pounded with fear and excitement.

"You're a big liar. You want me to be alone again. I hate being alone."

Amanda glanced around, expecting to see people staring at her arguing with a small child. To her surprise, no one even seemed to notice.

"No one can see me," Georgie said. "No one, but you. You want to stop me, I know, but you can't stop me."

Georgie reached out, and his wispy hand passed into Amanda's arm. The coldness felt as if it were burning her. It paralyzed her, and she was powerless to fight as Georgie disappeared.

"You can't stop me," Georgie said, his voice coming from Amanda's mouth. "Now, we will play a game."

"No!" Amanda's voice strained to come out.

"You're not supposed to talk back."

"I won't let you do this, Georgie," Amanda said, her voice becoming stronger.

"How can you be here with me?" Georgie cried out. "I'm here. You go away."

"No, Georgie. I will not go away," Amanda said, forcing back Georgie's influence. "You can't control me like the others. I'm stronger. I understand my abilities."

"I can! I can make you go away!" The words shouted from Amanda's mouth. "You can't stop me! I don't want to be alone again! I'll hurt anyone who tries to make me be alone!"

The strain on Amanda's mind and body increased. Her body began to shake. Even as she fell to the ground and blacked out she said, "I won't let you!"

Night brought with it a full yellow moon, below which the town of Fulton lay at rest—or seemed to, at least.

"I better get in," Suzy said, sliding across the car seat and holding her boyfriend's hand. The young couple sat surrounded by darkness in Mark's Charger. They were parked at the curb in front of Suzy's house. "You going to be all right?"

"Can't you stay for a few more minutes?" Mark asked.

Suzy glanced up at the illuminated picture window,

where a large shadow was cast against the curtain. "Maybe a couple more minutes, but that's all. You know, it's been hard on all of us. Ox and Karl were my friends too. But you have to get over it."

Even though Suzy kissed him, Mark stared straight ahead into the darkness. The night wind pushed an empty beer can down the street, and the rattle made Mark jump in his seat. Suzy kissed him again, but when her attempts to comfort Mark failed, she pulled away from him.

"We all take our chances every day," Suzy said. "It's not a pleasant thought, but any of us could be killed at any time. Living with accidents is just part of life. You can't lock yourself away."

"If they were accidents."

"What's that mean?"

"Just that. I don't think—"

"Suzy!" her father bellowed from the house. "Suzy, come in now."

"Yes, Dad!" she said. With a final kiss, Suzy left the car. "I'll talk to you tomorrow."

As he drove off, Mark saw Suzy disappear through the door and her father standing on the stoop staring back at him with his arms firmly crossed. Only one block away from Suzy's house, Mark shook his head. "Accidents. No fuckin' way!"

Caught up in his thoughts, Mark drove straight through a stop sign. When the loud screaming of a car horn blared in his ears, he stomped down on his brake, and his head snapped forward. The tires of his Charger bit into the blacktop with a tumultuous squeal, stopping the car in the dead center of the intersection. After a white Volvo swerved around the front of his bumper, Mark lifted his head from the steering wheel. All he saw of the Volvo were its red taillights moving farther and farther away.

"Sure," he said, taking a deep breath and wiping sweat from his eyes. "I'll probably end up killing myself."

After a nerve-racking ride home, Mark pulled up to his driveway, but stopped when he saw the rope across the entrance. He got out of his car, leaving the motor running. The car filled the air with heavy exhaust from the oil burning engine. The driveway was covered with a shiny black coat of tar sealer. Then Mark remembered his father telling him he'd have to park on the street tonight because their driveway was to be resurfaced.

"Shit." Mark stared down the street. There were cars parked on both sides as far as he could see.

With no other recourse, Mark drove around the block until he found a place to park. Once he turned off his car, it took Mark several minutes to build up the courage to leave it. But when he determined that the area was clear, he opened his door and slowly stepped out. His eyes scanned all his surroundings, moving back and forth looking for anything that was out of place; and he kept a sharp ear at for any noise that shouldn't be there. He slammed his car door, still watching, still listening.

He should go to the police, he told himself as he walked home. He should tell them everything about Bobby Cowal, about the beer, about Martin and Ox and the others. The police could help him; they could keep him safe. His friends were all dead—except for Martin.

Then a thought struck him hard. Could Martin be the one who was responsible for Karl and Ox's deaths? He had been the last to talk with Karl at Diana's party; and he had left the ball game for a few minutes after Ox had been ejected. Martin might have had enough time to kill Ox. And he would have the most to lose if they were made to pay for their part in the death. Martin had a pretty cushy life. He wouldn't want anyone to take it away. If he got rid of everyone who knew that they had been responsible for Bobby Cowal's death he would be in the clear.

"That's it," Mark said. He didn't need any more convincing. He dismissed the thought of going to the police. Doing that would only get him thrown in jail along with Martin. But since he'd figured it all out, he could take steps to keep himself alive. When he got the chance, he'd confront Martin and tell him all he suspected about Ox and Karl and use that as leverage to keep Martin away.

When Mark was almost to his house, the wind picked up with some force and hit him hard against his face. The bushes close to the sidewalk swayed back and forth, and a small piece of newspaper blew past him as he ran. Behind him, he thought he heard the sound of footsteps. But when he stopped to listen and the echoing steps also stopped, he tried to convince himself it was all in his mind—until a black shape darted between two houses.

"Who's there?" he shouted, but didn't wait for an answer before he began to run again. Full of fear, Mark raced on, and his lungs began to burn as if afire. From the corner of his mouth, a thin film of saliva dripped.

When he thought he spied the phantom shape again, Mark took shelter behind a large oak tree. Although it was poor cover, he peeked around the trunk and dug his fingers into the bark. As the wind whistled past his ears, he thought for a moment he heard someone whispering, "Hide-n-seek! Hide-n-seek."

Terrified, Mark backed away from the oak. His feet tangled with each other, and he toppled to the ground, landing on his back.

"Help me!" he shouted, then pushed himself across the grass as his feet kicked out. "Get away from me, Martin!"

Suddenly someone grabbed Mark's arm and pulled him to his feet. Mark screamed and struggled to regain his balance.

"Get away from me!" Mark yelled, tugging against the grip.

"Mark!" Another hand grabbed the boy's shoulder and shook his body. "Mark, calm down. It's me, son."

"Dad?"

"Yes, son."

"I thought someone was chasing me. I heard someone."

"There's no one here, son. Look for yourself. There's no one here except us."

Mark turned and visually retraced his steps. His father was right—there was no one there.

"I heard steps," Mark said. "I heard a voice."

"In this wind, son? Unlikely."

Mark allowed his father to lead him home. But the terror still welled within him. Someone had been out there in the night. The next time anyone came after Mark, he had to be ready. He didn't want to end up like Karl or Ox.

The Kilter house stood dark except for one window on the second floor that overlooked the lifeless street. Outside, a shadow crept closer to the structure, inching its way past the two expensive cars and along the narrow walkway leading to the house. There was a rustle, and the shadow froze dead still, melting into the darkness along the side of the house.

Judy's cat Caesar strutted out from behind the green bushes that lined the front of the Kilter house. The big tomcat stopped a moment, then hissed at the shadowy figure. With its back arched, its teeth exposed, the cat hissed again, then bolted off around the far side of the house.

Chapter Twenty-two

David Jensen sat, emotionally drained, in room 713 of St. Francis Hospital. His back hurt from the metal chair. No matter which way he turned, he couldn't get comfortable.

He began going over Amanda's notes for at least the twentieth time. She was lying unconscious in the bed next to him and couldn't explain what had happened to her. He let the notebook fall on his lap. His thoughts kept trailing back to the police reports. He found them so hard to believe. The police claimed that Amanda had suffered a breakdown while sitting on a park bench. The police had taken down several statements from bystanders who had all told the same story: one moment, Amanda was acting normal (some said they hadn't even noticed her at first); the next, she was screaming hysterically. The doctors at St. Francis had no explanation for why Amanda had not regained consciousness.

Distracted and overwrought, David returned to his reading. He had been in Fulton since the police contacted the university, and the longer Amanda lay comatose, the more he feared he was going to lose her. Thirty minutes had passed when he heard a sound he had been waiting long to hear—the sound of Amanda coming to.

"Judy," Amanda said, the word barely forming, but it was intelligible enough for David to hear. Frantically, he pushed the nurse call button.

"Amanda? Amanda? Can you hear me? It's David."

"David?" she whispered.

"Yes, Amanda. It's David."

"Where?"

"You're OK. You're in St. Francis Hospital in Fulton."

"How long?"

"Three days. Today is Friday. Amanda, can you still hear me?"

Amanda managed a brief nod. "Judy Kilter . . . warn . . . her. Dang-ger. . . . After her . . . will hurt her. Please, David. . . ."

As Amanda lapsed back into unconsciousness, a nurse entered the room.

"She spoke," David told the nurse, who lifted Amanda's wrist and began timing her pulse.

"That's a good sign, right?" David asked, but the nurse didn't give him any indication that he should get his hopes up.

Judy had been home from school no more than 30 minutes when David Jensen phoned and told her he needed to speak with her. At first, Judy thought it was a sick joke, then David had told her he'd found her phone number written on a matchbook from Maxie's Diner. When he explained about Amanda's condition and her warning, Judy agreed to meet him at St. Francis Hospital. After calling Peter and asking him to meet her at O'Brian's instead of picking her up at the house, she grabbed her purse and started toward the door.

Jessica stopped Judy before the girl had a chance to touch the doorknob. "Be home soon," she told Judy. "You need to decide on which dress you're going to wear to the dance."

"I don't want to worry about that now."

"When then?"

"Later."

"What time is later?"

"I'll be back when I'm back." Judy stormed out of the house.

At St. Francis Hospital, Judy held her breath, then knocked on the door to Amanda's private room.

"Judy?" David said. "Please, come in. Come in."

Like the rest of the hospital, the room had a disagreeable antiseptic smell. Judy's eyes fell immediately on Amanda lying in the bed. An IV needle was stuck in Amanda's arm and an oxygen tube ran up her nose.

"What happened?"

"Nobody knows," David said. "We can't talk here. Let's go to the visitor's lounge."

He gathered up Amanda's notes and the microrecorder, then guided Judy to the lounge. Inside, there were comfortable-looking couches and chairs along the perimeter of the room. Warm golden sunlight poured through large plate-glass windows.

Since the lounge was deserted, David could discuss Amanda's notes without the stares that such topics usually brought him. He knew that the two of them would have been too uncomfortable to talk openly in

Amanda's room. Still, he could hardly stand being away from her side, especially since she'd shown some signs of recovering. After they took a seat on the couch nearest to the door, David gave Judy a brief summary of all the information he had. Then he picked up the recorder and rewound the tape.

"I want you to listen to this carefully. It may be difficult, but tell me if you recognize any of the voices." He pressed the play button. At first there was only static; then came wails like an animal in pain, which were followed by a voice saying, "Could've broke his heart." Then just more animallike noises.

"Did you recognize that voice?"

Judy shook her head. "No, I don't think I've ever heard that voice before."

"OK, there's a little more." David fast forwarded the tape. He carefully watched as the tape-counter number increased, then stopped the machine. "How about this voice?"

"I tried to stop him," a man's voice said, but it was cut off by that same weird static again.

"Is there any more?" Judy asked.

"I'm afraid not. I'm not sure what happened to the tape. Those two spots are the only audible pieces. The rest is that same garbage."

"Can you play that last part again?"

"Sure." He rewound the last few seconds.

"I tried to stop him," the man's recorded voice repeated.

"I have heard that voice," Judy said. "I think. But I can't remember where."

"The first voice, I suspect," David said, "is a man named Delbert Oslow. I found his address in Amanda's things. That's how I found your number. I tried to speak with Mr. Oslow, but he flatly refused me. I hoped he could tell me exactly what he told her. Maybe even the identity of the second voice."

"This whole thing is about me, isn't it?" Judy said.

"I've gone over Amanda's notes several times," he said, knowing the next few minutes were going to be difficult for both Judy and him. "They're incomplete. My guess is that she didn't have time to make her final entries before . . . her accident. Amanda suggested that the deaths of your classmates are being, if you excuse the pun, executed by a malefic specter. You know, a ghost, a spirit, a poltergeist."

"You're joking?" Judy said.

"No. No, I'm not," he said in a serious tone. He could not let his own biases creep into his voice.

"Wait a minute," Judy said, still thinking David seemed a little off base. "I go to the movies like everybody else. I thought poltergeists just threw things around and screamed at you to get out. Not kill people."

"I wouldn't exactly use movies as a good reference point, but in this case, you're right. A restless spirit or poltergeist can, by itself, cause only very limited activities."

"By itself?" Judy asked.

"Yes, it needs a medium—a host, if you will—to do any real damage."

"Medium? You mean like in a seance?"

"You have been to too many movies," David said, forgetting that Judy was a high-school student, not one of his third-year graduate students. "A medium can be any sensitive person who opens himself up to the entity, either by accident or on purpose. People with a strong emotional charge make the best hosts. The poltergeist feeds on the energy, becoming stronger. Anger and hatred are the strongest and the darkest."

Judy's eyes shifted to the floor and she shook her head. "That doesn't explain my dreams. You don't really know, do you? No one can help me."

David felt sorry for the girl. There had been many times in his own life he had had that same helpless feeling. "Not necessarily," he said, trying to give her some hope. "There's a theory that when a surge of psychic energy is built up, then released in some type of occurrence, there is, for lack of a better term, a residue left over in the form of energy waves. The law of conservation of energy states that energy cannot be created or destroyed. It can only change form. This is just one example of how the physics world and the psychic world are linked."

"That's wonderful, but I still don't see—"

"Think of it like a TV signal. The energy wave carries the imprint of the event until it's picked up by a receiver. In this case, you."

Judy gave David a strange look, and he said lamely, "Well, it's a theory."

"If so," Judy said, "that explains the how, not the why."

David sat silently for a moment. Then he said, "You're right. I don't know why you're picking up on these events. Maybe because you know the people involved. I don't know. Amanda feels you have some very strong abilities. Some, I'm sure, are still untapped."

David took in a deep breath, then let it out. "But I really didn't call you down here to talk about theories and speculation. Amanda came to this morning for a brief moment. She spoke only a few words and those words were of you. She wanted me to warn you about some danger. That's all she said."

"Danger?" Judy said. "I'm not in any danger. How could I be in danger because of dreams? They scare me sometimes, but I always get over them. Anyway, I haven't had a dream in days, not since Tuesday."

"Are you sure? Tuesday?"

"Yes. Is there something special about Tuesday?"

"No. I don't think so. Amanda was hospitalized on Wednesday. I was just wondering if—"

"You were just wondering if there was some connection."

"Yes, I was."

Frightened by David's words, Judy quickly concluded their interview. She had to sort out her thoughts; she had to talk to someone she could trust. Fearful of her father's reaction, she headed for O'Brian's, where she was to meet Peter. Maybe he could make some sense of the terrifying mess.

A short while later, Judy sat in the first booth at O'Brian's Arcade pondering her discussion with David Jensen, keeping an eye out for Peter. The last few hours had only served to confuse her more. Confiding in Peter about her dreams had helped before. She wanted to tell him everything David Jensen had told her. But she didn't what to scare him off. The whole situation was too much on the edge. How much more could she take?

When Mona and Suzy appeared at her booth, Judy couldn't honestly say she was glad to see them.

"You should have told us you were going to be here," Suzy said.

"It was a last-minute change."

"Change?" Mona asked, sitting opposite Judy.

"I'm waiting for someone."

"For who?" Suzy asked, sitting down along with Mona.

"Peter," Judy said. With her two friends sitting across the booth hanging on her every word, Judy felt as if she were under interrogation and had just given the wrong answer.

"Look, there's Martin," Mona said and waved him over.

"Don't," Judy said, then started to slide out of the booth.

"What? A party?" Martin said, plopping down next to Judy, pinning her in. "No one invited me. Couldn't stay away from the old hangout?"

"I can live without it."

"She's waiting for—" Mona said.

"It's none of his business."

"Is that any way to talk," Martin said, his eyes moving down a menu, "with all we mean to each other?"

"You mean nothing. I should go."

"No, stay," Mona said. "We haven't really talked in days."

"Yes, please stay," Martin said in a sickly sweet voice. Martin set the menu down, then folded his hands. "Now what have you been up to—or down to—whatever the case?"

Martin's eyes opened wide as he spotted Peter sneaking a peek in through the glass of the main door. His mind started to race. Then he came up with an idea. He slipped his arm to the top of the booth just behind Judy's shoulders, careful not to really touch her. And when Peter had a clear view of them sitting together, Martin grabbed Judy and kissed her hard on the lips.

Judy, caught off guard, delayed for a split second

before she tried to push Martin away. That split second was all Martin wanted. After witnessing the kiss, Peter turned around and left.

Judy broke Martin's grasp with a slap, and the arcade echoed with the sound of her hand across Martin's face.

"Asshole! Let me out," she yelled at Martin when she saw Peter leaving. But he didn't move until she pounded her fist against his arm. "Let me out now!"

"OK, OK." Martin stood up, and Judy stormed out of the booth.

Martin heard the other teens laughing, but he didn't care. He was too impressed with his own sense of timing.

Desperately, Judy ran through the door leading outside, but Peter was nowhere to be found.

Later that night, an insistent tapping at Mrs. Romun's window woke the woman as she slept in front of her television set. The recliner had proved to be too comfortable, and she had slept through her favorite eight o'clock show, and through the next hour as well. Now the local news was on.

Tap, tap, tap.

Her head snapped toward the windows; her eyes shifted back and forth. But she couldn't determine the source of the noise.

"I hear you," she whispered. "You little bastards. I hear you."

She darted to one window, but only saw her reflection angrily staring back at her. Then the tapping came from the front door.

From the top drawer of her desk, she pulled a .38-caliber double-action revolver and released the safety. "You thought I was bluffing. Now I've got you."

Mrs. Romun tore open the door, expecting to be face-to-face with the trespasser, but there was no one there. She hunched forward, her eyes squinting to make out any images in the darkness. Off to her side, something moved, and she pulled the gun's trigger. The old woman had never fired a gun before, so the recoil came as a surprise and spoiled what aim she had. The whole experience stunned her for a moment. Before she could recover, the gun was ripped from her hand.

"You get away from me!" Mrs. Romun rushed back into her house, slamming the door behind her. She pressed her heavy body against the door to hold it shut, then put her ear up to the wood and carefully listened.

Hearing nothing she backed slowly away from the door and ran to her phone to call for help. When the emergency operator answered, Mrs. Romun pleaded, "Please come, I'm—"

Her eyes widened as she saw that her patio door was open.

"Please, help me," she whispered. In the earpiece she heard an eerie whine, then a double click. "Hello, is anyone there?"

A motion drew her attention away from the dead phone. The frame pictures on the walls began to sway back and forth. The collector plates in the oak curio cabinet began to rattle on their brass stands. The television set had nothing on but static.

Suddenly, the frames banged against the plaster, pulled out their hooks and went crashing to the floor. The curio cabinet was jumping and shaking. The plates flew around inside, slamming against each other and breaking into small pieces.

A hand grabbed Mrs. Romun's shoulder, but she

broke free and went screaming toward the front door. As she passed the TV, the picture tube imploded. Electric sparks flew in all directions, and a large puff of gray smoke puffed to the ceiling.

The woman yanked and tugged at the knob, finally tearing the door open. She saw the flashing light of squad cars coming toward her and ran down to the street. As the lead car stopped, Mrs. Romun raced to its door.

"You have to help me!" she yelled. "Something's in my house. Plates are breaking."

The officer stepped out of his car. "Please be calm, ma'am. I can't understand you. Did someone shoot at you?"

"My TV blew up," she said in a fit of hysterics. "The pictures fell."

"Ma'am you have to calm yourself. I can't help you if you don't relax a little."

"Whatcha you got," the other officer said, stepping around his squad car.

"I'm not sure."

Mrs. Romun pulled at the officer's shirt, tearing his pocket. "In my house . . . in my house . . . something. . . ." Mrs. Romun fainted.

The officer's reflexes kicked in and he grabbed Mrs. Romun. Her weight and body shape made it almost impossible for him to get a good hold. As she started to slip from his grasp, he took a deep breath and tried, to no avail, to hoist her up. "You want to help me here?" he pleaded with the other officer.

Mark Turner stood with the crowd around the flashing lights of the squad cars. He wasn't sure what had brought him to that street on the opposite side of town. Guilt? Fear? Lately, he couldn't tell the difference between the two. As the crowd gawked at the officers rushing in and out of the house, Mark's gaze was fixed on the house next door. He had been out driving simply to clear his mind, then found himself turning down the street where Bobby Cowal had lived. The lights caught his eye several blocks away, and something inside compelled him to stop.

Behind the long strips of yellow barrier tape, Mark listened as an elderly pair of women chatted about the attack. He didn't know of whom they spoke, but he thought the conversation seemed callous. It reminded him a little of the way Martin talked about Karl and Ox—cold with no feeling.

Mark's eyes fell to the ground. He felt the lack of sleep catching up with him. Then something by the bushes flashed in the spinning police lights. Something made of shiny metal.

He watched the officers controlling the crowds, holding back the curious. In the commotion, Mark slipped under the barrier tape. He knelt down and moved the lower branch of the bush.

Upon seeing the shining stainless-steel barrel, the black bone grip, Mark had to fight back the urge to pick up the .38-caliber revolver. First, he made sure he was unobserved. He knew the cops would want the weapon, but so did he. He needed protection. Certain he was in the clear, Mark quickly reached down and grabbed the weapon. Its weight surprised him. It didn't look as heavy as it was. He took the gun by the handle and carefully tucked it under his coat, a little afraid it would go off. Then he stood up slowly and scampered back to the long yellow ribbon.

"Hey, you!" a police officer yelled from behind

him and Mark stopped dead in his tracks. "Sorry, son, you'll have to stay on the other side of the line."

Even as the officer was shooing Mark away, the gun starting to slip out of place. Terrified, Mark held his ground until he could get a better grip on the gun.

"Come on. Get on the other side," the officer said, lifting the ribbon enough and Mark passed beneath, praying he wouldn't drop the gun. "I know it's tough to resist the excitement, but we have to start combing the area. You can watch from the sidewalk."

Without a backward glance, the cop trotted away, disappearing into Mrs. Romun's house. For his part, Mark grasped the gun firmly and hurried away. He had protection. He was going to escape his friends' fate. Mark rushed off so quickly that he didn't notice the dark shape dogging his every step.

"I'm home," Peter called out later that night. He kicked off his shoes before going to the kitchen. He found his mother sitting at the table drinking coffee with both hands wrapped tightly around the mug.

"What's going on. What's with the yellow police ribbon on old lady Romun's front yard and all the cops running in and out of her house?"

"It's been like that for an hour now. They think it was a burglar."

"Burglar? What would she have that anyone would want to steal?"

"I don't know," Sharon said, a slight tremor in her voice.

"They get anything?"

"I don't know." Her words quavered more.

"Mom? You OK?"

"I'll be fine. They had to call an ambulance to get her. I guess whoever broke into her house tore it up pretty bad."

"I don't think Mrs. Romun's worth getting so worked up over."

"It's not that." She leaned over and gave Peter a hug. "It could have been our house. It could have been me or you being taken away in an ambulance."

"I wasn't even home."

"That's not the point. Some stranger can just enter our home and. . . ."

"Mom, it's OK. You're safe. I'm safe."

"I don't know what safe is anymore. I always thought Bobby would be safe."

"That's different," Peter said, silently blaming himself for his failure to protect Bobby.

"Would you please get me a tissue?" Sharon said, pointing to a box on the counter.

"Sure." He got up from his chair and yanked a tissue from the box.

"How'd that happen?" Sharon asked when she noticed a small triangular tear on the shoulder of Peter's shirt.

"What?" Peter asked.

"Your shirt—it's torn on the shoulder."

"It's nothing. I must have caught it on something." Peter took the coffeepot and refilled his mother's cup.

"Thank you," she said.

"It'll be all right. Mrs. Romun will be back in a couple of days and be her own crab butt self again."

"Peter!" Sharon said, forcing back a tiny smile.

"What?"

Sharon took a sip of her rewarmed coffee. "Before I forget again," she said, "Judy stopped by."

"Really," Peter said, walking to the refrigerator. He opened it and pulled out a can of soda.

"She said something about a misunderstanding."

"There was no misunderstanding," Peter replied, and he meant it.

Chapter Twenty-three

In the early afternoon of the next day, a knock sounded at the front door of the Cowal house. Peter heard the sound from the kitchen and headed to the front of the house, where he peeked out the window to see Judy standing on the porch. She did look good, but Peter was still angry.

After Judy knocked again, she glanced over and saw Peter through the window. "Peter, let me in. I'm not leaving. I mean it, Peter. I'll stay here until you talk to me."

The door opened.

"What?" Peter said when he opened the door after a moment's deliberation.

"Nice to see you too. Can I please come in?"

She looked so pretty, Peter thought he would burst. "Why?"

"I want to explain about last night. I stopped by after you left, and your mother told me you hadn't got back yet."

"She told me. Why'd you stop by? To tell me you

302

and Martin are back together."

"No. We had a date, remember?"

"It looked different from where I was standing."

"You missed the best part. The part when I back-handed the creep."

"You did?"

"Yes, I did. Can I please come in?"

"Sure." Peter felt a little foolish. But as he held open the door, Judy walked through and kissed him on the lips.

"I only wanted to meet you at O'Brian's because I hoped it would save us some time. I . . . I had an errand to run. I didn't think that jerk would be there." Judy put her arms around Peter's neck and kissed him again. "I'm sorry. And I missed you."

"Don't be sorry. I'm a jerk," Peter said.

"Why?"

"I thought—"

"Shhhh." Judy covered his mouth with her finger. "It's over now. You know, I just thought of something. We're alone aren't we?" She smiled teasingly. One arm still around his neck, she pulled his face close to hers. "Show me your room."

"Yes, but—"

She pulled herself closer to his body, resting her head on his shoulders. He could feel her breasts against his chest, which made him feel pleasantly uncomfortable.

"Yes, but," he said sadly, "my mother will be back anytime now."

Judy gazed up at him with her dark brown eyes.

"Sorry," Peter said, and they both laughed. "You want something to drink?"

"Sure. Anything diet. I just realized," Judy said, looking around the kitchen, "this is the same house we played in when we were little."

"Yep, the very same."

"What's this?" Judy said, pointing at a crayon drawing hanging on the refrigerator door.

"Bobby drew it. A family portrait of sorts. It was in his room, but I moved it down here. He was very proud of it."

"Oh, I see. That must be you." She giggled.

"Don't laugh. I think it does look like me. A little."

"That's your mother," Judy said. "Is that your father?"

"No. That's Georgie. Bobby's imaginary friend."

Judy's face lost all expression. "What was his name?"

"Georgie. Why?"

"When I was a little girl, I had an imaginary friend named Georgie. The first time we met, I told you about him. Remember?"

Peter shrugged. "You want some ice? This pop is still a little warm."

"That's weird. I haven't thought of him in years. I remember him as being so real. But my parents told me he wasn't. I guess I must've believed them because I told him that and he went away. I remember crying. Isn't that silly?" When Peter's face turned cold, Judy said, "Well, I thought it was silly."

"What?" Peter said, breaking his concentration. "Sorry."

"Don't you think it's strange that Bobby and I both had an imaginary friend with the same name?"

"I'm sure it's just a coincidence," Peter snapped. "Can we just drop it."

"Yeah," Judy said cautiously. "Sure."

"I'm sorry," Peter said. "It's just when I think about Bobby I get. . . ."

"Peter, you home?" his mother called from the front door.

"Yeah, Mom. I'm in the kitchen."

"Come help me with these bags," Sharon said. "There was a sale on underwear, so I picked you up a couple pair."

"Mom!" Peter said, rushing to stop her from embarrassing him anymore.

"What?" Then she saw Judy coming from the kitchen. "Oh. . . ."

"Hi, Mrs. Cowal."

"Hi, Judy," Sharon said, and Peter prayed she wouldn't say or do anything more to embarrass him. To his regret, his prayer went unanswered. For, a moment later, Sharon pulled the briefs from her shopping bag and handed them to him. "Here, run these up to your room."

"Mom!" Peter said. He took Judy by the hand and headed out the door before more damage was done. "I'll do it later. We have to go."

"It was nice seeing you," Judy said, as she was pulled past Sharon and out of the house.

The night air whistled through the empty bleachers. Some of the loose boards rattled and banged. Clouds were moving out to the west, and the warm June night would be clear and starry. With the exception of the custodial staff, the stadium had been empty since the last baseball game, but that night it had two visitors.

"I'm really scared," Mark said, taking another hard drink from his beer bottle, then wiping his mouth on his sleeve. "Something's happening to us."

"Shut up," Martin said. "You sound like a baby."

"You shut up!" Mark yelled back. "You think you're really tough, don't you?"

"Tough enough."

"Ox was pretty tough," Mark said. "It didn't do him much good."

"The cops said that was an accident," Martin said, twisting the top from his second beer.

"Sure, an accident," Mark said, after another sip of beer. "Ox just happened to drop a hundred pounds of weights on his head, splattering his brains all over the floor. You bet! Ox could clear that weight no problem. And what about Karl? He's dead too. Can't you see there's something weird going on? Someone's out to kill us—kill us all!"

Martin laughed and took another swallow of beer, which infuriated Mark.

"Aren't you listening? Don't you get it? Don't you even care?"

"I'm listening," Martin said. "I'm listening to an idiot scared out of his mind. And, no, I don't care."

"I am scared," Mark said, putting his hand in his jacket pocket. "That's why I've got this." He pulled out and displayed the revolver.

"Where in the hell did you get that?" Martin said.

"That's my business."

"What in the hell do you plan to do with that," Martin said, "besides blow your foot off?"

"I been thinking about it all. I figured since only the four of us knew what happened at Crazy Man's Bluff and two are dead and I know I didn't kill 'em—that leaves one. Doesn't it?"

"You're crazy."

"I don't think so." Mark pointed the gun at Martin's head, his finger to the trigger. The hammer came back slowly. "Admit it, Martin. You killed them."

"Stop fooling around, Turner," Martin said. "You're crazy. I didn't kill anyone."

"Who else would? I figure I'll be the next die." The hammer came closer to its release. "But I'm not going to let that happen. Tell me you killed Ox and Karl and maybe, just maybe, I won't pull the trigger."

"No, I won't tell you that. I already told you I didn't kill them. They were my friends too!" Martin yelled.

"I doubt if you understand the word." Mark's finger came all the way back on the trigger, the hammer released.

Martin sprang up from his seat and leaped to the side. Mark laughed when the gun didn't fire. "Scared now, tough guy?"

"Asshole!" Martin said, trying to catch his own breath.

"You should have seen your face," Mark said, still laughing. "Bet you unloaded in your pants."

"You asshole!" Martin yelled. "What if it was loaded?"

"Relax, I took the bullets out." Mark reached in the other pocket and produced four bullets.

"That's it," Martin said, "I've had enough of you. I'm getting the hell out of here." Martin stomped off. "You're lucky I don't kick your ass for doing something so stupid."

Mark laughed to himself. Martin was the lucky one, and Mark wouldn't give him a second warning. If Mark felt the least bit threatened, the gun would be loaded next time.

Just outside the Fulton city limits, sounds of a car engine cut the night air. The full moon shone down, illuminating the lakeshore, and the car's headlights lit up the road. Peter carefully steered Judy's Probe down the bumpy stretch while her arms were wrapped tightly around his torso. They had spent the rest of the day together, and even though night had come, it seemed as if only moments had passed since Judy had arrived on Peter's doorstep.

Peter stopped the car at the edge of the road, only a short walk from the water's edge. Peter grabbed a blanket from the backseat and Judy took Peter by the hand. A few feet from the lake, Peter spread the blanket out on a strip of grass, and they sat close together on the blanket, the moon reflecting in the water.

"You're the first person I've ever brought here," Peter said.

"Really?"

"Not even Bobby," Peter said. "I kept this place to myself. Sort of my own private place to escape to."

"What do you have to escape from?"

"You'd be surprised. It's tough being a brain sometimes. People expect so much from me."

"Yeah, but look at you. Next fall, Ohio State on a full scholarship." She ran her fingers through his hair.

"You'll be going, too," Peter said.

"Yes, with my dad paying the bills. It's not the same. Don't get me wrong. I really appreciate my father doing it, and I know he's very happy to be able to send me. But to get there on your own is a real accomplishment."

"Hey," Peter said, bending over to kiss her, "you do what you have to."

Judy broke away from their kiss. "Let's go swimming!"

Peter saw a glimmer in her eye. "We don't have our swimsuits."

"Who needs suits?" she said, taking off the open blouse that covered her blue tee-shirt.

"Judy!" Peter said, thinking she couldn't be serious.

"Chicken?" she said jokingly and pulled the blue shirt over her head, releasing her firm round breasts.

Even through it was dark, Peter could still see her clearly. While Judy stood up and kicked off her shoes, he couldn't take his eyes off her. He unbuttoned his shirt and forced himself to maintain control of his erection as she stripped off her white cotton shorts. Her white panties seemed to glow in the moonlight.

"Will you hurry up?" She was standing by the water's edge, covered only by her small, silky panties. Peter remained silent and took off his sneakers and socks, jeans and underwear, then got to his feet. He felt a little foolish standing naked on the shore.

"You ready?" Judy said as she removed her final piece of clothing. Her naked skin against the backdrop of water made Peter think he was going to lose control and, as a result, become very embarrassed. Judy turned and ran into the water, calling out to Peter to follow. He smiled and chased after her.

They splashed each other and played in the water and kissed a few times. Peter couldn't help thinking how beautiful she looked with her long hair slicked back, dripping wet with water.

"What was that?" she said, standing still. Then, without warning, Judy's head disappeared under the water.

Peter waited for her to come to the surface to splash her a good one. But she did not come up. He waited a moment, then called, "Judy? Judy!"

Peter felt a surge of water behind him; then two

arms grabbed him around the shoulders, pulling him under. He twisted his shoulder to break the grip of his captor. When he swam up, breaking the plane of the water, Judy was there laughing. "I got you good," she said.

"Oh, yeah?" He grabbed her and dunked her under the water. She came up and continued to laugh. She wrapped her arms around his neck to prevent him from submerging her again. Then their lips met once more as they fell into a tight embrace. Their tongues touched, entangled in their passions. Peter felt her soft breasts against his chest, and her legs wrap around him under the water. His excitement could no longer be held back as he slipped gently inside her, the contrast of the cool water and the warmth of their flesh adding to their excitement.

Farther along the shore of Myer's Lake, Suzy and Mark had been parked for about 30 minutes next to a small inlet that fed the lake. They hadn't wasted a moment getting out of their clothes and into each others' arms. After displaying their affection, they lay close to each other, Mark curling Suzy's hair around his finger as she snuggled for his warmth.

"What's so funny?" Suzy asked, when Mark let out a small laugh.

"Nothing, really. I was just remembering the look on Martin's face."

"Martin? You're with me—like this—and you're thinking of Martin."

"Sorry." He kissed her forehead, then forced back another laugh.

"Do you love me?" she asked.

"What kind of question is that?"

"A simple question. Do you love me?"

"You're my girl, aren't you?"

"You've had other girls."

Mark knew where her words were heading, so he decided to head Suzy off. "Yes, I love you."

"No, you don't," Suzy said, then laughed.

"You're so funny," Mark said sarcastically.

"Funny or fun?" she said, her finger running lightly across his chest.

"Well, I don't know. . . ."

"Oh, yeah?" She began kissing his chest, then continued past his sternum, down to his hip. Finally, her tongue probed and teased his thighs.

"This may be a bad time to bring this up," Mark said, opening the door and jumping out, "but I've got to go pretty bad. Sorry."

"Don't go without your pants," she said, reaching to the floor to retrieve his jeans. "What if someone comes. . . ."

Suzy could see for a good ten feet, but Mark was nowhere in sight. A bush rustled on the other side of the car, but Suzy ignored it. Suddenly, the car door behind Suzy was yanked open, and she screamed.

"Nice body!" Mark yelled.

After throwing the pair of jeans at him and hitting him square in the face. Suzy said, "That wasn't funny!"

"Yes," Mark said, through his laughter. "Yes, it was. What a good joke."

Suzy folded her arms, covering her chest, and started to sulk. "Not a very funny one."

"You're right." Mark knew what he had to say if he wanted any more sex that night. "I'm sorry. It was stupid."

"Sometimes, I think you're crazy."

"I am," he said, "crazy about you."

When she smiled, Mark knew he was back in, or at least he could be back in.

"Get in here," she said.

"I wasn't kidding about having to go. I really do."

"OK, but make it quick. And put your pants on."

Mark covered himself with his jeans and started for the closest tree. He stopped and opened the car door. Picking his jacket up, he felt the reassuring weight in the inside pocket. "Forgot my jacket."

"Hurry back," Suzy said as Mark walked off to the tree.

Suzy lay back on the car seat, the cool air pouring over her bare skin. She closed her eyes, waiting for Mark's return. It wasn't long before those feelings she thought Mark had so wonderfully satisfied came back. With her eyes closed, she could almost feel his weight on top of her. The feeling intensified.

She sat up and peered out at Mark. He was quick when it came to those nature calls. She struck the sexiest pose she could think of. She wanted Mark back in the mood the moment he returned. He would open the door, the interior light would come on, and there she would be, waiting.

A slight distance from the car, Mark undid his pants to relieve himself. The sound of a twig snapping made him turn quickly, and he urinated on his foot.

"Shit." Even as he tried to shake his foot dry, another twig snapped.

"Suzy?" he called out. "Suzy? If this is how you think you're going to get back at me for scaring you, it's not going to work.

"Suzy?" he said when there was no response. At the same time, he pulled the gun from his jacket. He opened the cylinder, then reached in his outside jacket pocket for the bullets. He moved quickly, but his hands shook. Mark started to load the first bullet, but missed the chamber and his hand slipped forward dropping all the bullets.

As he got on his hands and knees and rifled through the sticks and leaves for the bullets, another snap came close.

The moonlight shone off something. Mark grabbed at it, hoping it wasn't a piece of glass or junk metal. He gasped as his touch told him he had found one of the lost bullets. He shoved the bullet in the chamber and snapped closed the cylinder. Then he turned and fired.

A sharp sound woke Suzy. She didn't know how long she had been asleep. A minute? Ten minutes? She sat up, but Mark was nowhere in sight. Her romantic feeling had been replaced by worry, which would turn to anger if Mark's disappearance was another joke. For the next two minutes, she stared off in the direction Mark had gone. She squinted, trying to penetrate the darkness, hoping to see Mark emerging from the trees.

She waited one more minute, then reached over and grabbed Mark's shirt, which was long enough to cover her body. She didn't want to be caught naked if Mark had been found by a Fulton cop patrolling the roads around the lake. That had happened to one of her girlfriends, and the ribbing didn't stop for some time.

She got out of the car, but the pointed twigs and sharp rocks told her she needed her shoes. After protecting her feet, she headed out toward the same thicket of bushes where Mark had disappeared to relieve himself.

"Mark," she called out. "Mark, this isn't funny."

No reply. No sound at all. If the police had found Mark, she surely would have heard voices—unless the cops had already taken him back to town. No. Fulton cops wouldn't believe he was out there alone. They would look for his car. Her face blushed as she imagined the officer shining his flashlight into the car where she was—the thought was too embarrassing to continue.

"Mark," she called out again when, with the help of the moonlight, she could make out the back of Mark's head through the leaves of some tall bushes. "What in the hell is taking you so long?"

Mark didn't answer.

"I was getting—shit!" she said when a twig snapped her across the bare leg. A small trickle of blood came from the broken skin and ran down her shin. "Mark, will you come out here?"

Mark didn't move.

Suzy worked her way through the leaves, then tripped over something heavy. She found herself lying across Mark's body. His detached head was mounted on top of a tree stump.

Suzy screamed until she fainted.

A little girl, wearing a white ruffled skirt and matching socks and leather shoes, skipped down the sidewalk and stopped beside a little boy bouncing a large red ball in front of an empty lot. She watched the boy bounce the ball up and down, up and down. The little boy didn't take his eyes off the ball as it bounced. Then he stopped and held the ball with both hands. He stared back at the little girl.

"Hi, Judy. Will you play with me?" he asked.

Judy shrugged her answer.

"We'll have fun. I have a lot of toys." The little boy smiled. "Want to see?"

"Sure," she said timidly.

"They're in my house. Come on."

"Is it far? My father told me not to go far."

"It's not far. It's right here," he said, pointing to the empty lot.

Judy turned her head and saw a large house standing in the lot.

"I'm not supposed to go in a stranger's house," she said.

"I'm not a stranger. I'm your friend. We've been together for a long time. Come see my toys."

The little boy took Judy by the hand. "Come see."

The sidewalk to the house was patterned with dirt-filled cracks. Judy stepped carefully, wanting to keep her white shoes clean. When the two children reached the front porch, the little boy opened the door. Judy looked in, but she could see nothing in the darkness.

He tugged her arm, wanting her to continue. Judy followed him through the doorway into a large hall. Her eyes quickly grew accustomed to the darkness. The hallway had several closed doors and a long winding staircase leading to the second floor. The sound of the door slamming shut behind her made her jump.

"Let's play a game," he said.

"What should we play?"

"I know! I know! Let's play hide and seek." A big grin appeared on his face as he ran off. "You're it!"

She had no time to voice an objection. She would just leave and not play his stupid game.

"You can't find me," the little boy's voice echoed through the hall. "Nah. Nah. You can't find me! You're scared."

"No, I'm not," she called out, knowing deep inside she was a little.

She searched the rooms off the hall. First a room with a large desk and lamp. He was not there. Then she searched the kitchen. Nothing. Next she tried the living room.

Judy heard a loud sound coming from the main hall—the sound of something falling down the stairs. She ran from the living room to the foot of the stairs The boy's red ball bounced down the stairs. It made a loud thump as it hit each step. Judy watched as the ball came down the stairs. The ball seemed to be moving in slow motion as it thumped against each step.

When the ball landed at her feet, Judy felt something wet soak into her white socks. She looked down at the ball lying still before her. She screamed as she saw the eyes of a severed head staring up at her, a trickle of blood coming from the mouth. Blood spilled from the torn tissue of the neck and pooled around her shoes, coloring them murky red. The blood seeped over the rims of her shoes and the white cotton drank in the fluid.

"Come and play, Judy. Come and play."

Judy didn't move. Her eyes scanned the room for the little boy.

"He was no fun," the boy's voice said. *"He didn't want to play any of my games."*

Judy turned and ran for the door. She grabbed the knob, but the door wouldn't open. She pulled the door with all her strength.

"Play with me," the voice said.

She tugged at the door once more. But her hands slipped off because blood on them made the knob too slick to hold.

"I know a good game to play."

"I don't want to play! I want to go home!" Her yell turned to a sob. *The front of her white dress was covered in blood. "I just want to go home."*

"Play with me, Judy! Play with me!"

"Judy? Judy, wake up," Peter said, gently shaking her. He couldn't imagine why she was screaming. Then, her eyes opened, but she kept screaming. "Judy, it's OK."

"Peter?" She wrapped her arms around him and pulled him close.

"Yeah, it's me. We fell asleep on the blanket."

"Oh, Peter," she said. She felt his bare chest touching her and realized they were both still naked.

"Must've been one bad dream," Peter said.

"They're getting worse. They start out normal, but then . . . then. . . ." She sobbed on Peter's shoulder.

"Don't worry. They're just dreams."

"No, they're not. I can't explain it, but they're not just dreams. That little boy. He makes me play games with him. Terrible games."

As they started to dress, Judy told Peter about the dream. It felt good to tell him and not keep it bottled up inside. She trusted Peter.

"You'll need this," he said, handing Judy her blue shirt while listening to her talk.

"Dr. Colins was trying to help me," Judy said, passing Peter his pants, "but now she's in the hospital. Nobody knows what's wrong with her."

Once dressed, Peter and Judy began their walk to the car. "Peter, I'm so scared." She stopped and hugged Peter again, burying her head against his chest.

"It'll be OK," Peter said, but his face had a blank expression. "I'd better get you home. Believe me, you have nothing to worry about."

Chapter Twenty-four

The following day, Peter stretched out on his bed, his head resting on folded arms, his white-stockinged feet dangling off the end. There was still a good hour before he and his mother would have to leave for the graduation services. After years of working hard at his studies, doing extra work to get better grades, he thought he would have been more excited about the afternoon's event. But his thoughts were of Judy and the night before. He wondered if she could tell it had been his first time. He wished he had told her, but hadn't known how to bring up the subject.

The noon sun poured through the open window along with light gusts of fresh early summer air. The room was still except for the slight motion of the curtains. Peter couldn't stop thinking about Judy, the lake, and her dreams until a loud thud came from his closed bedroom door. The startling sound caused Peter to jerk with such force that he felt a twinge in his right shoulder.

"Mom?" Peter called out, sitting up, rubbing his

sore muscle. When he heard the knock again, Peter put his feet to the hardwood floor.

"Who's there?" His mother would have entered by now. Then, he thought that it might be Judy playing a joke.

"Oh, who could it be?" he said in a sarcastic voice. He waited a moment to see if she would say something. When she didn't, Peter approached the door and asked, "Did my mom let you in? Judy, I know it's you."

Peter pulled the door open only to find an empty hall. Then something hit his feet and he jumped back.

A dirt-covered softball rolled into his room. Peter lifted it off the floor. He wiped off some of the dirt. Under the grime, Peter found one word written in black marker: *Bobby*.

Too stunned to move, Peter stared at the ball he thought had been buried with his brother. How in the world had it gotten there?

When his mother called to him, he quickly hid the ball. He didn't want to upset her. He'd solve the mystery later.

"Caesar," Judy called out, carrying the cat's red bowl, which was filled to the top with food. She walked around the side of the house, shaking each bush. "You hungry, boy? I've got your favorite— liver-and-chicken flavor. Yum, yum."

She moved around to the back of the house, but there was no sign of the tomcat. "Caesar, where are you?"

"Judy," Roger said, hanging half out the back door. "You almost ready?"

"Yeah, I thought I'd see if Caesar would come around for some food. I haven't seen him for days."

"He's probably found himself a new girlfriend. He'll be back when he gets hungry enough. Leave his food."

"I guess so." Judy put the food by the door as she entered the house.

"Jessica's doing her finally touch-ups," Roger said. "We'll be leaving in a few minutes."

The ride in Roger's white Lincoln Town Car was not a quiet one. The argument began almost the very moment the car pulled out of the driveway.

"It's too bad," Jessica said, "you decided not to have a graduation party. We could have invited all our friends. It would have been so wonderful."

"Wonderful for you maybe," Judy replied. "Not me. I didn't feel like entertaining your friends."

"I'm sure the Welths will be having a lovely affair. And don't you worry. Your father and I will understand if you want to leave us after the ceremony and go to Martin's."

"Obviously, you don't understand. I'm not seeing Martin anymore."

"You remember, darling," Roger said, trying to help his daughter. "Judy is seeing Peter now."

"Peter? Peter who? Do we know his family?"

"Peter Cowal," Judy said.

Jessica repeated Peter's name silently. She tried to remember where she had heard the name; then her eyes opened wide. "The boy at the house the other day? I should say not. What are you doing dating someone like the Cowal boy? The youngest is crazy, isn't he?"

"Jessica! Peter's brother has—had Down's syndrome. He wasn't crazy."

"What do you mean had? Was he cured?"

"No," Roger said, "the poor boy is dead. Remember, Jessica? It was in the paper."

"I don't waste my time on such grisly things,"
Jessica said. "Besides, I'm sure he's much better off."

"Jessica!" Roger said.

"I just meant—"

"Jessica!" Judy said, "That was the cruelest thing
you've ever said."

Although Jessica tried to keep up a conversation,
Judy refused to answer her, and Roger only responded
with short answers. By the time they arrived at the
stadium, no one was in the mood to celebrate.

The weather that day couldn't have cooperated more
for the Fulton High graduation ceremony. Rows of
folding chairs filled a portion of the stadium field.
Up front was a moveable stage draped with a
blue-and-white canopy. On top of the stage stood
the podium and several more chairs. Both the country
and state flags graced both ends of the stage. Hanging
over head, suspended between two steel poles, was a
large congratulatory banner.

But the sunshine and the cool breeze were marred
by the two enlarged photos of Karl Warner and Gary
Oxten that stood on stage. Thoughts for the two dead
classmates tinged the joyful occasion with a touch of
sorrow.

"I'm sure she didn't mean to sound so heartless,"
Roger told Judy as they walked in to the stadium.

"Yeah, look at her." Judy's eyes moved to Jessica
standing up by the stage with a group of well-dressed
women and men. She gabbed away as if she had
won the lottery. "Those aren't your friends, Daddy.
They're her friends. I wish we could go back to the
way we used to be. She's always trying to change me
and you."

"I know one thing that hasn't changed." Roger

kissed his daughter's cheek. "I'm very proud of you, and I know your mother would be too."

"I like to think she is," Judy said.

"Let's find our seats," Jessica said as she joined them. "Come on, Roger. Don't dawdle. I have the most interesting news."

Roger winked at Judy, who waved as he left her. "We'll see you later."

"Did you hear about Suzy?" Mona said, coming up behind Judy. "She's in the hospital in shock or something."

"Who told you that?" Judy asked.

"Her father. I called this morning to find out what color dress she was wearing." Mona repeated her conversation with Suzy's father. She seemed not to take a single breath between words. "Mrs. Kendell has been with Suzy since last night. I'm sure Mr. Kendell would be there too, but someone has to look after Suzy's little sister Annie."

"Yeah," Judy said, although she hardly realized she had spoken. Mona's words kept fading out, becoming lost in Judy's memory of a bouncing ball.

"Judy," Mona said, shaking her arm, "have you seen Mark at all?"

Judy tensed for a moment. "No, I haven't."

"I figured as much."

"Did Mr. Kendell say something about Mark?"

"No, not really. I guess the cops are keeping it quiet. They didn't tell Suzy's parents anything, except she was found wandering alone out on Clark Road. But I don't think it can be anything good. Why else wouldn't the police say what happened? You feeling OK?"

"I just need to sit down." Judy forced a smile as her classmates passed by. Some greeted her by name, and she returned the greeting with as much pleasantry as she could muster. When she spotted Peter and his mother entering the stadium, Judy leaped up from her chair and walked as fast as she could without looking like she was running. "Hello, Mrs. Cowal."

"Hi, Judy. Isn't this exciting? You both have worked very hard to get here."

"Yes, ma'am," Judy said. "Peter, can I talk to you?"

"I'll find myself a seat," Sharon said, excusing herself.

"What's up?"

Judy glanced around, making sure she would not be overheard. "It's happening again."

"What?"

"The dream I had last night. I think Mark Turner is dead."

"It was just a dream," Peter said.

"Haven't you been listening to me? I told you about Ox and Karl. I thought you understood. I thought I could count on you." Judy turned and began to sob.

"You can, Judy. You can." Peter put his hand on her shoulder.

First, the ball appeared—then, Judy breaking down. Graduation day was quite different from the way Peter had imagined it. He could only wonder what would happen next.

David sat next to Amanda's hospital bed. The room's silence was displaced ever so slightly by her shallow breathing. He gently held her hand and wished he could break through to her. But all he could do was watch her still form and pray.

For Amanda, there was only a void of nothing, neither dark nor light, surrounding her. But in the emptiness, there was awareness, and Amanda reached out to an unknown entity that summoned her.

"I don't understand you," she shouted into the void. "Where are you? I can't see you."

The murmuring came from the distance, and she tried to go toward the muffled sound.

"I'm coming. I'm coming. Wait for me. Don't go. What are you trying to say?"

As suddenly as it appeared, the mysterious entity disappeared, and Amanda was alone again.

Sitting alongside her bed, David nodded into a light doze, unaware of the mental struggle within his comatose friend.

Chapter Twenty-five

It was Thursday afternoon and Judy felt terrific. Four nights had gone by without any dreams, without the little boy, without the games. Graduation had come and gone, and she would put the past behind her, where it belonged. All she wanted was to spend a wonderful summer with Peter.

"Don't ask how I got the tickets, Peter," Judy said into the phone. "I just got them. . . . All right. . . . Seven will be great. . . . No, really, tomorrow is my treat. . . . No, I said my treat. . . . Me too. OK, bye."

"I hope you weren't making *those* plans for tomorrow night," said Jessica, whose arrival in the kitchen had made Judy cut her conversation short.

"That's none of your business."

"I'm afraid it is. We all have an obligation at the club."

Judy remembered the dance then, but she held firm to her plans. "I'm not going."

Jessica glared at her. "I don't understand."

"What's there to understand? I'm not going to a

stuffy dance with a lot of loudmouths bragging about how much money they have, made, or spent. I'm not going."

"You listen here, young lady. This is an anniversary dance at your father's club. You're not going to embarrass me or your father by not coming with us. I will not be pelted with questions if you're not there. You're going." Jessica's tone changed as if she had good news. "Martin Welth will be there."

"Another good reason why I'm not going."

"It will give the two of you a chance to make up. Martin's going to make a lot of himself," Jessica said. "After college, he'll have a good job in his father's business. You could do a lot worse. You need to think about your future."

"I'm not interested in Martin, his father, or his father's business. They can all go to hell."

"Judy! I don't want to hear that kind of language in this house. Wait until your father gets home."

"Wait until your father gets home," Judy said, mocking Jessica's words. "Please! I can't believe you said that. That's your trouble, Jessica. You think I'm some little girl you can order around." She started toward the stairs.

"Where do you think you're going? We're not through talking."

"We are as far as I'm concerned," Judy said and fled to the sanctuary of her room.

In her hospital bed, Amanda still lay in a coma. In her mind, she continued to float in a vast void. She had no fear of it. And if she had to choose words to describe how she felt, they would be peaceful and strangely safe. She had a sense that the void would protect her, keep her from harm.

A boy's voice suddenly broke the tranquility—the voice that Amanda had heard before. "Please, stop him . . . Georgie . . . hurt."

"Who are you?" Amanda shouted to the boy, who had appeared with her in the void. She couldn't make out the details of his face, but his features seemed different somehow—out of proportion with those of other children. "You've been calling to me. Why?"

"Please help . . . bad things."

Even from her distance, she saw the boy's mouth moving, but very few words escaped. He waved to her to come closer. But it didn't matter how many steps Amanda took; she couldn't get any closer to him.

"How can I help?" she called out in desperation. "I don't understand."

"He don't know . . . bad things . . . Peter . . . Stop Georgie." The boy faded. In the void, a speck of light appeared and floated where the boy had just stood.

"Amanda," a voice said from the speck. It burst forward and grew, surrounding Amanda, engulfing her in white light. "Amanda."

In the light came twists and eddies. Patterns of gray took shape, then quickly turned to swivels of black and white, which became browns and yellows. With each passing moment, more colors sprang free from the swirls. Then the swirling stopped, and the colors formed a soft blurry mass moving in slow motion across her line of vision. Finally, the mass moved faster and become more definite in shape.

"Amanda." As Amanda's eyes focused, she saw David leaning over her, and he said, "Thank God."

Other sounds burst into Amanda's consciousness— a door opening and closing, people rushing back and forth. David's face moved away to be replaced with one Amanda didn't know.

"You gave us all quite a scare," the man said. Another flash of light crossed her right eye, then her left. "Pupil response is good."

"Is he here?" Amanda said, then coughed because her throat hurt with each word.

David's face came back into view. "I'm here, Amanda."

"No." She coughed and tried to sit up. Immediately, she felt someone forcing her back down.

"Please, stay down, Dr. Colins," the man said.

"Listen to the doctors," David said "Stay still."

As she returned to the world of reality, Amanda wondered if the fading images of the boy were nothing but a dream. Soon, as she drifted into a peaceful sleep, she lost even thought.

Not long after her argument with Jessica, Judy was in her bedroom when there was a knock at her door. She didn't hear the knock because of the stereo headphones over her ears. Music had always helped her relax, and lately she needed a lot of assistance to relax.

When her father walked in, Judy removed the headset. "Hi, Daddy."

"Hi, kitten. What's this I hear about you not wanting to go to the dance tomorrow night?"

"I sort of have a date."

"Oh, I see," Roger said, rubbing his chin. "Peter Cowal?"

"Uh-huh."

"But you've known about this dance for a month. It's important to me for my best girl to be there."

"I know and I'm sorry, but can I skip it anyway?"

"I wish it was that simple. Jessica would not let either of us hear the end of it."

"Well, then, can Peter come to the dance?"

"I'm sorry, but it's for members only. You can spend the entire day with him and still go to the dance for me."

It was easy for her to see how important this was to him. "All right, but can we leave Jessica home?"

Roger smirked. "She knows her way to the club."

The elevator stopped on the second floor, and the passengers shifted to make room for a nurse carrying a tray of test tubes. Alex didn't notice her get off on the fifth floor because his mind was trapped on other matters.

The local newspaper had printed nothing about any more deaths, but Alex had learned about Mark Turner purely by chance. Raymond Hursch, the mechanic, had come to his house to return a spare set of garage keys. During their chat, Raymond mentioned a towing job he had done for the police. He thought it was strange because, unlike the many other towing jobs he did, the officers at the scene told him nothing except to move the car. When Raymond was hooking the car up, the lights from his truck shined on the remains of white fingerprint powder on various parts of the gray-blue paint. A day later, the car was picked up by Mark's father.

The lights over the elevator door stopped moving at the number seven. The door opened and Alex stepped out onto the seventh floor of St. Francis Hospital. He had never liked hospitals, especially not that one—the one in which he had recuperated after the local toughs had beaten him when he was a boy. But he had to put his personal feelings aside.

He had returned to the field several times over the last few days to speak with Georgie. He tried pleading, yelling, begging, but all brought the same useless result. He needed the help offered by Amanda Colins after all. She had told him she was in Fulton doing some investigation work for Frank Currie, so he reasoned she would have an office at city hall. He could have called her again at the number she had given him, but he decided it would be better to meet with her face-to-face. At the information desk in the city hall atrium, he found out about Amanda being hospitalized. He hadn't bothered to ask the cause. He knew.

As Alex walked to Amanda's hospital room, Peter came to his mind. Alex had called the boy, leaving messages with his mother. All had gone unanswered. He even went over to the house, hoping to catch Peter there, but with no success.

"Excuse me," Alex said, standing at the threshold of room 713.

David jerked in his chair, the old man's words pulling him from the verge of sleep. "Can I help you?"

"I'm acquainted with Dr. Colins. I was wondering how she is doing."

"Better, I'm glad to say, mister . . . ?"

"Alex Stein." The man made a motion of venturing farther into the room, but then pulled back. "Very good. I won't take any more of your time."

Suddenly recognizing Alex's voice through his grogginess, David bolted from his chair. "There's more, isn't there?"

"I must be going."

"You're the second voice."

"Please, I came to see how the young lady was faring. Nothing more."

"I doubt that," David said bluntly. "What do you know about all this?"

"Nothing really."

David stepped in front of the old man, blocking his progress. "What happened to Amanda?"

"Please, I said I know nothing."

"I don't like calling a person liar, Mr. Stein, but you're lying now. You wouldn't have come down to see Amanda if it was nothing."

"Can't an old man visit a friend?"

"I don't have a problem with that, but I don't think you're a friend. Please, tell me what you know. It could help me prevent whatever happened to Amanda from happening again."

Alex hesitated, but sensing that David wouldn't let him go until he had what he wanted, Alex capitulated.

An hour passed as the two men sat in the lounge, speaking of facts others would think of as fantasy or insanity. The younger, a student and teacher of the paranormal; the older, one who had inexplicable experiences of it. And both men realized that they were powerless against it.

"If you stopped him before—"

"He doesn't trust me. I've betrayed him." Alex rose and walked over to the window. He saw a tiny boy being led by a woman wearing a flowered dress. "Georgie doesn't know me anymore. He doesn't see me as his big brother. He sees an old man. He sees the face of our father when he looks at me. I can do nothing more."

"Why come to see Amanda?"

"Hope, nothing more."

"For what? That Amanda could still help you?"

Alex nodded. "A few nights back another boy was

killed. The Fulton Police are keeping the death out of the papers."

"How can you be sure that Georgie was involved?"

"I just know. It fits Georgie's pattern."

"Maybe the story got pushed back or buried on page thirteen."

"Mr. Jensen, I've lived in this town all my life. When a local boy dies, the story does not get buried on page thirteen."

"I didn't mean to imply—"

"There must have been something very tragic about the boy's death. Someone made a deliberate decision to hold back the information." Alex turned to face David. "I must go."

"Is there nothing else you can do? He is your brother, after all." David paused for a moment. "That didn't come out right. I'm not blaming you."

"I appreciate your concern. And to answer your question, I believe the avenue of a solution through Georgie is closed. But there may be another way."

"Tell me if I can help."

Alex signaled his thanks for the offer, but said, "Again, this is something I must do myself."

David nodded and rose from his chair. "I want to apologize for the way I acted earlier."

"Say no more. You must care for Dr. Colins very much."

As Alex walked down the hall, David couldn't shake his suspicion that there was still something more the old man was holding back.

Chapter Twenty-six

The next day, in the late afternoon, Peter held Judy's hand tightly as they strolled along a dirt trail. The city kept the piece of land in an almost untouched state for nature lovers. The tall, leafy trees, the birds and squirrels, the nearby river—all made it hard to believe that a long track of homes was only a half a block away.

"You have your favorite spot," Judy said. "This is mine."

A thin woman with two small boys walked past the couple. The boy in blue shorts turned around and stuck out his tongue, and his brother laughed.

"But it's so busy here," Peter said. He reached up with his free hand to remove a tiny leaf that had landed in Judy's auburn hair.

"Sometimes it gets like this. It's a public hiking trail, but it's still my favorite place. When I get upset, I can walk here for hours. It calms me down. I love being outside in the fresh air."

"I know what you mean. Bobby and I used to fly

kites on days like this all the time."

"Kites?" Judy said, sounding surprised.

"Hey, these weren't your drugstore buy-'em-and-assemble-'em kites. I designed and built them myself. Bobby loved to help me. He'd get so excited when we got them airborne, and even when we didn't, he still had fun."

"You really miss him, don't you?" Judy said, keeping up with his longer stride.

"Have you heard anything about your friend in the hospital?" Peter asked. He didn't want to talk about Bobby.

"You mean Dr. Colins?"

"Yeah, I guess."

"No, I haven't heard a word. I could call that David Jensen guy, but I haven't."

"How about your dreams? Have they stopped?" Peter asked as they strolled up to the bridge that crossed the river that fed into Myer's Lake. The rapid waters splashed against its banks 20 feet below.

"Here's the part I like the best," Judy said, not answering Peter's question. She didn't want to tell him that she had just had a dream the night before. She didn't want to ruin such a perfect day.

Judy dashed on to the bridge, and Peter followed her to the middle. His footsteps rattled the wooden planks.

Judy stood leaning over the railing of the bridge, looking down at the rushing whitecaps. "I love watching the water go by. And the way it sounds slapping against the rocks—it's so relaxing."

As Peter took a step closer to Judy, he reached out to touch the long hair draped gently down her back. He was close enough to smell the light fragrance of her perfume. When Peter touched her shoulder, Judy lurched forward and fell against the top of the railing. Then she screamed.

Peter grabbed her by the arm, just above the elbow. "Careful! You're gonna fall in!"

"Sorry, I was so caught up in the view."

"No," he said, releasing her arm, "I shouldn't have startled you so."

Judy gave him an embarrassed smile. "My heart's beating a mile a minute."

Peter ran his fingers through her hair and pulled the long strands off her shoulder. "We should go. The sun is starting to set."

"Five more minutes?" She looked at him with her big brown eyes.

"OK," he said and smiled, "five more minutes."

On the way back to town, a few minutes later, Judy rested her head on Peter's shoulder with her arm tucked under his. Her eyes were closed for a moment and the Buick seemed to be flying along the road.

"You tired?" Peter asked.

"No, not really. Just a little headache. Nothing serious." She opened her eyes and peeked up at Peter. He didn't notice her watching. "I hope you didn't mind the change in plans."

"No big deal. I'm with you now."

"I want you to know that I'm only going to the dance for my father."

"I know," Peter said. But when Judy suddenly winced, he asked, "You OK?"

"I'll be fine." She took his hand as a sharp pain shot through her head. Unconsciously, she squeezed down on Peter's fingers.

Soon enough, Peter pulled into the Kilter driveway. His tires squealed slightly as he made the turn. As he stopped the car, Jessica stared at him through the big bay window. He ignored the woman's gaze, dashed around his car, and pulled the door open for Judy. He took her by the arm, helping her to the front door.

"Maybe you need a doctor," he said.

"Don't be silly." Even through her pain, she couldn't hold back a tiny laugh at Peter's concern. She kissed him. "You're so sweet. I just need some aspirin. That's all."

"You sure?" he said, trying to keep the concern out of his voice.

"Yes, I'm sure. I'll still see you tomorrow. Right?"

"Only if you're better."

"I told you that I'll be fine." She kissed him once more and opened the door. "Thanks, Peter."

Peter smiled, but he wasn't sure why she thanked him. "I'll talk to you later. Just get better."

Judy gently nodded her head, then disappeared through the door. Peter stood there for a second until he saw Jessica still staring at him through the window. He had the urge to flip her the finger. Instead, he waved to her, then drove off.

Taking two aspirin and lying down for an hour did wonders for Judy. Now she had finished dressing and headed downstairs. She wore a yellow sleeveless dress with a ruffled knee-high hem line. She had her hair up, except for two strands that framed her face.

"I suppose I'll be chasing the boys away tonight," Roger said as Judy came down the stairs.

"I doubt that Dad."

"You've never been an eighteen-year-old male. I have. I'm not too old to remember what it's like. And with that in mind, I've been thinking." He took a step closer to his daughter and made sure Jessica was out of earshot. "I realize that spending the night at one of your old man's functions isn't your idea of a good time. And I understand. So, how about this? You follow us in your car, stay at the dance for an hour. Then I'll distract Jessica and you can slip out. She'll never notice once she starts talking, and if she does, I'll cover for you."

"Great!" She leaned over and kissed her father on the cheek.

"Don't let Jessica get wind of this, or we'll both be sorry."

"Right."

"Someone sounds hungry," Roger said when a loud meow came from behind the closed front door.

"It's about time he came home."

"Don't let him get you dirty. We'll be leaving in a few minutes." Roger disappeared into the living room.

Judy opened the door and found Caesar busily licking his paws and wiping his face. The cat stopped its grooming and stared up at Judy.

"Where have you been?"

Judy kneeled to pet the cat. He arched his back and hissed, then thrashed out his paw. Judy pulled back her hand, and Caesar just missed scratching her.

"What's the matter, boy? You feeling OK? Come here." She patted her hand against her knee. "Come on, boy. It's OK."

The tomcat cocked his head to the side as if understanding Judy's words. He hesitantly took a step forward, then another, making his way to Judy. He took a short sniff of her hand, meowed, and rubbed the back of his neck against her outstretched hand.

"That's a good boy."

*   *   *

Amanda woke on hearing her name. Her eyes were unfocused, but someone was standing alongside her bed. She thought the person was David until he spoke.

"You have to help Peter."

"You. You are real," she said, recognizing the boy from her dreams.

"Please, help Peter."

"Who are you?" Amanda said softly.

"My name's Bobby Cowal. Will you help my brother?"

"How can I?"

"Georgie. Georgie's going to hurt him. Stop Georgie."

"Do you know where Georgie is?"

"Yes. Please, hurry. I can't stop him by myself."

At that moment, David entered the room carrying a cup of steaming coffee. "You're awake."

Amanda sat up and lowered her feet to the floor. "Get my clothes."

He put his coffee down and rushed to her side. "Amanda you're still in no—"

"Get my clothes now! We have to prevent another death."

"Death? Amanda, listen to yourself. You're hallucinating." He tried to ease her back into the bed. "You need more rest."

"We don't have time to argue. We have to go."

"Let me call a doctor."

"No. I know what I'm doing, David."

David walked to the closet and got Amanda clothes. "I hope you're right."

"We'll stop him," Amanda said. "I promise."

"What?"

"I'm afraid you'll have to drive, David," she said, reaching behind her back, untying the laces of her hospital gown.

"Drive? Where?"

"I'll give you directions as we go."

Even hours after Peter had dropped Judy off, his thoughts were still full of her. He felt there was more to her sudden headache than she let on. He had never seen anyone get so ill so quickly as she did.

Darkness had overcome Fulton and he was on his way to Alex's house. Alex had asked him to go over as soon as possible because he had an emergency and needed Peter's help. Peter hoped it wasn't another water-pipe breakage like the previous summer. Even though Alex kept the house in good condition, the pipes in the walls needed some repair.

"Come in, Peter," Alex said when Peter arrived.

"What's the trouble, Mr. Stein? Should I get the toolbox?" Peter didn't wait for an answer and started toward the garage.

"No, nothing like that." Alex held the door open for Peter. "Please, come in. We must talk."

"All right." He followed Alex to the living room.

"I'm glad we have this chance to speak," Alex said. "I hoped we could have met sooner. You didn't return my calls."

"I've been spending a lot of time with Judy Kilter."

"Well, we're together now."

Something in the man's voice made Peter ask, "Are you OK?"

"Yes, I am, but it's not me I'm worried about. Please, sit."

Peter did as Alex requested. "Now you're starting to make me worry."

Alex didn't respond to the boy's comment. "Look at these clippings."

Peter picked up the newspaper stories. He read the first, then quickly scanned through the rest. "These are all about the guys from my school. The ones who died."

"Those boys, I believe, killed your brother."

Peter's eyes moved from the clippings to Alex's wrinkled face. "I know what I said before. I was just upset. I realize now that Bobby's death was an accident."

"No. Bobby's death was caused directly or indirectly by these boys. You know that to be true. And one by one, they are being killed for his death. I don't know how many, if any at all, are still alive. There have been three deaths, with the most recent being one week ago tonight."

"Three? No, you must mean two." Peter paused for a moment. "A week ago?"

"Peter," Alex said calmly, "tell me how you have been feeling."

"Great." Images of Judy and Myer's Lake flashed in his mind. "Really great."

"Nothing unusual, nothing different? No strange occurrences?"

"Well," Peter said reluctantly, "there was one thing, but you'll think I'm going crazy."

"It will be fine. Tell me."

"It was stupid, but I buried Bobby's favorite softball with him. I went to his grave and dropped it in before they finished burying him."

The elderly man sat silently, but his attention was focused totally on Peter.

"The weird part," Peter said, "is that I found the ball back at my bedroom door. I should really say it found me. And lately I've had the strangest feeling someone's been following me, watching me. Maybe I'm just cracking up."

"No. No, you're not. It's all connected. Don't you see? The killings started after Bobby's death. Can't you see the changes you've gone through? You're different now. Think about yourself before Bobby's death. Are you the same Peter Cowal you were then?"

"No, I'm not, but that has nothing to do with—"

"Peter, my boy, it does. What other explanation could there possibly be?"

"Why are you saying these things?" Peter yelled, wondering if the old man was having a mental breakdown. "What possible good could it do me to hear this garbage?"

"Peter, I do this to stop the killing."

"Then tell the police," he said, his anger increasing. "Leave me out of this."

"I can't. You're killing them, Peter. You're the one."

"You're crazy!" he shouted and stormed toward the door.

"Peter, stop! You may not even be aware of what you're doing. My brother Georgie is controlling you."

Peter stopped in his tracks. "What did you say?"

"It's not really you. Your body is being used as a instrument of revenge. The love of your brother is making it possible."

"What did you call him? Georgie?" The name raced through Peter's head—Georgie was what Bobby had named his imaginary friend.

"Yes, he was my brother," Alex said. "He can control others. I can help you, Peter. Let me try.

Since the first death, I have looked for a pattern. That pattern is you."

Peter hardly kept up with his own thoughts, let alone Alex's words. Judy had told him that she had had a friend like Bobby's. His name was Georgie too. What if Georgie was real?

"Peter, are you listening? I can help you."

"Yes, I hear you. And I swear to you that I am not the one you're looking for. I think I know who is. But it can't be possible. It can't be." Peter's words barely escaped his mouth before he dashed out the door.

"Stop, Peter!" Alex went after the boy. "It's too dangerous! Let me help you. You'll only get yourself killed."

Standing at the opened door, Alex watched Peter's car tear from the driveway; then he said a silent pray for Peter's protection. As the white Buick raced down the street, another car had pulled up to the curb.

"Was that Peter?" Amanda Colins shouted out to Alex as she opened the car door.

"Yes, I thought he—"

"Please, Mr. Stein," Amanda said, waving him to the car, "come with us. We don't have much time."

At the Ridgeport Country Club, Judy, Jessica, and Roger were sitting at one of the lavish tables closest to the band. Naturally, Jessica had had a hand in the seating arrangements.

"Doesn't everything look so nice? Oh, hello, Gladys. You look fantastic," she said to a heavily jeweled woman walking past the table. Then she whispered to Roger, "She's heading straight for the buffet table."

"There's certainly plenty," Roger said. "I wouldn't want to be in that kitchen tonight."

"What are you doing, dear?" Jessica asked him when he smiled at Judy and tapped his watch.

"Oh, nothing. I think my watch stopped." He held it to his ear.

"Look, the Welths have arrived," Jessica said, giving the family a brief wave. "I'm sure Martin will think you look lovely tonight, Judy."

"I don't care what Martin thinks."

"What kind of foolish talk is that?"

"You just can't get it through your head—"

Roger signaled to Judy, trying to get her to ignore Jessica's comments.

"The Welths are coming over. Straighten up, Roger." Jessica made a slight adjustment to his tie, then made sure her pearls were displayed properly. "Darwin and Amy, how lovely to see you."

"This must be our table for tonight," Darwin Welth said.

"Why, yes, it is," Jessica replied. "I placed you here myself. And how are you, Martin?"

"I'm fine. Thank you. Hi, Judy."

"Hi." She didn't bother looking at him.

"We noticed the new wing as we drove up," Darwin said. "The work seems to be coming along fine. What do you figure it will take to complete it? Another couple of months?"

"Six weeks," Roger said, "a month, if the weather holds."

"Men," Jessica said, "always talking about digging in the dirt."

"Why don't you two kids dance," Darwin said, "while us old folks talk?"

"Speak for yourself, Darwin," Jessica said, playfully slapping him on the hand.

The adults laughed, but Roger had to force his.

"Yes," Jessica said. "You two go dance. Don't they make a lovely couple?"

"I don't want to dance." Judy looked at her father, who tapped his watch again. "OK, I guess. A short one." It had to be better than listening to Jessica ramble on. Judy felt sorry for her father because he still had hours to go.

On the way to the dance floor, Judy didn't look at Martin once. She wanted to be done with the party and just get out of there. When Martin tried to take her hand, she pulled it away, making sure Martin knew she meant it.

"People are going to get the wrong idea," Martin said.

"I don't think so," Judy said, crossing her arms.

"It's going to be a little hard to dance if I can't touch you."

"One dance, Martin. That's it!"

"Fine," he said, "don't shit a cow."

Judy held Martin's hand limply and made sure there was plenty of room between their bodies. She kept her eyes on her father and the others. Several times, Martin tried to pull her closer, but she pushed him back every time. His anger and frustration started to grow because other club members, especially his father, could see him struggling with the girl.

"I've missed you." Martin waited a moment. "Say something."

"All right. How about this. I don't care. Happy now?"

"Come off it. You're not fooling anybody."

For the first time since being on the dance floor Judy meet Martin's gaze. "I'm not?"

"No, you're not. You can't tell me you didn't feel anything when we kissed at O'Brian's."

"You kissed me. I was an unwilling participant. Or couldn't you tell?"

"Admit it—you felt something."

"Besides disgust, not a thing."

"Still, it had to be better than Peter Cowal."

"Leave Peter out of this. He's none of your concern."

"He made it my concern when he stole my girlfriend."

"You don't get it, do you?"

"What?"

Judy shook her head. "I'm not going to waste my breath."

"Cowal's a creep. I'll give you one more chance. Forget him and I'll take you back. What could being with that weakling possible do for you? There's no comparison between the two of us."

"You're right."

"Of course, I am."

"He's a lot stronger inside than you'll ever be. If you ever had to deal with the misfortunes he's had to, you'd crumble into a crying heap."

"You mean like when his retard brother fell off Crazy Man?" Martin smirked. "Who really cares? No one, I'd say. It was no real loss."

A sharp pain drilled Judy through the back of her head. "You had something to do with Bobby's death."

"What?"

"You did. You were there—you, Ox, and the others. All of you."

Martin squeezed her wrist. "You shouldn't make accusations you can't prove. People might take them seriously."

"Don't touch me," Judy said, trying to pull away.

"You're making a scene."

"You want a scene? How about this: if you don't let me go, I'm going to start screaming at the top of my lungs." The pain in Judy's skull increased. "Let me go."

"Fine," Martin said, releasing his grip.

She stormed away, passing her father, Jessica, and the Welths without a word.

"Lover's spat, son?" his father asked when Martin strutted back to the table.

"You know how women get," Martin said.

All the adults except Roger laughed at the cute remark. Then Roger muttered something under his breath before saying aloud, "I understood you two have stopped dating each other."

"My, my," Jessica said, "where would you get such a foolish idea like that?"

"From Judy. She dropped him like a bad habit," Roger said, enjoying himself because he had never liked the Welths.

"Oh, my," Jessica said, avoiding Darwin and Amy's nasty looks. "The girl never makes herself clear. She's just like her father—so high-strung."

Martin quickly became bored with business talk and club gossip, but he had a diversion worked out for just such an occurrence. "I think I'm going to get some punch."

Martin slipped out behind the clubhouse. He made sure to stay out from under the street lamps that populated the access road around the building. Instead, he walked across the perfectly kept grounds down to the pond. It was dimly lit and isolated.

Behind him, a shadow moved out from its hiding place alongside the clubhouse and followed him down. The dark figure took cover each time Martin turned to make sure he was in the clear. The shadow watched Martin standing alone as it drew closer and closer.

Martin reached into his pocket and pulled out a joint, which had already been darkened on one end. When he struck a match, the flame lit up his face and he inhaled on the small roll, pulling the fire into the paper and leaving the tip a glowing red ember. Martin looked around, but his eyes, still not accustomed to the darkness, could not see very far into his surroundings.

Then a man's voice whispered, "I'm sure everyone's still dancing."

"Do you smell something funny?" a woman said, and Martin flicked the joint's ember out with his fingertip. Then he tried to wave away the smoke.

"No, I—" the man said.

"Oh, hello," the woman said, adjusting her blouse after discovering Martin standing there.

"Lovely night, isn't it?" Martin said.

"Yes, it is," she said.

"Well, good night," Martin said.

"Good night," the couple said, almost in unison.

Martin hurried off, before the couple got a good view of his face, but he could still hear the woman say, "I thought you said no one would be here."

As Martin started back to the main building, a rattling sound stopped him. Off to the far side of the building, a plastic tarp covering a brick pile flapped in the breeze. The new wing. "Perfect," he said to himself. That stretch of road had only one lamp on this side. It illuminated the new construction, but he figured the other side would be so dark that he would be undisturbed.

He entered, almost tripping on a short piece of lumber. He kicked his path clear. Farther in he found a dust-covered sawhorse. He brushed it clean and took a seat.

He put the joint in his mouth, then pulled the book of matches from his pocket. Martin struck another match, and the light burst in the darkness, making him turn his eyes away from the flame for an instant. He touched the flame to the rolled paper and drew a long breath. The glow reflected off something silky yellow.

To his surprise, Judy stood in front of Martin, holding something at her side.

In front of the clubhouse, Peter's car came to a screeching halt by the curb. He rushed out of the Buick, leaving the lights on and engine running, and flew up to the front door.

"I'm sorry," a large man at the door said. "Members only tonight."

Peter had to come up with something quick. He certainly wouldn't pass as a member, and he knew he was going to get only one shot to save Judy. "I have an important message for Roger Kilter."

"I'll see that he receives it."

"Nope. I was told to deliver it personally."

"Not possible."

"What's your name?" Peter asked.

The man gave Peter a questioning stare, then answered, "Henry Moszer, and what good will that do you?"

"Plenty good. When I go back to my boss and tell him Henry Moszer won't let me deliver his message to Mr. Kilter, that will pretty much take me off the hook. Though I suppose my boss and Mr. Kilter will be speaking with you tomorrow about it."

Henry cleared his throat. "Make it quick."

"No problem. I have other things to do tonight myself." Peter entered the club and let out a sigh. He quickly scanned the room, but he didn't know any of the faces. He did notice, however, that many of those faces were staring at him. He marched across the room as if he had a purpose, constantly looking out for Judy. He was about to make a second pass through the crowd when he saw Jessica sitting alone at her table.

"Excuse me, Mrs. Kilter. I'm—"

"For heaven's sake, what are you doing here?" Jessica said, looking at Peter as if he were trash.

"Is Judy here?" Peter asked.

"No, she's not."

"I need—"

"You're the one causing the trouble between Judy and Martin. She was a fine girl before she got mixed up with you."

"Ma'am, excuse me, but this is very important. Do you know where she is?"

"Don't tell me what's important, young man."

A strong grip on Peter's arm spun him around. Henry Moszer did not look pleased. "I figured you were lying. I just wanted to see what you were up to."

"What's all this about?" Roger said, walking up to the table.

"I'm sorry, Mr. Kilter. This kid gave me some cock-and-bull story about some message."

"I'm looking for Judy," Peter said, tilting his head around Henry's body. "Do you know where she went?"

"I think you should leave," Jessica said with a sneer

in her voice. "He's putting all those foolish ideas in our baby's head."

"The boy simply asked where Judy is," Roger scolded his wife and signaled Henry to release his hold on Peter's arm.

"Yes, sir," Peter said. "It's very important I find her."

"She's around somewhere, Peter. I don't know exactly where."

"Did she leave with Martin?"

"What business is that of yours?" Jessica snapped.

Roger glared at his wife and said: "I don't think so."

The Welths returned from the dance floor, and Darwin asked, "Is there any trouble here?"

"I'm looking for Judy," Peter said. He couldn't believe what he was about to say. "Or Martin. I need to find either of them. There's no time to explain."

"Martin left for some punch a while back," Darwin said. "He hasn't come back yet. He must be out on the grounds somewhere."

Peter said no more and dashed toward the door.

"He's a good for nothing," Jessica said, not noticing that Roger followed Peter. "Why Judy got involved with him in the first place, I'll never know."

Outside, Peter drove along the service road that surrounded the clubhouse. His eyes shifted between the road and the surrounding area. He passed a pond and came upon an area under construction. Suddenly somebody dashed across the lawn. It was too dark to make out anything clearly, but Peter thought it might be Judy.

He sped up some, hoping to find a turn off. When he found none, Peter made his own. One sharp turn of the steering wheel and his Buick jumped the curb. As his car drove across the dry ground, the beams from his headlights gave everything an eerie yellow glow. The bare support beams and the exposed cross beams gave off twisted and warped shadows in the light. After he stopped the car, Peter stepped out of his car and approached the skeleton structure.

"Judy?" he whispered, as if trying not to disturb anyone. "Judy, are you here?"

Peter stood still and listened for any answer, any response, any sound—anything at all—but there was nothing. Peter wasn't sure if that was good or bad.

"Judy," he called out again when he saw someone running. "It's me, Peter."

His footsteps rattled as he walked across the sheets of plywood that covered the floor, each stride producing moans and crackles. He walked under what surely must be the beginnings of a doorframe. As he worked his way deeper into the structure the light became dimmer. When a creak caught his ear, he stopped, but saw nothing.

"This is crazy," he told himself, as he leaned against a sawhorse. "I can't be right."

Then he noticed that the sawhorse was sticky, as if someone had covered it with a weak glue. Peter rubbed his hands together, trying to wipe away the mess. He moved to where light was coming through an unfinished window and was horrified to see that his hands were covered with blood. He stared at his palms and the dark sticky blood between his fingers, then glanced back at the sawhorse. His footprints had left a wet trail that led to the window.

From behind him, a blood-caked hand landed on Peter's shoulder. He lunged forward away from its touch. He wanted to scream, but fear froze the sound in his throat.

"Help me," Martin said. Those faint words stopped Peter from running away.

Martin was propped up against a wall for support. He held his right hand over his bleeding left shoulder. The other arm hung limp by his side, with several gashes crossing his forearm. Even in the bad light, Peter saw the blood dripping from between Martin's fingers and landing in a small pool. The left leg of Martin's pants was matted with splashes of blood.

"Help me," Martin said. "She's trying to kill me."

If it wasn't for all the blood, Peter would have laughed at Martin. Instead, he put Martin's good arm around his neck to give him support. "Hold on."

Finally making their way out of the new construction, Peter gently lowered Martin to the ground. "Rest for a minute."

"Rest? You're as crazy as Judy."

"Can't you be serious once in your life?"

"I am being serious." Martin stood up and stumbled over his first step. The pain on his face was obvious.

"Where are you going?"

"I'm out of here," Martin managed to say. "I'm not going to stick around here anymore. She's berserk. And who knows where she is right now."

Peter pulled Martin back down. "You're in no condition to—"

Before Peter could finish his sentence, Martin slugged him against the jaw. Even in Martin's weakened state there was some power behind the blow. It caught Peter off guard and he fell backward.

Peter quickly recovered and wiped the blood from his broken lip. Then he grabbed Martin by the arm. With one movement, he yanked Martin toward him, at the same time burying his fist into Martin's stomach. Martin dropped to the ground, where he lay gasping for breath.

"That was really funny," a little boy said. "Hit him again! Hit him again!"

"Who said that?" Peter turned, but couldn't see the face hidden in the shadows.

"It's me—Georgie. Remember me? Me and Bobby used to be bestest friends. But you didn't like that, did you? You didn't want Bobby to play with me."

"I don't believe you," Peter said. "Georgie was a friend Bobby made up. If you really are Georgie, come out so I can see you."

"Bobby was my friend. You didn't like me to play with him. Others played with me, but they got big and stopped playing. Bobby got big too, but he still played with me. Bobby was my only friend and they hurt him. Now I'm all alone. No one to play with me."

"You're not alone now, Georgie," Peter said. It was hard to admit to himself, but Peter started to believe that this thing was his brother's playmate.

"I am alone. She doesn't want me here. She tries to stop me."

"Who tries to stop you?"

"Judy. She was my friend a long time ago. She can see me sometimes, even though she's grown-up. She sees me, but doesn't ever want to play. I make her play now."

"Let her go and I'll play with you. We'll play any game you want, just let her go."

"No, you're a grown-up. You won't really play with me," Georgie said, his sobbing turned to anger. "You'll try to trick me. Bobby's gone. He's the one who hurt Bobby. I killed the others dead. I'll kill him."

"No, you can't." Peter stood between Martin and Georgie.

"You're just like them. You didn't want Bobby to play with me. You wanted him to stop. You don't let me hurt that bad guy. I hate you. And now you want to trick Judy away from me too! You won't want to play with me. You want Judy back. You'll take her away and make me be alone again. I hate you! I hate you! I won't be alone no more! You can't make me be alone. I won't let you take Judy away. I'll kill you too!"

Judy's body charged out from the darkness toward Peter. The front of her yellow dress was spotted in blood; red sprays on her arms. Georgie's voice came from her lips, saying, "I hate you! I hate you! I make you dead."

Peter's eyes shifted from Judy's enraged face to the large red-streaked carving knife held high over head. Peter had barely enough time to move before her arm came down in a swift strike.

"Judy!" Peter yelled. "Judy, you can stop him."

"She only plays with me now," Georgie said as Judy's body lunged at Peter, retreated, only to find himself flying backward, tripping over Martin.

"She's crazy," Martin gasped.

"Judy, stop!" Peter shouted.

"She's not listening," Martin said. "Do something."

The scowl on her face told Peter he was not getting through to her. Judy was in Georgie's control. The wild anger twisted her lovely figure into a grotesque creature, and she came closer with the knife clinched tightly at his side.

Peter tried to slide across the ground, but he was quickly overtaken by the possessed girl, who loomed over him. There was nowhere to go.

Georgie made Judy raise the knife. "Kill you, I will."

"Georgie, stop!" a boy's voice said from behind Peter. "I can play with you."

When Judy stopped and looked toward the voice, Peter breathed a heavy gasp and started to turn his head to see who had saved him.

"Don't hurt my brother," the boy said.

"Bobby?" Peter said, still not wanting to make any sudden moves.

"Hi, Peter," Bobby said from the shadows.

"Bobby? Is that you?" He knew his brother's voice, but was it possible? Then, seeing Georgie's anger on Judy's face, Peter realized anything was possible.

"Georgie, please don't hurt Peter," Bobby said, still talking from the shadows. "I can't let you hurt him. He's my brother."

"But he's bad. Like the others," Georgie said from within Judy.

"No, not Peter. He's not like the others at all. They were always mean to him and to me. They were bad—not Peter."

When Bobby fell silent, a woman Peter had never seen before stepped into view. Behind her were two men. Like the woman, Peter didn't know the younger man, but even in the bad light he recognized Alex. With all that was going on, Peter was surprised to find himself saddened for calling his friend a crazy old man earlier that night.

Judy's eyes followed the woman as she drew closer, and his surprise registered on Judy's face when the woman spoke with Bobby's voice: "It's all OK now, Georgie."

"Amanda, stay back," David shouted.

"I want the hell out of here," Martin said, frightened

still more by the last strange turn of events.

"Shut up," Peter said, awed at the sight of his dead brother's spirit channeling through the stranger. "She's . . . he's trying to help save our butts."

"Mr. Stein," Bobby said from Amanda's mouth. "Tell Georgie it's OK. He doesn't have to hurt nobody anymore."

"Yes, Georgie, it's OK. We're here to help you."

"See," Bobby said.

"Amanda," David said. "Amanda can you hear me?"

"Yes, David, I'm here." Amanda said. "We're both here."

Peter got to his feet and slowly made his way over to Alex, who took Peter by the arm and said, "Have faith, my boy."

"I didn't mean to—"

"We can discuss it later. Right now we have more important matters."

"Come with me now," Bobby's voice said, and Amanda motioned to the spirit of Georgie within Judy. "I know a real neat place to play. Come with me."

"Can we play all the time?" Georgie asked and Judy dropped the knife.

"Forever and ever," Bobby said from within Amanda.

Peter watched in amazement as a small boy, no older than six, separated from Judy's body, which fell limply to the ground. At first, he thought she was dead, but then saw her chest rise and fall with shallow breath.

"Go to her, Peter," Alex said. "She needs you."

Peter rushed to her side and wrapped his arms

around her, holding her head close against his chest. "Judy, can you hear me?"

She stirred a little, and her eyes flickered open. "Peter, I heard you calling me. I heard you. It wasn't a dream. I tried to stop him," she said, releasing a flood of tears. "I almost killed you."

"It wasn't you," Peter said, pulling her closer and gently kissing her forehead. He wiped away her tears. "It wasn't you."

All eyes were focused on Georgie as he reached out for Amanda's hand. The moment he touched her, Bobby slipped free. David managed to catch Amanda before she stumbled backward. She recovered quickly, but she stayed in David's arms.

"She's real pretty, Peter," Bobby said, facing his brother. He wore his favorite pair of black high-top sneakers and his favorite baseball cap.

"Bobby?" Peter said, looking up at his brother.

"It's OK, Peter. I've seen Daddy. He misses you and Mommy. Tell her not to be sad no more, OK? And I want you to keep my ball. That's why I brought it back to you."

"I will," Peter said, watching both Bobby and Georgie walk off hand in hand and fade away to nothing.

Then Peter heard Bobby speak one last time. "I really liked the baseball glove. It would've been a real neat birthday present."

Peter knew he had no more need to keep the wrapped box with the bow hidden under his bed. "Bye, Bobby. I'll see you some time," he whispered. The pain he had felt for his loss left with his brother. He smiled and held Judy, who had fallen asleep in his arms.

Amanda touched Peter's shoulder. "She'll be all right. She just exhausted. It's over. It's all over. How about you? You OK?"

"Sure. But do you know anyone who could use a baseball glove? Never been used." Peter looked back to the spot where Bobby had disappeared. "Never mind. I think I'll keep it after all."